THE PRODIGY

The author will donate ten percent of the profit from this book to support LGBTQ, racial, and women's justice issues.

THE
PRODIGY

BOOK 4 OF RIAN KRIEGER'S JOURNEY

ROGER A. SMITH

MILFORD
HOUSE
an imprint of Sunbury Press, Inc.
Mechanicsburg, PA USA

MILFORD HOUSE

an imprint of Sunbury Press, Inc.
Mechanicsburg, PA USA

For information about special discounts for bulk purchases, please contact Sunbury Press Orders Dept. at (855) 338-8359 or orders@sunburypress.com.

To request one of our authors for speaking engagements or book signings, please contact Sunbury Press Publicity Dept. at publicity@sunburypress.com.

FIRST MILFORD HOUSE PRESS EDITION: April 2025

Set in Adobe Garamond Pro | Interior design by Crystal Devine | Cover by Lawrence Knorr and Ashley Nichole Walkowiak | Edited by Sarah Peachey.

Publisher's Cataloging-in-Publication Data
Names: Smith, Roger A., author.
Title: The prodigy : book 4 of Rian Krieger's Journey / Roger A. Smith.
Description: First trade paperback edition. | Mechanicsburg, PA : Milford House Press, 2025.
Summary: 1838. In Philadelphia, an exploding steam engine sets back Rian Krieger's plan to one day run her father's locomotive factory. In South Carolina, Olivia Tucker rebels against a life of privilege built on the backs of the enslaved. The girls conspire long distance to burn the daily cruelties of the South's slave system into the American consciousness.
Identifiers: ISBN : 979-8-88819-290-0 (softcover).
Subjects: FICTION / Historical / General | FICTION / LGBTQ+ / Transgender | FICTION / African American & Black / Historical | FICTION / Historical /19th Century / American Civil War Era.

Designed in the USA
0 1 1 2 3 5 8 13 21 34 55

For the Love of Books!

To my comrades in the Brewster Writers Group

Kim Berner

Jeff Drake

Christine Jenkins

Margaret Rice-Moir

Michael Ryle

Ted Spevack

CHARACTERS

In Philadelphia

Rian Krieger: Fourteen-year-old tomboy

Otto Krieger: Rian's father; owner of Krieger Coach, partner in Krieger Locomotive and Krieger Rail

Kurt Krieger: Otto's youngest brother and Rian's uncle; ship's carpenter

Adrian Krieger: Otto's brother and Rian's uncle; founder of Krieger Locomotive but currently living in Saxony

Mila Krieger: Adrian's wife; soon to join him in Saxony

Jabez Howes: Son of the late sea captain Levi Howes; Adrian and Mila's ward; Rian's cousin

Seamus Gallagher: Former president of the No Name Fire Brigade; Rian's cousin through her late mother

Conor McGuire: Rian's best friend who sometimes lives with Rian and Otto

Jules Freeman: Owner of Freeman Hydraulics, one of the few Black-owned companies in Philadelphia; foreman at Krieger Coach; formerly enslaved, but self-emancipated in 1820

Maddie Freeman: Jules's wife; founding member of the Philadelphia Female Anti-Slavery Society; president of Freeman Hydraulics

Lucretia Mott: Outspoken Quaker abolitionist; Otto and Rian's next-door neighbor

James Mott: Lucretia's husband; abolitionist and member of the Bank of Industry's loan committee.

Hugh Callaghan: President of the Moyamensing Hose Company and Seamus's nemesis

Siobhan Callaghan: Hugh's daughter and Seamus's girlfriend

Harold Foote: Reporter for the *Philadelphia Independent*

Geoffrey Clifton: Publisher of the *Philadelphia Independent*

George Shippen: Chairman of the Board of the Bank of Industry; railroad entrepreneur

Trey Shippen: George's son

Edward Schiffler: President of the Bank of Industry

Billy Schiffler: Edward's son; a bully, and one of Rian's antagonists

Nicholas Biddle: Former president of the National Bank of Pennsylvania; financial genius

James Forten: Perhaps the richest Black man in America; owner of a sailmaking shop on the Delaware

Robert Purvis: Wealthy Philadelphia landowner who finances numerous abolitionist and Underground Railroad initiatives; James Forten's son-in-law

Braden McSweeney: Owner of McSweeney's Saloon

Ruben Hasselbach: Whiskey distiller

Richard (Dicky) Pricker: Philadelphia Harbor Master

Quinton Schott: Crane builder

Gamaliel Leonard: Co-owner of the Johns & Leonard Pier

James Hollingsworth: Maître d' at the United States Hotel

Jonas Longstreth: Partner in Ellis & Longstreth Lumber Company, and member of the Bank of Industry's loan committee

Delilah Winter (referenced but not seen): Poker player who was in the group that returned to America from Russia with Rian and Seamus; cleaned Rian out of much of her fortune on the last night of their voyage

In the Krieger factories

Heinrich Aldridge: Krieger Locomotive designer

Harry Vogel: Krieger Locomotive foreman

Jimmy Butter: Krieger Locomotive worker

Benny Holt: Krieger Locomotive worker

Joheim Fischer: Krieger Locomotive worker

Gerald (The Trout) Downing: New foreman at Krieger Locomotive

Aaron Bassinger: President of Krieger Rail; accountant for all Krieger companies

In Boston

Joseph Ingersol: Pier owner

Cyrus T. Newkirk: President of the Boston & Lowell Railroad

John Quincy Adams: Former president of the United States

In Utica and on the Hudson

Erastus Corning: President of the Utica & Schenectady Railroad
David Winter: Artist who painted Rian's portrait aboard the *Great Western*

In South Carolina

Randolph Tucker (The Squire): Owner of Long Pond, a rice plantation outside of Charleston
Penelope Hayne Tucker: Randolph's wife
Olivia Tucker: Randolph and Penelope's daughter; Rian's friend
Cook: Enslaved cook at Long Pond
Emblee: Enslaved house servant at Long Pond
Matilde: Enslaved house servant at Long Pond
Grafton: Enslaved field hand at Long Pond
Matthew Jaudon: Owner of Catawba Point plantation and neighbor of the Tuckers
Knox Boseman: Plantation supervisor at Long Pond
Dr. Elias Marks: Head of the South Carolina Female Collegiate Institute (Barhamville) in Columbia, South Carolina
Julia Marks: Dr. Marks's wife; teacher at Barhamville
Eugenie Allston: Olivia's roommate
Caldwell Montgomery: Olivia's classmate
Miss Edwards: Instructor at the South Carolina Female Collegiate Institute
Trevor Wilkinson: State senator; owner of Thousand Oaks, a cotton plantation outside of Columbia
Poppy Wilkinson: Trevor's wife
Barnwell Wilkinson: Trevor and Poppy's son
Topper: Olivia Tucker's enslaved half-brother
Ashbel Molineaux: Investigator

1838

1888

TUESDAY, OCTOBER 9

· RIAN ·

Rian Krieger quietly closed the front door behind her and descended the five porch steps. Anticipating the crisp October weather, she had donned a light coat over her standard factory clothing: nankeens[1] and a shirt. Her shoulder-length hair was tucked up into her flat cap, and that's the way it would remain until she went to bed. *All is good*, she thought.

The houses across the street were barely visible in the pre-dawn light. The stars, brilliant when she sprinted to the privy half an hour ago, were not nearly as spectacular. Rian was about to start her walk to work when her father stuck his head out the door. "*Liebling*," he called to her in a hushed voice.

Otto Krieger had called her *Liebling* since she was a child, and she considered it endearing when they were at home. But she was fourteen years old and striving to establish her right to work alongside the men in her father's factories. *If I were a boy, the workers wouldn't question my presence in the shop. But they resent me because I'm a girl—the boss's daughter, to boot. The fact that I have the skills to be there doesn't matter to them. When* Vater *calls me* Liebling *in front of men, it makes the impossible even harder.*

"*Liebling*," Otto called again, "if you wait five minutes, I will join you."

Loath to disturb the neighbors, Rian nodded and waved in assent, but irritation welled inside her. Waiting meant idleness, and idleness didn't suit her. Idleness became an opportunity for the dark thoughts to take control. *You're The Oddity*, they would say. *You're the only girl in the world who thinks like you do.*

Rian visualized her brain as a buckboard—a work wagon. Most of the time, she drove the buckboard by engaging in a demanding task. It didn't matter what it was—bookkeeping, building a wagon wheel, drawing a new part for a locomotive—when the work required concentration, she lost all sense of self, the time flew by, and her qualms remained securely tied down in the wagon bed behind her. During idle times, however, those dark thoughts gnawed their way

---

1. *Nankeens* are pale-yellow pants made of durable nankeen cotton. The cloth was originally made in Nanking (now Nanjing), China.

loose like rats escaping from a burlap sack. The rat-thoughts climbed over the back of the driver's bench and grabbed for the reins.

But her surroundings—this moment—helped her for once shove the rat-thoughts back into the sack. The weather was brisk and gusty. The wind in the elms and chestnuts already sounded different now that the trees had lost half their leaves. The fallen leaves, brittle and free, swirled off the sidewalk and into Ninth Street. A skinny stray dog—a large something in his mouth—trotted furtively between the houses across the street. A block to the south, Jason-the-lamplighter extinguished the coal gas flame of a streetlamp. A farmer leading his horse and a wagon that carried three milk cans gave Rian a perfunctory wave as he passed.

Come on, Vater. *Hurry up. I can't keep the rat-thoughts back there forever.* Her father finally exited the house, bounded down the porch steps, and pointed up Ninth Street with his old lumber estimating rule.[2]

"Why are you going in early?" Rian asked, hoping conversation would keep the darkness at bay. Father and daughter turned left out of their front walk and strode north.

"Today is voting day for the new Pennsylvania Constitution," her father responded. "Jules and I plan to head to the State House around ten o'clock. I think we will be away from the office for a few hours, so I need to do some work beforehand."

"Do you expect trouble?"

"Of course. The bully boys will be out in force. They will do everything in their power to prevent any Black man from voting. Those who know Jules by sight will give him special attention. No matter what, today's vote will be historic. It will decide whether the Black man retains the right to vote in Pennsylvania."

They turned left on Sassafras Street, joining a stream of Irish day workers trudging to the coal docks on the Schuylkill. Rian nodded to one of them—a nameless familiar face she often saw on her morning commute—but received no acknowledgment in return. "Will you vote as well?"

"If I am still standing, I will vote. Truth be told, I forget whether I am supposed to vote yes or no. They have changed the wording so many times . . . First there was no mention of Black freemen at all, which was good. Then some of the convention delegates—scoundrels, in my opinion—tried to inject a 'white freemen only' clause into the wording. Then that amendment was defeated. Then it was brought up again. Honestly, I have lost track of where it

2. Before Otto emigrated to America from Germany, he was trained as a forester. The tool of his trade was a lumber estimating rule—a calibrated stick that helped to determine the amount of usable lumber that could be derived from a standing tree. Otto now used his rule as a walking stick.

is. Jules will know, of course . . . What about you, *Liebling*? What is on your schedule today?"

Rian was about to tell her father he was supposed to vote against the constitution as written, but got detoured by his question. "Accounting in the morning . . . which reminds me: Have you heard from Erastus Corning recently? We've been expecting that contract for months."

"Corning and I have been corresponding. The *Utica & Schenectady* has had merger problems with a sister railroad that will extend the route to Syracuse . . . Legal technicalities, apparently, but they have caused delays. If the *U&S* buys locomotives and rolling stock, it will be from us. Corning asked me to be patient."

"Do you trust him?"

"I will trust him when I have a contract in hand . . . And your afternoon . . . Will you be working with Heinrich again?" Heinrich Aldridge was Krieger Locomotive's brilliant engine designer who had taken Rian under his wing.

Rian nodded. "I'm building a wooden pattern[3] of a gear for the *Standard* locomotive, even though it's more than two years away from production and your guy Corning hasn't signed a contract yet. The gear's a foot in diameter and has thirty-two teeth. It's the most demanding pattern I've ever worked on, and it has to be perfect."

"And Heinrich trusts you making such a demanding part?"

"Yesterday he told me I'm his best pattern maker."

Her father was silent for a few paces, obviously pondering the implications of this statement. "So I guess Jules and I taught you well."

Treasure this moment, Eena.[4] He doesn't praise you often. Vater *doesn't approve of me being out in the shop, but my love for the factories is his fault.* Rian had been kicked out of three schools by the time she was eleven. Otto started bringing her to work every day in hopes she could learn the "Three Rs" while woodworking. "You two *did* teach me well. And for that, I am grateful, because the factories are where I'm supposed to be." *And, because patterns have to be perfect, I concentrate so hard that the dark thoughts stay in the back of the buckboard.*

---

3. The fabrication of any cast-iron part started with a mechanical drawing—a visual guide that laid out precise dimensions as viewed from front, top, and side. A skilled artisan then used the specifications to fabricate a three-dimensional pattern—an exact, wooden version of the future part—out of American chestnut. The pattern was embedded in a box that had been hard-packed with sand. When removed, it left a negative impression of the part—a mold. Molten iron was poured into the mold. Wooden patterns could be used many times to create uniform cast-iron components.

4. Rian's cousin Jabez called her *Eena* when they were toddlers because he couldn't say *REE-in*. She still refers to herself as *Eena* in her thoughts.

Father and daughter left the stream of day workers and turned north on Broad Street.

"*Liebling*, I talked to your Aunt Mila yesterday. She has sold the house."

Rian suspected what was coming and knew it would change her life. "What did you two decide about Cousin Jabez?"

"Jabez has dug in his heels. He refuses to sail to Europe with her. I offered to take him into our home."

Jabez is a tortured soul. Living with him will be difficult. Father and daughter walked almost half a block before Rian replied. "I think this will be hard, but it's a good idea. I'm not happy about it, but I'm willing to do it." *Damn, I wish there was some other course we could take, but this is the one we're on for now.*

"You are sure? You are wholeheartedly on board for Jabez moving in with us?"

"If he refuses to go to Saxony with Aunt Mila, I see no other choice." *I'm afraid he will jump off Sparks Shot Tower[5] if pushed too hard, but of course I can't tell you that.* "I know he's difficult, but I believe we can handle him."

"Then it is settled. I will talk to Mila this evening. She plans to take the train to New York City on Thursday."

* * * * *

Rian broke from her bookkeeping when Jules Freeman entered the Krieger Coach office. His entry allowed the din from the shop to momentarily intrude on the relative quiet. Jules was her father's first hire when Otto started making carriages. He became the foreman as the business grew. His influence was pivotal during Krieger Coach's expansion into making railroad cars. Two years ago, Jules and his wife, Maddie, started Freeman Hydraulics, which made steam-powered fire pumps. Jules still spent most of his workday at Krieger Coach while Maddie ran their family business. Jules and Maddie were prominent members of Philadelphia's thriving Black middle class. Publicly, they were active in various anti-slavery societies and self-help organizations. Other activities were much more secretive: Jules and Maddie were stationmasters and conductors in the Underground Railroad.

Jules closed the door behind him. "Otto, get your coat. It's time to go vote."

Her father rubbed the nib of his steel-tipped pen inside the neck of his inkwell, cleaned the nib with a rag, set the pen down, then gave Jules his full

---

5. The 142-foot-tall Sparks Shot Tower was built in 1808 to manufacture bullets by dropping molten lead from a great height. By the time the lead hit a barrel of water at the bottom, it was a perfect sphere. In 1838, the tower was still the tallest structure in Philadelphia.

attention. "Jules, I confess, I have lost track of the politics of it all. Am I supposed to vote yes or no on this?"

Rian had studied Jules all her life. She could tell the moments when he masked his true feelings—be they anger, irritation, disappointment, or fear—when amongst whites . . . *even with my father, who is his best friend. Or at least his best white friend.* This was one of those moments. Jules had worked tirelessly for months to defeat the new constitution with its proposed white-voters-only wording. *Damnit, I should have told* Vater *how to vote on our way to work, but I got distracted.*

Jules responded to Otto in a measured tone. "The proposed version of the new constitution says only white freemen can vote, Otto, so we're voting against ratification." Then he brightened up a bit. "Are you ready for this? There are sure to be fisticuffs."

Oblivious to Jules's momentary irritation, her father rose from his chair and grabbed his frock coat off the coat tree. "I am only thirty-eight. I think I've got a few more tussles left in me. You know us Kriegers: Warriors by name and warriors by nature."

Rian rose from her desk. "*Vater,* may I come, too? I've never seen men vote before."

Her father shook his head. "I am not sure this will be an example of democracy at its finest, *Liebling.* But I will tell you what you could do for me. Walk over to Krieger Locomotive and tell Harry to give the men time off during the day if they intend to vote. I believe most of them know what is riding on this and will side with Jules and his race."

Rian wasn't sure her father was right, but . . . "Harry won't be happy to see me." *I disobeyed him so often that he banned me from the factory. Plus, he doesn't think a girl should work in the skilled trades.*

"You are only delivering a message, *Liebling,* not trying to worm your way back onto the floor." With that, Otto grabbed his lumber estimating rule and rested it on his shoulder, a sign of his readiness to fight and vote. All three walked through the office door into the noise and busyness of the Coach factory floor.

* * * * *

Rian entered the cavernous locomotive factory from the door in the alley and was engulfed by a delightful cacophony—workers hammering rivets into place, machinery whirring, men yelling, metal clanging on metal, and the steam engine rhythmically *choosh! . . . choosh! . . . chooshing!*

This used to be the "music" that accompanied my afternoons and I miss it . . . It's busier than the last time. To be expected, I guess. Now that the depression is over, Harry's installing new machinery and rehiring workers.

Rian spotted Harry right away. He was yelling above the noise to three workers near a hulking metal lathe—the first machine tool in a row of brawny machinery that ran the length of the factory. As she walked toward the group, she sensed something amiss with her music and stopped mid-stride. *The steam engine's* chooshing *too rapidly. Not a lot, but something's not right.*

She peered at the steam regulator, high atop the engine's mammoth boiler. What she saw sent a chill down her spine. Jabez Howes stood on the scaffold that flanked the boiler. He was staring at the regulator, and the balls of the regulator weren't spinning.

"Oh, sweet Jesus," Rian uttered. She ran to Harry, grabbed him by the arm, and pointed toward the boiler. "Harry! I think Jabez messed with the regulator! I'll fix it, but you should clear these guys out of the way in case the boiler blows before I get to it!"

Harry, at first irritated at the interruption, glanced toward where Rian was pointing, then bolted for the wrought-iron stairs that led to the scaffold.

"Clear out of here!" Rian yelled to the workers. "Something's wrong with the regulator!"

The workers shook their heads, as if the boss's daughter was yet again off on a wild hare, but they did start moving away. Rian ran after Harry, who was sprinting up the wrought-iron stairs.

Jabez turned at the sound of Harry's shoes clanging on the steps. "No! Stay away!"

Rian hit the stairs, taking them two at a time. It was as if she were in a dream, climbing as fast as she could but not fast enough. She yanked on the railing to speed her ascent, but it all happened so slowly.

Harry reached the top of the stairs, strode to Jabez, roughly wrenched him away from the boiler, and shoved him toward the stairs. Rian shouldered past Jabez.

Jabez tried to grab her but failed. "Eena, I don't want anyone else to get hurt."

Rian saw Harry reach for the boiler's release valve.

"Eena, I'm sorry! I want it to end!" Jabez yelled from behind her.

Rian didn't hear the explosion.

She never remembered being thrown backward toward the stairs. Never remembered ricocheting off Jabez and into the air fifteen feet above the factory floor.

Image courtesy of Alamy

(Three Months Earlier)
Wednesday, July 11

· RIAN ·

"Miss Krieger! Rian!" Harry Vogel yelled as he glared at Rian from twenty-five feet below. "You must come down right now! A fourteen-year-old girl should not be up there!"

Rian ignored him. *Miss Krieger, my ass.*

Rian placed one foot in front of the other as she worked her way along the catwalk, a series of narrow planks nailed end-to-end along the bottom chords of the factory's roof trusses. She maintained her balance by holding her arms straight out from her sides, her daring-do made a bit more difficult by the coil of rope draped over her left shoulder.

The lack of railings didn't intimidate her. The drive shaft mere inches above her head wasn't rotating. If she felt the need, she could reach up and grab it. Besides, the trusses offered a hand-hold every six feet.

"Rian, I ordered Jimmy Butter up there! I want him to handle this."

Asshole. She dodged left-right-left around pulleys and continuous belts that, minutes ago, had transferred power from the drive shaft to the machine tools below. Her flat cap occasionally brushed the drive shaft, an indication that she had grown taller since her last time up here.

"Miss Krieger! If you don't come down, I will be forced to go across the alley and get your father! He will not be pleased!"

"My father's in New York," Rian muttered to Harry, but she doubted he heard her, and frankly, she didn't give a damn.

Half an hour ago, the shop had reverberated with the pounding, clanging, and banging of twenty machine tools, all powered by the driveshaft that ran along the peak of the trusses. Rian loved the cacophony of it all. It was the music of her afternoons in the locomotive shop. When a team of men from the docks delivered a new riveting machine, Harry decided he wanted it hooked up right away. That work could only be done if the factory was temporarily shut down. The workers disengaged their machines. Harry pushed the giant lever that disconnected power to the drive shaft. Then he pulled the clutch to the two massive flywheels. They ever-so-slowly wound to a halt.

I wouldn't have hooked up the riveter in the middle of the workday because of all the lost production time, but that's Harry's problem. He's the foreman. Rian worked her way along the catwalk. With the machinery now idle, she could hear a driving rainstorm pounding on the roof a few feet above her.

The thirty machinists, journeymen, and helpers on the shop floor were now well aware of her fracas with Harry. They hooted and hollered up at her. *Most of them don't like Harry, and all but a handful hate me. Well, fook you all.*

"If you don't turn around by the time I count to three," Harry yelled from below, "I will re-engage the drive shaft!"

Rian pulled the coiled rope off her shoulder, held on to one end, and let the rope drop. Harry jumped back to avoid getting hit by the knotted end, causing her a moment of satisfaction.

"I won't give in to your defiance! Come down right now!"

Benny Holt—one of the few men in the factory who tolerated Rian—poked his thumb up at her. "Aw, come on, Harry, she's already up there."

If Harry shrugged some sort of acquiescence, Rian didn't see it. Benny grabbed the rope and tied it around one end of the new continuous belt—a heavy, five-inch wide, fire-hose-grade strip that, when sewn end-to-end, would become a fifty-foot loop. Benny gave a gentle double tug to signal "pull away."

Rian reeled up the rope. She grasped the end of the belt, draped it over a pulley on the drive shaft, and fed it hand-over-hand back down to the floor. Benny wrapped the belt around the pulley of the new riveting machine.

The riveter was the first new machine purchased by Krieger Locomotive since they sent half their machine tools to Russia last year. *The riveter is proof that the fooking depression is finally coming to an end.*

"Hang on a minute, Rian," Benny called up to her.

It would take a while for Benny to stitch the belt ends together. With no task to demand her attention, Rian found herself in her least favorite situation: time alone with nothing to distract her . . . an opportunity for that ever-present darkness that always lurked in the back of her brain to start gnawing: *You're The Oddity. The girl who hates dresses. Hates needlepoint. Hates manners. Hates anything to do with that girly-girl stuff. What's wrong with you?*

And that rat-thought had a buddy: *Fire follows you—fire that is out of control and fire you think is under control but isn't. Yana got the first part right, and a lot of people got hurt.*[6] *And what the hell is "fire that you think is under control but isn't?" What's wrong with you?*

You're The Oddity. Think, Eena, think. Shove these thoughts to the back of the buckboard.

Rian took a deep breath. *Well, you're up here. Make use of the time.* She looked up . . . ran her fingers around one of the support bearings that held the drive shaft in place. *It's dry. Can't even feel any tallow.*[7] *Whoever was supposed to lubricate the joints last time did a piss-poor job.* She walked to the next bearing. It was dry, too.

She surveyed the factory from her lofty vantage. *The factory I love, the factory I'll run someday. Yana predicted that, too. "First no, then yes."*

"You think you'll run this factory someday, don't you?" Harry yelled up to her as if he could read her thoughts. "Well, your daddy doesn't want that to happen, I don't want it to happen, and no one in this shop wants it to happen. So it's not going to happen. Not ever!"

Rian ignored Harry's rant. *Think, Eena, think.* At the far end of the giant room stood two huge sliding doors: one to accept raw materials from Broad Street, the other to discharge finished locomotives. A track ran the length of the shop in a U-shape and exited out the "finished locos" slider. Four spurs—work stations for engines under construction—branched off each side of the U. An axle and two thirty-six-inch drive wheels remained on one of the spurs to the left—souvenirs of a locomotive that a railroad in Indiana had ordered just before it went out of business. *Those wheels have been clogging up that workstation for three months. Harry should get them out of the way.*

She imagined what the factory would look and sound like when twenty new machines repopulated the empty spaces. *We'll have at least two of everything, the way it used to be. Lathes, drill presses, crimpers, grinders, shapers, shearers, metal saws, and probably ten more workers. And by the looks of the riveter, the new machines will be better than the ones we sold to Russia. That's progress, I guess. Things always change. More men. More machines. More music. Damn, if the depression hadn't knocked us back on our heels, this factory would already be too small.*

---

6. In *The Coachman*, a fire destroyed Tsar Nicholas I's magnificent, art-filled 1,500-room palace in St. Petersburg, Russia. In *The Blackmailer*, a Russian soothsayer named Yana predicted that fire would follow Rian: "All kinds of fire. Fires that are out of control. Many of them. Fires that you think you control, but you don't." Weeks after Rian returned to Philadelphia, a pro-slavery mob burned Pennsylvania Hall, which was built to host abolitionist conventions of up to three thousand people. Its life, from dedication to destruction, lasted four days. The following night, a mob burned the almost-completed Shelter for Colored Orphans.

7. In this pre-petroleum era, beef or mutton fat was rendered into a useful lubricant that was inserted between the moving parts of machine tools, steam engines, and locomotives.

Rian pivoted. To the north was the Finish Room, where almost-completed locos were wheeled to be painted and varnished in a dust-free environment. To the west the steam engine idled, and beyond that, on the other side of a wall, lay the shop office. Beyond that was an alley that separated this building from Krieger Rail. To the south was the door to the alley between Krieger Locomotive and Krieger Coach.

The door opened and Rian's cousin Seamus Gallagher entered the factory wearing a heavy brown rain slicker and a wide-brimmed hat.

"Give it a tug, Rian!" Benny yelled.

Seamus glanced up, saw Rian, and waved.

Rian returned to the pulley and pulled down on the belt with both hands, careful not to shift her center of gravity too far off the catwalk. The upper pulley rotated, causing the drive shaft to turn as well. Rian pulled on the belt again. The idler pulley on the riveter rotated exactly the way it was supposed to. *Amazing. We got it right the first time.* She gave Benny an okay sign.

While Rian was busy testing the continuous belt, Harry Vogel had walked back to the steam engine. He pulled the giant lever, which engaged the two massive flywheels.

Uh-oh. The next step after engaging the flywheels would be to start the drive shaft back up, which could be done with a mere pull of a lever. No one was supposed to be on the catwalk while the drive shaft and pulleys were running, but Harry was pretty ired. Rian looked back along the catwalk to the safety of the stairs that led down to the scaffold atop the steam engine two hundred feet away. *He wouldn't dare.*

With the flywheels rotating at full speed, Harry shifted the engine's continuous belt from its idler pulley to its drive pulley. The belt squealed briefly. The drive shaft an inch above Rian's cap started rotating, then spun faster.

Rian duck-walked toward the steam engine with her arms straight out from her sides, an awkward, moving squat that kept her away from the spinning shaft. She stole a glance at the floor below. Harry whirled his arm as he held it aloft—the signal to start all the machines back up again. *Jaysus, any one of these belts could take my head off, and there's fifteen of them between me and the steam engine.*

Rian quickened her pace, bobbing her head left then right around spinning belts and pulleys, her leg muscles starting to burn from the unfamiliar crouch. She took the steep stairs that led down to the wrought-iron platform that flanked the boiler two at a time, turned left on the platform, then sprinted down the final set of stairs. With every step, she built up more steam. By the time she reached the shop floor, she was ready to blow. She grabbed a two-foot piece of angle iron out of the scrap box and strode toward Harry, who was talking to Joheim Fischer, his back to her.

Joheim saw Rian coming. "Watch out, Harry. Here she comes."

Harry turned around with a smirk on his face that disappeared when Rian swung at his head with the angle iron. He had just enough time to dodge it. "Jesus, Rian, what are you doing?"

Rian again swiped at Harry, this time at chest height. "Fook you, Harry. You almost killed me!"

Joheim made a grab for the angle iron, but Rian saw it coming and gave him a warning swing. "Stay out of this, Jo. You know I mean it."

Harry retreated behind a wooden column. "I told you I was going to turn the drive shaft back on."

Rian swung at the column. "You said you would count to three!" Harry yanked back his hand a fraction of a second before the angle iron hit the column with a *thunk*. The metal vibrated so hard it hurt her hands.

Harry danced backward. Rian held the angle iron like a rounders bat and aggressively strode forward.

"You should have listened to me," Harry stammered. "I ordered Jimmy Butter to go up there."

Rian continued to stalk the foreman. "Jimmy's afraid of heights, you asshole. I could do the job faster."

Many of the shop workers gathered to watch the confrontation. "Good luck, Harry!" one of them yelled sarcastically. "We're pulling for you."

"Yeah, but no one's betting you'll get out of this alive," another said, which elicited many hoots and hollers.

Harry kept backing up, still holding his hands up defensively. "You're a girl. I've told you a hundred times, a factory is no place for a girl."

"I've heard that all my life! And do you know what happens?" Rian took another swing at Harry's head. "This happens!"

Harry dodged back, tripped over the long-neglected axle, and fell on his back, defenseless. At that moment, someone grabbed Rian from behind and jerked her entirely off the ground. "That's enough, Cousin," Seamus Gallagher said.

"Fook you, Harry!" Rian bellowed as she swiped at empty air. Seamus didn't release his bear hug. She kicked and yelled righteous defiance as Seamus hauled her through the door to the alley.

They burst out into the driving rainstorm. Rather than let her go, Seamus tore off Rian's flat cap and held her under a torrent of water streaming off the factory roof. "That's enough!"

Rian sputtered under the rainwater. "All right! All right! I quit. Lemme go."

"Are you done?"

In response, Rian held out the angle iron for Seamus to grab.

Seamus took charge of the weapon and allowed Rian's feet to return to the ground. "You could have killed him."

Rian stepped away from the torrent coming off the roof but made no attempt to get out of the downpour. She turned her face upward for a moment, allowing the rain to hit her full-on, then turned to Seamus. "I wasn't going to kill him, just make sure he thought twice before he fooked with me again."

"Well, you could have fooled me."

Rian bent over to rescue her flat cap from a puddle. "What took you so long?"

"What?"

"You probably could've grabbed me after the first swing."

Seamus smiled. "You were quite the tiger in there. I figured you needed to burn off a little of that anger first."

Rian moved into the shelter of the roof's overhang and stood with her back to the factory's brick wall. "Probably smart," she said. "I was ireful. I imagine it'll be a while before Harry pulls that kind of nonsense again."

"Rian, you're fooking crazy. Harry's never going to let you back into the factory. Why were you up on the catwalk anyway? Harry can order whoever he wants up there."

"Because he wanted Jimmy Butter to do it."

"So what? Jimmy could have handled it."

"Jimmy's drunk as a skunk. His wife died last week, and he's been drinking ever since. If he had gone up there, he would have fallen off and gotten killed. Then his four kids would be orphans. Harry's too stupid to notice, and even if he did notice, he still might have ordered Jimmy up there."

Seamus leaned into the factory wall and crossed his arms. "Why didn't you tell Harry that Jimmy was sozzled?"

"Because then Harry would have fired him."

"Well then somebody oughta get Jimmy to a temperance meeting."

Rian side-glanced at her cousin. "Seamus, what are you doing here, anyway?"

"Looking for your da. He wasn't in the Coach office."

"*Vater*'s on a sales trip—New Jersey, New York, then Montreal. What do you want him for?"

"I want Krieger Locomotive to build a still for me. I'm going into the whiskey business."

With something new to think about, Rian held out her hand. "Can I see your plans?"

Seamus shook his head. "Ruben Hasselbach made sketches. They're here in me pocket, but I'm not going to show 'em to you in the middle of a gullywasher."

Even though her cap was soaking wet, Rian put it back on her head. Her light brown hair, shaggy when she was a coachman in Russia, had grown out to be not quite shoulder-length—still too short to necessitate tucking up into her cap. "I guess I've cooled off enough. We can go over the plans in the Coach office. But Seamus, could you please go back and talk to Harry?"

"I'm not going to apologize for you, Cousin."

"No. Tell Harry that when I was up on the catwalk, I noticed that the bearings on the drive shaft need some tallow. My best guess is that whoever he sent up there the last time didn't do their regular lubrication very well."

* * * * *

· OTTO ·

"Don't promise more than we can deliver!" Those were Harry Vogel's parting words as Otto Krieger left the office for his sales trip. *"You have a habit of over-promising to our customers, and then we go crazy trying to fulfill your promises."*

Don't promise more than we can deliver, Otto repeated to himself as a young man ushered him into the Utica, New York, office of Erastus Corning. Corning wore two hats. He was both the owner of Rensselaer Iron Works and the president of the *Utica & Schenectady Railroad.* He appeared to be in his mid-forties. *A good half-dozen years older than me.* His opulently appointed office, fashionable clothing, and portly stature all bespoke the prosperous, well-fed life of a successful industrialist.

Corning shook Otto's hand and returned to his swivel chair. His desk was massive, built of dark mahogany, but its top was populated only by an ink well, a leather desk pad, and one sheet of paper. Two bookshelves flanked a credenza behind him, all filled with an orderly accumulation of books, files, ledgers, and papers. "Herr Krieger, I wondered if I would ever meet you. All my dealings to date have been with your brother, but I understand Adrian moved to Russia. Please, sit down."

Otto sat. He didn't think it would be helpful to add that Adrian's mission in Russia—building a railroad from St. Petersburg to Moscow and the factories to support them—had failed. "Yes, that is true. I am now in charge of both Krieger Coach and Krieger Locomotive. I have good people running both."

"Well, your factories have a sterling reputation. Quality craftsmanship. Innovation. Durability. Those are all things we railroad men value."

"Thank you," was all Otto said. *Let him do the talking in the beginning. I cannot sell unless I learn what his concerns are.* He waited for Corning to continue.

Predictably, Corning filled the silence. "Well, I have to admit, I'm a little concerned about your ability to complete an order in a timely fashion. Your fellow Philadelphian Edward Harris called on me yesterday—drumming up business, the same as you're doing now. He told me Adrian shipped half your machine tools to Russia and your factories are crippled."

Harris, dieser Hurensohn [that son of a bitch], Otto thought. *But now I know.* "Tsar Nicholas made us a generous business proposal when all of America was reeling from the Panic. Now that things have returned to normal, we are replacing the machinery." *But Harris did not lie. We are finally getting our feet back under us, but the lack of machinery has slowed us down.*

Corning leaned back in his chair. "I'm happy to hear that, Otto, because we're very confident about the future. I have some news I couldn't share with Harris. Last night, the board of the *Utica & Schenectady* voted to merge with the *Mohawk & Hudson.*"

Otto responded to this nugget with an ingratiating, gapped-tooth smile. "That is good news for you and the people of the Mohawk Valley."

Corning nodded in agreement. "When our third railroad, the *Utica & Syracuse*, is completed next year, passengers will be able to ride 150 miles from Albany to Syracuse without changing trains."

"It sounds to me that you will be needing new equipment."

Corning nodded. "We are about to send a request for bids for twelve locomotives to every locomotive manufacturer in the East. Since the Krieger companies also make rolling stock, we would be happy for Krieger Coach to additionally bid on twenty-four passenger cars."

Otto did his best to hide his surprise. So far on this trip, he had experienced encouraging receptions from the presidents of the *New York & Harlem* and the *Camden & Amboy* railroads, but nothing like this. *A contract for twelve locomotives and twenty-four railroad cars would put us back on our feet, even if no one else purchases a thing. Still . . .* "But no freight cars? Everyone I have talked to on this trip has said they expect freight to eclipse passenger revenue now that the depression is over."

Corning sat back in his chair and crossed his arms. "Not for us, I'm afraid. In order to make that happen, we'll have to bribe half the New York State Legislature."

Otto gave Corning a quizzical look.

His host continued. "Many of our state legislators are Erie Canal stockholders. They have banned our railroads from hauling freight for fear of competition with their precious canal. We have people working on that problem in Albany, but I'm afraid it will take years, numerous elections, and bucketloads of money before the right people are installed. Then, I assure you, we can get the laws changed." Corning picked the sheet of paper off his desk and handed it to Otto. "Here is the locomotive specification sheet we are including with our request for bids."

Otto scanned the paper. *Weight no more than sixteen tons . . . wood or coal burning . . . sustained speed of thirty-five miles per hour . . . haul gross weight of thirty-five tons up four-percent grade . . . minimum of ten miles between water stops . . . engine driver cab.* He slipped the sheet back onto Corning's desk. "We delivered the first of our *Eagle*-class locomotives to the *Philadelphia & Columbia* last month. It exceeds all these specifications by quite a bit."

Corning cocked his head as if he questioned Otto's statement. "When I met with Harris yesterday, he said he would have to talk to his engineers before committing to these numbers."

Otto ignored the opportunity to criticize his competitor's ignorance of his own business. A slight shake of his head and a shrug of his shoulders was sufficient. "When would you expect delivery?"

"The first locomotive? A year from the day we sign the contract. The remaining engines? One every other month after that."

Otto had heard enough. "I can meet that entire delivery schedule with my *Eagle*-class locomotives, but I think that would be a mistake."

"A mistake? Why?"

Otto ignored Corning's question. "The train I arrived on today was driven by a locomotive called the *Triumph*. How old is that machine?"

Corning gave Otto a rueful smile. "It's one of Harris's engines. Our most recent purchase, actually." He swiveled his chair, removed a ledger from the credenza, opened the book on his desk, and ran his finger down a column of entries. "We received delivery on January 5 of this year. We spent a month assembling it. It's been operating since February 15."

Perfect. "That engine labored to haul us up a few of your hills this morning."

Corning closed the ledger. "Harris called it an experiment. It was not our wisest purchase."

"Erastus, the railroad industry in America is only seven years old. Every locomotive made in America so far has been an experiment. But now . . . now we know what it takes to build a modern locomotive." Otto retrieved the spec sheet from Corning's desk. "I have a question for you. If you hope to eventually install legislators who will pass legislation favorable to your railroads, why order locomotives incapable of hauling freight?"

"Keep talking. . . ."

"I do not think this spec sheet is demanding enough. My chief engineer has a design on his drawing board right now that will maintain a speed of fifty miles per hour, even up your four-percent grades. If coupled with one of our tenders, it will run fifteen miles between water stops. It will be capable of hauling fifty tons, whether freight or passenger cars, whether summer or winter."

"If it's still on the drawing board now, this modern machine of yours won't be ready for three years."

"Two years," Otto corrected, ignoring his promise not to over-promise. *Harry will kill me.*

"But we need new machines within a year—as soon as the *Utica & Syracuse* is completed."

Otto leaned forward. He momentarily lowered his head as if he were formulating his words, but he already knew what he would say. *And the shop will be in an uproar because of it.* "Here is what I can do. I will deliver your first *Eagle*-class locomotive—the same machine we delivered to the *P&C* last week—a year after we sign a contract for twelve locomotives. We will deliver five more *Eagles* within the next year, one every other month. After that, every other month for a year, you will receive our newest locomotive—the one that Heinrich Aldridge is designing right now—the one that will exceed even more ambitious specifications for load capacity, speed, and water stops."

Corning removed two cigars from a humidor on his desk and offered one to Otto. "Herr Krieger—Otto—you talk with great confidence about this locomotive of the future. I would need guarantees for both performance and delivery."

Otto crossed his legs, sniffed at the cigar, and inhaled its pungent aroma. "This locomotive will set a new standard in the industry. It will be fast, powerful, reliable, and elegant. Your customers will eagerly anticipate their journeys as an enjoyable experience, not an ordeal that must be endured to get to where they are going. As the first purchaser of a locomotive in this line, I would grant you the right to name the series."

Corning struck a loco-foco, lit his cigar, then tossed the matchbox to Otto. "You're a good salesman, Otto, I'll grant you that. Let's use a word you have already thrown out there. Let's call it *The Standard.*"

Otto smiled at Corning's suggestion. *If he is naming the machine, he is already half-sold.* "*Standard*-class has a nice ring to it. I believe the men at the shop will be pleased with that name. You know we have a third company—Krieger Rail. Could I also entice you to commit to new track?"

Corning took a few contemplative puffs on his cigar and smiled. "I'm afraid you will have to curb your ambitions in that respect. My shop—Rensselaer Iron Works—is already gearing up to produce T-track for the entire system, and I expect I'll make a tidy profit."

Otto mentally noted that self-interest wasn't only the province of the New York State legislators.

Corning read his expression. "Otto, don't be so naive. Every member of a railroad's board of directors is in it to steer commerce to his own business. To make sure the railroad uses their surveyors, or buys their land, their picks and shovels, or in my case, my rail. Every member of a bank's loan committee directs loans to himself, his friends, and his legislators. It's how our nation works. You should position yourself to do the same. If you don't, competitors like Edward Harris will gladly do so, and then you'll find yourself without a whit of influence to control your fate."

Otto puffed for a few moments on his cigar. He was already dreading breaking the news to Harry Vogel and Heinrich Aldridge. *I just promised to deliver twelve new machines at a rate we have never attempted before, and we only have half the machine tools we had a year ago.*

He had planned to continue on to Canada to make a sales call in Montreal. However, with such a pivotal contract dangling in front of him, he shifted his focus to getting back to Philadelphia as soon as possible. He checked his pocket watch to see if he could catch the 3:15 back to Schenectady and then another train to Albany in time to catch a night paddle steamer to New York City.

Corning didn't seem to be in a hurry to end the meeting. "How is your son?"

"Hmm?" Otto responded. *This misconception happens all too often.*

"Rian, your son. When I was in your shop last year, your brother and I took a break to eat in your meeting room. Your son sat in to listen. I told Adrian that our engine drivers froze during the winter, even though they stood right behind the locomotive's boiler. Rian suggested we build a cab for the driver. I loved the idea. Adrian said Krieger Locomotive could do it. I put cash on the barrelhead before I left. I've told that story a thousand times since. Daresay, if any of my engine drivers ever meet Rian, they'll gladly buy him a beer."

"That may have to be a few years from now. Rian is only fourteen." For fear of scuttling their deal-in-the-making, Otto briefly considered allowing

Corning's misconception to go uncorrected. *But no.* "And Erastus, you have made a common mistake. Rian is my daughter, not my son."

Corning responded by chuckling and rolling his eyes. "Well, she fooled me," he said as he tapped his cigar in his ashtray. "I imagine she won't be able to get away with that for very much longer."

The fact that Rian allowed Corning to think she was a boy irritated Otto considerably. *This has been going on for years. I will take this up with her—yet again—when I get home.* And deeper down—so deep that he barely thought it—Rian's subterfuge made him afraid for her. *She is lucky. Most men are indulgent because she is so young. Her youth protects her. But as she grows older, people will shun her for these kinds of shenanigans.*

Otto rose from his chair to initiate his departure. "In any case, those beers may have to wait. I do not think Rian has much interest in alcohol."

* * * * *

· SEAMUS ·

Seamus entered the Krieger Coach office and shed his hat and coat. "It's still raining like cats and dogs out there," he said before he turned his attention to his cousin. The bond they had formed during their Russian adventure was still strong, but they had barely seen one another once a week since their return to Philadelphia three months ago.

Rian stood next to her bookkeeping desk. She had changed into a dry shirt and nankeens and was toweling off her hair with a clean shop rag.

As Rian grew older, Seamus wouldn't have been surprised had she shown some maturation toward womanhood, but he detected no changes at all. Her frame was still angular, with no hint of curves. She was clearly her father's daughter—tall, with wide shoulders and slightly olive skin. Seamus saw hints of Otto's strong jaw and high cheekbones—traits that made Otto Krieger quite handsome—but Rian's features were softer. Especially in light of her clothing, the uninitiated could not be faulted for assuming she was an adolescent boy.

And then there was the distinctive Krieger family trait: like her father and uncles, Rian was "blessed" with a wide gap between her two front teeth.

Rian unself-consciously ran a comb through her hair. "What did Harry say?"

"He said you are never to set foot in the locomotive factory again."

She dropped the comb in a drawer and shut it more forcefully than necessary. "Stupid . . . What did he say about lubricating the drive shaft?"

"He said to tell you thank you, but you still can't come across the alley." Seamus perused the office. Four desks were jammed into the room. Otto's desk was tidy. Next to it, rolls of paper stuck vertically out of a crate—designs for passenger cars, freight cars, flat cars, and tenders. Jules kept a desk here for when he needed to concentrate, but he spent most of his time out on the shop floor. The desk of Aaron Bassinger, the accountant who taught his trade to Rian before he became president of Krieger Rail, lay empty. Rian's desk held a ledger book and a short stack of papers. A nut and stubby bolt acted as a paperweight atop the pile. "Cousin, we need to talk."

Rian sat behind her desk as if preparing herself to conduct business. "Yeah, I know. This thing with the still is exciting. Let me see the plans."

"No, you idiot, I'm not talking about my still," Seamus said as he sat down in a chair on the other side of the desk from her. "Rian, you've been mad as a wet cat ever since we got back from Russia. What's going on?"

"Nothing's going on." Rian popped up and grabbed her flat cap, which had been shedding water on a nearby table. "Harry shouldn't have ordered Jimmy Butter up onto the catwalk. I climbed up there before he could stop me."

"Aye, and ired him considerably. Conor told me you got in another fight with Billy Schiffler."

Rian wrung the cap out over a wastepaper can. "It wasn't a fight like the time I punched him in the nose. We were playing rounders. Billy and I were on the same team. Billy wanted to be the server, but it was my ball, plus I'm a better pitcher."

"Really?"

"Well, he's bigger than I am now." She hung the cap on a peg near the door. "He pitches faster, but I'm more accurate. He was peeved that he wasn't the server. He called me a stupid girl, but I didn't hit him. Then Conor showed up, and Billy said Conor couldn't play because he's Irish, even though we were down one guy. We started yelling at each other, but I still didn't hit him. Conor and I left."

"With the ball?"

She returned to her chair and plopped down. "Of course."

Seamus leaned forward, his elbows on the arms of the chair. "Okay, that one I get . . . And I also heard you lit into the new guy you were teaching to sharpen chisels?"

Rian leaned back in her chair and crossed her arms. "He's a gump. He thought his chisel was good enough and it wasn't."

"You taught me to sharpen chisels on my very first day here three years ago."

"Yeah, but you kept at it until you got it right."

"Not at first. You were patient with me."

"Yeah, but . . ." Rian stopped. She picked the nut and bolt off the pile of paper and rotated the nut back and forth.

Seamus folded his arms, determined to wait her out.

Rian sighed. "In Russia everyone thought I was a boy. I liked that because they treated me different. Do you think Harry would have objected to me being up on the catwalk if I'd been a boy? Do you think *Vater* would give me that look every time I go out into the shop?"

"What look?"

"Conor and I call it 'The Look of Vague Disappointment.' He doesn't say anything to me anymore, but he looks at me like I've yet again failed to live up to his expectations. When Conor and I go out after supper to play rounders, he wishes I were staying in to practice the violin, or read, or do needlepoint. When I go out to the backyard and chop a few billets of wood, he says, 'Let Conor do it.' I like chopping wood, but *Vater* thinks it's not women's work."

"So that's it? You're always tetchy because everyone in Philadelphia knows you're not a boy?"

"Well, no. If you want to split hairs, I'm tetchy because everyone treats me like a girl."

"Well, at least we've made progress. You admit you're a tetch."

Rian rolled her eyes. "Show me your fooking plans."

"Not yet. There's gotta be more."

Rian placed the nut and bolt back on the desk, crossed her arms, and slunk down in her chair. "Come on, Seamus," she whispered.

Seamus pulled a folded sheet of paper from his jacket pocket and waggled it in front of Rian. "Spill, or I don't show you the plans."

Rian averted her gaze for so long, Seamus was afraid she wouldn't acquiesce. Finally . . . "We've been back for three months. I've been the first person in the office every single day. I work on the books each morning until they're current. Afternoons I go across the alley to help out. I help out because I want to learn everything there is to know about building locomotives. I want to run that shop someday, and everyone hates me."

Seamus stared down at his paper, running his finger and thumb along the crease, then returned his regard to Rian. "They don't hate you, Cousin, they just don't think a girl belongs in a factory."

"Girls younger than me work in the mills all up and down the Schuylkill."

"Those girls tend machines. Their shop bosses don't let them leave their machines for hours on end. None of them expects to run the mill someday. I'll bet you dollars to dumplings that everyone in the shop knows you think you could do Harry's job better than him."

Rian smiled ruefully and nodded, but didn't return his gaze. "I'm different."

"Yeah, you're no mill girl, that's for sure."

"No, I'm different from every girl in the world. I don't like dresses. I don't want to stay at home. I don't want to do girl things. . . ." Her voice became so soft that Seamus had to lean in to hear her. "Before we left Russia, I told Uncle Adrian I like it when people think I'm a boy—that I wish I were a boy."

Well, now we're getting somewhere. "So no one thinks you should run Krieger Locomotive, you're different from any other girl we know, and you wish you were a boy. Is that why you're so tetchy?"

Rian nodded.

Well, can I be surprised and not surprised at the same time? "Cousin, here's what I think. I think you will do a lot in life, whether it's over in that locomotive factory or someplace else. I'll be happy to help you anyway I can. Honestly, if I were a girl, I'd probably be ireful about it, so I'm on your side. As far as the wanting to be a boy part, I'm afraid there's nothing I can do to help you out there."

"Fook," Rian whispered as she shook her head.

She's said enough. Seamus scootched his chair toward Rian's desk. "Wanna see some plans?"

Rian merely nodded.

Seamus, who had never yet distilled a batch of whiskey, explained the process as best he could. Ruben Hasselbach, a distiller who recently moved to Philadelphia from western Pennsylvania, had described it to him, but he'd never seen it done. "You moisten the barley, which causes it to sprout, which creates sugar. You put this sugary malt into a tank with hot water and mash it up. You add yeast, which gobbles up the sugar and magically turns it into alcohol. You pour this potent wash into a copper pot for distillation. And this is where Hasselbach's design comes in. It's going to be a triple distillation. You heat the wash. You have to be gentle about it, because the alcohol will leave the mash before the water starts boiling. The alcohol becomes what Ruben calls a vapor, and it rises up the neck of the still, then down this tube, where it becomes a liquid again. Then we do it all over a second and a third time."

Rian eyed the drawings and flicked the paper disdainfully. "Seamus, these aren't plans. They're sketches."

Seamus chose to ignore Rian's disdainful tone. "What do you mean?"

"There are no dimensions, no specifications for the thickness of the copper. How long does Ruben want the tube to be?"

"I don't know."

"Does *he* know?"

"I guess so, but it's all in his head."

"Then I want to meet with Ruben. Krieger Locomotive can't make a still without proper plans. But I can draw them up if I can talk with him."

"Since when do you know how to make shop drawings?"

"Heinrich Aldridge is teaching me. We're drawing plans for the parts for the new locomotive. I'm good at it. I have to concentrate so hard sometimes I forget . . ." Rian stopped.

"Forget what?"

"Nothing."

"Cousin?"

Rian sighed. "I have to concentrate so hard I forget how different I am."

Poor kid. Well, at least now I know what's going on. "Since you can't go back over to the locomotive shop, wanna go visit Ruben Hasselbach and get some dimensions?"

* * * * *

· RIAN ·

The rain stopped while Rian and Seamus met with Ruben Hasselbach. By the time they left the man's third-floor apartment, Rian possessed a new set of plans and a much better understanding of the still's specifications.

Seamus checked his pocket watch as they exited the building onto East Pine Street. "It's two o'clock. I'm running late for me daily with Conor. Care to come along?"

Rian's best friend, Conor McGuire, was employed as a messenger out of the Merchants' Exchange Building. A consortium of businesses operated a series of optical telegraph towers that extended from the mouth of the Delaware Bay to Philadelphia and on again from Philadelphia to Wall Street in New York City. Using large mechanical arms, coded messages passed from tower to tower and could travel a hundred miles in fifteen minutes. Unbeknownst to the consortium, Conor and Rian broke the merchants' code before she ran away to Russia. Conor had been passing on useful bits of news to Seamus for over a year. They met daily at McSweeney's Saloon.

"Girls aren't allowed in McSweeney's," Rian muttered as they turned left onto South Tenth Street.

"It's early afternoon. Nobody will be there except for Braden. He won't mind if you're sitting with us. Besides, you're dressed in your usuals, and most folks'd think you're a boy."

Traffic along their route was so congested they walked faster than the wagons in the street. "I guess the depression is officially over," commented Rian as she stepped around a puddle.

"Seems to be. There's a lot of goods on the docks that are poorly guarded. That's working to No Name's advantage." Seamus had started the United No Name Fire Brigade two years ago. Like most Philadelphia fire companies, besides putting out fires, they also engaged in larcenous pursuits. No Name's "bread and butter" was incoming or outgoing cargo along the Delaware River.

Rian and Seamus crossed the street, dodging between two freight wagons, one carrying a load of carpets, the other a large wooden box stenciled with the words

FRAGILE

CHANDELIER

ABOARD THE BOLIVAR

They walked around street vendors who clogged the sidewalks, noisily hawking anything and everything out of wheelbarrows and carts—local strawberries, oranges from the Caribbean, radishes, pepperpot stew, matches, bread, oysters, and meat pies.

"Seamus, why do you want to build this still, anyway?"

"Hugh Callaghan says I can court Siobhan if I make something of myself."

Rian noted that Seamus said *myself* rather than the *meself* he would have used a few months ago. "Delilah Winter really hurt you, didn't she."

"Delilah Winter told me the truth. She said that an Irishman would never be allowed in the places she wanted to go. That me accent and me . . . *my* accent and *my* clothing would automatically exclude me. If changing my speech is a part of making something of myself, then I'm willing to do that."

"So you're going to stop being Irish?"

"Hugh Callaghan somehow does it. When he's on the street with his boyos, he talks like an Irishman. When he's behind closed doors, he speaks the Queen's English."

"Seems like a long time before your payoff. Start selling whiskey, make a pile of money, and only then start courting Siobhan again."

"Oh, we already see each other on the sly."

"And what'll happen if Hugh finds out?"

"I expect I'll get a thumping. It won't be pretty."

Conor wasn't in McSweeney's when they entered. Seamus pointed toward the back of the saloon. "Conor and I sit over there where it's dark, away from other customers, not that anyone's ever here this time of day." He walked around the bar and disappeared into the kitchen.

Rian sat in the back as instructed and surveyed the empty saloon. She didn't like sitting there and doing nothing. Without a task to distract her, she became . . . *oh God, don't tell this to Seamus* . . . tetchy. She tried to imagine the saloon crowded with men drinking, laughing, and telling stories. Imagining wasn't enough of a distraction. Billy's words during the rounders game kept seeping into the back of her head. *"You're a stupid girl."*

She unfolded the plans of the pot stills that would triple-distill the wash in batches. She pored over the paper—the bulbous shape of the copper pot, which fed vaporized alcohol into the graceful arc of the lyne arm. She used her finger to trace the spiral path of the vapor into the condenser.

She imagined herself drafting the shop drawing the Krieger Locomotive machinists would use to fabricate the stills. Without pencil and paper in hand, her mental exercise wasn't working, and Billy's taunting words crept back to haunt her. *"Hey, girly, if you're going to quit, at least leave us the ball!"*

Rian shoved the paper aside. *Think, Eena. Think. Think of something that gets Billy's fooking words out of your head.* She had returned from Russia with more than a thousand dollars[8] in her pocket. *Now that the depression is over, maybe it's time to figure out how to use my money to make more money.*

Making money—that was something she knew how to do. When she was in Russia, she charged a rental fee to wealthy nobles who wanted to read the latest installments of Charles Dickens's *Oliver Twist.* Members of the Tsar's Imperial Horse Guards paid her to exercise their horses. She endured freezing cold while pushing sleds off the Ice Mountain at the Winter Carnival. And—the easiest money of all—she played poker.

When she and Seamus sailed back to America from Russia, the passengers gambled incessantly. At night, the game was poker, new to everyone, but Rian excelled at it. Although she lost much of her winnings on the last night, the remainder of her rubles, riksdalars, pounds, and dollars were stashed under her mattress at home. She had offered to invest it in the Krieger companies, but her father had declined.

In a flash of inspiration, Rian realized her best investment opportunity was right in front of her. Suddenly, with plenty of things to think about, there was no room for Billy's taunts. Her mood brightened.

Seamus walked out of the kitchen with three mugs of coffee. "Not like Conor to be late," he said as he placed a mug in front of Rian and sat.

Rian blew a few times and took a tentative sip. The coffee was hot and strong. "Seamus, I want to help you with your distilling business."

8. A thousand dollars in 1838 had the buying power of almost $34,000 in 2025.

"I think this is a two-man operation, Cousin. Hasselbach and me is about all I can afford."

"Come on, Seamus. I've got time on my hands and I need to keep busy. I need something to fill my evenings. Let me help you out."

Seamus kept his eyes on the front door. "I've got to make something of meself—I'm talking serious money—so Hugh Callaghan will let me marry Siobhan. I can't be frittering it away paying staff."

"I don't want to be staff. I want to be an investor."

Seamus pulled his eyes from the door and glimpsed at Rian. "What do you have to invest? Delilah Winter cleaned you out at the poker table our last night on the *Great Western*."

"Yeah, I lost a bundle." Rian sipped her coffee. "But I never bet any of the money I won between St. Petersburg and London, plus I won some bets after we docked in New York. *Vater* has paid me to do the bookkeeping since I got home. I've got more than a thousand dollars back at the house. Think of what you could do with that kind of money."

Seamus contemplated the size of Rian's potential investment. "Hmm, if I had a little more cash, I could start on a grander scale."

Rian held out her hand.

He shook Rian's hand. "I think Gallagher's Fine Whiskey just got a little grander, partner."

Their attention was drawn to a commotion at the front of the saloon. Conor McGuire and Rian's cousin Jabez Howes bonked their way through the door together and bashed into a table. Jabez's arm was draped over Conor's shoulder, and he favored his left foot. A cut on his forehead had bled onto his shirt.

* * * * *

· SEAMUS ·

Seamus would have been happy to include Rian in his meeting with Conor. *But Jabez? Nah.* He relegated Rian and Jabez to a nearby table, then found himself musing about his cousin and her cousin as he sipped his coffee. Jabez, born two weeks before Rian, was an orphan. His mother—Uncle Otto's sister, Monika—died bringing Jabez into this world. His slave-trading sea captain father, Levi Howes, killed himself while at sea last December. Jabez was legally under the care of Adrian and Mila Krieger, but Adrian had hopefully been sprung from prison in Russia by this time and was making his way home. Uncle Otto had hired Jabez at Krieger Coach, but Jabez spent more time smoking cigarettes in the alley than working. Eventually, he drifted away from work altogether and caroused along the waterfront with his friends.

Every time I see Rian and Jabez together, thought Seamus, *I think they must be twins. Same hair, same coloring, same build, same gap between their teeth—except that now Jabez is holding a chunk of ice covered by a bar rag to his lip.*

"What happened?" Seamus asked Conor, who was savoring his first sip of coffee.

"I was delivering messages on the east side of town. The schooner *Bee* passed Cape May with a load of tobacco from North Carolina. The dispatcher at the Merchants' Exchange wanted me to alert Jacob Frishmuth at his cigar factory. When I got there, Jabez and two other kids were tearing out of the back of the building with Old Man Frishmuth hot on their tails. He clocked Jabez good before they got away."

Seamus shook his head. "What were they doing?"

"Stealing cigars. Not enough to sell, like you would be interested in. Enough to smoke."

Seamus frowned at the knottiness of it all. "Jacob's a friend. I'll have a little talk with Jabez before we leave to make sure he leaves Frishmuth & Son alone."

"I don't know, Seamus. No one else has had any luck with him. He can't even purloin a smoke without getting smacked around."

Seamus had heard enough about Rian's "twin." "What have you got for me besides tobacco news?"

"Folks at the Merchants' Exchange are excited. Forty-two ships have entered Delaware Bay in the last twenty-four hours. That's the most in a year. The harbor master is about tearing his hair out because he doesn't know where to put them all."

Seamus smiled. "So Dicky Pricker doesn't know what to do with all the ships that are sailing into his harbor. That's good for me, because the more confused our harbor master is, the easier it'll be for me and the boys to lift some goods off the docks. Anything promising?"

Conor sifted through some slips of paper. "Silver from Mexico."

Seamus shook his head. "That'll be too closely guarded."

"There's boots, shoes, and calicoes from Boston."

Seamus shook his head.

"Sugar from Cuba? Iron? Wine? Silk?"

Seamus stretched back in his chair and laced his fingers behind his head. "Let's think on the wine and the silk. Maybe we can pay the watchman to make himself scarce for a few hours."

"Oh, and one other thing." Conor drained his coffee mug. "I delivered a message to George Shippen's office at the Bank of Industry. He's all in a lather about something. I could hear him yelling right through the closed door to his office."

"Any idea about what?"

"Only that it's got something to do with bank stocks."

"Well, good. I don't like that man, even though I know he's friends with Uncle Otto."

* * * * *
· RIAN ·

Rian, her hands around her empty coffee mug, tried to lighten the mood by telling Jabez about her altercation with Harry Vogel in the locomotive factory. Then she stared across the table at her cousin. "Was it worth a couple of cigars to get beat up?"

Jabez shrugged while holding the rag-wrapped ice to his lip.

"Petty theft isn't working for you. Give working at Krieger Coach another try. Ask *Vater* to hire you again. He'll be happy to have you back if you put in a good day's work . . . even half a good day's work. You could get back to being the son he's always wanted."

That last quip made Jabez smile. Where Rian's father frowned on her fascination with the shop side of the Krieger businesses, he fawned all over his nephew—on the rare occasions when Jabez feigned even the slightest interest. "Maybe. But someday I'm going to inherit my father's fortune. I'll be rich. Then I can do whatever I want, and your father, Uncle Adrian, and Aunt Mila won't be able to order me around."

"I thought you didn't want anything to do with your father's money. Uncle Levi was captain of a slave ship."

"Well, I've changed my mind about that. Right now, there's a fortune in real estate sitting in New York City. Someone should benefit from it. Might as well be me."

"You don't turn eighteen for another three-and-a-half years. Are you going to spend all that time swiping cigars?"

"Dunno. It beats working and beats going to school." Jabez leaned back in his chair and folded his arms. "I'm not doing any worse than you are. That fortune teller in Russia said you would run Krieger Locomotive someday. After today, Harry will never let you in the door."

Ouch, how did he turn this around onto me so fast? "Yana told me that first I wouldn't run it, then I would. I figure I'm in the *not-run-it* stage, that's all."

"And the dresses. What about the dresses?"

"She told me I would have to wear a dress for a while longer, then I would never wear a dress again. I never once wore a dress when I was in Russia. I've barely worn one since I got back."

Jabez tossed the wrapped ice on the table. "You still believe an old hag got your future right?"

Rian shrugged. "She's done well so far."

"What? That part about fire following you? Eena, she was pulling your leg. Use your head. There are always fires. Ship fires, factory fires, house fires, warehouse fires. Your cousin is a firefighter, for God's sake. You never would have seen that palace fire if it hadn't been for him."

Rian felt the irritation well up inside her. "It's not just those kinds of fires. It's fire I think I can control but I can't." *Fire follows you. You're The Oddity.*

"I think that's a stupid prediction."

I don't want to talk about this. Rian glanced at Seamus and Conor, who seemed to be wrapping up their business. "Come on," she said to them, "I've been away from the shop long enough. We should get out of here." *A fire that I think is under control but isn't. What is that supposed to mean? Not only do I have no idea, it bothers the hell out of me.*

* * * * *

· OLIVIA ·

Long Pond Plantation,
on the Cooper River near Charleston, South Carolina

Olivia Tucker's limp, headless chicken was still warm and dank from the scalding, but she had plucked so many chickens in the past couple of years that the task was welcome and mindless. She was content to pluck away and listen to Cook rant.

"That raggedy-assed half-wit is useless as tits on a boar," Cook declared, referring to the field hand she had just shooed out of the summer kitchen. "What's he think? Cook was born last Sunday?"

Moments ago, a field hand named Nassau climbed the hill from the slave cabins to the kitchen, hoping to borrow one of Cook's wooden spoons because he had lost his and didn't have time to carve a new one. "More likely one of those other Misery Row bumpkins stole it," Cook spouted.

Olivia would have let Nassau borrow the spoon. Cook had extras, but she wasn't having any of it. "Ain't one of them worth a tinker's cuss, Little." Cook had called her *Little* since she could walk and Mammy-Rose would bring her into the kitchen so they could steal cookies together. "Don't trust 'em, never will."

Olivia kept her mouth shut, relishing the honor of being included in one of Cook's rants. Cook's mask was down—an unheard-of happenstance in the presence of a white person—and Olivia sure as heck wouldn't say anything to ruin that.

Cook's diatribe brought to light the gulf between the house servants and field hands. Call them what you want—servants or hands—they were all slaves, owned by Olivia's father, Randolph Tucker, Squire of Long Pond, one of the largest rice planters in the South Carolina Lowcountry. The house servants considered themselves the aristocrats of Long Pond's little slave society. They were better fed, better housed, better looking, better dressed, and more attuned to the righteous arrogance of their white masters. As far as the house servants were concerned, the poor wretches who labored in the fields from sunup to sundown six days a week, who lived in the mean cabins of Misery Row, were loutish, ignorant, and beneath contempt.

Olivia didn't know what the field hands thought of the house servants. She didn't know any of them, really. Those few she talked to treated her with the hat-in-hand, eyes-down deference her station allegedly warranted, even though she was only fourteen.

Olivia thought it all was a bunch of balderdash. All of it.

Unlike every other white South Carolinian she knew, Olivia hated the institution of slavery. But she mostly kept her thoughts to herself. *If I say anything to Papa, he yells and tells me I'm too young to understand. If I say something to Mother, she falls into a mood. I can't say anything to the servants—even Cook—because they'll get all agitated. And the difference between house servants and field hands? One more evil inflicted on them all to keep them in line.*

Olivia chose to shove all those thoughts to the side and enjoy her time in Cook's domain—plucking chickens, watching the comings and goings in the kitchen, listening to Cook rant. Sadly, the moment didn't last. Papa's voice sounded from the back door of Tucker Hall. "Olivia, come in here right now!" He didn't bother taking the ten extra steps to the threshold of the summer kitchen, although he couldn't possibly have seen Cook and her from where he was.

Olivia knew right away that she was in a bucket of trouble. Her father only called her *Olivia* when he was angry. Not long ago, he was wont to call her *Whiskey*, which was short for *whiskey in a teacup*.

"You're like whiskey in a teacup," Papa told her a thousand times when she was a sprout. "You're pretty as porcelain on the outside, but you sure do pack a punch. I'm proud of you."

Her father's praise—on the rare occasions she heard it these days—no longer carried the ring of truth. Olivia was skeptical about the *pretty as porcelain* part. A year ago, Mother described her as "coltish," a reference to her tendency to flit from one thing to another. But what Olivia heard was that she had spindly legs and kept bumping into things. That's when she started staring in the mirror. What she saw was a passable young woman with blue eyes and auburn hair who exhibited not a hint of a womanly curve. Twelve months onward, she still stared in the mirror, waiting in vain for the curves.

And she never heard the *I'm proud of you* part anymore. In fact, more and more often, Papa barked *Olivia!* in exasperation. She had lately skirted so many rules—some stated and some so baked into Lowcountry culture that they were considered common sense—she could only guess what she was in trouble for.

Cook fished a headless chicken out of the scalding pot. "You better get going, Little. Squire almost never come out that door, and he don't sound too happy."

Olivia thought plucking chickens in the summer kitchen was far preferable to getting yelled at by her father. She felt an ease with the house slaves that she could only show in the safety of Cook's domain. They slipped over there when they thought they could get away with it—to grab a few scraps of leftovers or flirt or laugh or merely get off their feet.

That ease didn't exist two years ago.

* * * * *

Olivia began gravitating to the kitchen after Mammy-Rose and Topper—the two most important people in her world—disappeared from her life. Mammy raised Olivia, and raised her mother before that. Topper was her half-brother and best friend. With them gone, there wasn't anyone left at Long Pond who Olivia could talk to. *Not Mother. Certainly not Papa. Not those three mindless Jaudon girls from Catawba Point, the next plantation upriver.*

Time passed. Despite Olivia's frequent visits to Cook's kitchen, she could tell the slaves didn't like seeing her there. Why should they trust her? She was the only legitimate child of planter Randolph Tucker. She was a privileged scion of the master class, a girl whose family's wealth was built off the backs of eighty people held in bondage . . . a hundred if you considered the house servants.

The house servants would enter the kitchen all loose and laughy. Then, when they saw Olivia, the mask would go up in a blink. She could feel their resentment . . . well, she knew it was resentment, but the mask rose so fast that it came across as the slightest bit of vexation. Then they would smile, nod slightly to acknowledge her presence, and do what they came into the kitchen to do, but without a quarter of the animation with which they first entered.

Five months after Mammy ran off—in December of 1836—Olivia made a big leap to break the logjam. She remembered it like it was yesterday. "Cook, do you remember when Mammy bolted when we were in Philadelphia?"

Cook didn't look up. She was counting while kneading the dough for her famous rice and flour bread, and kneading had to proceed for eight solid minutes. Cook didn't have a watch, but she sure knew how to count up to at least four hundred eighty. "How would I remember that, Little? I've never been to Philadelphia for your mama's social season."

Olivia had hung around Cook's kitchen long enough to know a barb when she heard it. For years, the Tucker family summered in Philadelphia. Cook had never been brought North to impress the Yankees with her cuisine. Northern dinner guests wouldn't have appreciated Cook's Gullah fare, so Mother always hired a local chef to work the kitchen during the ten weeks of summer socials.

Meals at Long Pond were dictated by whatever bounty the sea, the Cooper River, the fields, and the gardens offered up each morning, but almost always contained at least one Lowcountry staple: shrimp, crab, rice, peas, okra, or greens. "It's the food your daddy was raised on," Cook told her many times. "It's what he loves, so that's what I cook."

At the moment, Olivia wasn't concerned about Cook's barb or the hurt feelings it concealed. Her heart was pounding. She leaned toward Cook and whispered, "Mammy didn't escape on her own."

Cook kept counting and leaned again into her dough. "Figured."

"Three of us helped her escape. Me, a girl named Rian, and a boy named Conor. We had to because it was the day before Mother, Mammy, and I were supposed to leave Philadelphia and come back here."

"Seventy-eight, seventy-nine, eighty," Cook muttered, then glared at Olivia. "Rose never told anyone at Long Pond that she was fixin' to bolt. Did you put that idea in her head?"

"No, it was her idea. Remember Topper? Mammy's grandson? You know he's my half-brother, right?"

Cook returned her attention to her dough. "Course I know that. You shouldn't be talking about it, though."

"Topper was supposed to come North as Papa's groom, but Papa lost him in a card game. Everyone else in Mammy's family had been sold off, so she had no reason not to try to get away."

Cook wiped her hands on her apron and stared at Olivia for the first time. "She told you this?"

"Yes, on the steamship on our way North."

"Why'd she trust you?"

"I reckon she already knew what I'd say."

Cook lifted the dough, placed it in a big ceramic bowl, covered it with a towel, and parked it near the stove. "Who else at Long Pond knows this?"

"No one."

Cook turned, grabbed a wet rag, and wiped the butcher block table. "You make sure you keep it that way."

"You won't tell any of the other house servants?"

Cook kept wiping even though all the flour had disappeared. "Are you crazy, girl? A juicy story like that'd travel 'round the Lowcountry like wildfire. If your daddy ever finds that out, he'll tan your hide good."

Olivia put her hand on Cook's to stop her wiping. "But I want the others to relax when they come into the kitchen. I love being here . . . love being with you . . . with them . . . but I don't want them to feel uneasy when I'm here."

Cook looked Olivia in the eye. "You can tell?"

"Of course. That's why I'm telling you about helping Mammy-Rose get away."

Cook went back to wiping, only slower. "Topper. She loved that boy. You loved him, too, didn't you."

"Of course. We grew up together, closer than peas in a shell."

Cook smiled even though she made a show of still wiping.

"We played spies in Tucker Hall, caught tadpoles in the creek, mucked stalls together, walked Mr. Boseman's horse when he brought him back in a lather, read *Robinson Crusoe* to one another. . . ."

"You shouldn't be talking about slaves knowing how to read, Little, even if they ain't living here no more. Your daddy wouldn't appreciate it."

"I hate my father. He had his way with Mammy's daughter, then sold her when he tired of her. He lost Topper—his son!—in that card game. When he's drunk, he gets mean."

Cook turned, swished her rag in the washtub, wrung it out, then turned again to face Olivia. "You shouldn't talk about your daddy that way. It'll lead to trouble, and that trouble somehow always flows downhill to us . . . And never tell another soul what you done. Let Ol' Cookie deal with your little problem in the kitchen. I'll let the others know what's what. But I sure as hell ain't gonna tell 'em what you done."

* * * * *

"Tellin' you, Little," said Cook, bringing Olivia back to the present. "You'll get a lickin' if you don't jump."

Cook might have been right. *Papa hits, but only when he's been drinking.* She rose from her stool, leaving a half-plucked chicken on the chopping block. "I'll come back unless he confines me to my quarters. I can't believe I'm fourteen years old and I still get sent to my room."

Cook ruled the kitchen even though Papa owned her and Grampa Tucker owned her before Papa. Mother only entered Cook's domain to coordinate the menu if they were entertaining at Long Pond, otherwise the cuisine was Cook's to determine.

Tucker Hall—what the slaves called the Big House—was Mother's domain, although Mother let Papa think he ran things. She often referred to him as The Squire, a nod to his legal training, though he had never practiced law. Even though she probably had a better head for figures than Papa, he kept Long Pond's books. Mother always deferred to him during social occasions, but in private, she tore into him furiously for his liberties with the comeliest slave girls.

Truth be told, Olivia despised her father for much more than what she had mentioned to Cook. He bought and sold individuals rather than an entire family, thus tearing them from their loved ones. He allowed his human chattel to be treated brutally. He developed a greater fondness for his racehorses than he did for the human beings their family had enslaved since his father's time.

Olivia entered Tucker Hall through the back door. She followed the silence and the wide-eyed oh-you're-gonna-catch-it-now expressions on three different servants' faces through the pantry, the kitchen, the dining room, the solarium, the tea room, and into the parlor. Mother sat on one of the settees. Colonel Jaudon, the father of the three stupid girls who joined Olivia at Long Pond five days a week for tutoring, sat on another settee opposite Mother. The Squire stood at the unlit fireplace, holding a copy of *The Liberator* . . . the June 8 issue, to be precise.

The Liberator was William Lloyd Garrison's abolitionist newspaper, printed in Boston. Intercepting abolitionist material sent through the mail was illegal, but postmasters in many Southern states ignored the law and threw the publications away. They were never punished for it. As far as Olivia's family was concerned, *The Liberator* might as well have been written by the devil.

Papa held out the newspaper. "Olivia, tell me about this."

Olivia checked around for the signs. *No whiskey bottle. No drink glasses. Good. Papa doesn't hit when he's sober.* "It's a newspaper."

"Now is not the time for sass, Olivia. Did you give it to Carlotta Jaudon?"

"Yes, Papa. Yesterday." *Tarnation, I was stupid,* Olivia thought to herself. *I thought it might be a dumb idea even as I was handing it over.*

"Why did you give it to her?"

Olivia tried to inject enough truth into her response to make it at least a little bit plausible. "There's an article on the front page about a riot in Philadelphia," she said in the sincerest voice she could muster. "A mob burned down a new meeting hall. I walked by the site before they started construction two years ago. I guess I wanted Carlotta to be impressed . . . to think I was worldly . . . that I had actually seen a place that they wrote about in newspapers." *But I really wanted her to start thinking. To become an abolitionist like I am. I thought* The Liberator *might do the trick. Damnation, that was stupid.*

Colonel Jaudon stood and turned to Olivia. "Did you know that was an abolitionist newspaper when you gave it to my daughter?"

Olivia didn't like Jaudon. Every week or so, he wandered over from Catawba Point with a bottle of spirits. He and Papa would drink until dawn. Whatever Papa was supposed to do the next morning wouldn't get done. *The man is a drunken buffoon, but now is not the time to treat him that way.* "Yes, sir. But I only wanted her to read the article about the mob because—"

"Did she read the other articles?"

"No, sir." *Not quite true. She might have read the first paragraph of some of them.*

Her father stepped forward, his grip crinkling the newspaper. "Where did you get this?"

"I found it in a trash can at the post office." *A lie. Rian Krieger sent it to me because she saw the riot. She even ran into the building to save some man's papers. But I sure as heck didn't tell Carlotta that, and I'm not going to tell you, Papa.*

"What were you doing in the post office?"

"Picking up the mail." *Sending a letter to Rian.*

"Did that Krieger girl send this to you?"

"No, sir." *Yes.*

"Did any of the slaves see it?"

"No, sir." *Yes. They had it for a day. Some were able to read it. I read it to others.*

The Squire gave Colonel Jaudon a raised eyebrow, as if to ask if this interrogation had gone far enough.

Jaudon nodded. "I think we've heard enough, Squire. Let's chalk it up to your daughter's naivety. It is time for me to return to Catawba Point and tell my wife that, in all likelihood, our fifteen-year-old is not an abolitionist." Then he smiled. "God forbid."

The Squire turned to Olivia. "Your mother and I are not done with you yet. Do not leave the room." Then, to Colonel Jaudon, he said, "Matthew, as I walk you out, I have some concerns about some things I'm hearing from my brother in Burma. It seems the Brits have opened up that area and started building dikes. . . ."

Olivia paid little attention as her father's voice faded into the ballroom and disappeared completely in the foyer. *He's not drunk yet. I don't have to worry.*

Mother fumed on the settee. "Olivia, you really must stop this nonsense. The Squire tolerated your shenanigans when you confined them to Long Pond. Now you have involved the neighbors. That is unacceptable. If you keep this up, Barnwell Wilkinson will have nothing to do with you when the time comes."

Barnwell Wilkinson was the son of her father's oldest friend from college. From the moment the two children were born, the parents joked that they would someday get married. As Olivia and Barney reached their teens, cementing the alliance between one of the largest rice plantations near Charleston and one of the largest cotton plantations near Columbia seemed inevitable.

Olivia's attention drifted as her mother prattled on. *Rian could have clipped that article out and mailed it to me, but she sent me the entire* Liberator. *She wanted me to read the whole newspaper. I bet she even wanted me to show it to the slaves.*

". . . there won't be a suitor in all of South Carolina who comes near you, despite our wealth . . . Olivia, are you listening to me?"

"Hmm? Yes, Mother. No one will want to marry me."

"Olivia, your list of transgressions is growing. You showed that filthy anti-slavery rag to Carlotta Jaudon. You yelled at the overseer in front of the field hands. You spend more time in Cook's kitchen than in the parlor with me. This has all got to stop."

Randolph Tucker's footsteps grew louder as he strode through the ball-room. He re-entered the parlor, slammed the door behind him, kept coming straight at Olivia, and slapped her hard on the face.

The blow knocked Olivia back a half-step.

"Never embarrass me in front of a neighbor again!"

Stunned, Olivia stared back at her father in defiance, struggling not to show the fear that had taken hold.

The Squire retrieved the newspaper off the table and crumpled it up. "These people are a threat to our way of life. I do not want you reading their filth. You are only fourteen years old. You are too young to understand. I tell you, wait a few years. You will comprehend we live in an earthly paradise. South Carolina is the wealthiest state in the Union for a reason."

Olivia glowered at her father in furious silence, but waves of new truths cascaded into her consciousness. *He hit me and he hasn't even started drinking yet. He hit me because I embarrassed him. This changes nothing. I'll keep on doing what I do. He will do what he does. If it means he hits me again, so be it.*

* * * * *

· RIAN ·

Rian left McSweeney's Saloon and walked back to the Krieger Coach office, where she found Jules Freeman working at his desk. Word of her confrontation with Harry in the locomotive factory had already leapt across the alley.

Jules put his pencil down and leaned forward, elbows on the desk. "We should tell your father."

Jules played many roles in Rian's life: mentor, confidant, protector, inspiration. His walk through life would have been noteworthy had he *only* been the foreman at Krieger Coach. In Philadelphia, a Black man who gave orders to whites was unusual, though not unprecedented. However, Jules had also started his own manufacturing firm: Freeman Hydraulics, which built steam-powered fire pumps. When Jules was asked to complete the construction of Pennsylvania Hall earlier this year, his wife, Maddie, assumed the day-to-day running of the business and continued to do so to this day.

Jules and Maddie were also stationmasters in the Underground Railroad. Rian used to help them out by conducting self-emancipators to their next station, but her father put a stop to it because it was too dangerous.

"No, this is my fight," she responded. "*Vater* doesn't think I should be out in the shop, so what's the sense of telling him about Harry?"

"You could have been killed. You and I both know Harry's not a very good foreman. Maybe this should be the excuse to get rid of him."

The thought of getting rid of Harry made her smile. *But* Vater *would replace him with some new gump who would throw the same obstacles in my way: "You're a girl. You don't belong here."* Rian decided to change the subject. "How's Maddie doing at Freeman Hydraulics?"

"Apparently my wife was born to be a businesswoman. Here we are, in the middle of a depression—"

"Coming out of a depression," Rian interrupted.

"—coming out of a depression, and sales of our fire pumps are steady. She's hired more men. If we could borrow money from a bank, we could buy the machinery we need to fabricate the boilers rather than subcontracting to Krieger Locomotive. Of course, no bank will loan to a Black-owned business."

"I've got some money left over from my Russia trip, but I told Seamus I want to invest in his new distilling business."

"How much are you talking about?"

"A little over a thousand dollars."

"I'm afraid we'll need three times that much. Give it to Seamus."

"What are you going to do?"

"What every Black business owner has to do: save up until we can pay for a machine in cash. Then start saving again. It takes longer. It's not as efficient. But that's the way it is."

* * * * *

· OTTO ·

Otto bought a ticket from Albany to New York on the river steamer *Victory*. Late to the ticket queue, he secured the last private cabin available for the night voyage down the Hudson River. With a good sleep and a little luck schedule-wise, he could catch the first train out of Amboy, New Jersey, and be back in Philadelphia less than twenty-four hours after his meeting with Erastus Corning. *If I am lucky, I will arrive fresh enough to put in some work in the afternoon.*

Now, in the darkness of his cabin, arriving well rested appeared to be a fantasy because sleep eluded him. Even though he had paid extra for the private cabin, he was disappointed to find his minuscule accommodations were situated directly above the ship's engine room. His berth was hot and noisy. He tossed in his narrow bunk for what felt like the hundredth time.

On this night, he could have expected his promises to Erastus Corning— delivering a locomotive every other month once the contract was signed—to be what kept him awake. But no. What he kept coming back to was Rian. *Corning thought she was a boy. If she continues this way, she will end up like my . . .*

"This is ridiculous," he muttered. It was long after midnight. He dressed in the dark, left his cabin, climbed the stairs, and emerged onto the main deck to find a balmy, cloudless night. The light of a waning gibbous moon danced off the Hudson. With his elbows on the rail, he soaked in the solitary peacefulness for ten minutes or so, but his thoughts kept returning to Rian.

The shore was vaguely visible in the moonlight, and one lighthouse and an occasional navigation lamp marked the *Victory*'s methodical progress downriver. With the rhythmic *choosh . . . choosh . . . choosh* of the ship's steam engines now barely audible, Otto became aware of the tinkling airs of a piano emanating from the saloon behind him. Although tempted to return to his cabin and attempt to sleep, he chose the saloon instead. Inside, a piano man plunked away, a gentleman and a lady huddled in a corner, and four men played cards at a table. A bartender read a newspaper behind his station.

Otto ambled to the bar. "*Guten Abend* [Good evening]. Is it too late to get a beer?"

The bartender folded his newspaper. "It is never too late to get a beer on this boat." He drew a glass from the tap and placed it in front of Otto. "When did you come over?"

"Hmm?"

"I'm guessing you were born in Germany. By your accent, I bet you're from Württemberg, like me."

Not yet ready to chat, Otto raised his glass to signify that the man's guess—the Kingdom of Württemberg—was correct.

The bartender freshened his own glass with beer. "I was born in Ebhausen. My parents brought me over when I was seven in 1816 to escape the Hunger Year."[9]

Mention of the Hunger Year conjured up all sorts of emotions for Otto. He tried unsuccessfully to stuff them down. "A sad time. My brothers, my sister, and I lasted a little longer. We came over in 1820."

"If you lasted that long after the famine, why'd you come over?"

"A lot of reasons. The short answer is that we landed on the wrong side of a constable's sensibilities."

"I'm going to be on duty until three. How about the long answer?"

Otto was usually irritated by Americans' propensity to ask personal questions, and resisted giving in to their impertinence. But this man was a fellow

---

9. The volcano Mt. Tambora in the Dutch East Indies erupted in April 1815, the largest volcanic catastrophe in recorded human history. The explosion threw a vertical mile of the mountain into the atmosphere. Ash traveled hundreds of miles before it came to rest. Worse, millions of tons of sulfur dioxide worked their way into the Northern Hemisphere, circled halfway around the world, and blocked out sunlight in parts of the United States and Europe. In the subsequent "Year without Summer," crops failed. Württemberg, already ravaged by successive invasions during the Napoleonic Wars, was especially vulnerable. During the "Hunger Year," the starving population was reduced to eating rats and tree bark. The connection between the eruption of Mt. Tambora and "The Year Without Summer" was not made until decades later, when it was first proposed by the physicist and atmospheric researcher William Jackson Humphreys.

German. Otto was sure he would never see him again, and he had committed to drinking at least one beer.

He sipped his beer. It was warm, the way he liked it. *Where to start?* "My father was born in 1775. He trained as a blacksmith in Stuttgart. A blacksmith had great status in those days, even though the smithing guilds' power was on the wane. The guilds' jealously guarded what influence they still had left. After my father married my mother, she assisted him in the forge. He taught her many skills."

"And that didn't go over very well with the blacksmith guild?"

"No, not at all. My father pushed back and told them to mind their own business. He was headstrong. Our surname is Krieger."

The bartender regarded Otto with new interest. "Warrior? I've never met anyone with that name before."

Otto nodded. "I heard my father say, 'I am a Warrior by name and a warrior by nature' a hundred times. He and my mother were often in a kerfuffle with one neighbor or another. My parents were liberal thinkers. They were both attracted to the new ideas coming out of France at the time. Liberty, equality, and fraternity all seemed like worthy concepts to them."

"To them? Your mother as well?"

"Oh yes. Mother was as bullheaded as my father . . . feisty. Too feisty for many of our neighbors. Then the King of Württemberg joined Napoleon's coalition. My father enlisted in the cavalry."

"So Krieger became a warrior."

Otto smiled at the thought. "Indeed. And when he was away, my mother put food on the table by keeping the forge open."

"And the guilds . . . ?"

"Ostracized her. As did more of our neighbors, but not all, at least for a while. In between wars, Papa would come dragging home and return to the shop. Mother would continue to assist him. When he went back to war, she took his place again. She became independent. Some people kept going to her because her smithing skills were significant and she was honest. Of course, she could never call herself a blacksmith because she was a woman."

The bartender sipped his beer, his eyes encouraging Otto to continue.

"The other blacksmiths shunned her. Our shop was repeatedly vandalized. No one came to our defense. Mother never knuckled under. In fact, she became even more outspoken and defiant."

"How old were you at the time?

Otto shrugged. "Fourteen or so. Old enough to understand what was going on, too young to do anything about it. My father was one of the few military men from Württemberg who survived the Russian campaign. He came home and licked his wounds. Then, in 1813, our beloved king left Napoleon and changed sides to the Sixth Coalition, and my father was gone for another year. He finally came home for good in 1815."

"And your mother kept blacksmithing all this time?"

Otto sipped his beer and nodded. "She did. My father returned from France wounded in body and spirit. It took him years to recover. Mother kept the forge open. Then the Hunger Year struck. Hard times do not bring out the best in people. Business dropped off. The guilds and even more neighbors shunned my family."

"And that's why you came to America?"

"No, that came later. After my mother died of starvation in 1817. After my father married another woman and had two daughters. But part of me has always felt that it was not the starvation that killed her. I think she really died because she was too far outside the norms Stuttgart was willing to tolerate. The ostracization wore her down, then finally killed her. That is why . . ."

"Why what?"

Otto found himself surprisingly on the verge of tears. He tried to speak the words but couldn't. *That is why I fear so much for Rian. I see so much of my mother in her. Where strength in a man is viewed as laudable, in a woman it breeds ostracism and pain.* "That is why . . ."

"Could I have another root beer, please."

Otto glanced to his right to find one of the men who had been playing cards when he entered the saloon.

The bartender nodded and turned to grab a bottle from the shelf behind him. "Hold that thought, Herr Krieger."

The card player turned to Otto. "Krieger . . . Three months ago, I painted a portrait of a young man named Rian Krieger aboard the British steamship *Great Western*."

Verdammt noch mal [Damnit]. There it is again. My daughter posing as a boy. This is so maddening. He reluctantly offered his hand to the man. "You have made a common mistake. Rian Krieger is my daughter, not my son. Your painting hangs on the wall of her bedroom. I am told by those who know more about art than I do that it is excellent work."

"My name is David Winter. I must confess, I am in a bit of a shock. I could have sworn Rian was a boy."

Otto had no desire to talk about Rian's propensity for masquerading as a boy. "And you were involved in Rian's notorious poker games?"

"Sadly, yes. She is a better poker player than I am."

"Poker. Is that what you and your friends are playing over there?"

Winter shook his head. "Not many people know the game yet. We're playing *vingt-et-un*. Would you care to join us?"

Otto checked his pocket watch. *Two o'clock.* "*Vingt-et-un.* I have heard of that game but never played."

"The rules are easy. Come join us. You can tell me how my friend Rian is doing."

Otto never returned to his cabin. He left the table a modest winner as the sun was rising. He never returned to the bartender to tell him that his mother's feistiness—and the shunning that resulted—was perhaps what most shaped him as he grew toward manhood.

My mother's greatest trait was her feistiness, and it was the source of her undoing. That is a fate I will do everything in my power to help my daughter avoid.

THURSDAY, JULY 12

· OTTO ·

Otto managed to sleep on the train from Amboy to Camden. Still, he trudged the last leg of his journey from the Walnut Street ferry dock to Krieger Coach with mixed emotions. The likelihood of a contract for a dozen locomotives and twenty-four passenger cars was exciting. However, Krieger Locomotive foreman Harry Vogel was sure to be irate when he heard the news. On top of all that, he had renewed his vow to rein Rian in. During his long evening with David Winter in the steamship's saloon, he heard stories of Rian's shenanigans on the trip from St. Petersburg to New York. *Winter referred to Rian as* he *so many times that, after a while, I stopped correcting him. This has been going on for far too long. It has to stop.*

Rian and locomotive designer Heinrich Aldridge barely acknowledged Otto when he entered the Krieger Coach office. *What is Heinrich doing over here? His office is across the alley.* Then Otto realized that Rian and Heinrich were engaged in an argument.

"No, no, no!" Rian said forcefully. "If we make the main rod symmetrical, we can use the same pattern on both sides of the engine."

"But if we make each rod unique—the left-hand one a mirror image of the right-hand one—we will have more upfront cost but save money on materials in the long run."

Otto often encountered his daughter in conflict with someone—himself, her best friend Conor, Harry Vogel, men in the shops—but arguing with Heinrich was a new one. *Rian would never have the temerity to argue with Heinrich.*

Heinrich was a steam engine genius, Krieger Locomotive's initial hire three years ago. Since then, rapid innovation in the sciences and arts of metallurgy, combustion, precision manufacturing, and power generation meant that what was considered state-of-the-art a few months ago would be outmoded tomorrow. Heinrich Aldridge was the man who kept Krieger Locomotive leapfrogging ahead of its competitors.

Then Otto noticed that Heinrich and Rian were . . . smiling. "*Was geht hier vor sich?* [What is going on here?]" he asked.

Heinrich glanced up from the desk. "*Otto, willkommen zuhause* [welcome home]. Your daughter and I are haggling about the nitty-gritty of my latest design. We have some ideas, but there are disagreements."

"Apparently," was Otto's only comment. *I have been gone for a week, and this is the only reception I get.*

"Hello, *Vater*. You're home earlier than we expected," Rian said, but then she turned her attention back to Aldridge. "Who's going to make the extra pattern? We don't have enough pattern makers as it is."

"We'll have to hire them," said Heinrich.

"We don't have enough money to hire anyone new. We can barely make payroll as it is."

"Aha," said Otto. "If either of you would ask me how my trip went, I could help inform your 'disagreement.' The *Utica & Schenectady* wants us to bid on a contract for twelve locomotives. If we land this contract, we will have more than enough money to hire all the workers we want. Here is the *U&S* specification sheet."

Although Otto handed the sheet to Aldridge, the steam-engine genius shared it with Rian and they read it together. Heinrich finished reading and shrugged. "Otto, the *Eagle* already exceeds all these specifications. The locomotive we are haggling about right now will make the *Eagle* obsolete. How soon do we have to get our bid in?"

"Two weeks. The first locomotive must be delivered a year after we sign the contract—if we get it, that is—and then one locomotive every two months after that." Otto resisted the impulse to shut his eyes as the inevitable storm broke over his head.

Heinrich put his hands to his head in dismay. "Otto, this is exactly what Harry pleaded with you not to do. We have never produced locomotives at that rate, even when we had twice the men and machinery."

Otto walked behind his desk as if it would be a sufficient barrier to this onslaught. "Well, you may not like it, but my job is to sell. Your job is to figure out how to fulfill the contract."

"Technically, it will be Harry Vogel's job, but . . ." Aldridge glanced at Rian. Rian shrugged, picked up a pencil, and started making calculations. "Otto, this is madness," Heinrich said. "Yes, we have a design—a wonderful design—for the new machine. And we can certainly build our next *Eagle* in a year, especially if we continue to purchase new machine tools. But a new locomotive every two months after that?" He turned to Rian. "What did you come up with?"

Rian put her pencil down. "We know from experience that, counting patterns and molds, the first locomotive will take forty thousand man-hours to build. With Krieger Locomotive's current payroll of thirty skilled men, we can make the first deadline. Once the patterns and molds have been created, the number of man-hours drops to about thirty thousand. However, if we're building a new locomotive every two months after that, with a sixty-hour week, we would have to double our payroll . . . to sixty-two men—plus or minus—if my calculations are correct."

Heinrich nodded, supporting her estimate, and glanced up from his own calculations. "You should talk to Harry, but my gut tells me that even if we can repopulate our current shop with new machine tools, we will be too cramped. In order to manufacture at this volume, we will need at least 125,000 square feet. We will need to build a new factory."

Heinrich's statement—"we will need to build a new factory"—crowded out all other thoughts from Otto's mind: the brief notice Otto had taken about his daughter's contribution to the discussion, his question about why Heinrich and Rian were meeting in the Krieger Coach office rather than the Krieger Locomotive office, or his chagrin at promising too much to Erastus Corning. *This is it*, he said to himself. *I can see it. That land I bought across the street will be the site for the new locomotive factory. Krieger Locomotive is back on its feet. I must talk to Shippen. I need to borrow more money. Lots more.*

In his excitement, he forgot that he also intended to rein in Rian.

* * * * *

· OLIVIA ·

Olivia sat alone on the Long Pond's Cooper River dock, killing time until she met Emblee in the summer kitchen for a reading lesson. A steamboat gave a friendly *toot* as it churned upriver. She waved back, but her mind was elsewhere, contemplating the path her relationship took with Cook after she revealed her role in Mammy-Rose's escape.

Cook started saying and doing things in front of Olivia that no enslaved individual would do unless they knew they could trust her. The other servants certainly noticed. As they became more comfortable with Olivia in the kitchen, she occasionally caught a glimpse of a copy of *The Liberator* being passed from one house slave to another. If Cook saw the transfer, though, she would shoo the perpetrators out of the kitchen and tell them to conduct their mischief down at the cabins.

Olivia learned that one of the issues of *The Liberator* had been handed off by a free Black man on a boat loading rice at Long Pond's landing on the Cooper River. Another came from a plantation on the Ashley River when Mother spent an overnight and took Matilde, her current favorite, along to attend to her. The others' provenances were mysteries, but in all cases, the issues were wrinkled, tattered, and months or even years old.

Then, a new indication that the house slaves were beginning to trust her: Emblee, who tended to Olivia's toilet, worked in the kitchen, and served the family's meals, approached her in the summer kitchen. She held out a copy of *The Liberator.* "Can you teach me to read this?"

Olivia liked Emblee. After Topper left, Emblee kind of slid into his place, but not really. They spent a lot of time together but never shared their innermost secrets like Olivia and Topper had. Emblee could draw better than Olivia and even taught her some things. She could take a piece of charcoal and draw a person's likeness on an old shingle, and you could tell who it was without a hint. Didn't matter who it was on the plantation; she could capture the essence of a person with a few deft strokes. Of course, if Mother or Papa ever caught her doing that on any day but a Sunday,[10] she would get a licking.

Close as they were, when Emblee asked Olivia to teach her to read, Olivia first side-glanced to Cook for a *yes* or *no.* Teaching a Black person to read— free or enslaved—was punishable by as much as a hundred-dollar fine and six months in prison. And that was if the teacher were white. If the teacher were a free Black, the punishment would be a fine, prison, and as many as fifty lashes.

Cook considered this for quite a bit, then nodded. "Not when anyone else is around, though—Black or white."

Olivia turned to Emblee. "Can you read any of it?"

"No, but I want to."

Emblee's tutoring began immediately. Weeks in, Olivia retrieved a copy of *McGuffey's First Reader* from the nursery. The nursery had been turned into Mother's sewing room but still had many mementos of Olivia's early years. About the only maternal task Olivia could remember her mother doing was teaching her to read. Mammy did everything else. But then again, Mammy raised her mother, too. *And now Mammy is free someplace in the North, or maybe even Canada.*

Olivia rose from the dock and started walking up the hill toward the summer kitchen.

* * * * *

Emblee stumbled her way through a McGuffey lesson. When she hesitated too long on a word, Olivia would prompt her, "Sound it out."

---

10. Sunday was allegedly a day of rest for field hands, but in reality was far from it. The enslaved tended their garden plots, ground their ration of corn for the week, and did what they could to earn a little money—take on odd jobs or make things like brooms or preserves.

"Ma-ry had a lit-tle lamb, Its fleece was white as snow, And ev-er-y where that Ma-ry went . . ."

Olivia and Emblee were concentrating so hard on the lesson that neither one heard Cook talking to someone in a raised voice out at the clothesline.

"The lamb was . . . sure to go," Emblee read, then beamed at Olivia.

The Squire suddenly loomed over Olivia and Emblee. He slapped Emblee hard, and the book flew out of her hand and landed near the kindling pile.

Papa rubbed his fingers with his other hand and leaned in close to Olivia, the smell of whiskey on his breath.

A spasm of fear coursed through Olivia's body. *This is bad right now, but it will be okay. He'll rant and threaten. Maybe he'll hit me like he did yesterday. Then he'll drink into the night. And tomorrow he won't do anything about my transgressions.*

"You know," said Papa, "I blame myself for this. The first time I caught you teaching this African to read, I threatened to sell her away, but I didn't."

Because you were drunk. You never follow through on your drunken threats.

"I should have proved to you that there are consequences to your actions." Papa grabbed Olivia by the arm, yanked her out of the chair, and dragged her into Tucker Hall. He berated her through the house, up the stairs, pushed her into her bedroom, and slammed the door. "Now stay there!"

An hour later, the unmistakable *clink* of bottles coming from Papa's office meant he was rooting through the liquor cabinet for a new bottle. The following morning, he meted out no further punishment. There were no further "consequences to her actions."

* * * * *

· OTTO ·

The dining room of the prestigious United States Hotel pulsed with activity. A hundred diners—politicians, bankers, industrialists, and other members of Philadelphia's elite—conversed, laughed, and plotted. Silverware tinkled against china. Waiters slipped deftly between tables while holding trays aloft.

Sometimes Otto had to pinch himself—after years of dining regularly at the hotel, he was now an accepted member of this elite club. He ran his last hunk of bread around his plate, sopping up the remaining streaks of his beef stew gravy.

Otto's dining companion today was George Shippen, chairman of the Board of the Bank of Industry and motivating force behind numerous railroads. Shippen had listened intently to Otto's recapitulation of his successful sales trip, and Otto was warming up to make his pitch for a substantial new loan.

"George, now we know the configuration of a modern locomotive and what it will take to build it. Our newest engine will have five thousand separate parts. Each part will be cast, or forged, or pressed, or milled based on its function. I will need special machine tools for each step of the process. We will still have blacksmiths in the shop, but they will not spend their days beating molten iron with a hand hammer; our blacksmiths will use steam hammers. Our machinists will drive lathes and planers that shape components with tolerances of a sixty-fourth of an inch. If we land this contract, we will have to double our staff in a year."

Shippen put up his hand. "I can see where this is going, Krieger, and your news is heartening. Now that we're climbing out of this damnable depression, I'm sure the Bank of Industry's loan committee would have supported a request."

Otto's heart sank. "Would have?"

"The bank's future is muddy. Something has happened in the past few days. All of Philadelphia smells an end to the depression. As you know, the Panic almost broke the Bank of Industry. The price of our stock still hasn't recovered—the same as stock in my railroads. While you were in New York, someone bought up a huge percentage of the BOI's stock at a bargain price. So much stock that I can tell what is coming: I've lost control of the bank's board and, more to the point, the loan committee."

"And you fear that will mean poor investments?"

"Perhaps, but let me give you a quick lesson in how the world really works. In our relationship so far, you have benefited from a loan committee, with timely prods from me, of course, that favored the Krieger companies. Oh, admittedly, your hiring practices—putting that African in charge of your carriage shop and hiring Irish—didn't work to your advantage, but you trimmed your sails when you had to. It's safe to say that our relationship with the Krieger companies is a fine example of how the system should work."

"Should . . . but does not?"

"Not all the time. These days, not a lot of the time. The loan committee in every bank is charged with the responsibility of directing finite resources to those enterprises most likely to justify the bank's investment. All too often, the committeemen instead make loans to their own enterprises or those of their friends, whether they're sound investments or not. They make bribes described as loans to state legislators, who then pass legislation that favors them."

Otto wasn't much surprised by this. It was essentially the same conversation he had with Erastus Corning, the president of the *Utica & Schenectady Railroad*. And Otto had always assumed that Shippen had directed bank funds to his own railroads. "So there is no sense in making a loan application to the Bank of Industry?"

"No, I think you should apply, but I'm telling you, it seems that I won't be able to influence the newly configured committee's decision, no matter how worthy your application is."

"Who are the new committee members? Perhaps we know them?"

Shippen glanced around the vast dining room. "That's the thing. I don't know who they are. I don't know who has bought up all my stock. For all I know, it's someone in this room. It seems that half the money in Philadelphia is eating here today."

* * * * *

· RIAN ·

Rian knew her father would get around to chastising her about the incident with Harry Vogel, but hoped he wouldn't ruin their first dinner together in almost a week. He didn't even wait through the soup course.

"Harry told me he banned you from Krieger Locomotive yesterday."

I bet he didn't tell you he almost killed me. "He never told me directly, but Seamus passed on the word."

"You openly defied him in front of the men."

Rian knew this discussion would take a while. She placed her spoon on the plate that held her soup bowl. "He was about to make a bad decision. One of the men could have died."

"And what was this bad decision?"

He wanted to send Jimmy Butter up onto the catwalk. Jimmy was drunk. "I can't say."

"Cannot . . . or will not?"

"Will not." In these types of conversations with her father, this was the point where he would explode, chastise her for keeping secrets, and ban her from doing something she had been doing. *Then I figure out how to circumvent the ban. Then Vater storms around about it. These disputes occur every once in a while, then they blow over.*

But this conversation took an unexpected turn.

"I played cards on the steamship from Albany with a man named David Winter. He said to say hello."

A flood of mixed emotions engulfed Rian. On one hand, Winter had painted the portrait of her that was her most prized possession. On the other hand, the day he finished the portrait, Rian exposed him for cheating in a poker game. "How is he?"

Her father nodded. "Well, I think. Looking for a place to set up a portrait studio. It was interesting, what I learned. Two voyages: St. Petersburg to London, then Bristol to New York. All that time, he thought you were a boy."

Rian knew her father hated it when people mistook her for a boy. She was unapologetic. "I'd been masquerading as a boy in Russia. I figured it would be easier to travel home as a boy. I had all the clothes. . . ."

"Erastus Corning thought you were a boy."

"When I met him, I was dressed in my shop clothes."

"But there is a common thread here. You dress like a boy. You never correct people when they misperceive you as a boy. Rian, this has to stop."

The rat-thought started gnawing. *The Oddity. There it is. You're The Oddity.* Rian rose to clear her unfinished soup bowl.

"Please do not walk away from me, *Liebling.*"

"I can't wear a dress in the shop," Rian called over her shoulder as she entered the kitchen. "It will get too dirty."

Her father's voice followed her into the kitchen. "You have been banned from Krieger Locomotive."

"But not from Krieger Coach." Rian felt her position crumbling. Rather than continue to defend the indefensible, she placed her dishes in the wash tub and left the kitchen.

"Rian," her father called from the dining room, "we are not finished with our supper or this discussion."

"You may not be, but I am," she shot back over her shoulder. She mounted the stairs, entered her bedroom, and slammed the door. She plopped down on her bed and stared at her portrait. Her thoughts went back to those days on the Atlantic. Like everyone aboard the ship except for Seamus, Winter thought Rian was a boy, a former coachman, the erstwhile companion to Grand Duke Konstantin, a card sharp. After experimentation with numerous poses, David Winter had placed Rian's top hat at a jaunty angle on top of her head. He wrapped her in the voluminous navy blue greatcoat that the Tsar's Imperial Horse Guards had given her in honor of their fallen captain.

You can't be The Oddity, she whispered to the figure in the portrait.

The young man in the top hat stared back at her, the wide, spit-worthy gap between his front teeth, the knowing smile insinuating a shared secret, the strong jaw implying confidence and capability. Winter had made his subject appear older in the painting—perhaps seventeen—which had intrigued Rian from the first moment she saw the portrait.

Who am I going to be? What will I become? She asked the young man. *You can't be The Oddity. You're too . . . perfect.* Most nights, the young man's confidence radiated out to her, filled her. But this time, she felt nothing emanating from the portrait, leaving her to fill the void. *You're The Oddity,* she thought for the hundredth time that day.

FRIDAY, JULY 13

· OTTO ·

James Forten entered the Krieger Coach office unannounced. Otto rose and walked around his desk to greet him. Forten owned the largest sailmaking operation on the Delaware and, at age seventy-one, was reputed to be the richest Black man in America. He had commissioned a well-appointed cabriolet from Krieger Coach several years ago that Otto occasionally saw on the street. It was one of his better creations.

Otto felt warmly toward Forten, yet wary. Forten was an astute businessman. He contributed both money and articles to William Lloyd Garrison's anti-slavery newspaper. He made loans to individuals—both Black and white—whom he deemed worthy of his support. *But most of his visits since he purchased that cabriolet have been to request a contribution to one of his many causes.*

Otto gestured for Forten to sit in the chair in front of his desk, then retreated to his own swivel chair. "What brings you here, James?" *How much will this cost me at a time when I can ill afford it? What more can the Black community ask of me? I no longer sell any Krieger products to slaveholders. I occasionally escort fugitives to the next station on their Underground Railroad.*

Forten placed his top hat on a side table and sat in the proffered chair. "Let's call this a combination of business and pleasure, Otto. Two months ago, the mob that burned down Pennsylvania Hall dealt a huge blow to my brethren. . . ."

"Yes, I am well aware. I purchased three shares in that enterprise at your behest."

"We built that building to be a beacon for the anti-slavery movement until the sin of slavery is banished from America. It lasted four days, from dedication to destruction. Rather than hole up and lick my wounds, I've decided to take another tack."

"And this new direction somehow involves me?"

Forten nodded. "I understand your business has suffered in recent months because of certain moral decisions you've made."

Otto wondered momentarily who had been speaking to Forten. *My next-door neighbor Lucretia Mott? Jules Freeman? Jules's wife, Maddie? Hell, it could even have been Rian.* He gave Forten a wry smile and leaned back into his desk. "Yes, I sold two small locomotives to sugar plantations in the Caribbean and expected to sell many more. Lucretia pointed out the hypocrisy of my actions, although she was tactful enough not to call it that. If I hate the sin of slavery—which I do—she asked me why I would support it by selling locomotives that make slavery more viable. With Lucretia's clarity of thought to buttress me, I decided to stop doing business with companies that use human chattel. I have not contacted any such outfits since then. I have no regrets."

"How is your business otherwise?"

"The depression set us back on our heels, the same as everyone else. But I believe we are finally on the other side. Right now, we are putting together bids to build twelve locomotives and twenty-four passenger cars for the *Utica & Schenectady Railroad*. If we land that contract, it will change our companies forever. I want to build a new factory on the land I bought across Buttonwood Street. I am projecting three acres all under one roof, solely dedicated to building locomotives. Our staff will double to more than sixty. We will invest in machine tools that did not exist when we opened the Krieger factories two years ago."

Forten crossed his legs and removed a pipe from his pocket. "You'll need more capital."

Otto nodded. "George Shippen at the Bank of Industry has thrown a bit of cold water on my plans. I already have significant loans with them, and I don't think they will offer new ones. A while back, I would have been happy to talk to Nicholas Biddle at the Pennsylvania National Bank, but sadly, that no longer seems advisable. Apparently, Mr. Biddle has been loaning heavily to plantation owners in Mississippi, which, of course, is inconsistent with my newfound moral ground, but also a poor business decision. I hear his bank is on thin ice."

Forten nodded, affirming Otto's take on the situation. "I have a question for you. Three board positions have recently opened up at Shippen's bank. All three individuals would also sit on the bank's loan committee. Would you be interested in taking one of them?"

Otto picked up his pipe from his desk, dumped its spent ashes into a waste can, and started tamping in new tobacco. "Why would anyone offer such a position to me? I know nothing about evaluating loan applications."

"Otto, you are one of the noteworthy, up-and-coming businessmen in our city. You have weathered a depression that drove three of your competitors into bankruptcy. You're a natural fit for the task."

"How do you know about all the doings at the Bank of Industry? Shippen doesn't even know who bought up all his stock."

Forten leaned back in his chair. "I know about it because I am now the bank's largest stockholder. There are laws that prevent a Black man from sitting on a corporate board, but there are no laws that ban him from buying so much stock that he can dictate which men . . . which *white* men . . . sit on the board."

James is Shippen's mystery stockholder. Otto's eyes widened at Forten's audacity. Then the impact of Forten's offer sank in. He lost interest in his pipe and placed it back on his desk. "Why are you interested in having me sit on the board?"

"Because of your decision to stop abetting the institution of slavery by trading with slaveholders. I believe that if you can make such a decision that directly opposes your economic well-being, the least I can do is support you. The same with James Mott."

James. My Quaker neighbor. Also a businessman who has stopped trading in slave-tainted goods. "It would be an honor to work with James. And the third position?"

"Jonas Longstreth of Ellis & Longstreth Lumber Company. Jonas was very supportive of Jules when he oversaw construction on the Pennsylvania Hall project."

Otto had never met Longstreth but knew him by reputation. "George Shippen will not take well to losing control of the board. This may be awkward because I consider him a friend."

"I met with him yesterday afternoon. He agreed to endorse my nominees—I have the power to unseat him otherwise—but I made my own concessions. When I die, the Bank of Industry can purchase all my shares from my estate at the prevailing rate."

"How long would my position on the board last?"

"As far as I am concerned, as long as I own the stock, which means as long as I am alive."

"James, your timing could not be better. As a member of the loan committee, I could advocate for loans to be made to my own Krieger companies."

Forten shrugged. "That seems to be the way business is done these days. But beware: If you take out more loans, you will be further in debt to the bank. Otto, there is one other important aspect to this offer. . . ."

Uh-oh, here it comes.

"I would like you to advocate for Negro[11] loan applicants, business owners who previously were not deemed worthy of consideration because of the color of their skin."

The real motive behind Forten's bold powerplay became clear. *You sly, old fox. You sprung your trap perfectly.* "James, you test my mettle. My support of the Black community heretofore has been mostly under the covers."

"Yes, I daresay you will become a less-popular dining companion at the United States Hotel. Pro-Negro sentiment is not common among that set."

Otto's thoughts raced. If he accepted the board position, he could expand his business. But most of his dining companions would disapprove of making loans to Negroes. It had taken him years to feel like he belonged in the dining room of the United States Hotel, and this would put it all in jeopardy. He picked up his pipe, struck a loco-foco, and took a few draws. "James, when I emigrated to America eighteen years ago, I did not know of the existence of bank boards, and even if I had, I would not have imagined myself sitting on one. I would be honored to serve on the board."

* * * * *

As Otto watched the door close behind Forten, his thoughts wandered back to his mother and how the people of Stuttgart ostracized her because she was different. *If we had been rich, they would have overlooked her differentness. Rich people can do things—say things—that are unpopular, but they get away with them because they are rich.*

If I am rich, I will still find dining companions at the United States Hotel. If I am rich, all of Rian's differentness—her clothing, her stubbornness, her defiance—will not matter. Men of good breeding will flock to my door, asking for her hand in marriage.

* * * * *

· RIAN ·

Rian stood at a workbench in Krieger Coach, using a rat tail file to remove the last minuscule snits from the wooden pattern of the thirty-two-tooth gear. The pattern would eventually be pressed again and again into a sand table to

---

11. A note to readers: With the wish to keep this narrative as historically appropriate as I can, I employ three terms that African Americans used in the 1830s to describe themselves. In order to justify the use of terms that have since lost respectability or even become offensive, I cite African American civil rights icons who used those terms with dignity. James Forten identified himself as colored, W.E.B Dubois called himself a Negro. Martin Luther King used that term as well and also called himself black. In recent years, the term *black* has been capitalized to *Black*. I have chosen to use that more modern form throughout Rian Krieger's Journey.

make molds for cast-iron gears. She set the pattern on its edge, closed her eyes, and felt around for imperfections. She found none.

"What number pattern is that?" Conor's voice came from over her shoulder.

Rian remained focused on her fingering. "I dunno. Forty or fifty. I think it's perfect. Heinrich will be pleased. . . . Done with your messages for the day?"

"Yeah, that's why I'm here. I thought you might want to climb Sparks Shot Tower and watch the sunset."

"I can't. I've gotta help Seamus at the distillery."

"Come on, Rian. Take some time off. All you do these days is work."

Rian sighed. "I've told you a hundred times. When I'm concentrating on something, I'm not thinking about being different. My bad thoughts stay in the back of the buckboard."

Conor sighed in exasperation.

"So everybody wins. I'm happier because I'm not thinking. Heinrich gets another pattern. Seamus gets a distillery."

"But what do I get? I don't get you at all anymore."

"Then come with me to the distillery."

* * * * *

· OLIVIA ·

Five days a week, the Jaudon girls walked to Long Pond to join Olivia for French lessons under the tutelage of the spinster Miss Petty. Olivia found all three Jaudon girls to be tiresome, especially that twit Carlotta who squealed on her about *The Liberator*. Olivia no longer shared any personal details with the Jaudon girls and certainly nothing about her abolitionist sentiments. Today her antipathy got so bad that she silently wished they would all have to go home for some reason so she could retreat to the summer kitchen.

As if to answer her prayers, today's lesson came to an abrupt halt when Miss Petty keeled over right in the middle of their conjugation of the verb *avoir*. Not that Olivia wished Miss Petty any ill will, of course, but Mother shooed the Jaudons back home, then ordered Matilde to prepare a guest bedroom for Miss Petty, who would be staying for the night or who-knows-how-long.

With Mother distracted and the Jaudons blessedly gone, Olivia slipped upstairs to change out of her good taffeta dress and into a day dress more suitable for Cook's kitchen. She opened the top drawer of her bureau to grab a more appropriate pair of stockings and came upon a forgotten newspaper article she had clipped out of the *Charleston Courier* two years ago. It had lain in her drawer ever since.

* * * * *

Olivia first read the article on a Sunday. She was helping Cook put up string beans from Cook's own garden. Cook blanched her beans and stuffed them into a jar with garlic and vinegar so she could sell them to the general store a mile down the road. Cook liked to add a sprig of dill into her beans before she poured the melted paraffin on top to seal the jar. The Squire didn't like dill, so she didn't do that for the beans she put up for the Tucker pantry. The paraffin hadn't melted yet, and Cook couldn't talk to Olivia and tend to the paraffin, so Olivia glanced around for something to do and spotted the *Charleston Courier* in the kindling box. The newspaper was dated September 9, 1836. She silently read an article on the back page.

On this date 97 years ago, South Carolina, already the most prosperous British colony in America, was shaken by a rebellion. A perfidious slave by the name of Jemmy led a revolt of his ilk out of the Stono River, 20 miles SW of our fair city. Their first act was to raid Hutchinson's Store, which sold firearms and ammunition, and kill the proprietor and another unfortunate soul. Thus, armed and filled with the lust for blood, they marched south in the hopes of making their way to Florida, which at that time was a Spanish colony. Cutting a 10-mile-long path of destruction, the hellions burned 6 plantations and killed 23 innocent citizens.

Their rampage, however, ended before the sun set on that sad day. A hastily gathered militia caught up with the iniquitous devils and shot and killed 14 of them. Those who cravenly asked for mercy were immediately executed by hanging. Others who fled the scene of the battle were hunted and summarily hung.

Olivia re-read the piece aloud to Cook as Cook poured melted paraffin into jars, but omitted words like *perfidious* and *iniquitous*. "Did you know about this?" she asked Cook after she finished reading.

"Of course, every slave in the Lowcountry know about that day," Cook said as she poured. The silence stretched between them, then she muttered, "The day they strung up my great-great-granddaddy."

Olivia stared at Cook's back. She was about to ask more questions when the head gardener entered the summer kitchen and told Cook that The Squire's string beans were ready and he had ordered some of the boys to start picking. The gardener didn't give a hoot that it was the slaves' day off because The Squire wanted his vegetables picked at their absolute best. "More string beans than you can shake a stick at," he said. "You should drop whatever you're doing and get your kitchen ready to put up The Squire's beans."

Olivia could tell Cook was a little put out. Cook fussed and muttered a bit as she cleared space on the butcher block—"This is Sunday. Sunday afternoon's s'posed to be my time"—then settled herself down. Finally, she turned to Olivia. "Little, I want you to help the men bring in all those beans they've picked."

It was almost dusk. The gardener surely didn't need extra help trucking beans to the kitchen, but Olivia hopped to it. On her first trip back with a peck basket overflowing with beans, she noticed something odd. Cook was talking to a raggedly clothed field hand named Grafton, a noteworthy occurrence given Cook's general higher-than-thou attitude toward the farm help.

Cook wasn't lecturing or berating Grafton like she was wont to do with those folks. She and he were cooking something up together, keeping their eyes on both Tucker Hall and the shacks down on Misery Row. Both of them held an unlit candle. Olivia was curious but doubted Cook would give her a straight answer, so she didn't bother asking her what was going on. Back in the kitchen, Olivia snipped the Stono Rebellion article out to someday send to Rian Krieger, but then Rian ran off to Russia.

Then last year, Olivia was helping Cook pickle string beans on a Sunday. It was definitely a Sunday because Cook had a mound of dill sprigs on the butcher block to put in her jars. It was definitely early September because those beans always came on in the first two weeks of that month. Grafton, that same raggedy field hand, stuck his head in the summer kitchen and started to say something to Cook. He spotted Olivia and his mask went up in a blink.

Olivia remembered something odd from that day. Grafton indicated with a jerk of his head that he wanted to talk to Cook outside. Cook wiped her hands on her apron and followed the man out. Now, this sort of thing just didn't occur. As far as Cook was concerned, folks like Grafton were "raggedy-assed field hands," and no raggedy ass would have the nerve to order Cook around, especially in her own kitchen.

A minute later, Cook returned, slipping off her apron as she approached Olivia. "I forgot I was supposed to do somethin'. I'm gonna be gone for a bit." She hung her apron on the peg and walked out the door without another word. A moment later, she returned, opened a drawer near the door, pulled out a candle stub, and departed a second time.

Olivia rose from her stool, exited the summer kitchen, and watched as Cook and Grafton walked down toward Misery Row. She followed over the crest of the hill enough to see them enter the largest of the slave shacks, which probably housed six or eight men, but she had never been in one to know for sure. Three other slaves shortly followed, Matilde and two field hands.

* * * * *

With the two-year-old *Charleston Courier* article in hand, Olivia exited Tucker Hall from the back door and found Cook hanging rags on her line outside the summer kitchen. Olivia stooped to pull a rag out of the wicker basket, but Cook slapped her hand away and grabbed the next rag herself.

Olivia straightened in surprise. "Let me help you, Cook."

Cook attached the rag to her line using one of the clothespins a field hand named Damian carved out of willow on Sundays. "Don't think hangin' laundry's a job your daddy would like to see you doin', Little. You can take the basket back to the laundry in a minute, though. I've gotta get back to my stove."

"I will, but I want to talk to you about something."

"If you wanna talk, you better do it out here, and you better hush yourself."

Olivia glanced around. "Why? Nobody's nearby."

"Shadrach's in the kitchen scarfin' that leftover piece of pie you didn't eat last night."

Shadrach was a house slave who swept and dusted Tucker Hall before Olivia's mother arose in the morning, then helped the gardener outside in the kitchen plot. "That's okay. I like Shadrach."

"Well, I don't trust him, and you shouldn't either."

Olivia watched Cook pin the next rag to the line. Cook told her a lot more plantation gossip if she buttoned her lip and listened.

Cook pinned up another rag. "How do you think The Squire knew you was in the kitchen teachin' Emblee her ABCs the other day? Your daddy never come out here, yet he stormed right by me like it was nobody's business and cuffed Emblee good."

Dumbstruck, Olivia stole a glance toward the summer kitchen.

"Someone in the Big House told on you. I don't know who it was, but Shad was in the kitchen when you and Emblee was fixin' to get started. Maybe he went back inside and told your daddy, or maybe he told one of the others and they passed it on. Maybe it was Damian after he dropped off these new clothespins, but I can't figure how he coulda got word into the Big House. But what you gotta know, Little, is there ain't no secrets on a plantation. When those rats inside the house whisper in The Squire's ear, he gives them a little somethin'. Might be a hard candy from the dish on his desk. Might be some time off. Might be he looks the other way when he finds 'em loafin'. If you don't want The Squire to smack you again, you can't trust nobody inside."

"Then who can I trust?"

"Me, I s'pose. Matilde, even though she dresses your mama every day. Emblee, to a point, but I know what you two girls is like when she's dressin' you. You talk your girlie talk like she's your friend. Well, you can talk all the girlie talk you want, but if you even think of tellin' her what you did for Rose—helpin' her escape and all—you might as well be lightin' a fuse to a keg of black powder."

Cook's upset. Maybe this isn't the right time to ask her about this newspaper article. Instead, Olivia started the discussion a different way. "Cook . . . tell me about Grafton."

Cook hung another rag on the line before she answered. "Grafton? He's a no-account, same as the rest of the field hands." In a normal conversation, this would have been the point when Cook asked, *Why? Why you askin' about him?* Instead, she leaned over, picked another rag out of the basket, and pinned it on the line. Silence.

"I noticed that every once in a while, around string bean season, I see you and Grafton talking. I know you don't like the field hands much, and I wondered what you talk about."

"Don't you worry about Grafton and me. We ain't doing nothin' you need to concern yourself with."

Olivia wanted to believe Cook, but she didn't. Something was fishy. Disappointed that Cook shut her out, she turned on her heel, returned to her room, and stashed the article about the Stono Rebellion back in her stocking drawer.

But string bean season, Cook conspiring with a field hand she normally wouldn't give the time of day, and the Stono Rebellion all remained somehow connected, and the mystery simmered in the back of her mind.

THURSDAY, AUGUST 9

· OTTO ·

"The regular weekly meeting of the Bank of Industry's loan committee is called to order," George Shippen said with a light tap of his gavel. "I would like to introduce our three new committee members: Herr Otto Krieger of the Krieger companies; Mr. James Mott, wool merchant; and Mr. Jonas Longstreth of Ellis & Longstreth Lumber. Clerk, please note the presence of the other two committee members: president of the Bank of Industry, Mr. Edward Schiffler, and myself, Chair of the Bank of Industry Board."

Otto sat with his four fellow committee members and the clerk around a large table in the center of the Bank of Industry's boardroom. His back was to the only door. To his right, sunlight streamed in through three floor-to-ceiling windows that faced Broad Street. To his left, cabinets and shelves full of ledgers lined the wall. Directly ahead of him, a breakfront held a silver coffee service and a tray of biscuits.

Never in his wildest dreams did he think he would be placed in such a position of power. At these meetings, he and his four fellow committee members would decide the fate of businesses throughout Philadelphia and beyond, some of them—for the first time in the Bank of Industry's short history—owned by Black businessmen. *And today, I will ensure that Freeman Hydraulics is among the first of the Black-owned businesses to get a loan.*

"There is only one loan application before us today," Shippen continued. "We should be able to make short work of this, and then you gentlemen can be on with the rest of your busy day."

Otto knew a loan from the bank would make a big difference for Jules. With an infusion of capital, he could purchase the machines he needed to make boilers for his steam-driven fire pumps.

"If you open your folders, you will find a copy of an application for two thousand dollars from Long Pond plantation outside of Charleston, South Carolina, to build dikes to increase the acreage for rice cultivation."

Otto opened his folder, assured himself that the Long Pond application was the only one inside, and glared at Shippen. "I was under the impression that Jules Freeman had submitted a loan application."

"Mr. Freeman's application was rejected," Shippen responded, his words clipped.

Otto made eye contact with James Mott, then Jonas Longstreth. Both of them gave him a nod that implied, *Go ahead.* Otto returned his attention to Shippen. "Rejected by whom?"

Shippen folded his hands in front of him, then stared at Otto. "By Schiffler and myself."

"On what grounds?"

"Applicants are required to submit three letters of endorsement by members of the business community."

Unsatisfied, sensing Shippen's unease, Otto bored in. "Was Mr. Freeman told this in advance?"

Shippen shuffled his papers as if searching for an answer to Otto's question. "He may not have been."

"Does this application from Long Pond have three letters of endorsement?"

Shippen leaned back in his chair and folded his arms in front of him. "Long Pond is known to us. We have made two previous loans to them."

"Have the loans been paid off?"

"No."

This is how business gets done in this world. It is unfair, but it is the river we are swimming in. Otto forged ahead. "Is Long Pond current with its payments to the previous loans?"

"No, but this new loan will increase their acreage and thus their income. Our research indicates that the price of wholesale rice is up this year."

"And the source of this research?"

"Mr. Randolph Tucker of Long Pond—"

"Mr. Tucker is the applicant for this loan?"

"Yes."

Oof. Your duplicity is maddening. . . . "And your brother-in-law, I believe? "Yes."

"What collateral did Mr. Tucker offer for his previous loans?"

Shippen consulted some papers. "For the first loan of five thousand dollars, ten field hands. For the second—"

"What was the loan for?"

"The price of rice dropped in 1833. He needed a bridge loan to get him to the next season."

"Did the price of rice rise the next season?"

"Yes."

"But he did not pay off the loan."

"No."

The meeting went on like that—Otto barraging Shippen with questions, Shippen curtly supplying the information—for two more hours.

* * * * *

· RIAN ·

Rian was leaving the house when her father's younger brother Kurt mounted the last step to the front porch, his wide grin exposing the Krieger gap between his front teeth.

"Uncle!" In years past, Rian would have jumped into Uncle Kurt's arms and wrapped her legs around his bulk, but now, as a fourteen-year-old who had run away to Russia and returned with stories of her own, she gave him an affectionate embrace without the enthusiastic leap.

Kurt was the tallest and beefiest of the Krieger brothers, which intimidated many people but belied a gentleness Rian loved. He was clean-shaven for the summer, and his sun-bleached blond hair was pulled back into a ponytail. A ship's carpenter aboard the itinerant coastal schooner *Starling*, his visits to bunk at 134 North Ninth Street occurred on short notice. The *Starling* sailed to wherever the next cargo needed to go—anywhere from Halifax to New Orleans and the Caribbean—so Kurt could be gone for weeks or months. His overnight stays were always special occasions filled with stories of far-off cities.

Kurt held Rian at arm's length and eyed her up and down. "Still wearing boy clothes, I see," he said without a hint of judgment. "I guess my brother yet again didn't follow through with one of his periodic paternal proclamations."

Rian smiled at her uncle's alliteration as she pulled his sea bag off his shoulder. "I guess he figures it's more peaceful around the house when I get my way on this particular position. . . . Come on. I'm gonna visit my distillery. You've gotta see it."

Kurt relinquished his bag and watched as Rian opened the front door, tossed the bag over the threshold, and shut the door again. He turned and followed his niece down the porch steps. "Your distillery?"

"You bet. I'm a one-quarter investor, so it's twenty-five percent mine. I'm on my way there now. Seamus and Ruben are making their first batch of whiskey today. Some of the guys at the locomotive factory made the still. I was supposed to help, but Harry won't let me in the shop anymore."

"I can't wait to hear that story," said Kurt as he matched strides with Rian.

The story kept the two occupied for the fifteen-minute walk to the brick warehouse near the Schuylkill that housed Gallagher's Distillery. Rian pounded *bang-bang . . . bang* on the large sliding door with the ball of her fist.

Moments later, the door rolled aside to reveal Cousin Seamus. "Ah, I see my primary investor has brought her seafaring uncle! Come in, come in! Welcome to Gallagher's Distillery." Seamus hugged Kurt, then pulled him into the building. "Your timing's perfect. The first drops of our inaugural batch are making their appearance. Let me show you our little operation."

The day was hot, and the distillery was hotter yet. Rian's eyes were drawn to the first component of the still, a large copper pot topped by a graceful swan neck. This long spout fed into the condenser, which in turn led to the collecting safe. She inhaled the sweet, pungent odor of barley mash. "It smells good in here, Seamus. I could get used to this."

Seamus nodded in agreement. "Two weeks ago, this place smelled more like freshly threshed rye. Since I've been malting the barley, it keeps getting better."

Rian scanned a row of sixteen oaken barrels stacked two high along the back wall. "When did Mr. London deliver the barrels?"

"Yesterday. He even charred the interior of them like Hasselbach instructed."

"Who's Mr. London?" asked Kurt.

"A local cooper. Jules made that connection for me," said Seamus. "An up-and-coming Black craftsman. Jules thought we might be able to do some business together."

Rian put her nose to the bunghole of one of the barrels and pulled back sharply. "Whoa, he really did char them up. Very smokey."

"Why are the barrels charred?" asked Kurt.

"I'm taking Ruben's advice on this," Seamus responded. "He says it adds to the flavor. Some guy in Kentucky has been doing it for a couple of years now."

"Where is Mr. Hasselbach?" asked Rian.

"He hasn't been feeling well lately, darlin'."

Kurt surveyed the warehouse with a complete rotation. "Rian says that Hasselbach is the brains of the operation."

"Oh, I believe he knows the distilling business right enough, but he's not nearly as keen on setting up a factory, which is really what this is. That skill and a chunk of money are what I bring to the partnership. I've had to plan how this place will function two months, two years from now. Where the barrels will be stored. How we keep track of the product. Anyway, he's been sick more than he's been well. I'm afraid I'm on my own more than I bargained for. His daughter brings him over barely enough to tell me when I'm heading down the right trail or when I've wandered into unknown territory. So, I have to say, these first batches will be a bit more of an experiment than a sure thing."

"What kind of experiment?"

"Well, the whiskey Hasselbach brought with him from Pittsburgh three months ago—which was the best I've ever sipped—was made with a combination of rye and barley. He claims that eighty percent rye is a good target, but you can vary that combination. I'm experimenting and keeping careful notes, varying the malting time for the barley, then varying the roasting time to generate different amounts of sugar."

Kurt ran his hand over a barrel. "How many different batches do you plan to create?"

"Hasselbach says that each barrel's likely to be different, but with all me machinations, I figure that, in a year, I'll have sixteen batches to sample. When I settle on one that I really like, that's what I'll concentrate on, but I suspect I'll always do a bit of experimenting as I go along."

"Seamus," said Kurt, "I'm seeing a lot of expenses here for processes I can't even fathom—"

"I'll say," interjected Rian. "Rent for this building, sixteen new barrels every month, barley, rye, tanks to hold the grain, the still, a furnace, not to mention coal for heat."

Kurt turned to his niece. "Are you keeping the books for Gallagher's Distillery, too?"

Rian held her arms out wide, as if the answer were obvious. "Of course, but I'm learning the distilling trade right next to Seamus. Well, a bit of it, at least."

"Where's all this money coming from?" asked Kurt.

Seamus bent over and threw a small shovelful of coal into the pot's firebox. "Well, I've used all the money I brought home from our Russian adventure, and Rian's kicked in a chunk. But still, I'm becoming a mite stretched. I've had to return to my former pursuits of firefighting . . . and lifting whatever I can off the docks at night. My life's busy at the moment."

"So no sales for a year. When do you figure you'll start making some money on this operation?"

"Serious money? Well, in a year I'll know which of my recipes pleases me customers the most. That's when I'll start making it in big batches. In two years, on this date in 1840, I'll start selling one-year-old whiskey in quantities that keep me afloat. Four years from now, once my first big batch is three years old, I'll be selling the best whiskey this side of the Atlantic in quantities that will make me a rich man. And even then, I won't sell the entire batch. I want to see what happens if I age it even longer."

"Lofty ambitions," commented Kurt. "You sound different since you came back from Russia. You've dropped a touch of your mellifluous Irish brogue."

"Only a touch, I hope, and only for some people. I'm still getting used to it, and sometimes I forget."

"Why the change? Seems like a lot of effort."

"Rian and I traveled back from Russia with a beautiful lady who had made something of her life on her own terms. She told me that the Irish were a dime a dozen."

Kurt crossed his arms. "Ouch."

"It felt a tad harsh at the time, but I've taken it to heart. I figure I'll be a rich man soon enough, but if all me riches—all *my* riches—still don't get me past the maitre d' in the United States Hotel because of the way I talk, then I'm limiting myself. That's not how I want my life to go."

"What does Siobhan say about that?"

"Siobhan grew up speaking the Queen's English at home and swearing like a sailor on the street. She's content enough with all these changes to let me call her my girlfriend again. Changing the way I speak is certainly better than me gallivanting off to Russia."

"And her daddy?"

"I think Hugh's amused. He'd rather have me making whiskey than making trouble for him in the firefighting business."

* * * * *

An hour later, Ruben Hasselbach arrived. Gaunt, incapacitated by consumption, and wracked by repeated spasms of coughing, he was nevertheless in an ebullient mood. "Good evening, Rian, so happy you could join us for this momentous occasion." Hasselbach started to shake Kurt's hand but then retreated a step. "I am pleased to meet you, sir, but my doctor says that what I have may be infectious, so I will keep my distance. But come on now, let us see if this grand experiment will work."

By this time, a gallon of liquid had trickled from the condenser into the collecting safe. Hasselback lifted the cover, dipped a ladle into the alcohol, and poured an inch or so into four glasses. "Only sip this. It will be quite powerful."

Seamus held his glass up to the light. "There's no color to it."

"Worry not, Seamus. The color will come during the aging. This liquid will interact with the oaken barrels. The longer it ages, the darker it will become."

Kurt sipped cautiously. "I think you could sell this right now at most taverns along the coast and do quite well. It does have a bit of a bite, though."

Hasselbach sipped. "Yes, this will do very well. Seamus, we are in business."

Showing more bravado than brains, Rian took a healthy slug of the clear liquid and swallowed. It burned all the way down. She exhaled sharply. Her eyes watered. "Whoa . . . Is it okay to be an investor in a whiskey business and think the product is not for me?"

All three adults laughed, but then Hasselbach came to his product's defense. "Whiskey is a bit of an acquired taste, dear Rian. Perhaps you should wait for this batch to age a year or two before you come to a definitive conclusion."

* * * * *

· OLIVIA ·

The heat and humidity had been relentless for weeks, and the family had lately taken their suppers in the gazebo. Outside meals were generally more relaxed, and the "a child is to be seen and not heard" rule was often bent, at least a bit.

But not tonight, Olivia knew. The signs were as plain as the nose on your face. Papa had already downed a couple of bourbons before dinner, and he arrived with a glass filled almost to the brim. *Don't say a peep. Don't give him any excuse to blow up.*

Olivia and her mother had successfully navigated the dinner without precipitating any explosions, even as Papa ranted about his three favorite grievances: that devil John Quincy Adams, the proliferation of Asian rice, and the cursed tariffs.

"The tariffs can't drop fast enough, if you ask me," Papa said as he spooned the last smidgins of his okra and stewed tomatoes. He wiped his mouth with his napkin. "That was delicious."

"Thank you," Olivia said. She knew she had made a mistake as soon as she heard the sound of her father's spoon clattering into his bowl.

"What do you mean, 'thank you'?" Papa asked. His tone turned malevolent in a heartbeat. "Did you cook this meal?"

"No. Cook did."

"Were you in the summer kitchen when Cook was cooking?"

"Yes, for a little bit." *Idiot. All you had to do was shut up.*

"Did you help her?"

"I sliced the onions." *I made almost the whole stew. Cook was teaching me.*

Her father turned his attention to his wife. "Penelope, how many servants work in the kitchen?"

Mother's face turned stony. "Cook works by herself, mostly. If we are entertaining, Emblee and Matilde help."

"Anyone else?"

"If Matilde is attending to me, I suppose Cook might pull Nan in. Peg, maybe, but she's young yet."

"How old is Peg?"

"Twelve, I imagine."

"Two years younger than Olivia."

"Yes . . . Squire, I believe Cook has prepared some berries and cream for dessert. Wouldn't that be nice?"

"Cook!" yelled Papa. He glowered at Olivia—breaking his gaze only once to take another slug of his bourbon—until Cook arrived, still wiping her hands on her apron.

"Go get Emblee, Matilde, Nan, and Peg," Papa ordered.

"Yessir, Squire," said Cook, but she hesitated a moment, peeking ever so briefly at Mother.

"Go!" Papa exploded.

Cook turned and slow-walked back to the summer kitchen.

Mother made eye contact with Olivia, then shifted her gaze to Papa. "Randolph, please don't do this."

Ten agonizing minutes crawled by before the four servants could be found and lined up at the edge of the gazebo. Papa took a swig of bourbon and stared at Olivia. "Pick one."

"No," Olivia responded.

"Pick one, and Boseman will take her to auction tomorrow."

Mother placed her napkin on the table. "Randolph, please, Olivia knows she made a mistake."

"Apparently she does not. She persists in doing a slave's work. If she thinks we're keeping slaves to have them sitting around while she does the work, then she thinks we have too many slaves. If we have too many, we should sell some of them off. Pick two, Olivia. If you say 'no' again, I will order you to pick three. We'll see who can play this game longer. If we get to five, it'll be Cook."

Olivia glanced at her mother.

"Don't look at her. Look at me, and name two of these slaves so that we can get on with our evening! . . . Five! . . . Four! . . . Three! . . ."

Olivia gaped at Emblee, Matilde, Nan, and Peg. They were all petrified. A puddle of urine grew between Peg's bare feet.

"Two! . . ."

"Good evening, Squire. I'm sorry to interrupt your repast." Colonel Jaudon had walked around the side of the Big House with a bottle in his hand. "I apologize for barging in unannounced. I had no idea you would be dining so late, but I wonder if you might be interested in sharing some of this fine whiskey with me. My brother-in-law swears this is from a batch of a hundred gallons they found in Mount Vernon when Washington died."

Olivia thought the man to be a buffoon, but tonight he was a godsend. Papa shifted his attention from her to Jaudon. A moment of boozy confusion clouded his gaze, then he shifted again, this time to the bottle. "I think that is a capital idea," he said, his voice devoid of the least bit of ire. "Let's go to my study."

Olivia and her mother eyed one another. Olivia breathed a sigh of relief. *Papa and Colonel Jaudon are likely to drink until dawn. By that time, he won't remember any of this.*

Mother sat for a moment, then followed the men into the house.

She will spend the rest of the evening in her boudoir. Olivia turned her attention to the four servants. "I'm sorry this happened. Go back to whatever you were doing. No one will be sold away from Long Pond tomorrow."

As the four slaves turned to leave, Olivia shut her eyes hard, but the tears ran down her cheeks anyway.

* * * * *

· OTTO ·

Otto approached James Forten's three-story townhouse at 92 Lombard Street with a bit of trepidation. He knocked, and moments later, Forten's wife, Charlotte, opened the door. "Herr Krieger, we got your note. We've been expecting you. Please come in."

Otto doffed his top hat, entered, and was struck by the presence of more than a dozen individuals, young and old, all Black, reading or sewing or chatting. James and Charlotte were well known for housing a series of indentured servants and employees they mentored before helping them move on to better things. Some were former slaves, some the sons and daughters of neighbors. Some gave Otto a gander and smiled but showed no inclination to engage. Others were so preoccupied by their activity that they were oblivious to his presence.

"James is expecting you," said Charlotte. "He's trying to get some Vigilant Committee work done out back. There are too many interruptions inside."

"I hope I am not one of the interruptions."

"Your note said you wanted to report on your first loan committee meeting. He is very keen to hear about it."

Forten sat at a table in a waning patch of sunlight between the townhouse and a two-story back building that housed overflow members of his household. He glanced up at Otto and waved him to another chair at the table. "Otto, how good of you to pay this visit. Tell me, did George Shippen fuss and fume?"

"Dodged and weaved would be a more accurate description. James, the new committee members and I made a decision during the heat of the meeting that I think you should know about."

"And what is that?"

"Shippen blocked Jules's application on the made-up grounds that he did not include letters of endorsement. I assume he blocked others, as well. Meanwhile, he tried to ram his brother-in-law's application through without the same standards."

"And you called him on it?"

"It took me a while to get there, but yes. We have three votes. We can accept or reject any applications that come before the committee, and there is nothing that George can do about it. . . ."

"But?"

"But we cannot act on what we do not know about, so I proposed a compromise."

"I sense I won't like this."

Otto nodded. "In exchange for Shippen and Schiffler not obstructing the applications from Black businessmen, I okayed a new loan to Long Pond."

"A plantation . . . And what did Long Pond put up for collateral?"

"James, you have cut right to the heart of the matter. He put up five field hands and three house servants."

"And what happens if Randolph Tucker defaults on the loan?"

"Then the Bank of Industry ends up owning eight slaves. If that were to happen, the bank would most likely sell them to satisfy the loan. The bank would be in the slave business."

Forten bowed his head and said nothing for a long moment. "So in order to better the lives of my brethren here in Philadelphia, we have made the lives of our enslaved brothers and sisters in South Carolina more precarious."

"The irony of these unintended consequences was not lost on us."

"How did Shippen react?"

Otto noted the sun passing behind the back building, enveloping the two men in shadow. "I think he is a horse trader by nature. He pulled me into his office afterward and we smoked cigars. I consider him a friend, even though we do not agree about slavery or fair treatment for your brethren. Remember, he is the first person from the set who frequently dines in the United States Hotel who gave me the time of day. It is because of him that my carriage business thrived. He supported my expansion into the railcar and locomotive business."

"I caution you, Otto. That man is not your friend. He is a snake who only looks out for his own interests."

Otto heard Forten's words but . . . *George would never do me dirty.*

SATURDAY, AUGUST 18

· OLIVIA ·

Earthly paradise. Hogwash.

Olivia had never seen a debate, but she had heard of them. Even though she was only nine at the time, she remembered her father and Colonel Jaudon talking about debates between Andy Jackson and representatives from South Carolina about the Nullification. These days, her father read articles at the dinner table describing debates in South Carolina's capital, Columbia, and the nation's capital, Washington City.[12] She knew debaters armed themselves with facts. *Facts are indisputable. I will engage Papa in a debate, and I will be armed to the teeth with facts.* The problem was that she had no other person she dared talk to for guidance.

Since Long Pond grew most of the food it needed, market days were a once-a-week affair. Olivia often accompanied Cook and Emblee into Charleston to buy provisions: local shrimp, salt from New York or Virginia, molasses and sugar from the West Indies, maybe some salted cod from Boston. Cook always tended to business without dilly-dallying. That way, if there was time, she could steal off to visit her son, who had been sold years ago to a man who hired him out to a blacksmith shop on Water Street. While Cook was visiting, Olivia and Emblee shopped for cloth or ribbons or candies. One time, Olivia bought sketch pads for Emblee and herself.

The shortest route from the produce stalls to the blacksmith shop and the stores that sold ribbons and candies was past the slave auction on the shady side of the Customs House on Market Street. Olivia hated this part of their expedition and always tried to get through the crush of mostly men as quickly as possible. It broke her heart to see those despondent human beings on the auction block. Men and women, young and old, all bereft of dignity and hope. Olivia knew no mind was paid to separating a mother from her child or a husband from his wife if the auctioneer thought he could get more by doing so. Only the

---

12. Washington was commonly referred to as Washington City until the passage of the District of Columbia Organic Act of 1871.

fortunate few were sold in pairs or a family group. *A low definition of fortunate*, Olivia thought to herself.

Most of the crowd, both bidders and gawkers, were already liquored up. The bidders stood with their hands in their pockets, merely nodding to the auctioneer if they were still in the game. The gawkers, who Olivia's mother referred to as "the lesser elements," got their jollies from tormenting the slaves, especially the women. They yelled out what their new master would do to them . . . or their daughters. And even though Olivia was only fourteen with not a hint of a womanly figure, those same lesser elements would leer at her and blurt a boozy greeting like, "Come on, honey, have a drink with ol' Charlie."

On this day, though, as Olivia led Emblee and Cook on the path of least resistance along the crowd's periphery, Olivia stopped. "Emblee, wait for me outside the candy store. Cook, we'll meet you at the blacksmith shop in an hour."

Emblee and Cook nodded, clearly anxious to get as far away as possible from the bidders, gawkers, and despair. Olivia watched the pair get safely to the street corner, then changed direction and maneuvered her way to the front of the crowd. A man with an open ledger book stood at a tall desk to the left hand of the auctioneer. Olivia tugged on his sleeve. "Mister, what's the average price for a slave?"

The man ignored her until he finished making an entry. "Depends," he said without taking his eyes off his ledger. "Healthy bucks and breeder women do better than the old, the lame, the one-eyes, anyone with a lot of lashes on their back."

"Just give me an average."

"Be gone, missy. You're bothering me."

"Come on, Mister, give me a number."

The auctioneer forced a female slave to take off her shift and display her back to assure a bidder about her docile temperament—having no lashes was a good indication she was compliant. Olivia could tell the gawkers loved this part of the show because they greeted the woman's nakedness with lewd comments and whistles and catcalls.

"Five hundred dollars," the clerk muttered to Olivia as the lull stretched to a minute. The bidding resumed and the clerk returned his attention to his ledger. Olivia turned to leave.

"Used to be higher before the depression," the man muttered before she was a step away, but Olivia had heard enough.

On the next shopping excursion a week later, Olivia entered the Library Society's new building on Broad Street while Emblee waited outside. Olivia approached a man sitting behind a desk and asked to see a copy of the 1830 U.S. Census. The man had no intention of allowing some presumptuous girl to touch his edition until she mentioned that her last name was Tucker and her father had been a major contributor during the construction of this building.

After she had copied down the census information she was searching for, she gathered up Emblee and they walked to the sweet store. Olivia made a point of taking her time so Cook could gaze at her son as he worked in the blacksmith shop. *Lord knows the smith won't give the man a moment to talk to his mother.*

* * * * *

The timing of Olivia's confrontation with her father was more a matter of opportunity than a plan. Her parents were supposed to entertain the Jaudons for dinner, but in the late afternoon, Colonel Jaudon sent a runner over with a note that said his wife had come down with something. Thus, Olivia was dining with her parents on a Saturday evening, a highly unusual event. As she sat, she slipped the folded paper that held her numbers under her butter plate.

Cook had prepared she-crab soup and shrimp and gravy—two of her father's favorites—and since Papa didn't much like Mrs. Jaudon anyway, he was in an unusually good mood. "Evening, Whiskey," he said as he sat down at the head of the table. "Thanks for joining us this evening."

Papa and Mother exchanged news of the day while Emblee brought in a tray of soup and bread from the summer kitchen. The Squire shifted not a jot as Emblee reached around him to place his soup. "The overseer and I tested the new floodgate[13] for the first time today. It worked perfectly," he announced.

"I saw the men working on the trunk last week," Olivia chimed in, testing the "children should be seen and not heard rule."

The Squire ignored her comment. "The freshwater backed up into the rice field slick as a whistle. So as of today, we have added another two acres of rice fields merely by opening a floodgate."

"Thank you," Olivia said reflexively as Emblee placed a soup bowl in front of her. The Squire scowled at her. He had told her a thousand times that one does not thank a servant for doing their job properly. His words rang in her ears: *They are here to serve you, Olivia, not do you favors that deserve your gratitude.*

Idiot, Olivia thought. *Irritating Papa is not the way to start a debate.*

Mother's news was a bit more mundane. She had tended to two sick slaves. She volunteered to host her Garden Club's Fall Festival at Long Pond. Cook was

---

13. The Cooper River is an estuary. The rising tide pushes back at the river's freshwater, causing the water level to rise predictably twice a day. Enterprising rice farmers took advantage of this fact of nature by installing floodgates, or trunks, to irrigate their fields with fresh water.

in a bit of a crosspatch because now that the Jaudons had backed out of dinner, she had made too much soup.

"What about you, Whiskey? What did you do today?" Papa asked.

Okay, Papa has abandoned the "not heard" rule for the evening. This conversation is sure-as-eggs-is-eggs going to change his mood. "Today was uneventful, but yesterday was market day. I stopped at the new library your donation helped build."

"I didn't know females were allowed in the library," Papa said as he sprinkled some salt into his soup.

Olivia slipped her calculations out from under her butter plate. "I wanted to see if they had a copy of the last census. Papa, did you know that in 1830, there were 257,863 white people who lived in South Carolina?"

The Squire was about to take in a spoonful of his soup, hesitated, then put his spoon back in his bowl. "No, I didn't know that."

"And there were 7,921 free Blacks and 315,401 slaves. There are more Blacks than whites in this state."

Emblee arrived with the shrimp and gravy, noted that the family hadn't finished their soup yet, and stood at her place by the door. The Squire, ignoring her presence, stated, "As it should be. They are here to serve us."

Olivia's stomach churned, both from the callousness of her father's comment and the direction she was about to take the conversation. "Did you know that the average value of a slave is five hundred dollars?"

Her father pushed his bowl away and gave it a brusk wave that meant *clear this*. He sat back in his chair and crossed his arms. "Is that also something you learned at the library?"

"I asked the clerk at the slave auction last week."

Olivia's mother patted her mouth with her napkin. "What were you doing in that crowd, Olivia? You know how I feel about you being in the presence of the lesser elements."

Olivia ignored her mother's comment. "I multiplied five hundred dollars by 315,401 slaves, and I got over 157 million dollars. A couple of weeks ago, you said South Carolina is the richest state in the Union. But if my calculations are correct, most of that wealth is in human beings."

Emblee cleared the soup bowls and served the shrimp and gravy. She could have taken the dirty bowls back to the wash house but instead stood in attendance near the door.

"Land is the source of most of our wealth. But what is your point, Olivia?"

Olivia had no idea if her father was right, but she realized that sparring with him at the dinner table was a fool's errand. She tried to regroup. "How many families in South Carolina own a hundred slaves or more?"

Her father sighed, his impatience close to boiling over. "I have no idea. We members of the gentry sometimes refer to ourselves as *The Hundred*. That is probably as good a measure as any."

"Okay, so let's say the average number of slaves owned by one of The Hundred is 125. That means that 12,500 slaves of South Carolina are owned by one hundred families."

"Likely so . . . Olivia—"

"You said we live in an earthly paradise. If South Carolina is an earthly paradise, it is so for only a hundred families, and it comes at the expense of their 12,500 slaves. It may be an earthly paradise for us, but do we have to enslave people to give us a paradise? It certainly isn't a paradise for them."

"Their paradise will come in the next world, assuming they behave themselves."

"So let me get this straight: A hundred families in South Carolina get an earthly paradise at the expense of thousands of slaves. Do you honestly believe that is God's plan?"

Olivia's father nodded. "I *do* believe it. God placed the land before us for the taking. He killed the unworthy, heathen Wando Indians with smallpox to make way for us. Now we feed the world with our rice and clothe the world with our cotton. Can there be any doubt of our righteousness?"

"We clothe our own slaves with Negro cloth, the coarsest cloth there is. Have you ever felt it? You might as well be sticking needles into them. The supervisor issues two shirts and trousers to a field hand for a year. It's only July, and some men out at the dike last week were dressed only in a shirt. They were wearing no pants because they had worn them into tatters months ago. They should be treated better than that."

"I treat our servants better than the cotton planters upcountry. They are certainly better off here than working on a sugar plantation in Alabama."

Olivia was aware that Emblee had been standing by the door all this time. She forged ahead. "But it's wrong—"

"Wrong? Really? Olivia, we live in the greatest state in the greatest nation on earth. The South's cotton economy drives American prosperity. Drives the mills of Lowell, Massachusetts. Drives the shipbuilding economy of your precious Philadelphia. That is as it should be. If you studied history the way I have, you would know that slavery was integral to the greatest civilizations in history. Slavery is a time-proven practice."

"Egypt fell. Greece fell. Rome fell."

Her father's cheeks reddened. "They didn't fall because of slavery. Olivia, these people cannot care for themselves. Use your eyes. There are two farms owned by free Africans along the road to Charleston. Those people are doing worse than any slave at Long Pond."

"They aren't doing well. But that's because they aren't allowed by law to learn to read. They aren't treated equally by the laws. They can't take jobs reserved for whites, who, by the way, aren't doing very well either. The general store down the road makes all the Black people pay cash."

"Once again, that is as it should be. They can't be trusted."

"But the general store offers credit to the planters. I was there at the same time as Mrs. Jaudon. I overheard Mr. Rife putting the screws to her. The Jaudons have been carrying a balance at Rife's for sixteen months. He said she had to settle up her account because if they don't, he'll go out of business."

"America has been in a depression since last year. It has been difficult for the Jaudons."

"But not so difficult that they don't throw a shindy after the rice is harvested. Do they pay their bills? No. Do they treat their slaves the way they deserve to be treated? No. And frankly, neither do we."

Her father flung his napkin onto the table. "Perhaps you should have paid better attention to Reverend Bushy's sermon last Sunday. 'Both thy bondmen, and thy bondmaids, which thou shalt have, shall be of the heathen that are round about you; of them shall ye buy bondmen and bondmaids.'"

His voice became more insistent as he rose from his chair, his eyes fiery with righteousness. "'Moreover, of the children of the strangers that do sojourn among you, of them shall ye buy, and their families that they begat in your land shall be your possession.'"

He turned and gazed out the window toward Misery Row. "'And ye shall take them as an inheritance for your children after you, to inherit them for a possession; they shall be your bondmen forever.' Leviticus 25:44-46."

"So that's it? The justification for your life . . . our life . . . Grampa's life before us . . . comes down to a couple of Old Testament verses that Jesus's teachings contradict?"

Her father turned, his face distorted. "You want Christ's teachings? 'Servants, be obedient to them that are your masters, with fear and trembling, in singleness of your heart, as unto Christ. Slaves, be obedient to your human masters with fear and trembling, in sincerity of heart, as to Christ.' That's Ephesians 6:5. I suggest my daughter take that admonition to heart as well."

"Those are Paul's words, not Christ's. . . . No, slavery—our peculiar institution—is evil, and so are those who perpetuate it." Olivia's eyes burned into her father's. "Nothing you ever tell me, no Bible verse, no riches, will ever change that."

The Squire picked up an unlit silver candelabra and threw it against the wall. "That's enough! Olivia, this is the last straw. You must learn there are consequences to your words and consequences to your actions."

Mother remained mute at the foot of the table.

Olivia rose from her chair, almost daring him to slap her again. "Papa, no matter what your consequences are for me, they won't be as bad as the evils you inflict every day on the human beings you enslave! I hate you and I hate this place!"

"Go to your room!" The Squire bellowed.

Olivia turned to leave the dining room. "Thank you for serving us tonight, Emblee," she said loud enough for her parents to hear.

She didn't go to her room, of course. She left to sit in the shade of her secret tree. Outside, away from the anger and privilege of the Big House, an errant thought raced through her mind. *Rian Krieger wouldn't stay here. Rian would run away to Russia. But I can't run away because if I do, there will be no one left to protect the servants. I'm caught.*

* * * * *

· SEAMUS ·

Seamus stole a glance over his shoulder before he opened the door to the engine house of the Fairmont Waterworks. The couples strolling along the pebble path around the reservoir were too engrossed in themselves to notice. Even though his breaking and entering days were mostly behind him, it sure felt like that's what he was doing. It was seven o'clock. The sun had just set across the Schuylkill. *It'll be pitch dark by the time we leave.*

He was pleased with his choice for this particular rendezvous. The engine house was open to the public most days—it was quite the mechanical marvel, after all—but they locked it up at five. *It helps to have a friend who is paid to guard the machinery.*

Seamus entered onto a cast-iron platform, waited until his eyes adjusted to the dark, and peered over the railing down into the cavernous room. "Ssst! Siobhan, are you down there?"

The sounds were mesmerizing. The Schuylkill River's current did all the work. It powered a bladed wheel that turned a water wheel, which lifted hundreds of gallons of water out of the river each second. A pair of enormous air compressors, also powered by the river, rhythmically pumped up and down, pushing the water up even farther, where it entered a thirty-six-inch pipe that led to the reservoir.

"Of course I'm here," Siobhan spoke from down below. "I've been here for fifteen minutes. Get your Irish ass down here."

Seamus hurried down the stairs, his steps clanking on the metal. He couldn't tell from his girlfriend's tone what he would get when he got to the bottom. The black-haired, black-eyed beauty was capable of great affection and fits of ire. He found out which right away.

Siobhan's voice struck even before he reached the last step. "Seamus, is this the best you can do for a romantic rendezvous?"

Seamus responded into the dark. "No one will see us here. The falling water makes a bit of a soothing sound. I like it—"

"The water wheel creaks and squeals. There's not a soft edge in the whole room. I can't even lean into a railing because of the mold. Jaysus, you are so stupid sometimes."

"Whataya want? Your daddy said he'd kill me if he caught us together."

"Hugh said you had to make something of yourself. You've got a plan. A great plan. I think it's time you met with my father and told him what's what."

"Wait a minute. Are you saying you will marry me?"

"I will if you propose to me. But not here, you big dope. Pick someplace nice and do it properly. I want you on your knee. Don't worry about the ring. Anything will do."

That was when Seamus figured out that his almost official fiancée was capable of both ire and affection at the same time. *Hang on, Boyo. This will be a hell of a ride.*

* * * * *

· RIAN ·

It was the first time Rian had been invited to Shippen House. George Shippen and his wife, however, weren't at home. They and Rian's father were attending a play at the Walnut Street Theatre, *Metamora, or the Last of the Wampanoags*, starring Edwin Forrest. With the adults occupied for the evening, the Shippens' son, Trey, had invited Rian and Conor to play cards. "Jabez Howes says you played poker in Russia and you're good at it," Trey had commented when he extended the invitation. "You and Conor should come over. It won't be anything big . . . just penny-ante stuff. I've also invited Jabez, Billy, and Emmanuel."

Penny-ante poker didn't interest Rian much because the stakes were virtually inconsequential. But she accepted because Wilhelm (Billy) Schiffler would be there. Years ago, Billy gave her the name *Barn Door* in reference to the gap between her front teeth. *Relieving Billy of some of his money would be a real pleasure.*

Rian surveyed the table: Trey, Conor, Jabez, Billy, and Emmanuel Rauch, a boy she liked but didn't know very well. From the moment the first hand was dealt, she knew that, with the exception of Conor, each of her opponents had played enough poker to think they were good at it. *I will soon be disabusing them of that notion.*

The table was littered with half-pennies, pennies, half-dimes, and dimes. Rian had written out a sheet of ranks that rested between Jabez and Billy: Royal Flush / Straight Flush / Four-of-a-Kind / Full House / Flush / Three-of-a-Kind / Two Pair / One Pair / High Card.

As the evening progressed, the stacks of coins in front of Rian and Conor grew taller, and those in front of Trey, Billy, Emmanuel, and Jabez shortened. The losers became noticeably more frustrated.

"Okay, it's ten o'clock," announced Trey. "This is our last hand. My parents will be home soon, and they can't know you were here."

"Yeah," said Billy. "What were you thinking, Trey? A girl and a mick."

"I guess it was a big mistake, Wilhelm." Rian called Billy *Wilhelm* because he didn't like his given name and she knew it irritated him. "This girl and that Irish lad are taking all your money."

"Deal the cards, Emmanuel," said Billy.

Rian opened her new hand and found three twos. She ditched two losers, and Emmanuel dealt her a two and a three. Jabez picked up the sheet of ranks, glanced at it, and let it waft back to the table.

Betting was heavy from the beginning. Conor and Trey folded. Rian, Billy, and Jabez continued to raise. *There's less than two dollars in the pot. There was more than five thousand dollars in the pot the night Delilah Winter cleaned me out on the* Great Western.

At the end of the betting, Jabez and Billy had pushed all their coins to the center of the table.

"Full house," said Billy as he laid his hand down. "Queens over jacks."

Jabez fanned his cards onto the table. "I've got you beat. Aces over sevens." He confidently started to rake in the pot.

"Not so fast, Jabez," said Rian. She laid down her four twos. "It's my pot."

"Damnit," yelled Jabez. He stood up so fast that his chair fell over backward. He kicked the chair and stormed out of the room. A moment later, they heard the front door slam shut.

"I guess Jabez doesn't like to lose," said Conor.

"I'm not sure what Jabez likes these days," said Rian. *What is the story with my cousin? He hates to work. Refuses to go to school. True, he never lorded it over me when* Vater *treated him like the son he's always wanted, but when you come right down to it, my cousin is a mystery. Will I ever be able to figure him out?*

SUNDAY, SEPTEMBER 9

· OLIVIA ·

Cook worked seven days a week, although her responsibilities on Sundays usually ended after she cleaned up from dinner, which the Tuckers always ate at one o'clock. After that, her time was her own, so Mother cooked their supper using ingredients Cook left for her in the Big House kitchen.

This Sunday evening, however, was different. Mother's Garden Club was holding a special meeting at the Jaudons. Mrs. Jaudon had imported a plant from the Dutch East Indies that only bloomed at night, and Mrs. Jaudon wanted the women to smell it. Dinner for Olivia and her father would be catch-as-catch-can. At twilight, Olivia made her way to the summer kitchen to see what she could scare up. The butcher block in the middle of the room was loaded with string beans and a mound of dill sprigs, but Cook wasn't there.

Sunday . . . String beans . . . dill . . . early September . . . I wonder if there'll be more shenanigans between Cook and Grafton.

Olivia was heating last night's mutton and carrots in a cast-iron pan when Cook entered the kitchen, opened the drawer near the door, grabbed the stub of an old candle, and turned to leave. She hadn't noticed Olivia at the stove.

"Cook, what's going on?"

Cook stopped, hesitated, then turned. "Nothin'. Need some light is all."

"Are you doing something with Grafton?"

"You keep your nose where it belongs—outta my business. Sunday is my time."

Olivia had spent two years trying to get Cook to trust her, and here was the proof that she didn't. Cook was hiding something. "Cook, tell me what's going on. You know you can trust me."

"Little, there's trust and there's *trust*. You don't need to know what we're doing. Like I said, it's my day of rest, what's left of it. I can do whatever I want."

"Are you planning something?"

Cook leaned against the counter, dropped her eyes, and sighed. "We ain't doin' nothin' you need to worry about. We ain't fixin' to hurt nobody."

"What's going on? You can tell me."

"Look here—your people own us, lock, stock, and barrel. At least let us keep a few memories alive."

Cook had never spoken to Olivia that way. Olivia wondered if she had ever spoken to any white person that way in her entire life. "Fine," Olivia said. *But I don't feel fine. I'm worried.*

Cook marched out of the summer kitchen. Olivia followed her the few paces necessary to observe her walking toward the big shack in Misery Row. *And what a surprise: there's Grafton.*

Then, in a flash, the disparate bits of information came together like the pieces of a puzzle, and the key piece was something that happened ninety-nine years ago today: The Stono Rebellion. Olivia relaxed. *This is none of my business. Let them do what they need to do.*

* * * * *

The solarium was starting to cool now that the sun had gone down. Olivia sat in a wicker chair, her plate of mutton and carrots untouched in her lap. Rather than eat, she pondered what it must be like to have your memories destroyed.

Footsteps echoed through the foyer. Her father's voice wafted into the solarium. "How many?"

In response, Knox Boseman, the overseer, said, "I'm not sure. Perhaps a dozen. I know Cook's involved."

"Should I alert the Jaudons?" Papa asked.

Olivia couldn't hear Boseman's response because they had entered The Squire's office. She placed her plate on a side table, rose, and tiptoed toward the foyer, but before she got to the door, Papa and Mr. Boseman strode through the foyer toward the stairs to the second floor. Papa held the ring that looped through the key to the bedroom he had converted into an armory after the Southampton Insurrection[14] in 1831.

Papa's office had a fireplace and was directly beneath the armory. A grate in the office ceiling allowed a modicum of heat to filter upstairs on cold nights.

---

14. In August of 1831, a slave named Nat Turner led seventy enslaved and free Blacks in bloody attacks on households in Southampton County, Virginia. Their hope was to ignite a wider slave rebellion. The insurrectionists killed approximately sixty whites, including Turner's enslaver and his family. The rebellion was put down within two days. Some of those suspected of participating were beheaded, and their heads placed on pikes along county roads. Turner remained at large for a few weeks before he was captured, tried, and subsequently hanged. Aftereffects of the rebellion coursed through the South for years, sending successive waves of panic through the white populace every time a whiff of slave rebellion was detected.

Olivia and Topper used to eavesdrop on Papa through the grate from above when they were playing Spies. She now assumed the reverse could be true. She tiptoed into the office, pulled out a chair, and used it to climb onto Papa's desk and get her ear near the grate.

The floorboards creaked above her. Knox Boseman said, "What ones do you want?"

Papa: "All four pistols. The shotgun. The two long guns . . . Oh, hell, we'll take everything. I'll stay here and get all the guns loaded. You run and get Jaudon."

Boseman: "What are we going to do with them?"

Papa: "I'll whip the ringleaders myself, then we'll hang them, no matter who they are. You'll make the rest of them watch, then we'll pass around the whip until we can't lift our arms anymore. I'll let Aubry Richards have them on consignment. He'll walk them into Georgia, and before they know it, they'll be cutting sugar cane and wishing they had never thought about rebelling. I can't believe Cook is involved."

Boseman: "Every lash you lay will reduce what someone is willing to pay for them."

Papa: "Every lash we lay will pay benefits down the road. No slave will dare revolt in this neck of the woods ever again. Go now. Get Jaudon. I'll find Whiskey and make sure she holes up until this is properly over."

Olivia was certain that what Cook and Grafton were doing wasn't a rebellion. *But Papa sure as shootin' won't take kindly to it. If his blood is up, there will be plenty of whippings handed out before this is all sorted . . . I've got to warn Cook.* She climbed down from The Squire's desk, placed the chair back in its usual place, walked into the foyer, and was about to run down to Misery Row.

Bang . . . bang . . . bang! The door knocker sounded, not with the *bang, bang, bang* urgency of an impending slave rebellion, but more an *I'm-here-on-a-social-call-please-answer-the-door* sort of way.

Olivia opened the front door to find Colonel Jaudon. He held a half-empty bottle of brandy and was swaying slightly.

"Good evening, Olivia. Is your father in?"

Our neighbor has no idea what he's walking into. Olivia smiled and did her best to act as if all hell wasn't breaking loose. Things were piling up so fast that she felt herself on the verge of panic. "I think Papa's in the armory. Feel free to go upstairs. Second door on the left."

If Colonel Jaudon thought Olivia was remiss for not leading him upstairs herself, he didn't say anything. She waited until his feet disappeared, then returned to her father's office, put the chair next to the desk, again climbed onto the surface, and put her ear near the grate.

Jaudon: "Good evening, Squire. Olivia let me in. I'm afraid my home is not my castle tonight. The Garden Club has driven me out. I was hoping to share some brandy."

Papa: "Jaudon! A godsend. Your timing could not be any better."

Jaudon: "Well, thank you, Squire . . . What's going on?"

Papa: "Here, grab a pistol. There's trouble down in the slave quarters. I want to nip it in the bud, and your military background will be useful. If all goes well, we'll be lucky to finish off your brandy, but I assure you, it will be in the wee hours of the morning before all their evil work is dealt with. I have one more charge to load, then we can get going."

Olivia had heard enough. She again alit from the desk, again put the chair back in its place. Creaking floorboards above indicated that her father, Mr. Boseman, and Colonel Jaudon were leaving.

Olivia had only enough time to concoct half a plan. She grabbed the mammoth family Bible off the podium where Papa kept it on display, cradled it in her arms, ran through the foyer to the sound of footsteps in the hallway above, raced through the small parlor, through the kitchen, and into the pantry. She grabbed a candle, ran out the back door into the almost-dark, past the summer kitchen and down the hill toward Misery Row.

The high-pitched trill of a screech owl sounded from near the smokehouse, but Olivia knew it wasn't an owl making that sound. It was a signal from a lookout that danger was coming.

Lord, I hope this works. Olivia kept running, which was awkward with the big Bible.

A field hand standing guard outside the largest of the slave shacks thumped three shorts on the door, then put out both his hands. "Miss Olivia, you can't go in there."

Olivia did her best to catch her breath. She didn't know the man's name. "I don't have time to argue. Let me in. My father is coming down here with two men and guns. You should come in with me."

The man hesitated for a moment, then opened the door. Olivia entered to find Cook, Grafton, Emblee, and six other slaves, all clearly in a state of panic, scurrying about in the light of one candle that had been stuck to a table. The shack smelled of sweat, mold, and just-snuffed candles.

Olivia grabbed the lit candle off the table. "Light your tapers. Do it quick. My father's coming."

Cook gaped back at Olivia, mute.

"Do as I say right now and nobody gets a whipping tonight." *Except for maybe me.*

One by one, the slaves lit their candle stubs.

Olivia held out the heavy Bible toward Emblee. "Hold this so I can read it."

Emblee did as she was told. Olivia opened the Bible, unknowing and uncaring about what she was about to read as long as she was reciting something. "And the Lord spake unto Moses, saying, If a soul sin, and commit a trespass against the Lord, and lie unto his neighbor. . . ." She glanced nervously toward the door, then continued. "In that which was delivered him to keep, or in fellowship, or in a thing taken away by violence, or hath deceived his neighbor. . . ."

Footsteps sounded outside the shack, but Olivia kept on reading. "Or have found that which was lost, and lieth concerning it, and sweareth falsely; in any of all these that a man doeth, sinning therein: Then it shall be, because he hath sinned, and is guilty. . . ."

The door burst open and Olivia's father, Mr. Boseman, and Colonel Jaudon stormed in brandishing pistols. "On your knees, you disloyal rebels!" her father yelled before he absorbed the totality of the scene before him. "Olivia . . . What are you doing here?"

"Teaching Bible class."

Her father lowered his pistol. "Are you teaching the hands to read?"

"No, Papa. No one is learning to read."

* * * * *

The amazing thing was that Papa bought the ruse hook, line, and sinker. "It's not that we disapprove of your Bible classes," he told Olivia at breakfast the following morning. Olivia was surprised her father made it to breakfast. He and Jaudon had returned the guns to the armory and didn't leave the room until the colonel's bottle of brandy was finished. "Bringing the slaves a little religion is a good thing, actually. But you never told us what you were doing." Papa eyed Emblee, who was waiting in attendance near the door. "Emblee, my coffee is cold. Run and get me a fresh cup."

Emblee retrieved Papa's cup and turned toward the kitchen.

"You were an innocent young woman amidst men of no moral character," Mother said as she buttered her toast. "You jeopardized your safety." As far as Mother was concerned, the servants might as well have been wallpaper. She couldn't have cared less what Emblee heard or didn't hear.

Papa waited until Emblee was out of earshot to voice his major concern. "Now you have embarrassed us for a second time in front of Colonel Jaudon.

Oh my God, I can hear it now . . . 'Poor Tucker thought he had a slave rebellion on his hands, and it turns out it was only that little hellion of his, reading Leviticus to the darkies.' At least it was Leviticus," he said, his first hint of humor since last night's hullabaloo.

"Your father said that Emblee was holding our family Bible. Are you sure she wasn't reading along as you read, dear?"

You're not out of the woods yet. This is not the time to be snippy. "No, Mother. As I told Papa, it was Bible class, not reading class."

Papa sopped up his last bit of grits and gravy with his toast. "All these doings have stirred up the slaves. I think your Bible classes are a good idea, but you shouldn't be the person to give them. I'll tell Knox to take it on."

This will be one more obligation the slaves will have on their supposed day of rest. "Mr. Boseman has enough responsibilities. He won't appreciate giving up Sunday evenings to do more. I would be pleased to continue with the classes. I'll make sure Cook is always there. I'll be safe."

"No, my decision is final. I have been saying for ages that you get too close to the servants. Olivia, your intimacy with them and your involvement with the Bible classes has to stop."

* * * * *

That afternoon, when Olivia visited the summer kitchen, Cook sat at the butcher block, de-stemming string beans. The stems fell into a heap onto her apron. Olivia stood by the door and crossed her arms. "May I help?"

In answer, Cook leaned over and pulled out a chair.

Olivia sat and reached for some string beans to de-stem. "Are you okay?"

Cook just kept working on her beans, dropping the stems onto her apron-covered lap. "We don't want to forget, that's all. Is that so bad?"

"How do you know about the Stono Rebellion?"

Cook de-stemmed another handful of beans before she answered. "To you, it's an article in one of your newspapers. To us, it's family history."

"Us?"

"My great-great-granddaddy was named Josie. He wanted to be free. Grafton's granddaddy was Jemmy, the leader. Scipio's was Primus. Every person in that shack the other night had an ancestor who was free for fourteen hours ninety-nine years ago. All we was doing was rememberin' their names, rememberin' that moment, tryin' to think about what freedom must feel like."

"You would have been whipped."

Cook snorted. "Course we woulda been whipped. We thank you for sparing us from that."

Olivia and Cook worked on their string beans in silence for a few minutes.

Cook sighed. "All they wanted was their freedom and those folks hung 'em like they was useless pieces of trash." She rose from her chair, cradling the stems in her apron, then allowed them to cascade into the bucket of kitchen waste that would be fed to the pigs.

Thursday, September 20

· RIAN ·

The locomotive factory, which had been deafening minutes before, moved to *noisy* because ten workers had disengaged the belts that drove their machines. Rian—tallow pot in hand—grabbed her cousin Jabez by his shirttail as she walked by him on the shop floor. "Come on," she yelled. "You can help."

Jabez, who was reading something rather than sweeping up as he should have been, remained stationary. "I need to finish this letter first."

Rian stopped, pivoted, and returned to Jabez's side. "What is it?"

Jabez continued reading, then handed the letter to Rian. "It's from Uncle Adrian. He wants Aunt Mila and me to move to Germany."

30 June 1838

Beloved Mila,

I am still at Count Sheremetev's estate in Saxony. My imprisonment in St. Petersburg is already a distant memory.

I suppose I should start with the most important news. In my previous letter, I told you that the count had put forth my name to lead the construction of a railroad from Leipzig to Dresden. Well, the committee has offered me a very attractive contract. Both of my competitors for the job were English. Apparently two of the deciding factors were that I'm an American industrialist and I speak fluent German. I guess the committee chose to overlook my Württemberg accent.

I am going to take the job. It is beautiful here. I hope you and Jabez can join me as soon as possible. When Jabez was supposed to accompany me to Russia, he and Rian switched places, and I got that ball of fire instead. I assume Jabez will be equally resistant about coming to Leipzig. Please do your best to get him to come, but if he still digs in his heels, talk to Otto. Perhaps my brother will take Jabez in for a while until the boy finds an even keel.

I will write again tomorrow.

With love,

Adrian

Rian finished reading and handed the letter back to Jabez. "Are you gonna go?"

"To Saxony? Not a chance. I may have to pull a 'Rian Krieger' and run away." Jabez regarded Rian's tallow pot. "What do you want me to help you with?"

Rian held up the pot. "It's three minutes to twelve. The workers break at noon. That will give us time to do some maintenance on the regulators for the steam engines in all three factories."

"I don't care about that. Do it yourself."

"Oh, come on, Jabez. Don't you want to learn about how all this works?"

"I've successfully avoided it so far."

"Well, help me just because then."

"Why do you like all this? You could stay home all day and do nothing. That's the life your father wants for you anyway. He still doesn't pay you."

All the hammering and banging had come to a halt, and the workers started putting their tools away in advance of the noon whistle, so Rian could now talk in a normal voice. "You're right, I'm not getting paid to do this stuff. I do it because it's fascinating." *And because it keeps my mind so occupied, the rat-thoughts don't take over.* "I still get paid to do the bookkeeping, though."

The steam whistle blew two brief blasts, and the cavernous room turned quieter.

Harry Vogel shoved the giant lever that disengaged the steam engine from the belt that looped to the drive shaft near the factory ceiling. Harry saw Rian, eyed the tallow bucket, and pointedly ignored her.

"Come on, Jabez," Rian repeated. "It's time to get to work."

Jabez followed Rian up the wrought-iron stairs to the platform that flanked the steam engine's mammoth boiler. "I thought Harry didn't let you in the shop."

"There's no work going on. I'm doing a task most men hate. He doesn't bother me, and I don't bother him."

Jabez viewed the factory from the height of fifteen feet. "You really love all this?"

"All of it. It's what I'm going to do with my life . . . You won't run away. You're too lazy to do that."

Rian thought for a moment that Jabez would fire back, but he turned his attention to the steam regulator as if seeing it for the first time. "What does this thing do, anyway?"

Rian spun the balls of the regulator and watched them rise. "The more pressure there is in the steam chamber, the faster this thing rotates. The faster it rotates, the more centrifugal force makes these balls go higher. The higher the balls go, the more steam the regulator lets out. That reduces the steam pressure. So it's self-regulating. If this is working properly, there won't be an explosion."

"What would happen if something prevented the balls from rising or the regulator from rotating?"

"Sooner or later the boiler would blow up."

"Now that would be interesting."

"What?"

"Getting blown up. You'd be alive one moment and dead the next."

Rian stopped her lubricating task and eyed Jabez. "You're crazy."

"Maybe. Maybe not," Jabez responded with an expression Rian couldn't interpret.

* * * * *

· OLIVIA ·

For eight days, Olivia felt an unfamiliar yet welcome connection with the nine enslaved individuals who were merely trying to keep the memory of their ancestors alive. The difference was subtle, but it was definitely there. They made eye contact for a moment longer. They smiled ever so slightly. Their masks remained down, or at least down a bit.

Olivia assumed the story of the sham Bible class was kept within a tight circle. After all, The Squire would likely reward a rat with significant benefits for such a tale—extra rations, light duty, or maybe permission to visit a loved one at a nearby plantation. But somehow, even without the full story being told, word had traveled that Miss Olivia could be trusted.

Olivia basked in that subtle glory for those eight days. And since her parents didn't punish her for teaching Bible classes without their knowledge, she breathed a little easier.

Then she entered her bedroom to find her mother staring into the wardrobe. "Mother, what are you doing?"

"I'm packing your trunk."

"Where are we going?"

"It's you who is doing the going. Your father and I have reached the limit of our tolerance for your shenanigans. We have enrolled you in the South Carolina Female Collegiate Institute in Columbia."

Olivia's first thought was, *If they force me to leave, who will protect the slaves?* "Mother, please don't do this."

Penelope Tucker folded a day dress Olivia wouldn't wear until it started to turn cold. "The Squire told you there would be consequences for your actions. Now you will find out what those consequences are."

"Is this about the Bible classes?"

"Your Bible classes were the straw that broke the camel's back. You are too close to the servants. You said yourself that you hate it here. Your father and I think it would be best for you to get away from Long Pond for a while."

"Mother, no, please don't do this."

Her mother continued folding. "We will ship your trunk today. You and I will leave tomorrow. I suggest you start saying your goodbyes to the Jaudon girls and your precious servants. You won't be coming home anytime soon. Columbia is a hundred and twenty miles from here."

* * * * *

The trip from Charleston to Columbia should have been a three-day trip, wholly by water. The steamboat should have stopped at Long Pond's Cooper River landing and taken Olivia, her mother, Matilde (to serve Penelope), and Emblee (to serve Olivia) upriver to the Santee Canal, through the canal, then onto the Santee River, then the Congaree River, and on to Columbia.

But it had been a dry summer. Word from upriver was that boats on the Santee Canal were bottoming out and the canal was impassable. So Penelope changed plans to an onerous day-long train ride from Charleston to Hamburg, then two days by stagecoach to Columbia. Travel by stagecoach was arduous—bumpy, dusty, and punctuated by frequent stops to change or water horses. Besides, the inns along the way were far beneath Mother's standards. Given all these newly anticipated trials, Penelope informed Olivia that Matilde and Emblee weren't coming along.

"We can do without the added expense, and besides, neither of them travels well," Mother said. "They would be more trouble than they're worth."

Olivia and Penelope rode the train from Charleston to Hamburg without incident, save the occasional glowing cinder that blew out of the locomotive's smokestack and was sucked into the passenger coach. Olivia was used to the lush, swampy rice fields of South Carolina's Lowcountry. The scenery changed rather dramatically as they traveled farther inland. The dominant crop became cotton—planted right up to the train tracks and every road and crossroad. Thousands of rows of cotton followed the contours of the fields, and it was almost harvest time. Three feet tall, the cotton now shaded out any chance a weed had of growing.

Hamburg, the northern terminus of the *Charleston & Hamburg Railroad*, was a new, rough-hewn village built on the South Carolina side of the Savannah River across from Augusta, Georgia. Penelope Tucker could find no one at the train station to lug her carpetbags, so searching for a room while manhandling her own baggage around became a burden too great to bear. She settled for a scruffy rooming house tended by a proprietress who smoked cigarettes and showed no interest in helping the travelers with their luggage. Olivia and her mother slept in the same bed.

The next morning, they walked to the stagecoach office at seven o'clock, only to learn the schedule had changed and stage service to the east was only offered on Mondays, Wednesdays, and Fridays.

Marooned in Hamburg for the day, they returned their bags to the rooming house and strolled around the village. The most prominent business by far was a slave market that was thriving for one reason: to supply Georgia, mere steps away across a bridge, with slaves. This happened out in the open, despite a Georgia law banning the importation of slaves into the state.

Olivia stood on a plaza and stared at eight poor wretches already on display on a narrow porch in front of the slave house—six men from their mid-teens to late forties and a young woman pressing a seven-year-old to her side. A nearby sign declared

MORE STOCK ROUND BACK
INQUIRE WITHIN

The unwelcome reminder of buying and selling other human beings—familiar as it was to Olivia—dug hard at her. "You lived in Philadelphia on and off for half your life before you married Papa," she said to her mother. "That city is a hotbed of the abolition movement. Didn't any of that rub off on you? Don't you understand how wrong the institution of slavery is?"

Penelope stared at the humans-for-sale for half a minute. "No," she said, then turned away. "Let's go find a cup of coffee."

It turned out that there were no cafés in Hamburg, and by this time, the rooming house proprietress was nowhere to be found. "Try Singer's across the river," a man sweeping the wooden walkway in front of his barbershop told them.

Augusta, across the bridge, was quite a bit larger than Hamburg but still nothing compared to Charleston. Singer's Restaurant had tablespace to serve twenty people, but this early in the morning, the cook seemed reluctant to make a pot of coffee when she didn't officially open until noon. Mother flashed a condescending smile and waggled her purse. The cook acquiesced.

Olivia and her mother sat at a table for two next to a window. With no one else in the room, Olivia could hear the cook rattling around in the kitchen. Perhaps she was the Singer named on the sign out front, perhaps not; she wasn't inclined to introduce herself. After ten minutes, the cook came out with two cups of coffee, which she clattered down on the table so carelessly that the coffee sloshed onto the saucers.

Penelope lifted her cup, hunted for a napkin to scuff the bottom of the cup onto, but the cook hadn't bothered to give them one. She tsked, poured the slopped-over coffee from the saucer back into the cup, took a tentative sip, winced, and set the cup down. "It's the life I agreed to when I married your father," she said, expanding on the "No" she had uttered twenty minutes beforehand.

Olivia stared back at her mother. *This may be the last chance I have to talk about this subject.* "But it is so wrong."

Penelope refused to return Olivia's gaze. "I don't think it is."

"You think it's right to allow that woman and her child to be sold off to some sugar plantation down in Georgia?"

Her mother slid her cup and saucer toward the center of the table. Finally, she looked back at Olivia for the first time. "Yes . . . I do."

"And what if they get bought by two different buyers. Is that okay?"

"No, of course not."

Olivia leaned in, thinking she finally found a crack in her mother's defenses. "Then where do you draw the line?"

"It is not for me to draw the line," her mother responded. "It is within the law."

"Then the law is wrong."

Penelope returned her gaze to her cup and saucer. "You shouldn't be so hard on your father."

What? Why? Where is this coming from? "Papa has his way with the slave girls."

Mother reacted not a jot to the *slave girl* comment. *That's a surprise. I've overheard my parents argue about Papa's dalliances ever since I can remember. He promises to stop, but he always keeps slinking back down to that cabin by the river.*

"Papa gambles," Olivia continued. "He gets mean when he's drunk. He gives the slavedriver license to punish the field hands unmercifully."

"He is under pressure. It's the depression."

"The depression? The depression is over. I got a letter from Rian, and she said Krieger Locomotive is building a new factory."

"Well, it's not over in the South. The price of cotton fell by twenty-five percent last year, and it has already fallen another twenty-five percent this year."

"But what does that matter to us? We grow rice. Rice . . . it's Carolina Gold."

"The price of our Carolina Gold is falling, too."

"What do you mean? I've heard Papa say a thousand times: 'The world's gotta eat.' Even poor people buy rice."

"Apparently the world is producing a lot more rice than it used to. Your father received a letter from his brother in Burma. The Brits are all over that area. They've built dikes and flooded land in Burma, Java, and India. In the past couple of years, they've produced so much rice that the price has fallen. Europe is importing less Carolina Gold and buying cheaper rice from Asia instead."

Olivia's parents never shared the ins and outs of Long Pond's business with her. She was surprised her mother broke precedent. "What's Papa doing about it?"

Penelope Tucker shrugged as if this sort of decision was also out of her province. "He asked your Uncle George for another loan."

"Uncle George's bank in Philadelphia? He can lend money to us in South Carolina?"

"He has already done it twice before."

"How far in debt are we?" The thought that Long Pond was in debt came as a shock to Olivia. The Tuckers were in the upper echelons of The Hundred, the families who controlled South Carolina's politics, economy, and social life.

"We can still afford to send you off to school in Columbia."

"But we're living beyond our means?"

"For the moment. Your father is doing his best to preserve our way of life. We live in a paradise, and you don't appreciate it."

"What is Papa doing to preserve our precious way of life besides asking Uncle George for a loan? Even I know that can't go on for very long."

"He told Knox Boseman to work the slaves harder. We're selling off a few."

"Field hands or house servants?"

"Both."

A feeling of dread coursed through Olivia. "Who from the house?"

"No one you care about." Penelope continued to stare at her coffee.

"I care about all of them."

"But not your precious Cook or Emblee." Her mother wrapped her hands around the coffee cup as if in need of its warmth. "The Squire probably would have sold Emblee off to teach you a lesson, but he can't."

"What do you mean, he can't?"

"He used her and seven other slaves as collateral for the loan."

"What's collateral?"

"When you borrow money, the bank demands you list something they can claim if you don't pay back the loan. The Squire has already mortgaged the two farms he inherited when his brothers died. Now it's the servants."

"What happens to those people if Papa doesn't make the payments on the loan?"

Her mother sat back and crossed her arms. "Uncle George would probably extend another loan."

"But what if he doesn't?"

"Then I assume the bank would confiscate the slaves, walk them to the auction in Charleston, sell them for the highest price they can get, and satisfy the loan."

"Would a neighbor buy them?"

"None of the rice planters. They're in the same position we are. Maybe cotton growers upland. Maybe sugar growers in Alabama."

Olivia felt like she'd been punched in the gut. She rose from the table and walked out into the rising heat and humidity. She had not taken a sip of her coffee.

* * * * *

Olivia and her mother returned to the stagecoach office the following morning only to learn that the stage had more U.S. mail than usual and there wasn't space for all their luggage. Penelope lit into the clerk to no avail. She made Olivia return to the rooming house and leave a bag. "Tell that useless proprietress I'll pick it back up when I pass back through town in four days," her mother said.

As anticipated, the first day of travel by stagecoach was arduous, but coupled with Olivia's ill-concealed anger toward her mother, it felt like forever. The only scenery was cotton—the same as before, planted right up to the roadside. The only break in the cotton was when they neared a plantation house. First, Olivia noticed how the cotton fields stopped and the cornfields began. Then came a few acres of vegetables. Then the plantation house. "They always plant their corn and vegetables near the house," said one of their fellow passengers. "That's so they can keep an eye on 'em. Otherwise, the slaves'll grab more than their allotment. They're shifty that way."

* * * * *

The stage stopped for the night at an inn in the middle of nowhere. Olivia and her mother wordlessly carried their bags up a flight of stairs, changed out of their dusty dresses, and returned to the lobby, which also served as the dining room, a post office, and a hardware store. The room smelled of smoke, cooking grease, and unwashed bodies. The only dinner offering was ham, potatoes, string beans, and coffee for twenty-seven cents.

After minutes of silence and no other diners to distract them, Mother folded her hands and leaned into the table. Had her head been down and her eyes shut, Olivia might have assumed she was about to say grace, but her glare drilled into Olivia across the table. "Tomorrow is our last day of travel. You have not been inclined to talk, so I will fill the silence with everything you need to hear before we part. You can either respond or continue to frost me out—at this point, I no longer care. Olivia, you can decide what your future brings, but no matter what, your future goes through the South Carolina Female Collegiate Institute. Let me map this out for you. You will attend that school, where you will receive the best education for young women in the country and, hopefully, they will file off your many rough edges. If you behave yourself, next summer we will sail to France and polish you up for your eventual marriage. The following summer, when you turn sixteen, you will come out at the Charleston Cotillion, thus declaring you are eligible for courting. You will return to the school and graduate. The only way you will not graduate is if you and Barnwell are married beforehand, at which point you will become his problem."

Olivia considered not responding, but the holes in her mother's argument got the better of her. "And where on this 'map' of yours is a place where I make a decision? When do I determine my own future? What if I don't like Barnwell . . . or he doesn't like me?"

Her mother shrugged. "Not likely. Poppy Wilkinson and I have been planning this since you were born. But, if Barnwell won't have you, then after you graduate, we will take you to Philadelphia for the summer social season. With your pedigree, you should get snapped up by the son of one of the city's industrialists. However, if you continue to show this defiant streak up North, it may take you two social seasons to find a husband. If it goes longer than that, you will be declared a spinster and hopeless as far as marriage prospects go."

Olivia picked up the fork to use it as a pointer. "So let me summarize my options." (Fork to the left.) "Marry Barnwell, who will become a plantation owner and slink off to his concubine down by the creek like Papa does." (Fork to the right.) "Marry the son of some prosperous Philadelphia businessman, where the high point of my year will be planning galas for the summer social season." (Fork back to the left.) "Or become a spinster."

"I doubt Barnwell will slink off—"

"Mother, you know as well as I do: All the rice planters in the Lowcountry have their way with their slave girls. I assume all the cotton planters around here are the same. Why would Barnwell be any different? Why do you want a life for me that drives you half-mad with anger?"

"It's not ideal . . . but yes, those are your options."

Olivia tossed her fork down on the table with a clatter. "Then I'll take Philadelphia."

* * * * *

As Olivia stepped out of the stage, she didn't know what she had expected of the state capital, but this wasn't it. She only knew two other cities well enough to compare it to. Its streets were straight as a die, the same as Philadelphia. But where Philadelphia's streets bustled with commerce and busyness, Columbia was sleepy. Like Charleston, there were more Blacks than whites, but that wasn't a surprise; Olivia was used to being outnumbered by Blacks.

The clerk at the stagecoach office sent a runner to the South Carolina Female Collegiate Institute, and an hour later, a landau arrived with its leather top down. A young man reined the horses to a stop, jumped out, introduced himself as Jeremy, loaded their bags onto the rear-facing seat, and offered his hand to Penelope to assist her into the coach. Olivia followed. Given Jeremy's sunny demeanor and occasional direct gaze, Olivia wondered if he was enslaved or free but came to no conclusion.

After fifteen minutes of riding with only the *clip-clop-clip-clop* of the horses' hooves and the thrum of the wagon wheels to accompany them, Jeremy pointed to a large edifice on a hill in the distance. "Barhamville," he said. "It's what they call the school, named after Dr. Marks's dead wife." He placed a bugle to his lips and produced two loud, blaring blasts.

Circling around the hill, the landau climbed a winding driveway and drew up to the school, which consisted of a large three-story Georgian Colonial center with two equally impressive wings. A man in his late forties, with generous side and chin whiskers, bounded out the front door and down the porch steps. He opened the landau door before Olivia's mother had gathered her things.

"Mrs. Tucker, Miss Tucker, welcome to Barhamville. I am so happy you're finally here. My name is Dr. Elias Marks, founder of the South Carolina Female Collegiate Institute. Please join me in my anteroom. You must be parched from your travels. I've asked our cook to prepare a pitcher of lemonade. Please, follow me."

Once Olivia and her mother were ensconced in a settee, lemonade glasses in hand, Marks settled opposite them in a wingback chair. "Well, Miss Tucker, now that you've finally arrived, we have completed our enrollment of one hundred twenty-one young women. Given your father's description of your tutelage so far, we waived the need for a preparatory year and placed you in our first form. I assure you, our curriculum is rigorous. Over the next four years, you will study algebra, geometry, botany, chemistry, mineralogy, astronomy, ancient and modern history, religion, literature, and natural, intellectual, and moral philosophy."

Olivia was fully prepared to hate this school, but the thought of learning all those subjects—the stimulation, the knowledge—turned her head.

"I am sure you will be impressed by our faculty," Marks continued. "They are of the highest caliber, graduates of the finest schools in both the North and Europe. Their resumes allow us to offer electives that include all the high arts: painting, sculpture, architecture, music, and poetry. Then there's languages. Our faculty includes men and women born in France, Spain, and Italy. Also, this year we're introducing an additional elective: horseback riding—sidesaddle, of course—"

"Dr. Marks," interrupted Penelope. "The Squire and I do not doubt the quality of education Olivia will receive here, but I must be frank. My daughter is a willful child. As she sits before you, her father and I believe she will be unfit for marriage . . . unfit to manage a plantation household as we believe is her destiny. Olivia has many positive characteristics. But if you and your prized faculty do anything, it must be this: You must temper her willfulness. In four years, I want to encounter a finished young woman who will submit to the will of her husband."

I will never knuckle under to my husband's will. Either I'll be an equal partner or I'll be a spinster my entire life.

Dr. Marks crossed his legs and leaned forward, clasping his hands around his upper knee. "Mrs. Tucker, I have every confidence we will accomplish that and much more. Our graduates include the daughter of Senator Calhoun and numerous other members of South Carolina's gentry. Like your daughter, our young women are destined to take their rightful places at the sides of the men who will rule this state—and this country—for a generation. I pledge to you that we will do our part. And Olivia, you will be very happy here."

Maybe, maybe not.

Dr. Marks rose from his wingback chair. "I'm afraid your late arrival has complicated things, Mrs. Tucker. All your daughter's classmates settled in over the past few days. The first day of classes is tomorrow. Our carriage will take you back into town, and Jerry will stick with you until you find suitable accommodations. I suggest the Capitol Hotel."

Penelope rose. "A hotel won't be necessary. My husband's college roommate is Senator Trevor Wilkinson of Thousand Oaks. I've arranged to spend the night with the senator and his wife. My understanding is that they live only a few miles outside of town."

Dr. Marks gave a subtle bow. "The Wilkinsons are esteemed pillars of Columbia society. I would be pleased to have Jeremy take you to their home."

Olivia's mother gave Olivia a brief hug and whispered in her ear. "Behave yourself, dear. No more shenanigans." She turned and walked out the office door without looking back.

* * * * *

The woman proffered folded bed linens, a towel, and a washcloth to Olivia. "Welcome to Barhamville, dear. I am Mrs. Marks. I'm sure you will be very happy here."

Olivia, holding a carpetbag in each hand, clamped the linens between her left arm and waist. She remembered how Jeremy had mentioned Dr. Marks's dead wife, so she assumed this woman was a new Mrs. Marks.

The woman turned and started walking upstairs, making no effort to relieve Olivia of any of her burdens. "I will be teaching you algebra and ancient history this year," she said over her shoulder.

"Very exciting," said Olivia. "I know very little about either subject."

"Your trunk arrived yesterday. It's waiting for you in your room."

"I can't wait to get out of this dress. I've been wearing it for three days."

"That's good to hear, dear. You are expected to wear a hoop skirt, corset, and flat heels to dinner. Dinner begins promptly at six, so you have a little time to change your clothes and make up your bed."

"Make up my bed?"

Mrs. Marks arrived at the top of the stairs, turned, and waited for Olivia. "You've never made a bed before?"

"No. Emblee—a servant—she always did it."

Mrs. Marks led the way down a long corridor. "Well, there are no servants here to pamper you. How will you ever run a household if you never learn to do these chores for yourself? We will teach you to keep the highest standards so that, one day, you can demand those standards of your staff. . . . Here we are. Room 27, your home for the school year." Mrs. Marks knocked on the door and opened it before any call to enter was heard.

An attractive young woman Olivia's age arose from her bed. She was shorter than Olivia, slim and smiley. She wore her auburn hair in shoulder-length ringlets, as was the style, and appeared to be dressed for dinner. Like Olivia, she had not yet developed a womanly figure, but the hint of her curves to come was enhanced by a dress with a wide bodice that tapered to a thin waist and then flared out in a bell shape.

Mrs. Marks waved her hand toward the young woman. "Miss Eugenie Allston of Columbia, this is your roommate, Miss Olivia Tucker of Long Pond. Miss Tucker has never made up a bed before. Please teach her and help her into her corset before dinner time." With that, Mrs. Marks left the room, closing the door behind her.

* * * * *

Olivia learned a lot while Eugenie was teaching her to make up her bed. "The school isn't full. They are so desperate that they've admitted me. I grew up right here in town." "You don't have to wear a hoop skirt like they say you do. If you prefer petticoats, you can get away with it." "Most of the girls are nice, but a couple are very snooty." "This is how you miter the corner of the bed sheet. It's like wrapping a Christmas present." "My father is the pastor at the Methodist church in town. He says the Yankees are trying to take away our slaves. I think he's right." "I hate corsets. You and I are both skinny. Maybe we can skip the corsets together and see if Mrs. Marks notices. I bet she'll let it go." Olivia liked Eugenie, but her slavery comment meant that if they became friends, their friendship would only go so far.

At dinner, Olivia and Eugenie joined four other girls from her form at a round table and waited for dinner to be served. Three of the girls resembled Eugenie and her, with undeveloped figures. This was not the case for Caldwell "Caldie" Montgomery. Caldie already had a womanly silhouette. "I attended my first cotillion three weeks ago," she volunteered before soup was served, "even though I was technically too young. My dance card filled before some of the debutantes'."

Olivia dreamed of finally being able to attend balls the summer she turned sixteen. When the Tucker family used to summer in Philadelphia, her mother's "Philly in Flower" event always kicked off the social season. Olivia had only been allowed to peek in to see the dancing in the ballroom before she was sent to bed.

Caldie was already maneuvering to become the queen bee of their form. She dominated the table with a flood of information that trumped every other girl's story. Before and during the salad course, Olivia learned: "My father is the representative from Richland County, where we are right now." "Our plantation is called Brae Loch. It's only a mile from here, but Dr. Marks suggested that I live in the dormitory because it will help me establish my place as a leader in the Institute." "Senator Calhoun is my godfather."

During the entree: "I can walk home any time I want." "The year after next is my debutante year. I'll come out at the Columbia Cotillion. Not every girl from Columbia comes out. You have to be nominated." "Mrs. Marks teaches the girls everything they need to know beforehand. She recruits local boys to be our partners for dance classes." "I can already do the St. James Bow."

During dessert: "My mother already has me almost engaged to Mr. Yancy Howard of Signal Point. His family owns a hundred slaves." "My father owns two hundred slaves." "We spent the summer in Tuscany. Florence was magical."

Olivia decided she really didn't like Caldie Montgomery. *As much as I hate slavery, right now I wish Papa owned three hundred field hands so I could shove that little piece of information right in Caldie's face.*

FRIDAY, SEPTEMBER 21

· OLIVIA ·

It was the first day of classes. Olivia, Eugenie, Caldwell, and eight other young women awaited the arrival of their moral philosophy teacher. Olivia chose a desk in the last row of the classroom.

"My parents enrolled me here because it is the finest school for young women in the country," Caldie told whomever would listen. "Isn't that wonderful? That it's right here in Columbia, so near to Brae Loch? My father says the teachers here will help shape our thinking so we become ideal helpmates to our planter husbands."

Shape? Olivia thought to herself. *Mother says, "temper her willfulness." Caldie says, "shape." Call it what you want. Nobody will shape me. When that old battle axe walks in the door, she'll find she has a worthy opponent in Olivia Tucker. No one will shape me. No one.*

A young woman who appeared to be in her early twenties breezed into the classroom, closed the door, and leaned into her desk. She wore no corset, nor was her skirt particularly puffy. "Good morning, ladies. My name is Miss Edwards. I am a native of the Commonwealth of Pennsylvania and a graduate of Oberlin College in Ohio. Who here is in your first year at Barhamville?"

All eleven girls raised their hands.

"Good, then we all have something in common. Let's get started, shall we?"

Miss Edwards handed a newspaper clipping to a girl in the front row. "This is an article from the *Columbia Telescope*—right here in South Carolina—published earlier this year. Please stand, announce your name, and start reading aloud."

After a minute, she directed the young woman to hand the article back to the next girl in line, and so on. While each girl read, Miss Edwards gazed down at the floor with folded arms and bowed head.

After the last girl in line finished the *Columbia Telescope* article, Miss Edwards handed another article to another girl in a front desk. "This next article is from the *Philadelphia Independent*. It describes the same event, but from a different perspective."

Both articles covered the Grimké-Weld wedding in Philadelphia the previous May. They mostly agreed on the facts: Angelina Grimké and Theodore Weld were the darling couple of the abolitionist movement. Miss Grimké detested the institution of slavery even though she was the daughter of Charleston enslavers. *Same as me*, Olivia thought to herself. Mr. Weld trained agents to travel the land and speak about the evils of slavery. The couple was married by two ministers: one Black and one white. Both Blacks and whites attended the wedding and the reception that followed. The bride purposefully omitted the words "to obey" from her wedding vows. The groom renounced his right to *feme covert*, which meant that even though he had a legal right to take possession of Angelina's fortune, he chose not to do so.

But the two newspapers drew dramatically different conclusions. The *Columbia Telescope* condemned Miss Grimké as a traitor to her class. The writer was appalled at the fraternizing of the races and disdainful that the bride and groom were married by a Black and a white minister. He belittled Miss Grimké's unwillingness to obey her husband and Mr. Weld's ridiculous decision to not assert his God-given right to her wealth. The *Philadelphia Independent*'s perspective was quite different. The author—a reporter named Harold Foote, whom Olivia had met—found it laudable that the races mixed amiably. Although the wedding vows seemed somewhat outré to him, the reporter applauded the newlyweds' willingness to flaunt convention.

"Okay, ladies," said Miss Edwards, "you have been presented with two divergent viewpoints of the same event. This year—together—we will have numerous opportunities to learn to think critically, examine a set of facts, and come to our own conclusions."

Miss Edwards paused. Olivia surveyed her classmates. No one moved a muscle. They were enraptured by this new, charismatic force.

"Today, let's start by grappling with a momentous concept. What you have learned so far in your young lives might not be the only way to view the world. . . ."

Olivia admitted that, apparently like her classmates, she was already infatuated. *If Miss Edwards is an example of the battle axes who will teach me for the next four years, I'm in with both feet.*

"There is an alternative to your Southern slave system," Miss Edwards continued, "and to the way you are preparing for marriage."

Caldie Montgomery raised her hand and stood. "Are you saying slavery is wrong?"

"There is no need to stand as we engage in discussion. I want this class to be more of an open forum. But to answer your question, I am saying you shouldn't take what your fathers or older brothers espouse as the gospel. You were issued a brain at birth. I urge you to use it to come to your own conclusions."

Another girl started to stand, then smiled and sat back down. "Are you saying we shouldn't get married?"

"Not at all. Angelina Grimké, a free thinker to be sure, chose to marry, but she and Mr. Weld have molded their marriage to their own standards, not to someone else's. I urge you to do the same."

Debate for the rest of the class that day was spirited. Most of the girls were appalled at any criticism of what Senator Calhoun had called the South's *Peculiar Institution*. They also had no intention of deviating from their destiny of becoming perfect wives to men of the South Carolina gentry or possibly new Philadelphia money.

Olivia occasionally contributed to the discussion, but mostly she sat awash in a flood of gratitude. Miss Edwards's words validated what Olivia believed about herself: *I am an independent thinker by nature. I already figured out for myself that slavery is sinful when not a single white South Carolinian guided me there. Miss Grimké and Mr. Weld's wedding decisions make perfect sense to me.*

However, Olivia walked out of class that day with another conclusion that she doubted her classmates shared: *Philadelphia. Where my mother lived on and off until she married Papa. Where my family used to summer to escape Charleston's heat and malaria. Where we bought a house so Mother could become a pillar of the social season. Where Papa and Uncle George still huddle to plot their mutual business interests. If Angelina Grimké and Theodore Weld are typical of what's happening in Philadelphia, then that city is where my destiny lies.*

* * * * *

Caldie Montgomery didn't attend dinner that evening. "I need to go to Brae Loch," she announced. "I've got to talk to my father about something."

The next day, Olivia and the rest of her classmates awaited Miss Edwards' arrival. Olivia had taken a seat in the front row. Caldie, seated at the desk next to hers, prattled on about something ignorable. Then Dr. Marks entered and closed the door. "Good morning, young ladies. I will be your moral philosophy teacher for the next few weeks—"

"Where's Miss Edwards?" Olivia blurted out.

"Please stand when addressing the instructor, Miss Tucker."

Olivia stood. "Dr. Marks, where is Miss Edwards?"

"She has been dismissed."

Olivia saw Caldie Montgomery turn and smirk at the girl behind her.

* * * * *

That evening, the first form elected Caldie president of the class. Olivia watched as Caldie received congratulations from her classmates. She acted as if the presidency was her birthright.

"What does the president do, anyway?" Olivia said to Eugenie.

"She gets to order us around. First-form girls serve meals and clear the tables. We're also responsible for delivering messages."

"Doesn't seem like a big deal."

"Yeah, but it could be. Delivering is easy because you spend most of your time in Dr. Marks's anteroom waiting for a message that needs to be delivered. You can read or study while you're sitting around. Dining Hall duty is different. Serving and clearing are messy and busy."

"I don't mind doing that."

"Yeah, but the president can assign the tasks however she wants. She can give her friends messenger duty, and the girls she doesn't like get Dining Hall duty."

"That's not fair."

"Nope, but that's the way it is. One thing for sure: Don't irritate Caldie. If you do, you'll find yourself on Dining Hall duty five days in a row."

THURSDAY, OCTOBER 4

· RIAN ·

Rian, Conor, and Jabez occasionally climbed to the top of the Sparks Shot Tower to watch the sunset and talk. Today, Conor had to work a double shift out of the Merchants' Exchange because a lot of the messengers were sick, so it was only her and Jabez.

The routine was always the same: wait until the workers left for the day, pull the key from its hiding place, and shut the door behind them. This evening, Rian and Jabez started climbing minutes before sunset. Rian found the circular stairs a little more difficult to navigate since they were lit only by Jabez's candle. "Are you sailing to Germany with Aunt Mila or not?" she asked.

"Not," Jabez said over his shoulder. "I don't want to move to Saxony. I won't know anybody. I don't speak German. I don't want to go to school there. I don't want to help Uncle Adrian start his railroad."

"That's a lot of reasons."

"Mila's meeting with your father. She's going to ask him if I can move in with you."

Rian still didn't like the thought of Jabez moving into her house but had reconciled herself to it. *He's a terrible worker. I can't imagine he'd be any better as a housemate.* "You'd have to share a bed with Conor."

"I don't care."

"Things will be different in our house. *Vater* will give you a choice: Either show up to work regular as clockwork, or go to school. He won't let you fool around with your friends down on the waterfront all day."

"Yeah, like he does such a great job keeping you in line. You do whatever you want. I imagine I'll be able to do the same."

The truth in Jabez's assertion struck home. Rian chose to say nothing. *Living with him will be tough. He's so lazy.*

Jabez reached the smelting room first while Rian navigated the rest of the stairs. He held the candle so its light illuminated her remaining steps. "Maybe I'll run away."

Rian joined him and surveyed their surroundings, where molten lead was dropped through a hole in the center of the room. *One of these days, I want to watch the men make bullets.* "Where would you go?"

Jabez handed the candle to Rian and started climbing the ladder toward the trap door in the roof. "I'll become a gambler on a Mississippi riverboat."

Rian snorted. "You can't play poker worth a damn. I take your money every time."

"Well, that's the plan." Jabez unlatched the trap door and climbed through. "Holy shit," he said.

The sudden rush of wind from outside blew out the candle. Rian followed Jabez up the ladder. "What?" she called up to him.

"They tore the railing off."

Rian kept climbing, hoisted her way onto the roof, then stood. "Whoa, this changes things. It's dangerous up here now. Why the hell would they remove the railing?"

"Dunno. I like it."

It was a lot windier on the roof than at ground level. As she usually did, Rian walked around the roof of the tower, but this time, she kept a wide berth from the edge. With the sun now set, the colors of autumn were mostly muted. The church spires and factory chimneys to the west were mere silhouettes. Ships' masts in Camden across the Delaware could have been mistaken for the edge of a forest. Faint sounds of revelry wafted up from Water Street to the north. Dim cones of light from gas streetlights plotted straight lines along Second and Third Streets.

By the time Rian finished her walkaround, Jabez stood with his back to the void, his heels dangerously close to the edge, his arms out wide.

"Jabez, what the hell are you doing? Get away from there!" *Jaysus, he's crazy.*

"Don't come near me," he said in not much more than a whisper.

Rian stayed rooted near the trap door. "Be careful. If you lose your balance, you're dead."

Jabez closed his eyes and leaned his head back. "Would that be a bad thing?"

"Of course it would. Jabez, it's gusty tonight."

"You're right. One gust in the wrong direction, and I'm flying."

"How about taking one step toward me." *This is bad. This is really bad.*

"I like this. It could all be over."

"What are you doing? What are you saying?"

Jabez lowered his arms, but only a little. He opened his eyes and looked at Rian. "I'm saying that if I died, I would finally have . . . peace."

"Peace from what? You got even with your father. You burned his slave ship. Its evil days are over."

"The *Bridger's* evil days will never be over. It made four trips from Africa with slaves, two of them under my father. Eena, you never heard the wails from down in the hold. You haven't smelled the stink."

"But your father's dead. And the *Bridger* is gone. You did your best. You, Jules, Logan, my father. It's over now. The evil that happened aboard that ship is in the past."

"No, it's not. I live with it every day."

"You were only thirteen. You couldn't do anything to help those people."

"They weren't the only ones."

"Who else?"

Jabez didn't answer. He shut his eyes again and raised his face to the darkening sky.

"Jabez, what other evils happened on that ship?" *Grab him! Grab him right now while his eyes are closed.*

A gust of wind forced Jabez to adjust his footing. "Don't do it, Eena. I'll hear you if you step any closer."

"Something happened to you, didn't it?"

His face still to the sky, Jabez wiped tears from both his cheeks, then held his arms back out wide again.

"Jabez, tell me what happened."

Jabez shuffled backward a few inches. Then, "There was a sailor on the ship. He did things to me."

"What did he do?"

Finally, Jabez lowered his arms, and his shoulders sagged. He averted his gaze as if he couldn't bear to meet Rian's eyes as he revealed the truth. "He hurt me. I couldn't do anything to stop him. He said that if I told Captain, he would kill me. That's the real reason I burned the ship. I thought that would end it, but the hurt didn't go away. It's still there. And if I take one step back right now, I will finally end it."

Think, Eena, think. "Maybe running around the waterfront with your friends isn't such a bad idea after all."

"You just said Uncle Otto wouldn't let me do that."

Say something. Say anything, quick, before he blows off the fooking roof. "Jabez, I'll make you a deal. Come away from the edge. Come down the stairs with me, and I'll . . . and I'll teach you everything I know about poker."

Jabez lowered his arms the rest of the way. "Everything?"

"Yeah, everything. I never told you this, but I know when you're sitting on a bad hand because you flick your cards. You only do it once, but you do it. It's called a tell."

"Do I do something when I've got a good hand?"

Keep him talking, Eena. Keep him talking. "Yes. If you come down the tower with me, I'll explain. Most people have tells if you study them. There're other things I can teach you."

"You can't tell Aunt Mila what I said. You can't tell anyone. Promise me."

"Okay. All this is just between you and me. But you have to promise me you won't come up here and jump."

"Okay, I can promise that."

It was only after the two had parted for the evening—Jabez to return to his home with Aunt Mila, and Rian to 134 North Ninth—that she started contemplating all she had learned about Jabez that evening. *He was only twelve years old, and that sailor abused him terribly. He's been tortured by those memories all this time. There may be nothing I can do to take away his pain. I will never forgive myself for every time I have judged him, but I will never judge him again.*

* * * * *

Rian thought of nothing but Jabez's pain for most of the walk home. When she saw Conor pass through the light of a street lamp half a block ahead of her, she whistled through the gap between her two front teeth. Conor turned and waited. He waved a letter in Rian's face when she caught up to him. "I've got a letter for you. Guess who it's from."

Rian grabbed the letter from Conor's hand and read *Olivia Tucker.* Momentarily forgetting about Jabez, she picked up her pace the final block to the house.

By the light of the parlor's whale oil lamp, Rian broke the wax seal with the letters *OT* pressed into it and started reading aloud.

September 26, 1838

Dearest Rian,

 My parents have finally become fed up with my "abolitionist devilry." Well, that was really Papa. He got so mad at one point that he slapped me in the face. Mother's motivation—as stated to her Flower Club friends—sounds different, but it isn't. She wants me to become the perfect wife for Barnwell Wilkinson (who will become a planter like his father). I've been shipped off to the South Carolina Female Collegiate Institute in Columbia, and whatever the school can do to temper my willfulness will be fine with her.

I don't know about marrying Barney, but if I do, I won't knuckle under to him like Mother does to Papa. Papa's mean when he's drunk.

I was ambivalent about leaving Long Pond. Even though I'm only fourteen, the house servants have been treated better because I occasionally intervene. I wish I could say the same thing for the field hands, but Papa gives the slavedriver a free hand to squeeze every ounce of labor he can out of them. I'm going to miss Cook and Emblee and some of the other servants.

I won't miss my parents' bickering. Papa bought a rather comely young woman at the slave auction and is keeping her in a cabin down by the river. Same cabin, different concubine. Mother raised a fuss as she is wont to do. Father told her he wouldn't go down to the river anymore. That lasted for a couple of weeks, then he started up again. Mother knows, of course. There are no secrets on a plantation. The stories fly around the farm, but in whispers.

Now that I'm in Columbia, at least I'm closer to Topper. Mama hates it when I call Topper my half-brother, even though I'm only saying out loud what everyone in the county knows but doesn't talk about (those whispers again): Papa had his way with a slave girl named Rachel when Mother was pregnant with me. Of course, all the other planters do the same thing.

I don't like this school very much. Some of the subjects are interesting, but they already fired the only teacher I liked. If it gets really bad, I'll take my inspiration from you and run away. Is there an Underground Railroad in Philadelphia that takes fugitive white girls? Ha ha. That was a joke. Or maybe not.

Say hello to Conor, if he's living with you, and your father.

Love,
Olivia

By the time Rian finished reading, she and Conor had climbed the stairs and were sitting on Rian's bed.

"She always does that," said Conor.

"Does what?"

"Signs her letters with the word *love*. 'With love.' 'With affection.' Is that what girls do?"

"How the hell would I know? I don't have any girl friends except for Olivia, and I haven't seen her since before Russia."

* * * * *

· OTTO ·

Otto sat with Mila in the parlor of his sister-in-law's home when Jabez arrived from his walk with Rian. The room held only three straight-backed chairs now that Mila had sold most of her furnishings and shipped a box of items to a wharf in New York City. Mila was excited about reuniting with Adrian in Saxony after a year apart. Jabez seemed excited about . . . nothing.

"It is settled," Otto said. "Jabez moves in with Rian, Conor, and me next Wednesday."

Mila nodded. "Jabez, are you sure you want to stay in Philadelphia? You have never been to Germany. You might like it."

Otto knew Jabez had seen much of the world in his young life: the Caribbean, South America, China, Africa, but not Europe. He turned his attention to his nephew for a response. He got . . . still nothing.

Otto's sister died giving birth to Jabez. Mila and Adrian took him into their home and treated him like a son while his seafaring father traveled the world. Jabez and Rian were peas in a pod. They played together, even looked alike, both filled with exuberance and mischief. But after eight joyous years, Levi Howes, then captain of a Baltimore clipper, blew into town and whisked Jabez away to be his cabin boy. When Jabez returned to Adrian and Mila's care five years later, he was a different child: sullen, withdrawn, more prone to a new kind of mischief that was darker, harmful, thoughtless.

Finally, Otto could not tolerate the silence any longer. "Jabez, are you okay with this plan?"

Jabez didn't say anything for a long moment, nor did he return Otto's gaze. Finally, he uttered, "The plan makes me feel . . . trapped." He rose and left the house.

Otto watched the door close and turned to his sister-in-law. "Mila, he will be all right. You cannot delay any longer. This house is sold. Your furniture is sold. If you are not on the *Great Western* the day after tomorrow, it will be weeks before your next opportunity, and no one wants to be on the North Atlantic in November."

* * * * * * * * * * * * * * *

Our narrative has now caught up to the book's opening scenes, in which Rian and Otto walk to work, Jules enters the office to accompany Otto as they vote, and the boiler at Krieger Locomotive explodes, blowing Rian into the air.

TUESDAY, OCTOBER 9

· JULES ·

As far as Jules was concerned, the stakes of the vote on the proposed Pennsylvania constitution couldn't have been higher. It would be close. On this day, more than any other election he had ever participated in, it was vital that he and his compatriots exercise their legal right to vote. Otherwise, this might be the last day he ever cast a ballot.

He knew the scene inside the State House would be chaotic. On election days, officials set up temporary voting windows for each ward—an ungenerous nine-by-nine-inch square—inside the mammoth State House vestibule. In theory, to perform his civic duty, a voter waited in his ward's line, then handed his vote through the window. In reality, the room was always so crowded that there wasn't even a semblance of a line. Those closest to the window—monitors, both Whig and Democrat—held no legal standing but never yielded their place. They watched for friends and offered to hand their votes through the window for them. If the monitor didn't know you, you had to fight to the front and thrust your vote through the window before you were shoved back.

Today, though, the chaos had spilled outside. A gauntlet of partisans—pro on one side, anti on the other—harangued arrivees in last-ditch attempts to sway the undecided. They armed their potential converts with ballots and plied them with fliers, apples, and hard cider. If a voter was indiscreet enough to identify himself as for or against the new constitution, allies and opponents lined up to either push him through the State House doors or prevent him from getting there.

When Jules and Otto arrived along with a dozen other Black men and as many white allies, there was no doubt in any of the haranguers' minds how the group intended to vote. Rather than wait for them to wade through the gauntlet, the gauntlet descended on them. Jules warded off blows and accepted encouraging tugs toward the door. The group beat, clawed, bit, punched, and pushed their way into the vestibule. Jules lost track of his allies, as each was forced to make his own way through the mob toward his ward window.

One of the larger men in the room, Jules bulled his way to the front and, ignoring both friendly and hostile monitors, thrust his ballot through the window. Blows rained down on his head and shoulders. He swung blindly at his tormentors, connecting a few good shots, taking as many. Someone—he had no idea whether friend or foe—was knocked to the floor and rolled into Jules's legs, forcing him to go down on all fours. An ineffective kick glanced off his shoulder, but his assailant was pulled back. A pair of hands roughly grabbed him by the jacket and, despite his bulk, picked him up.

"Play your role here, Jules," a voice yelled in his ear. "I'm saving you from a thrashing, but I don't want my boys to see it that way." Hugh Callaghan, his frequent antagonist but occasional ally, propelled him toward the door. Jules turned and swung at Hugh, glancing a blow off his shoulder. Hugh returned one in kind. The two grabbed at each other, dancing a charade of a fight until they shouldered their way out the door and down the steps.

"Have you had enough?" Hugh yelled.

"Not even close!" Jules responded, his blood up, his frustration and confusion overwhelming his usual ability to control himself. He charged at Hugh, shouldering into his belly, and the two tumbled to the pea gravel. They traded blows as they rolled around the walkway. A ring of men formed around them, mostly shouting encouragement for Hugh.

Then Jimmy Butter, a worker at Krieger Locomotive, shouldered his way through the circle and yelled, "Jules, stop!"

Thankful to have a semblance of an excuse to end their fight, Jules and Hugh desisted, rose from the pea gravel, and dusted themselves off. "Let that be a lesson to you!" Hugh yelled, his last act in the charade.

Jimmy grabbed Jules by the sleeve and pulled him close. "Jules, this doesn't matter right now. There's been an explosion at the locomotive factory. Rian's been hurt. We need to find Otto."

* * * * *

· OLIVIA ·

Olivia begrudgingly admitted that since Dr. Marks had taken over the Moral Philosophy class from the short-tenured Miss Edwards, he had helped the girls learn the fundamentals and art of debate. But there was a problem. Although the topics had helped the girls hone their skills, the propositions were underwhelming. For instance, the proposition two weeks ago was: *More stimulating conversation will occur at a dinner party of six guests than twelve.*

Olivia had warmed up to last week's topic: *Government funds should not be used to dredge the Santee Canal*, and she willingly joined the opposition side. She felt her team won the debate, but that is not how the class voted.

When Dr. Marks announced that class debate would center on slavery this week, Olivia fantasized about wrestling with the issue of emancipation, or teaching slaves to read, or—*oh glory, could you imagine?*—the morality of helping slaves escape. However, when Dr. Marks announced the proposition of the week—*Free Blacks in South Carolina should be forced to relocate to Africa*—she was disappointed to the point of distress.

Dr. Marks strode into class, shut the door, and said, "Good morning, ladies. You have had time to prepare yourselves for this week's proposition. It's time to choose our teams. Who would like to take the affirmative side?"

Four girls, including Eugenie, raised their hands.

Before Dr. Marks could ask for volunteers for the opposition, Olivia stood and said, "Excuse me, Dr. Marks. I have a comment."

Dr. Marks sighed, as Olivia often had comments. "Yes, Miss Tucker?"

"I believe this week's debate topic has a flawed basic premise. I think we should be debating that."

Some of the girls were amused when Olivia drew the class off on tangents. Others viewed her banter with Dr. Marks as an opportunity to whisper and pass notes. This morning, the whispering mostly entailed who would take which side of the proposition.

"Very bold of you, Miss Tucker. And what is the flawed basic premise you are referring to?"

"We're discussing exiling free Blacks to Africa with the underlying assumption—the basic premise—that slavery is good. If we're going to debate the topic of slavery, we should start by establishing the validity of our basic premise. I propose that an appropriate proposition for today should be: *Slavery is evil.*"

Whatever buzz was going on to determine which of the girls would volunteer to oppose the deporting of ex-slaves to Africa immediately ceased. All eyes went to Dr. Marks.

Dr. Marks stared at Olivia for a long moment. "We will stick to the curriculum I have established. Miss Tucker, please stay after class. I would like to have a word with you in private."

＊ ＊ ＊ ＊ ＊

Only Eugenie sat with Olivia during the noontime meal. None of her classmates approached their table. No one asked, "What did Dr. Marks say to you?" No one said, "That was brave of you to say that."

"You shouldn't have done that," Eugenie said after one of their classmates delivered two plates of salad to their table.

"Why not? You should always establish that your basic premise is valid. Dr. Marks taught us that."

"You shouldn't have done that because you'll never make any friends in this school. Even me."

"Despite every word you've said, I don't believe you really think slavery is acceptable. Your father is a minister. He doesn't own any slaves."

"We don't own slaves because we can't afford them. My father is about as pro-slavery as you can get. And because of you, I had to examine that basic premise. And do you know what? I think slavery is fine the way it is."

* * * * *

Back in their room that evening, Olivia and Eugenie were reading on their beds. The door was open. Caldie Montgomery appeared and said, "Abo, you're serving breakfast, lunch, and dinner tomorrow because Patricia is sick."

Olivia glanced up from her bed. "Who are you talking to?"

"You, stupid. I've decided to call you Abo, short for abolitionist. You thought you were real smart talking that way to Dr. Marks in class today. Let's see how smart you feel when you have no friends. Good night, Eugenie. Good night, Abo."

FRIDAY, OCTOBER 12

· RIAN ·

Darkness.

Pain. . . . It even hurts to breathe.

Conor's voice broke into Rian's consciousness. "Lucretia, I think she's waking up!"

Time passed, but whether it was minutes or hours, Rian had no idea.

Someone pressed on her chest. "Ow! *Scheisse!* [Shit!]" she protested.

A stranger's voice said, "Well, that's good news. She's conscious."

"Dr. Boswell, I apologize for my daughter's language," her father offered. "She has spent too much time with the workers at the shop."

"In this case, it's quite useful," the doctor responded. "Now I can get a handle on her internal injuries." Another prod, gentler this time, but it still sent a shot of pain into Rian's chest.

"Jaysus! Stop."

More pressing. More swearing. Dr. Boswell removed a bandage that had covered Rian's eyes. He held up two fingers. "Good morning, my dear. How many fingers am I holding up?"

Rian noticed her father hovering over Dr. Boswell's shoulder. "Two," she said. Conor leaned into the wall at the doorway, his arms folded. She could hear her next-door neighbor Lucretia ordering someone around in the kitchen downstairs.

Dr. Boswell pointed to Conor. "Who is that person over there?"

"Conor McGuire . . . my best friend."

"Tell me how you two became friends."

"My mother and both of his parents died on the same day during the cholera epidemic." Rian winced. Speaking was an effort. "*Vater* said he could stay with us for a while. . . . We haven't been able to get rid of him," she added as a joke.

Conor snorted. Dr. Boswell smiled. "Well, it's good to have you back. We were a little worried but a lot less worried now."

"What happened?" She tried to prop herself up to ease her breathing a bit, but a knife-like pain shot through her right shoulder. Her left arm was swaddled in a bandage.

Even though every motion hurt, Rian allowed Dr. Boswell to help her rise to a sitting position. He placed a pillow behind her. "Whatever position you can find to help you breathe easier is the best position for you. Feel free to keep experimenting." The doctor straightened and crossed his arms. "The boiler for the steam engine that drives the machinery at Krieger Locomotive blew up. You were thrown from the boiler scaffold onto the shop floor. You are lucky to be alive."

"Is everybody else okay?"

Her father sat down on Rian's bed. "We can talk about that later. You were foolish to do this. I do not know what you were thinking."

Rian momentarily shut her eyes. "What have I done to myself, Dr. Boswell?"

Dr. Boswell started talking to Rian's father. "Otto, this is a critical time—"

"No," said Rian, who found breathing in an upright position to be a little easier. "Speak to me."

Boswell received a nod from Otto, then addressed Rian quietly. "Your wounds are significant, my dear. You received a nasty bump to your head. Escaping steam from the explosion caused severe burns on your left arm from your wrist to your biceps. You have a deep wound on the left side of your neck—I suspect from a flying shard of metal. I apologize for the pushing and prodding, but I have confirmed what I suspected. You have a broken clavicle, numerous broken ribs, and probably a punctured lung. But you are fortunate in a way. If that is the extent of your internal injuries, all these wounds can heal without further intervention from me."

Rian looked away, and that motion alone was like a knife poking into her shoulder.

Boswell held a glass to Rian's lips. "Here, drink this."

Rian realized she was thirsty and drank gratefully, but grimaced at the liquid's bitterness. "That's awful. What is it?"

"Laudanum. It is a tincture of opium. Quite miraculous, really. Now that you're awake, regular doses of this will dull your pain. But be careful. It can develop a power over you. People have become slaves to its effects."

Dr. Boswell placed a new, smaller bandage on Rian's head and another loosely around her neck. He wrapped her chest tightly with long strips of cloth and then bound her arm to her chest. After a few more formalities, he made his goodbyes and Otto escorted him downstairs.

That left Conor the only other person in her bedroom, for the moment at least. He sat on her bed. "We've been worried."

Rian moved her shoulder to check the degree of pain. It had already lessened. She also felt somewhat lightheaded. "How long have I been out?"

"Three days. Rian, you were struggling. Dr. Boswell told your father you might not make it through that first night. That cut on your neck is pretty deep. You almost bled to death."

"Was anyone else hurt?"

"Rian, Harry's dead. He was killed instantly."

"Oh, no. . . ." *Harry. Harry hates me. Hated me,* she corrected. *But Jaysus, I never wanted this.* The laudanum haze further enveloped Rian's senses. "What about Jabez?"

"He's okay. You were right in front of him. Your body saved him from getting hurt. Rian, it's a miracle no one else was killed."

Rian shook her head. "I've got to talk to Jabez."

"Jabez? Why?"

"He tinkered with the regulator somehow. That's why the boiler blew. Conor, he was trying to kill himself."

Conor gazed out Rian's window. "That explains it."

"I messed up his plan when I alerted Harry."

"No, that's not what I meant. All of a sudden, Jabez changed his mind. He was all set to move in here with you, me, and your father. Then the explosion. Then he decided he wanted to go to Saxony after all. He and your Aunt Mila left on the train to New York yesterday. I think they board the ship to Bristol today."

Rian shook her head ever so slightly, careful not to disturb the bandage on her neck. "How bad is the shop?"

"It's a mess. The steam engine and boiler are destroyed, of course. It blew in the office wall. A quarter of the drive shaft along the ceiling got mangled. They think they can repair the lathe and the drill press that were nearest to the boiler."

"How long will it be out of commission?"

"Dunno. Three weeks maybe? Your da has already bought a steam engine and boiler from a business that went belly up a couple of weeks ago. It's supposed to be delivered in parts sometime next week."

"I've got to get better. I can help put that mess back together. It's the kind of thing I'm good at." Rian attempted to get out of bed, but even the dulling effect of the laudanum couldn't mask the shots of pain that coursed through every part of her body. "Uh!" she moaned and slumped back into her headboard. "Not yet, I guess."

"Yeah, you should probably wait a few days before you try that."

"Did *Vater* and Jules get in any fights when they were voting at the State House?"

"Oh, yeah. Apparently a couple of doozies. Bigger than the last time, but all our guys voted."

"Did they vote down the new constitution?"

Conor sat at the foot of Rian's bed. "No. It got ratified. It was close. We lost by a thousand votes.[15] As of three days ago, Black men in Pennsylvania no longer have the right to vote."

Finally, the full effect of the laudanum kicked in. "Conor, this is too much. I've got to sleep."

* * * * *

· OLIVIA ·

Olivia had been at Barhamville for more than a month before she was invited to Thousand Oaks, the Wilkinson plantation outside of town. On Friday afternoon, she read in her room, awaiting the arrival of . . . someone—the arrangements had been made through Dr. Marks, and the exact plan was not entirely clear to her.

At last night's dinner, when Olivia told the girls she was going to visit her father's college friend and his family for two days, she had purposely omitted two key items. First: reference to the Wilkinsons' son, Barnwell. Knowledge of his existence would become the source of incessant teasing by Caldwell. Besides, Olivia hadn't seen Barney since they were ten years old. She could barely remember what he looked like. Second, and even more important: Topper. She and Topper had grown up together at Long Pond until they were twelve . . . she, the daughter of planter Randolph Tucker and his wife, Penelope; and he, the son of the same man and a slave girl named Rebecca. Topper's parentage was unacknowledged by her father, certainly by her mother, but whispered about when members of the Lowcountry gentry socialized. Randolph Tucker added ownership of his son to a pot in a card game and lost him to Trevor Wilkinson two years ago. Olivia had heard nothing from or about him since.

Smirky Caldwell Montgomery appeared at her door. "Abo, Mrs. Marks says you're to come down to the parlor. Mrs. Wilkinson is here . . . You didn't tell us there was a son involved. He's gawky, but even so, I think you should have dressed a little better."

---

15. The final tally was 113,971 to 112,759.

Now second-guessing her decision to wear a day dress, Olivia arrived in the parlor, holding a carpetbag in each hand. Mrs. Wilkinson, seated in the settee opposite Mrs. Marks, interrupted her conversation to turn and give Olivia an assessing regard. "Olivia dear, how good to see you. You have grown so."

Olivia assumed The Squire hadn't told his old college roommate about her willfulness or her abolitionist tendencies. Such information would certainly diminish her value on the marriage market—and her family's reputation—here in the midlands of South Carolina.

Tall, skinny Barnwell unfolded himself from his chair, strode to her, and said, "Let me take those for you." He promptly set the carpetbags down, grabbed Olivia's hand (which she had not proffered) while he was still bent over, lifted it to his lips, and kissed it. This wasn't just a brush on the lips. He kissed it with such verve that she could hear the smack of it.

Mrs. Wilkinson ignored her son's gracelessness. "Olivia dear, we look forward to hearing all the news from your family. Come. Our carriage awaits."

Mrs. Wilkinson led the way and Olivia followed. Barnwell brought up the rear with both carpetbags, even though Olivia had tried to wrest one from him. A landau with its top down was parked in the circular drive. Standing by the landau's half-door was . . . *oh glory! It's Topper.* Topper: dressed in nankeen pants and a white collared cotton shirt, taller, more filled out, looking more like their father . . . And his mask was up.

Before Olivia had a chance to react to his presence, he dropped his mask for a fleeting instant—just enough time to give a subtle shake of his head, indicating she should not acknowledge him. Mask back up, Topper offered his hand to Mrs. Wilkinson to assist her into the carriage. He did the same for Olivia, giving her the opportunity to smile at him with her eyes, the only gesture of recognition the moment offered.

"Sit opposite me, dear," said Mrs. Wilkinson. "You will be much more comfortable facing forward."

Topper relieved Barnwell of Olivia's carpetbags and lashed them to the boot. Barnwell climbed into the carriage. His mother gestured with her hand that Barnwell should sit next to Olivia in the front-facing seat. He followed orders.

* * * * *

Olivia grew up knowing her family was rich. *Or at least I thought we were rich until Mother told me we were in debt.* But her perception of her family's wealth didn't prepare her for the mansion at Thousand Oaks. Every plantation house she had visited during her childhood, every mansion she and her mother had glimpsed from a distance during the three-day trip from Charleston to Columbia, all paled in comparison to this elegant, palatial manor.

"Whoa," Olivia blurted when she first glimpsed the Wilkinsons' stately home, then chastised herself for being too transparent. Her utterance elicited a wry smile from Mrs. Wilkinson.

The house was huge. It was obvious even from a distance that the stories weren't a standard height. A two-story covered portico and balcony surrounded the central core on all four sides. Eight pearly-white pillars buttressed the front facade. The middle two pillars bracketed a large green double door on the first floor. Smaller than the core, but adding to its sense of opulence, a cupola jutted from the roof and added another story's height. *Well done*, thought Olivia. *The cupola will bring light into the building no matter where the sun is but also create plenty of ventilation during the summer.*

"I'm glad you're impressed," volunteered Mrs. Wilkinson. "Hopefully, you will be spending a lot of time here."

Two hounds rollicked down the driveway to meet them. They escorted the carriage up the lane, barking all the way. A female slave stood at attention when Topper pulled the carriage to a halt in the circular driveway, grabbed Olivia's carpetbags off the boot of the carriage, and disappeared into the house. Topper offered his hand to Mrs. Wilkinson as she descended from the landau, then did the same for Olivia. Neither gave the other any sign of familiarity.

Mrs. Wilkinson smiled contentedly, shut her eyes, and briefly raised her face to the sun. "I've been looking forward to this moment for years. Now it's finally here." She turned her attention to Barney, who still sat in the carriage. "Show Olivia to her room, Barney."

Olivia detected a hint of impatience in Mrs. Wilkinson's voice. It took a few moments for Barney to gather his wits and get out of the landau.

"Olivia, my dear," said Mrs. Wilkinson, "your room benefits from the prevailing wind most of the year. When you're here, I want you to call it your room, because from now on, that's how we will refer to it."

The manor's interior was a testament to wealth. Following Barney, who was mute the entire time, Olivia marveled at the grand foyer, the grandfather clock *tick-tock-tick-tock*ing, the curved staircase, the second-floor view back down into the foyer, the sunlight streaming through the cupola, and finally, her bedroom. Her bags had been placed on a padded bench at the foot of her bed, but the slave who put them there was nowhere in sight. "Her room" was sixteen feet square with ten-foot ceilings. French doors opened on two sides to the balcony that wrapped around the house. Olivia walked out the door to the front. A wicker chair and small, circular table to her right momentarily distracted her, but then the view captured her. Two rows of stately live oaks flanked the driveway, which stretched a quarter mile to the road. Beyond the road, a field of cotton stretched to the horizon.

Barney followed her out onto the balcony. "You have a wicker chaise lounge and another table around the corner. You can come out here whenever you want, even to sleep. Tell Hanna and she'll make the chaise into a bed for you."

"Do you ever sleep out here?"

"During the summer sometimes. Depends upon the mosquitoes."

"Where's your room?"

"In the front on the other side of the house . . . My parents want us to get married."

Olivia thought that was a stupid thing to say at this moment. "How come?"

"Because our fathers were roommates in college. Because a cotton fortune would be marrying a rice fortune. Because you're pretty."

I've known forever that my parents want Barney and me to get married. But do I have any say in the matter? My future husband is an oaf.

* * * * *

Half an hour after the arrival at Thousand Oaks, Olivia descended the curved staircase to the foyer, hoping to slip out and find Topper. The grandfather clock sounded six o'clock, its chimes sonorous and reverberant.

"Olivia dear," came Mrs. Wilkinson's voice from the sitting room, "are you refreshed?"

Olivia slowed and entered the room to see her hostess sitting at a Louis XVI desk, quill in hand. Mrs. Wilkinson looked up. "Dinner is in an hour, dear. You should go right back upstairs and change. Hanna is up there somewhere and she can help you."

Damnation. "I was hoping to walk around a bit first. It's so beautiful here."

"There will be plenty of time for that tomorrow. Perhaps you and Barnwell can ride over to the farm tomorrow and see the fields of Thousand Oaks in all their glory. The hands are still picking cotton. They'll be at it for another week or so, and they'll be baling long after that. It's quite impressive."

"I would like that." *I have no desire to see slaves mired in their involuntary servitude. I need an excuse to find Topper.* "Do you know what horse I would be riding? Maybe I can go see it now."

"Probably Ginny. She's steady . . . Barnwell." Mrs. Wilkinson barely raised her voice, and Barney promptly appeared through the other door—so promptly that it was obvious he had been listening from the other room. "Take Olivia out to the barn and show her Ginny. Don't be long because supper will be served promptly at seven o'clock."

Last week, Caldie had told the table at dinner that the best thing you can do when you're with a man is to get him talking about himself. Because Caldie had already developed a womanly figure,[16] her pronouncements—which implied extensive experience—carried great weight

"Where do you go to school?" Olivia asked Barnwell as they descended the front portico of Wilkinson Hall.

"I don't go to school. I get tutored. Here on the farm."

According to Caldie, the man would take this opportunity to continue talking about himself, or, if he were skilled in the art of gentlemanly conversation, he would ask her a question about herself.

Nothing.

"What subjects do you like?" Olivia asked to fill in the silence.

"I don't know. History, I suppose." He steered them toward the barn but failed again to keep the conversation going.

Topper was brushing down one of the horses that had hauled them from Barhamville to Thousand Oaks. "Topper, Miss Tucker would like to ride Ginny tomorrow. She would like to see her."

Topper continued to brush the horse. He barely looked at Barnwell and avoided gazing at Olivia completely. "Ginny came up lame yesterday, suh. How about one of the others?"

"You know the horses better than I do. Which one do you recommend?"

"That's up to you, suh."

"No, I order you to recommend one."

Topper quit brushing, looked down, then regarded Olivia as if assessing her riding capability as she stood there. "How about Turtle?" he asked Barnwell.

"Which one is that?"

"He's the chestnut gelding, white blaze on his face."

"Go get Turtle," Barnwell ordered.

Topper set his brush on a bench, walked down the corridor, and disappeared into a stall a hundred feet away. Olivia remembered Turtle. She had ridden him many times until Papa lost him in the same card game that he lost Topper.

Topper certainly knows that, but he sure won't mention it to Barnwell. "Turtle. I like the name," she said to Barnwell.

Barnwell didn't respond.

Five minutes later, Topper returned, guiding Turtle with a lead. Turtle approached Olivia and gave her a nudge of familiarity with his nose. She scratched

---

16. There is little documentation about when girls reached puberty in America as the 1830s came to a close. Most historical studies speculate that menstruation first occurred between the ages of fourteen and seventeen with the curve skewed toward seventeen.

him on his face and neck. "Hello, Turtle. Do you want to go out for a ride with me tomorrow?"

"Here, Miss," Topper said as he held out the lead. "Walk him around a bit. Then I'll return him to his stall."

Olivia grasped the lead and, at the same time, felt Topper insert a slip of paper into her hand. She gripped the paper, her palm increasingly sweaty as she led Turtle out of the barn and then back again. She resisted reading the note as she and Barnwell returned to the mansion, and as she climbed the stairs to her bedroom. She shut the door to her room and unfolded the sliver of paper. Two words were scrawled in pencil.

"HERE. MIDNIGHT."

* * * * *

Olivia tried to memorize which steps squeaked as she descended the stairs to dinner. She claimed that she forgot her fan and tested them again on the way up, then again as she returned.

Hours later, the only sound in the mansion was the *tick-tock-tick-tock* of the grandfather clock in the foyer. The Wilkinsons' home was pitch dark. The moon had set when Mr. and Mrs. Wilkinson, Barnwell, and Olivia ate supper. Now, as midnight approached, all candles had long since been doused and masters and servants were in bed.

Olivia felt her way down the stairs, opened the heavy front door, slipped out onto the portico, and closed the door behind her. She navigated her way to the barn with cautious steps and sensed, rather than saw, the barn's presence. The sliding door was open enough for her to slip through.

A call sounded from the far end of the corridor, near Turtle's stall: the *hoo . . . hoo . . .* of the great horned owl that used to be Topper's secret signal when they were playing Spies at Long Pond.

"Topper!" she whispered.

"Back here!" he whispered back.

The two met and hugged. "Topper, I missed you so much. Are you okay?"

"I'm fine. Better than most of the slaves around here. It helps to know horses. But as soon as they know what's important to you, they use it against you. It's better that no one here ever learns how close we used to be. How is Gramma-Rose?"

Olivia pulled back from Topper's embrace. "Oh my goodness. You don't know. How could you know? Mammy-Rose bolted when we were in Philadelphia the summer you were sent here."

"Did she get away?"

"Sure did. Rian Krieger and I helped her."

"Rian . . . that girl who dressed like a boy?"

Olivia nodded but realized Topper couldn't see her in the dark. "Yes, with you gone, Mammy had no tethers to Long Pond. She was sick of being a slave."

"So you still hate slavery?"

"More than ever."

"Then I've got something for you. I've been keeping a record. All the evil-doing these devils inflict on my brethren. Didn't have any idea how I was going to get the word out until I saw you come out of that school building. Can you get my notes up North? I want them to be printed so people can read what goes on down here."

"It's been a long time since we read *Robinson Crusoe* together. You were pretty stumbly. I don't remember you writing much."

"I'm a lot better at both reading and writing than I was then. Master leaves copies of the *Columbia Telescope* around. He doesn't know I can read, and I doubt he would care if he caught me because all that newspaper does is laud the planters, agree with Senator Calhoun, and promote the right of the post office to intercept abolitionist pamphlets."

"Glory, Topper, you learned all that from reading the newspaper?"

"Just seemed to come to me naturally. Then I started practicing my writing."

"Of course I'll get your notes up North somehow. I would be honored. But Topper, if anyone finds out. . . ."

"If anyone finds out, I'll be sold to some sugar plantation in Louisiana. I'll be dead in five years . . . You go to that school now?"

"Since September. Papa caught me teaching Emblee to read. There were other things. Some he knew about, some he didn't. I got sent away."

Topper hesitated as he absorbed all that news. "Do you ever go into town?"

"Sometimes my friends and I walk there, yes. Why?"

"Master Wilkinson's a senator. Sometimes he rides his horse into Columbia. Sometimes he has me drive him, especially on market days. Sometimes I do the buying. Sometimes Essie sits up with me and does a big shop. After we're done with market, those of us who are enslaved to the big-bugs wait around outside the capitol for our masters to finish for the day. Course, we can't sit on any of the benches, but we all know full-well it's a lot better than picking cotton. There's a big rock in a shady grove of trees to the west side of the capitol build-ing. There's a crevice in the side of the rock. I'll leave my writing there for you."

SUNDAY, OCTOBER 21

· SEAMUS ·

Although the Gallaghers and the Callaghans both belonged to St. Philip de Neri Catholic Church on Queen Street, they tended to keep their distance. Problems started three years ago when Seamus got blackballed from Hugh's Moyamensing Hose Company. Most of the Moya boys didn't approve of his sympathies for the Black folks in the neighborhood. In response, Seamus started the United No Name Fire Brigade, which put out any fire in Moyamensing, whether the building was owned by Black, white, or Irish. Both outfits also engaged in darker, larcenous pursuits: theft on the docks along the Delaware, extortion, and problem-solving when a little muscle was helpful.

The Moya/No Name rivalry got stickier when Seamus started seeing Hugh's daughter Siobhan, which Hugh forbade. The only reason the rivalry didn't return to all-out war was because Seamus started feeding Hugh information gleaned from optical telegraph messages that Conor intercepted.

After Sunday mass, members tended to socialize in front of the church. As usual, Hugh, the rooster with his hen and four chicks, held court on the steps. Seamus and his ma, three sisters, and brother kept their distance more toward Third Street. Seamus of the Gallaghers and Siobhan of the Callaghans made eye contact but otherwise showed no hint that they saw each other frequently. The two lovers' rendezvous were still clandestine for fear of Hugh's ire. *We might as well be the Montagues and the Capulets*, Seamus said to himself.

Uncharacteristically, Hugh indicated with a jerk of his head that he wanted to parlay.

The thought crossed Seamus's mind that Hugh had found out about him and Siobhan, but if that had been the case, it was more likely that Hugh and a couple of his boyos would have ambushed him when he left McSweeney's late some night. He sauntered toward neutral territory, halfway between their families' habitual after-mass stations.

A toothpick dangled from Hugh's lips. He didn't face Seamus directly. He scanned the crowd, scanned the street, scanned the traffic a block to the north. "How's your cousin?"

"Mending. Making noise about going back to work." *Whataya want, Hugh? You aren't here to talk about Rian.*

"I don't much like that little brat, but I've gotta admit, she's a tough nut. The pennies love her. 'The Heroine of Krieger Locomotive?' A bit extreme, don't you think?"

"No, I don't think that at all. I think she's a genuine hero. She put her life on the line and got blown up for the trouble. Not sure I would have made the same decision."

"Said the firefighter who enters burning buildings to save Africans on a regular basis."

Seamus shrugged. *Come on, Hugh, what did you call me over here for?*

"Was she still spiriting Africans out of town before she got blown up?"

"I don't think so. Uncle Otto put a stop to that a while back when he found out."

"Shyte."

"What?"

"I owe a friend a favor. He's cashing it in. It's a job more suited for your Underground Railroad."

"It's not *my* Railroad. Talk to Jules."

"That's just it. I can't. Moya's already bought two of his steam-powered fire pumps. Negotiating a price with him was my excuse for meeting with him. We don't need another one just yet, so I don't have an excuse. Can you do it for me?"

"Since when do you need an excuse? Just go talk to him. You live three blocks from his house."

Hugh shook his head. "I'm in a bind. I'm getting some heat from me boyos for guarding his factory. We started during the trouble last May,[17] and we haven't stopped. I shouldn't be helping him out."

"Hugh, Jules pays you protection money."

Hugh shrugged. "The only Black man in Philadelphia we protect. I shouldn't have staged that fight with him at the State House, either. That was a stupid decision made on impulse. I think my affection for Jules is affecting me judgment."

"Your judgment? Or your sense of what's right and wrong?"

---

17. On May 17, 1838, four days after it was dedicated, a mob burned down Pennsylvania Hall, the Pennsylvania Anti-Slavery Society's "Temple of Freedom." On May 18, an equally arson-minded mob heading to Lucretia Mott's house was lured in a different direction by a "family friend." They burned the Shelter for Colored Orphans instead. On May 19, a mob attacked Bethel AME Church. These real-life events form the backdrop for the climactic scenes of Book 3 of Rian Krieger's Journey, *The Blackmailer.*

"Will you help me out or not?"

"I want to marry Siobhan."

Hugh pulled the toothpick out of his mouth and stared at Seamus. "You're asking me for my daughter's hand in marriage?"

Seamus nodded.

"I told you five months ago that when you start making something of yourself, I'll consider it. I'm hearing rumors that your first batch of whiskey is pretty good. When will that start paying dividends?"

"Not 'til August of '41—it'll have aged for three years, and it'll be the finest whiskey this side of the Atlantic."

"Too bad, kid. That's a long time to wait, but that's the deal."

"What if I do you this favor? Go talk to Jules?"

Hugh finally stopped scanning the horizon and drilled in on Seamus. "I'll tell you what. Siobhan's been making noise about going back to work at Mc-Sweeney's Saloon. I'm not crazy about the idea, because that's where your No Name boys congregate, but I'll say yes to that. You'll have more occasion to see her. That puts you on the inside track, and I don't have to listen to her bitching at dinner every night. And you know what, Seamus? If I was you, I'd start selling some of that whiskey sooner rather than later."

"Seems like we're making progress here, Hugh. Tell me about this favor you're doing for a friend."

"Well, it's not a friend, really. It's me wife."

* * * * *

· RIAN ·

Rian's father returned home after work each day and caught her up on the doings at the shop. The remains of the ruined steam engine had been cleared away. They were rebuilding the caved-in wall of the office. The lathe nearest the explosion, which they thought they could fix, was declared junk. The drill press would be usable once they fabricated a new part, but that couldn't happen until the factory was back up and running. Otto asked Seamus to become the new foreman of Krieger Locomotive. Seamus declined, but he did agree to supervise the repair of the ruined drive shaft since he had installed it three years ago when the factories were new. The used steam engine was delivered. It would take a lot of work to reassemble it. It was bigger than the old one but not as powerful as you might think.

Conor helped Rian slip her wounded body into her shirt at the beginning of the day. He brought news from his days of delivering messages. In the evenings, he did whatever he could to help. He changed her dressings and adjusted her sling. He read to her. At bedtime, he helped her out of her shirt and into her nightshirt. He blew out her whale oil lamp after she had crawled into bed.

Dr. Boswell's optimistic predictions began to manifest. Rian's assumed punctured lung must have healed on its own, because she no longer felt short of breath. Her broken collarbone started to knit together. Her ribs still hurt, but not so much that she felt the need to ease the pain with a few drops of laudanum. *The scar on my neck will be ugly*, she thought as she examined herself in the mirror.

On Wednesday, eight days after the explosion, the aroma of baking bread lured her downstairs for the first time. Although feeling somewhat woozy and despite her right arm being in a sling and her left arm in a bandage, she intended to eat dinner. *In the dining room. With* Vater *and Conor. I'm famished.*

A *Philadelphia Independent* dated October 10 sat on a side table in the parlor. A front-page article proclaimed

Man Killed in Steam Engine Explosion
Heroine of Krieger Locomotive
Saves Others from Certain Death

On Thursday morning, Rian walked around the block, then did it again in the afternoon. On Friday she walked a little farther, and on Saturday she walked farther yet.

"I'm ready to go back to work tomorrow," Rian declared on Sunday evening, twelve days after the explosion. She and Conor were in her bedroom. He was doing his best to cut her hair by the light of a whale oil lamp. She sat in a chair facing her portrait, which had now hung on her bedroom wall for five months—long enough that she often went days without really noticing it.

"Quit moving," Conor growled. "I almost cut your ear off."

"My deal with *Vater* was to my shoulders," Rian responded. "Take off about two inches. It was getting difficult to fold into my cap even before the explosion."

Conor impatiently pushed at her jaw, returning her head to a front-facing position. "I can't cut your hair if you keep rooching. Settle down and look at your painting."

Conor's order allowed her to gaze with great affection at the figure David Winter thought was a boy and had purposefully aged to look like a young man, not an androgynous adolescent. "I suppose I should consider myself lucky," Rian said.

"I'd say so. You're not dead."

"No, that's not what I mean. All my wounds can be covered by clothing. I can still become the boy in the painting."

"Except for the little, insignificant impediment that you're a girl."

"No, but I can still look like that Rian. That older, grown-up Rian who looks like he's seventeen."

Conor clipped away in silence for a few moments, then said, "Rian, you know I thought that old hag in Russia was pulling your leg when she told you your fortune."

"Thought . . . .?"

"Remind me what she told you that night."

"She said first I wouldn't run Krieger Locomotive, then I would. She said I would have to wear a dress every once in a while, then I would never wear one again."

"What else?"

"She said fire would follow me all my life."

"And what kind of fire?"

"Fire that's out of control. And fire that I think I can control, but can't."

"And what kind of fire is in the firebox of a boiler?"

"Jaysus," Rian said, but her mind raced to the obvious next conclusions. "Conor, if Yana's predictions about fire were right, then the rest will come true as well. A day will come when I'll never wear a dress again. I'm going to run Krieger Locomotive."

"Yeah, I can't believe I figured that out before you did. Maybe that explosion knocked some of the smarts out of you."

"Harry's dead. *Vater* hasn't hired a new foreman yet. Maybe he'll pick me."

"Rian, you're fourteen years old. You don't have a chance."

"Just watch me." She gazed anew at the portrait. The older, masculine Rian stared back. His lips were parted slightly, as if he were about to reveal a secret that would amuse both him and his confidante. *This is who I am destined to become*, Rian thought for the thousandth time. *This is what I'll look like when I finally get to run Krieger Locomotive.*

MONDAY, OCTOBER 22

· JULES ·

Jules was preparing a lumber order at his desk in the Krieger Coach office. Five feet away, Otto worked on a mechanical drawing of a new passenger car.

Blessed silence reigned until Seamus Gallagher entered, bringing the racket from the shop with him. "Hello, Uncle. Hello, Jules."

"Shut the door," Jules said without lifting his eyes from his work.

Seamus did as ordered, then sat in the straight-backed chair in front of Jules's desk. "Jules, how are you feeling about your relationship with Hugh Callaghan these days?"

Jules peered over at Otto, who rolled his eyes but returned to his drafting, saying merely, "I am here, but I am not here."

Jules put down his pencil and gave Seamus his attention. "Complicated. I pay him protection money so my factory doesn't get burned down. His hose company goes out of their way to torment my brethren. I saved his life when we burned the *Bridger*. He prevented Austin Slatter from killing me. He saved me from a thrashing at the State House when we voted." *The last time in my life I'll ever vote.* "I think we're pretty even. Why?"

"He needs to smuggle a self-emancipator out of town."

Jules side-glanced at Otto. Underground Railroad business was conducted on a need-to-know basis, but Otto's anti-slavery sympathies were well established through word and deed. Otto kept his nose in his drafting.

Jules returned his gaze to Seamus. "Now that's a surprise. Do you know any details?"

"If this weren't an issue of a self-emancipator getting assaulted, it would be comical. Hugh's wife was walking home from market, having just purchased a brand-new cast-iron frying pan. She spied a white man assaulting a Black woman in an alley. That got her hackles up, even though she doesn't have much sympathy for your brethren, same as Hugh. She set down her other packages, walked up behind the guy, and brained him with the frying pan. Dropped him right there in the alley. Asked the young woman if she was all right. The young woman blurted out her story. Mrs. Callaghan took a shine to her and brought her home. She's in Hugh's house right now."

Jules smiled for just about the first time since Black men lost the vote. He leaned forward at his desk. "So Hugh Callaghan, president of the Moyamensing Hose Company, is harboring a fugitive slave?"

Seamus smiled as well. "Hugh was adamant about splitting hairs in that regard. It's his wife who's doing the harboring. Hugh says you would be aiding his domestic tranquility if you helped him out."

"How can I refuse a man in such desperate circumstances?"

"I daresay this will put Hugh back in your debt."

"There aren't any passengers currently at my house. I can shelter her for a day or two. The problem is that I'm up to my ears in alligators right now. . . ."

Otto put down his pencil. "Perhaps I can help. I leave for New York tomorrow to make some sales calls. If I delay one more day, I can personally deliver the passenger car that's in the Finishing Room to the *New York & Harlem Railroad* on Wednesday. This woman can hide in the car all the way to New York City."

Heretofore, Otto had been only an occasional participant in Jules's Underground Railroad activities, and he had never previously volunteered. The thought of having him as a conductor would be a significant boon to the cause. He traveled frequently. He had resources. His mind was nimble when things got sticky. "Are you sure you want to further involve yourself in railroad business, Otto? Once you get in, it's hard to get out. The self-emancipators' stories will pull at your heartstrings."

"It is time, Jules. I have delayed this long enough. Seamus, tell Hugh that Jules and I will help to return tranquility to his domestic life. This will become one more favor in a growing back-and-forth."

* * * * *

· OLIVIA ·

As the school year progressed, the first form's pecking order began to sort itself out. Sadly, Olivia's proposition in Moral Philosophy class, that slavery is evil, changed the trajectory of her status at Barhamville. All her classmates except one used it as an excuse to treat her as a convenient outcast—someone they could step upon as they clawed their way up the Barhamville social order. Caldie Montgomery, the queen bee, seemed to tolerate her presence, but mostly to use her as a target for a string of humiliations.

But throughout Olivia's autumn of troubles, sweet, likable, vulnerable Eugenie never abandoned her. Despite Olivia's gratitude toward her roommate, she knew there would always be a moral chasm between them: She on one side, abhorring slavery, and Eugenie on the other side, with her unquestioning acceptance of the peculiar institution.

Olivia had walked into Columbia on three occasions with Eugenie, Caldie, and a couple of the other girls in the first form. The first two times, she couldn't break away to see if there was a note from Topper in the secret rock near the capitol building. This afternoon, however, while Eugenie and Caldie shopped for bonnets on Lady Street, Olivia snuck down to Capitol Square, walked by some coachmen lounging in the sun near a magnolia tree, approached the rock, spied the crack, turned, leaned into the rock, and found a folded scrap of oilskin that contained a slip of paper. She put the paper in her purse, folded the oilskin, placed it back in the crack, and returned to the store before the other two girls noticed she was gone.

That evening, alone in her room, she read Topper's message. Its depiction of slavery was upsetting, not because it was graphic, but because it was of everyday things that she already knew—*and if I'm aware of them, then every adult in South Carolina must know of them. Our willingness to tolerate such sins is just plain wrong.* It took Olivia half an hour to transcribe Topper's notes into a letter. She folded the paper and addressed the letter to:

Rian Krieger

134 North Ninth Street

Philadelphia, Penn.

She dripped a few drops of rose-colored wax—the color befitting a young lady of means—to seal the letter, then pressed the brass stamp with her initials *OT* into the wax.

Eugenie, who had been socializing down the hall, stuck her head in the door. "Dinner time, Roomie. Time to hear Caldie talk about herself some more." Hungry from her expedition to town and subsequent transcription, Olivia rose immediately, leaving the letter on her desk.

After dinner, it was Eugenie and Olivia's turn to clear and wipe the tables and set them for next morning's breakfast. When they returned to their room, Caldwell Montgomery was holding the still-sealed letter.

"Abo, who is Rian Krieger?" she asked.

WEDNESDAY, NOVEMBER 7

· RIAN ·

Rian sat on the catwalk high above the locomotive factory floor, her legs dangling in the air. The factory lay quiet. Once the workers had cleared away the debris from the explosion, all but a skeleton crew had been laid off until the factory was ready to resume production.

Rian had been working with Seamus all afternoon. They were using lag bolts to fasten bearing brackets near the peak of each truss. The bearing brackets, in turn, would cradle the new drive shaft when delivered tomorrow.

Now Rian waited for Seamus to return with more lag bolts. They had both fumble-fingered so many bolts—the fasteners bounced off the catwalk and onto the floor below—that Seamus had to go back down to get a new supply. She flexed her left shoulder to keep it limber until Seamus returned. It still hurt, but not nearly as much as it did when she first came back to work two weeks ago.

As usual, when Rian found herself without a task to distract her, she descended into a place of unease. But this time, it wasn't her usual rat-thought that gnawed at her, that sense of being The Oddity—the girl who hated girly things, who was pursued by fire and now horribly scarred on her left arm. This feeling was vague, unsettling, but lurking. *Something's wrong. Something new. Think, Eena. What is it?*

Rian mused about the past ten days. She had returned to the factory in time to help install the used steam engine, but when the first *choosh!* sounded during its test fire-up, adrenaline surged through her body. She excused herself, claiming that her pain had worn her down. Rather than walk across the alley to Krieger Coach—whose steam engine was always *chooshing* during the workday—she walked home. *What's wrong with you, Eena?* The sound of the steam engine—any steam engine—was music to her ears before the accident, but now was . . . what? *Disconcerting? Discordant? Ominous?*

Give yourself time, Eena. You'll get used to it.

Rian heard distant voices and scanned the length of the factory to find Seamus talking to locomotive designer Heinrich Aldridge. *Come on, Seamus, quit your jawing and get back up here. Fooking Irish*, she thought, ignoring the fact that she was half Irish. *They can stretch a five-minute conversation into twenty without taking a breath.*

Seamus finally finished with Heinrich. Holding a tin can with the resupply of lag bolts, he waved and smiled at Rian as he walked below her. Seamus mounted the newly reconstructed wrought iron stairs and platform next to the new/old steam engine, then climbed the second, steeper set of stairs to the catwalk. Rian rose from her sitting position, wincing a bit as she used her left arm to get her feet under her.

"You're healing up," Seamus commented as he approached. "You couldn't have done that maneuver a couple of days ago."

"Yeah, the laudanum did a great job of dulling the pain, but I had to get off it. I didn't trust my body. I didn't even trust my decisions."

"So you're off that stuff altogether?"

"Hundred percent."

Seamus smiled and shook the can, which jangled with the sound of more than enough lag bolts to finish their task.

Rian held out one of the bearing brackets that would soon cradle the new drive shaft. "What did Heinrich want?"

Seamus fished a lag bolt out of the can, stuck it through a hole in the bearing bracket, and held the bracket and the bolt up to the hole they had drilled into the truss just before he bobbled their last bolt ten minutes ago. "Nothing. Wondered when you were going to get back to pattern making."

Rian used a box wrench to screw in the bolt. "I can't be in two places at once. I can't help get this factory back up and running and work on patterns at the same time."

"Down, darlin'. Heinrich knows that and appreciates that you've been doing what you've been doing. Everyone in this shop knows we wouldn't be this far along in the resurrection of this manufactury if you hadn't crawled out of your deathbed and joined us."

Rian gave a final torque to the lag bolt. "I'm still angry at Heinrich. I asked him to support me when I get around to telling *Vater* that I want to be the new foreman. He refused."

Seamus fished the next bolt out of the can and fed it through the hole in the bearing bracket and into the hole in the truss. "Of course he refused, you idiot. The timing's wrong. For starters, you almost got killed by that steam engine— or, to be more precise, its immediate predecessor. When we were all in fear of you dying, your father blamed himself for allowing you to be in the shop and in harm's way. Once we hook up the drive shaft and fire up that yonder beast again, he'll pull you back into the office faster than you can say Jack Robinson."

Rian started screwing in the bolt with her left hand, but reaching above her was too painful, so she switched back to her right hand. "So that's it? *Vater's* never going to let me run Krieger Locomotive?"

"You're a smart cookie, darlin'. You gotta give Uncle Otto a little time. But you still have a lot to learn."

"What are you talking about? I'm already the best pattern maker in this shop. I can run every machine down on that floor. I understand production schedules, I've helped Heinrich design parts for the *Standard*, I know when a part should be made of cast iron or wrought iron or steel—"

Seamus held up his hand—a signal for Rian to slow down. "I'd say most everyone would acknowledge all those things, and probably a few more, but. . . ."

Here it comes, he's going to say, "You're fourteen" or "You're a girl."

"You're not ready to lead a crew of men."

Rian picked up the can of lag bolts and the last bracket and walked six feet to the next truss, her back to Seamus. "Why not?"

Her cousin followed with his bit and brace. "You're arrogant. You lord your proficiency over others. You're impatient. You'd rather do a task than teach someone else how to do it. You try to order folks around, and you've got no authority to do so."

Rian was about to blow. She held the bracket up to the truss with her good arm and waited for Seamus to mark the placement of new holes with a pencil. "Is that all?"

Seamus made the marks. Rian removed the bracket. Seamus lifted the bit and brace over his head and started drilling the holes—a maneuver Rian was not yet healed enough to execute.

"I could probably think of some others," he said as he rotated the brace around and around and the bit dug into the truss. "Look, you've worked with Jules since you were a mite. You've seen the way he runs Krieger Coach. He rarely gives orders—he makes suggestions. He never loses his temper, even when he should let a man have it good. He never lords his superior knowledge over the others."

"Well, if he did, the men would call him uppity . . . and more, probably."

Seamus finished the holes and lowered the bit and brace. He shrugged, acknowledging the accuracy of her statement. "And soon enough, you'll become a grown woman. Do you think your situation will be much different?"

A grown woman: That's never happening to me. "What do you suggest I do?"

"Make nice with the new foreman, whoever your da hires. Make sure you don't ire him the way you did Harry so he allows you in the shop. Work with the men. Don't lord your superiority over them. Keep working on your skills. And every time you have a success—big or small—find a way for your da to hear about it."

"What if the new foreman doesn't know as much as I do?"

Seamus checked his pocket watch. "Then help him along a bit. Rian, we're at a good quitting point here. I've got some business to attend to at the distillery. We'll need a slew of men to install the new drive shaft tomorrow. How about you report to your da across the alley and tell him to call in about ten or so men for first thing tomorrow. With any luck, we'll have the drive shaft ready for testing by noontime."

Rian and Seamus descended the stairs together and exited the factory through the alley door.

Seamus started walking down the alley toward Broad Street. "See you tomorrow, Cousin," he said with a wave.

Rian walked ten feet to the side door of Krieger Coach. An uncrystallized sense of unease cast a pall that contradicted all of Rian's accomplishments over the past two weeks. *Something is very wrong, but I can't put my finger on it.*

As she opened the door, the *choosh . . . choosh . . . choosh* of the Krieger Coach steam engine greeted her, and her knees almost buckled. She backed out and slammed the door. *Jaysus, it's been three weeks since the accident. My body is well along the way to being healed. But I'm afraid of steam engines. How will I ever run a factory if I soil my drawers every time I walk into one?*

1839

1839

WEDNESDAY, JANUARY 16

· RIAN ·

Rian tried to resume her former schedule—bookkeeping in the mornings and shop work in the afternoons—but tasks away from the factories' *chooshing* steam engines kept calling to her. Today was cold, cloudless, and windy, a perfect day to walk about town in her navy blue Russian greatcoat. She loved enveloping herself in the coat's thick, felted-wool, double-breasted heaviness. She loved that the coat's brass buttons and red epaulets made it distinctively unique in the city. She loved that each wearing represented an homage to its previous owner, Captain Stepanov. *Plus, I'm taller now—it fits me better than last spring.*

Much like other recent outings, Rian had several errands in mind for this excursion. First on her list: Reporter Harold Foote at the three-man office of the *Philadelphia Independent.*

As Rian walked to the office, she reflected on many fond memories from previous visits. The work there was brisk, quiet, and purposeful. The office's focal point was the cast-iron flatbed Columbian Press, a beastly but elegant man-powered contraption of compound levers and counterweights that could produce a hundred printed papers an hour.

Work on the Columbian Press was much too repetitive for Rian, but it was fun to watch for a few moments: ink the type-set plate with a roller, place the blank newspaper on the inked plate, fold the tympan over the paper, roll the carriage under the platen, pull the two-foot toggle, press the platen onto the tympan, release the toggle, roll the carriage back out, lift the tympan, peel off the newspaper, admire your work, do it all over again.

Foote was the only reporter in the firm. He patrolled the streets of Philadelphia for stories, but also traveled to Harrisburg and Washington City, which gave the *Independent* a certain gravitas throughout the North. The anti-slavery publisher, a man named Geoffrey Clifton, rarely left the office. He scoured mounds of papers from other cities for articles to reprint.[18] One thing that sepa-

---

18. The Postal Service Act of 1792 was an enlightened piece of legislation. It encouraged the flow of information around the country by, among other things, allowing newspapers to send their publications to other newspapers free of charge.

rated the *Independent* from other newspapers, however, was its unwillingness to hyperbolize salient points from those out-of-town articles.

The third man in the office was the typesetter. His hand flashed over a job case, pulling individual metal letters from little compartments and placing them upside-down left-to-right in one of five columns on the plate. Foote and Clifton could do the typesetter's job but not as fast. Two of the three men ran the Columbia Press. Everyone in the office was ink stained.

When Rian arrived at the office, a typeset sheet in the window said:

MOVED!
TO A BIGGER AND BETTER OFFICE
700 WALNUT STREET

Rian walked to the new location and found quite a new atmosphere. The main room was larger. The beastly Columbia Press had been moved, a significant task in itself, but was clearly no longer the showpiece it had been in the old office. The new center of attention was a steam-powered printing press Rian considered a marvel of engineering. The steam engine—there hadn't been one in the old office—was minuscule compared to the mammoth engines in the Krieger factories. As opposed to the *choosh . . . choosh . . . choosh . . .* like the one that almost killed her, this one sounded more like *pocketa . . . pocketa . . . pocketa . . .* and *(thank heavens)* barely caused her heart to race.

A continuous belt that looped from the steam engine to the printing press—essentially a little brother of the belts in the Krieger factories Rian was so familiar with—fed power from the engine to the press. All of the parts of this new press were recognizable to Rian, but . . . different. Rather than a platen that pressed onto the inked page, this was a large roller that fed and pressed the blank paper in coordination with a typeset carriage that rolled back-and-forth, back-and-forth underneath the roller . . . blank pages in one side, printed pages out the other.

Rian watched this mechanical marvel, mouth agape, for the better part of a minute until Harold Foote rose from his desk and approached her.

"Do you like it?" he asked, his voice barely raised above the *pocketa . . . pocketa . . .* of the steam engine.

"Love it," said Rian. "How come?"

"You think the Krieger factories are the only ones who innovate in this town? Clifton's been eyeing this machine for a few years now." He pointed to the Columbia Press in the corner. "With the old machine, two of us working would be lucky to print one hundred sheets an hour. We had this one shipped from England. It takes one man to run it, and it can produce more than a thousand copies in an hour."

"Harold, I'd love to get a tour of your new office, but I'm on confidential business."

Harold pivoted as soon as he heard the word *confidential.* "Rian, it's so good to see you up and about," he stated as he ushered her to his desk at the back wall. "We ran an article right after the explosion. I would love to do a follow-up. How are you feeling?"

Rian remembered that an article had been written, but the memory was vague, dulled by a laudanum-induced haze. She had no interest in an article about her. Sooner or later, that would lead to more scrutiny. At best, people would increasingly view her as The Oddity. At worst, they would start poking into the cause of the accident. Rian felt a huge amount of guilt that her attempt to foil Jabez's suicide led to the death of Harry Vogel. "As well as can be expected, thank you, Harold. I'm back at work now."

Foote indicated with a sweep of his hand that Rian should sit in a chair next to his desk. He resumed his seat and picked up a quill pen. "What prompts your visit?"

Rian settled into her chair. "Do you remember my friend Olivia Tucker?"

"Of course. You and she helped her Mammy escape from Olivia's parents' house on Spruce Street. The bully-boys turned Moyamensing upside down, searching for her. I helped muddy the waters by mailing a fake letter from Harrisburg. Are you two up to more shenanigans?"

Rian nodded in confirmation, then held Olivia's letter out to Foote. "She's written me a letter. She's attending a boarding school in Columbia now. She thought I should send this letter to Mr. Garrison in Boston. I figure the *Independent* should publish it first, then Mr. Clifton could send your paper to Mr. Garrison. I know you trade papers with Mr. Garrison anyway."

Foote read the letter, which Rian had read many times, except the details about the brutalities inflicted upon the enslaved, which she only read once and had no desire to read again.

October 22, 1838

Dearest Rian,

I received your letter dated October 15 and was horrified to hear you had been injured by that cursed steam engine. I am so happy you are recovering.

The Wilkinsons finally invited me to Thousand Oaks. I saw Topper for the first time in three years. He has been keeping a journal of the many tortures and deprivations suffered by the slaves in the region. He intends to leave new notes for me in a secret hiding place in hopes that I can get them published in The Libera-tor. That's where you come in. I can freely send letters to you but fear that any letter I send to Mr. Garrison would be intercepted and read. Could you please forward the following entry to Mr. Garrison?[19]

> *Field hands on the plantation in which I am enslaved are issued a peck of corn at the corn crib door every Sunday evening. From that corn, they must bake their own corn cakes each night for the following day's three meals. Most slaves here divide their week's allotment into sixths, add water to it, knead it into a mush, wrap it in green leaves, and place it in the embers of a fire. They have nothing but corn cake three times a day, six days a week. They are issued no salt to provide flavor to these cakes, although most have been able to barter for their own salt at Rife's General Store down the road by selling articles they have made on Sundays. Sundays are not a day of rest, even though that is what the strawboss calls it. On Sundays, field hands are expected to feed themselves from food they have cultivated in their own gardens, which they can only plant, water, weed, pick, and preserve on Sundays. Slaves too old to work in the field tend these gardens as best they can, and also tend some of the young children.*
>
> *Each male slave is issued a shirt and trousers for warm-weather months and a shirt, trousers—all of Negro cloth—and woolen jacket for the cold. Women are issued two shifts for the year, plus a jacket. By harvest season, all these clothes are in tatters, leaving both man and woman half or completely naked. Children under five, and many older than that, go completely naked until they are old enough to be helpful in the fields.*

Thank you, Rian, for any help you can give to Topper and me. You once told me that a hero is a person who risks life and limb to do that which is right. I think you were talking about Jules at the time. But you have already been a hero many times in your young life, as has Conor. I hope that through the small act of getting this sort of information to people who can send it out to the world, Topper and I can follow in your footsteps.

Please don't get blown up again.

With love,
Olivia

---

19. Note to readers: Topper's entries have a basis in actual events as related by Charles Ball (1780 to ?) in his memoir, *Fifty Years in Chains*, and by Harriet Jacobs (1813 to 1897) in her memoir, *Incidents in the Life of a Slave Girl*. Frankly, some of the images are quite disturbing (at least they were to me). I would not be insulted if you skipped over them. The takeaway? Slavery is a brutal, dehumanizing system. Man's willingness to inflict suffering on his fellow man is appalling. Topper's (and Ball's and Jacobs's) vignettes merely supply a few specifics.

Foote looked up from the letter. "Your friends are already heroes. Topper is an eloquent young man. His words will move many people. Will you write Olivia back?"

"Of course."

"I have a few recommendations. First, I think his notes are too specific. He shouldn't include names like Rife's General Store. The *Philadelphia Independent* sends copies of its papers to a hundred other papers around the country, including down South. One way or another, that sort of information will lead back to Topper's neighborhood. Please encourage Olivia to tell him to make up a persona—a fake, a composite. Tell him to write about things he has seen and heard, but specifics like names and places have to be changed."

"Thank you, Harold. I'll tell her."

Foote smiled. "You've made my day, Rian. I think Topper's notes will cause quite the sensation. I'll get on this right away."

"And you'll make sure Mr. Garrison gets them?"

"Yes, he's on our courtesy list. He gets everything we publish, same as we do of his. Sadly, he won't know you're part of the pipeline that got them to him. It's too bad. I know you two have a history . . . You and your friends, how old are you?"

"We're all fourteen."

"Our country needs more heroes, Rian. Black, white, male, female, young, old . . . it doesn't matter. We need more heroes."

Rian didn't feel like a hero as she left the *pocketa . . . pocketa . . .* of Foote's office. *I can handle being near that little baby steam engine, but that beast of a steam engine in Krieger Locomotive scares the bejaysus out of me. Heroes aren't afraid of steam engines.*

* * * * *

Rian returned to her lair—a room she had built for herself as far away from the new/old steam engine as possible—to find Conor sitting in her office chair. He was studying a sketch of a *Standard* locomotive she had left on her desk. *Shit, I haven't shown that sketch to Heinrich yet. I don't know what his reaction will be when he finds out I've tinkered with his baby.*

She closed the door behind her, shutting out the whir and whine of machinery as well as the more distant *choosh . . . choosh . . . choosh . . .* of the steam engine. She indicated with her thumb and a frown that Conor should get the hell out of her chair, then turned her back to him to hang her greatcoat on its peg. "What are you doing here?" she grumbled over her shoulder. *This isn't a social call. No one ever comes in here.*

Conor ignored Rian's command to cede the chair and spoke to her back. "Checking up on you. Where've you been?"

"It's none of your business, but if you must know, I met with Harold Foote, then I walked to the *Philadelphia & Trenton* railroad station in Kensington."

"Long walk . . . I guess you're all better now. When you got to Kensington, which street did you take, Penn or Beach?"

Rian turned toward Conor. "Still none of your business, but Beach."

Conor put his elbows on Rian's desk, then his eyes drilled into her. "You're not fooling anybody, you know."

Uh-oh, here it comes. "What are you talking about?"

"You're afraid of steam engines."

"I am not, I just—"

"Three months ago, you get blown up by the steam engine at the other end of this shop. You help Seamus install the new one and repair the rest of the damage. But where's Rian when Seamus fires up the steam engine and new drive shaft for the first time? Down here, putting up walls for this new hidey-hole, as far away from that steam engine as you can get and still be in the locomotive shop—"

"I needed some peace and quiet, that's all. The new engine was too noisy, and it's right next to the office."

"The new engine is only slightly noisier than the old one, and when the men rebuilt the wall between the shop and the office, they used a double layer of brick. The office is quieter than it used to be, even with the new steam engine."

"Well, the brick wall reduced the amount of space in the office. There wasn't room for another desk. . . ."

Conor rose from Rian's chair and walked around the desk to meet her eye-to-eye. "Yeah, I heard you tell your father that. That's a pile of shyte. The Locomotive office is bigger than the Coach office, and there's four desks over there. Why didn't you return to the office over in Coach? I'll tell you why: You'd have to pass right by the steam engine to get there. Why haven't you helped Jules make any rolling stock deliveries to the *Camden & Amboy*? Because you'd have to board the *Falcon*, a ferry with a steam engine . . . that you helped install, for Crissakes. Why did you take Beach rather than Penn Street? Let me guess. Because you would have had to walk by Cramp Shipyard and its three steam engines, one of which is right there on the street and undoubtedly *choosh, choosh, chooshing* away, just like a hundred other steam engines in this city—"

"All right! Enough! Stop!" Rian started to pace back and forth in the confines of the small room. "I'm afraid of steam engines! I admit it! Are you satisfied?"

"No, I'm not satisfied at all. What are you going to do about it? The old Rian Krieger wouldn't have allowed herself to be afraid of anything for this long."

Rian stopped pacing and leaned, half-sitting on her desk. "This is what I'm doing. I built this office. It's near all the machines I need to carve patterns for the *Standard*. I can shut the door and design new parts in peace. Sometimes I go out . . . to do research."

"What kind of research?"

"I talk to engine drivers and firemen after they finish their shift. I figure who better to talk to about locomotives than the men who use them."

"Why would they be willing to talk to you?"

Rian smiled for the first time. "A small bottle of Gallagher's Fine Whiskey is a pretty good incentive." *Please, Conor, don't keep going where I know you're going.*

"What about the bookkeeping? When do you attend to that?"

Damnit. "I get here even earlier than I used to. I can do most of it before they fire up the steam engine at Coach. I finish it up after the factory shuts down at the end of the workday."

"When do you sleep?"

Rian nodded her head toward a cot in the corner. The absurdity of her new habits was now glaringly obvious. *What was I thinking?*

"This is what you'll do for the rest of your life?"

Rian shut her eyes and bowed her head. Her shoulders started to convulse. Despite her best efforts to prevent them, tears flowed down her contorted face. *Shit, shit, shit.*

Conor rose and wrapped his arms around her. "It's going to be okay."

Rian, grateful for the embrace, buried her head in Conor's neck. "It'll never be okay," she blubbered, her voice muffled by Conor's shirt. "How will I ever run a factory that makes steam engines if I'm afraid of them?"

At that moment, Heinrich Aldridge entered Rian's hideaway without knocking. Conor released Rian from his embrace and stepped back. She wiped the tears from her face with the palms of her hands. "Hi, Heinrich . . . What are you doing here?"

Heinrich hesitated, then smiled slightly and sat in the one chair other than Rian's in the room. "I came to see if there's anything I can do to get you over your fear of steam engines."

Rian stiffened and glared at Conor. "Jaysus, does everyone in the shop know about this?"

Conor shrugged, ceding the response to Heinrich.

"Pretty much," said Heinrich. "I have some thoughts, if you're interested."

Rian fought back the urge to start crying again, then nodded.

"I grew up in Württemberg—not far from your father. When I was a boy, a dog bit me, so I grew up afraid of dogs. My uncle raised sheep on a farm about a mile from my house in Mannheim. He owned a big sheepdog . . . huge . . . My uncle asked me to become his helper, but I initially refused because I was afraid of his dog. My father figured out what was going on. He demanded that I walk to my uncle's farm every day for six weeks, each day spending more time watching the dog work, getting closer, closer, then sitting next to the dog for longer periods until my fear went away. Now I love dogs."

"What are you suggesting?"

"Today, climb those stairs to the platform next to the steam engine boiler—the one you got tossed from. Right now would be best. Spend two minutes, no more, no less. Tomorrow, spend four minutes. The next day, six minutes. When you can spend an entire workday there without fear, then you'll know you're cured."

Rian did quick math in her head. "I can't do that. It would take almost a whole year."

Heinrich shrugged. "And yet apparently you would be willing to spend the rest of your life crippled by your fear."

"If I sat up there longer than ten minutes, I would go crazy with nothing to do."

"You can do what you've been doing here for the past few months: Designing parts for the *Standard*. That drafting table in the Coach office isn't being used. You could move it up to the platform."

"I'd never be able to concentrate."

"Stuff cotton in your ears."

"Lucretia Mott would kill me if I used cotton." As soon as Rian said those words, she knew all of her protestations emanated from fear. The last straw was her assertion that her pacifist Quaker neighbor, who had helped to establish the free produce movement,[20] might throttle her for using an ounce of slavery-tainted cotton. Now it sounded ridiculous even to Rian. She shook her head. "Okay, that was stupid. Did you two cook this up together?"

"Not exactly," replied Heinrich, "but we've talked."

---

20. Lucretia and James Mott were early proponents of the free produce movement, in which people were encouraged to purchase only products untainted by the sin of slavery or go without them altogether. Cotton cloth, molasses, sugar, and rice—all more expensive than their slave-created kin—were sold in free produce stores. Sadly, the free produce movement never gained much traction and had little effect on the institution of slavery.

Rian fished her watch out of her pocket and headed toward the door. "I can't believe I'm doing this."

"Rian, do you want me to come with you?" Conor called after her.

"Of course I do. If I'm going to get blown up again, I'm taking you with me."

* * * * *

Rian returned to her lair seven minutes later to find Heinrich examining the locomotive sketch on her desk.

"How did you do?" Heinrich asked.

"Depends. If you count the time I was on the stairs, both up and down, a minute and thirty-seven seconds."

"Can you do longer next time?"

"Yeah . . . Probably . . . Maybe."

"That's good . . . Tell me about this sketch. It looks like a *Standard* with a bogie."[21]

Okay, Eena, your sketch may not be ready, but there's no going back now. "It *is* the *Standard* . . . the one we should be designing now. I've been talking to engine drivers and firemen on the *P&T* and the *P&C*. Matthias Baldwin is including bogies as an option on some of his locomotives, and the railroad men love it."

Heinrich shook his head. "It's too late to change the drawings. We would have to extend the chassis . . . maybe make them more rigid . . . Half the patterns have already been made. Hell, you've carved most of them."

"I don't think it's too late. We haven't started production yet. Most of the molds are for parts that wouldn't be affected if we added the bogie. That's why I drew this sketch—to see what else we would have to change."

"Your father won't like it. It'll add to the cost. We haven't even landed the contract from the *Utica & Schenectady* yet."

Rian shook her head. "But the *Standard* would be a better machine . . . safer. The last thing we want is news of a Krieger Locomotive derailing. "

Heinrich stared at Rian's sketch for another thirty seconds. "Okay."

"Okay, what?"

"Okay, I think we should proceed with your enhancements to the *Standard*, but this will keep our feet in the fire from now on. We must get these changes right, and despite your sketch—which at first glance seems well thought

---

21. A bogie was a set of pilot wheels placed at the front of a steam locomotive to help guide it around curves. Speculation during this era, which turned out to be accurate, was that these unpowered lead wheels would cut down on derailments.

out—the addition of the bogie will necessitate numerous other changes you may not have identified. There will be no room for any more of your modifications once we create a new set of shop drawings."

"Fine."

"And Rian, we'll have to figure out a way to get the cost back down. Put your thinking cap on."

* * * * *

Finally at home after a long day, Rian leaned back in the chair next to the Franklin stove and closed her eyes. *I feel like a juggler with too many balls in the air. And each ball is a heavy one.*

Ball No. 1 was the always-lurking rat-thought that had grown in size: she was The Oddity, but because of the explosion, now she was The Ugly Oddity.

Ball No. 2: She wanted to run Krieger Locomotive. But that got very complicated when you considered Ball No. 3: She was afraid of steam engines.

Ball No. 4: Fire followed her.

Ball No. 5: Heinrich had accepted her idea of adding a bogie to the *Standard*, and she had to figure out how to get costs back down.

Ball No. 6: The fight against slavery. Topper's notes, transcribed by Olivia Tucker in South Carolina, meant more secrets to keep, more errands to run. And now, Olivia's latest letter, waiting for her on the porch when she arrived home, added a whole new wrinkle in things. That was Ball No. 7:

Wednesday, December 19, 1838, 10 p.m.

Oh, what a tangled web I weave. I thank you for willingly abetting me in my conspiracy to get you-know-who's notes to you-know-who, but I have more favors to ask of you. I made a bit of a mistake. One of the nosy girls on my floor asked me who I write to so often, and I said my parents. She snuck into my room later on and read the address on my last letter to you. Thank God she didn't break the wax seal and read the letter. Anyway, I had to make up a story on the fly, so here's what I said. Prepare yourself.

There's this BOY named Rian in Philadelphia who I am sweet on, and I think he's sweet on me but I'm not sure. I haven't seen him since we were thirteen and he ran away to Russia, but he's back in Philadelphia now. He is the heir-apparent to his father's fortune in the railroad business. He's very good-looking. (I tried to stick to the truth as much as possible because I know this will get sticky. Thank goodness Rian can be either a girl's name or a boy's name.)

There are no locks on the dormitory doors or my desk. I have no place to hide my correspondence, so I have to assume Nosy Caldie Montgomery will keep snooping.

Now, here's the favor I need: return letters. I don't care what you write to me, but you have to write things that imply you might be interested in me (and of course that you are a boy). It would be best if you tell me you received my letter dated ?? so I know you got the latest notes from you-know-who, but NEVER tell me that you forwarded my information on to you-know-who because what you-know-who and I are doing down here could have grave consequences if we are ever found out. If you wanted to do me the best of all favors, you would tell me what you're REALLY doing rather than make something up, because I am sure you are doing interesting things. You always do. BUT! Don't mention anything about your abolitionist leanings or any anti-slavery activity at all! I would likely be thrown out of school merely for associating with you. (Just kidding. Or maybe not.) Even my roommate, who I like, is so pro-slavery that she doesn't understand there is another way of thinking about it.

I expect this grand conspiracy of mine (ours, I hope) will last until I graduate in May of 1842. So, as far as I am concerned, if you agree to this, we can take our time with it and maybe we'll fall in love via the mail. Then, shortly before I graduate, you will write one final letter, confessing you have fallen in love with another, which will break my heart. Then I will run into the consoling arms of Barnwell Wilkinson—well, probably not Barney because he is a bit of a lummox, and he will be a slave owner someday—so a metaphorical Barney. "Barney" and I will be married and live happily ever after.

Be prepared, I plan to write similar letters back to you. They will be short, with plenty of white space at the bottom. I'll write you-know-who's notes at the bottom in vinegar. When you pass the letters back and forth over a candle, the secret messages will magically appear.

Disappearing ink. Don't you think I am very tricky?

With love, (I don't really love you, well, I do love you, but not in the "I'm in love with you" way, but you should get used to me closing this way, because, although it will take us more than three years to get there, that's where we are headed.)

Olivia

P.S. Papa is still testy about Mammy-Rose fleeing her bondage from Philadelphia three summers ago. Even though he hates being away from Cook's Gullah cuisine, he wants to avoid Charleston's beastly summertime heat and humidity. His last letter confirmed we are going to Paris instead of Philadelphia. I assume Mother's nose will be out of joint for quite some time about The Squire's decree, since that means yet again no Philadelphia social season.

Anyway, no Philadelphia for me this summer. The closest I will get to you will be when we steam past the Delaware Bay on our way to New York, from whence we will steam to England and on to France. I'll wave as we go by.

* * * * *

It had been two months since Conor last cut Rian's hair, and it now grazed her shoulders—far too long as far as she was concerned. She and Conor were ensconced in her bedroom, she on a wooden chair with a towel around her shoulders, he behind her with a pair of scissors. "Cut off at least two inches. I need to be able to tuck it up into my cap."

The silence was comfortable. Rian had already confided everything she was juggling.

"Did you write Olivia back yet?" Conor had been privy to all the letters Rian and Olivia had exchanged since Rian had returned from Russia.

Rian leaned over and fished her completed letter off the bed. "Yeah, I finished it right after dinner. Do you want to read it?"

Conor grasped the letter and sat on the bed. Rian watched him read and interpreted every *hmm* and *unh* as either a positive or a negative sign.

January 16, 1839

Dearest Olivia,

1839—it still feels so odd to be writing the new year, even though I have been making such notations in the Krieger factory books for weeks now. Things in the locomotive factory are now back to normal after the explosion. We were totally out of commission for more than three weeks. I helped put things back together again once I could do the work without a lot of pain.

I was pleased to receive your letter dated December 19. My wounds from the steam engine explosion have mostly healed, although my right arm will always be scarred by the burn. Conor says nobody would notice, but I do when I look in the mirror.

Today I showed Heinrich Aldridge an idea for a design change on a new locomotive we hope to sell in a year or so. He liked it.

I am very disappointed your family will not be coming to Philadelphia for the social season. Even though you are not old enough to attend a ball yet, we could still attend regattas and picnics together.

Fondly,
Rian

Conor let the letter waft back down to the bed and picked up his scissors. "You're doing it again."

"Doing what again?"

"Pretending to be a boy."

Rian signed in exasperation. "Of course I'm pretending to be a boy. She asked me to."

"But you're kind of happy to be doing it."

"Is there anything there that isn't true?"

"Nope. Nothing." Conor *snip-snipped* with the scissors. "How long will you keep this up?"

"I dunno. I guess until she leaves that school. Leaves Topper."

"Just don't get in too deep." More snipping. "Remember what happened last time."

"Last time I was in Russia. I gave the grand duchess too much information. I was practically living at Anichkov Palace. This is different. Columbia is six hundred miles from here."

"Perfect," said Conor as he snipped. "What could possibly go wrong?"

Friday, January 25

· RIAN ·

Rian checked the time, stuffed her watch in her pocket, picked up her end of the drafting table, and started backing her way up the wrought-iron stairs. She and Conor had already walked the table out of the Krieger Coach office, past the Coach factory's *chooshing* steam engine, down half the length of the factory, across the alley, and into the Locomotive shop. The table was top-heavy, and muscling it up the stairs was difficult.

"C'mon, lift!" Rian grunted.

"I am lifting. This son of a bitch is awkward," said Conor. "How much time are you supposed to be up there?"

Rian took another backward step up. "Eighteen minutes. I hate it."

"How are you going to work up there, Rian? It's too noisy to think."

Another step, the fooking steam engine *chooshing* to her right and making her want to drop the desk, jump to the shop floor, and flee to her lair. "I told you, I'll stuff cotton in my ears . . . even if it was grown by slaves."

"How long will this experiment take?"

Rian glanced behind her to gauge the next step. "It's not an experiment. If I'm ever going to run this shop, I've got to get rid of my fear. The only way to do that is to spend so much time up here that the sound of a steam engine . . . the closeness of a steam engine . . . doesn't bother me. The *choosh* of a steam engine used to sound like music to me, but not anymore. If I could get back to that, it would be a miracle. I'd settle for getting close to a boiler and not feeling like I'm about to have a heart attack."

She climbed another step. "I add two minutes every day. Yesterday I spent sixteen minutes up there with nothing to do and too much to think about. I almost went crazy. That's why I need this table."

"What were you thinking about?" Conor grunted out.

"You know, the usual." Another step. "I'm The Ugly Oddity."

"Rian, I've got news for you. You've always been ugly."

Another step. "No, you idiot. I've got a scar on my neck and a burn down my left arm. Plus, I still don't know if I hate Jabez or not for doing this to me and for killing Harry."

Conor shifted his hold on the desk and disappeared from Rian's view behind the table. "That's a new one. Is that it?"

Rian thought for a moment as she continued to walk up the stairs backward. "I'm pretending to fall in love with a girl who lives in South Carolina."

"I think you secretly like that particular conundrum," came Conor's disembodied voice. "Jaysus, Rian, slow down!" Conor's head reappeared as he reached the platform. "You never answered my question. How long are you going to do this *not-experiment*?"

"If I follow Heinrich's advice, it'll be a year."

"Stupid," Conor muttered. "You know, the workers will think you're crazy."

Rian backed her way past the stairs that led to the catwalk and set the desk at the very end of the platform. "They already think I'm crazy. This will just make me seem crazier."

Conor put down his end and surveyed the factory from this lofty vantage. "What will you do up here, anyway?"

"Make mechanical drawings of parts that Heinrich assigns me." Rian shoved the desk around ninety degrees with her hip. "Then once Heinrich approves the drawing, I'll build the pattern out of chestnut down near my lair."

Conor turned and started walking back along the platform. "Well, it's been a pleasure, Rian. I've gotta get back to work. Me messages aren't going to deliver themselves."

Rian glanced down the length of the factory. "Thanks for your help," she called after him.

Conor waved without turning around.

"Deserter!" Rian called a little louder, eliciting another wave but still no turnaround. She pulled out her pocket watch and glared at the second hand as it slowly *tick . . . tick . . . tick*ed.

Well, that took four minutes and thirty seconds. Thirteen and a half minutes to go. Damn, it's hotter than hell up here. The urge to shoulder past Conor and flee down the stairs washed over her.

Hell. Now that's an appropriate name for this place.

TUESDAY, JANUARY 29

· RIAN ·

Rian walked south on Asheton Street, within spitting distance of the Schuylkill River. It was cold and windy, and the sun played hide-and-seek behind clouds that scudded east. She acknowledged that her out-of-shop research trips were originally an excuse to get away from the frightening *choosh . . . choosh . . . choosh* of the steam engine. However, now with a plan in place to get over her fear, she chose to continue her impromptu conversations with railroad men. For each excursion, she carried a leather messenger's satchel containing pints of Gallagher's Fine Whiskey and a notepad. The whiskey got the railroad men's attention. The notepad indicated that their answers were important. *Almost every time I go out, I learn things, and what I learn can affect the design of the* Standard. *And if it's too late to make changes to the* Standard, *then we can incorporate them into the next locomotive we design.*

She had already visited the city's three train stations[22] once, and two of them twice. Today was supposed to be her second *Philadelphia, Wilmington & Baltimore* day, but there was a problem. Three nights ago, a heavy rainstorm far upstream had sent unseasonably high water and foot-thick slabs of ice down the Schuylkill, creating a battering ram determined to find a way to the Delaware. The freshet of ice first swept away the floating bridge that had served the lower Schuylkill since the Revolution. Then bridge debris and ice combined to take out a pier and two of the six spans of the *PW&B*'s year-old covered railroad bridge. Reaching the *PW&B*'s depot on the west side of the river would require a significant detour until the bridge was rebuilt.

---

22. As locomotives notoriously spewed glowing cinders that frequently started fires, they were not allowed in the city proper. Thus, Philadelphia's three train stations were situated on the city's periphery. The *Philadelphia & Columbia* on North Broad Street served destinations to the west, the *Philadelphia & Trenton* in Kensington went north, and the *Philadelphia, Wilmington & Baltimore* progressed to the southwest. *PW&B* locomotives were unhooked from their cars on the west side of the Schuylkill. Horses then hauled the cars across the river and another mile to the *PW&B*'s station at the intersection of Broad and Pine Streets. Connections between stations were provided by horse-drawn carriages or omnibuses.

Eager to see the destruction, Rian followed Grays Ferry Road to the Schuylkill and positioned herself on a hillock upstream from the bridge to survey the damage. Chunks of ice still floated down the river, but the water level had dropped. Branches, sticks, leaves, and the shattered remains of a rowboat and an outhouse were piled high up the four still-standing piers. The Philadelphia side of the covered bridge, railroad tracks on the left paralleled by a roadway on the right, was intact, but on the far side, the roof sagged where the fourth and fifth spans had been ripped away.

Eight hundred feet from where Rian stood, on the other side of the river, workers had erected a crane to clear debris and eventually replace the stout beams that would span the piers. The crane was big. *Bigger than they need for this job. As a matter of fact, I don't think I've ever seen a crane that big.*

Curious, Rian left the hillock and descended an embankment to the bridge's entrance. Ignoring a sawhorse—the sole warning to keep out—she chose the bridge's track side, calibrating her strides in the semi-darkness to always step on the railroad ties. The engineering that went into the bridge's construction fascinated her. Struts and counterstruts built of massive timbers formed a series of X's that were framed by equally massive queenposts. She reached the damaged end, entered the sunlight, and surveyed the destruction from a much closer vantage twenty feet above the flowing river.

Two spans were missing, and the pier that once held them up had toppled to the water line. Two pieces of track, still attached to their railroad ties, bent down toward the water, their distorted arcs a testament to the power of ice and debris from last Saturday. To the left, remains from both the floating bridge and the covered bridge were strewn along river-right.

"Hey!" Rian called to a man standing next to the crane on the opposite shore. "How much can your rig lift?"

The guy gaped at Rian like she was from Mars. He hesitated for ten seconds, then called "Quinton!" to another man reading a set of plans laid out on the back of a freight wagon. The first man jerked his thumb toward Rian. "Some gump with a question!"

Rian ignored the *gump* comment. "How much weight can your crane lift?" she yelled to Quinton.

"This one?" Quinton responded. "Ten tons, I figure." He returned his attention to his plans. Then, without looking up but still loud enough for Rian to hear, he said, "Who wants to know?"

"My name is Rian Krieger. Is it your crane?"

Quinton seemed to ponder whether this conversation was worth his time. After a few seconds, he placed a rock on the plans, left the freight wagon, entered the covered bridge from the opposite side, and walked until he faced Rian from across eighty feet of missing bridge. "Yes, it's one of my cranes," he called above the sound of the flowing river below. "My name is Quinton Schott."

"Mr. Schott, could you build a bigger one? Maybe on one of the docks on the Delaware?"

"I've already built two over there. One for Britton and one for the Lehigh Coal Company."

"Could you build one that can lift twelve tons?"

Schott crossed his arms and leaned into the wall of the gaping covered bridge. "Reckon so."

"How about fifteen tons?"

Schott shrugged. "Whataya wanna lift that's that heavy?"

"A fully assembled locomotive."

"You said your name is Krieger. Are you Otto's kid?"

"Yes, I am."

"The girl who wears boys' clothes?"

Shit. Why does it always have to come down to this? "Yup, that's me."

Schott straightened, signaling an almost-end to the conversation. Given his previous question, Rian was surprised when he smiled. "You tell your daddy I can build a crane that can lift his engine, but how will you get it to the docks? That kind of weight will crush any wagon ever built."

"Thanks, Mr. Schott. I expect my father will get back to you some time."

"When?"

"Dunno. I haven't told him about my idea yet."

Schott shook his head as if he had just wasted the last ten minutes. Then he surprised Rian again, this time with a question. "What pier?"

"Dunno. You got any ideas?"

Schott turned away and started walking back into the shadows. "Check with Gamaliel Leonard at the Johns & Leonard Pier!" he yelled, his words echoing back at Rian from inside the opposite end of the broken bridge. "He's usually willing to try something new and he's got money."

Rian watched the man for a few moments. "Hey, Mr. Schott! Do you drink whiskey?"

Moments later, Schott's disembodied voice resonated from the darkness. "If it's good whiskey!"

Rian pulled the notepad from her sack and wrote, *Send a pint of whiskey to Mr. Quinton Schott.*

* * * * *

· RIAN ·

Rian entered the front door and felt the warmth radiating from the cast-iron stove. "I'm home!" she called.

"Alice just left," her father called from the dining room. "She made kidney pie. Conor and I are about to eat. Want to join us?"

Rian opened the stove door and lit a taper. As she mounted the stairs to the second floor, she spied a letter from Olivia on the windowsill. "Yes. Give me a minute to wash up, though." As Olivia's letter was likely to be written to an imaginary boy named Rian, she felt it would be best not to read this one to her father. She climbed the stairs two at a time, threw the letter on the bed, poured water from the pitcher into the bowl on the washbasin, unbuttoned her shirt, gave her armpits a quick wipe with a washcloth, buttoned herself back up, and flew down the stairs.

She was so preoccupied with what the letter might say that she forgot to tell her father and Conor about meeting Quinton Schott.

"There is a letter for you on the windowsill," her father said between bites.

Rian blew on a forkful of steaming kidney pie. "I saw it. I haven't read it yet."

"You and Olivia have started quite the correspondence lately."

"Yeah, I think she's lonely." She stole a quick side-glance at Conor, who gave her a conspiratorial eye roll. "She's at a boarding school in Columbia. I think she's having trouble making friends, so she writes to me. I feel obligated to write her back."

"Well, the next time you do, please give her our kindest regards."

After they washed and dried the dishes together, Rian excused herself, returned to her bedroom, and broke the wax seal on the letter.

January 1, 1839

> *Happy New Year! How strange it feels to be writing that date.*
>
> *I miss you terribly and read with great hunger every bit of news you send from Philadelphia.*
>
> *Please continue to write about your progress as you mend. Trying to prevent that boiler from exploding was very brave of you. I am sorry the foreman was killed.*

It is difficult to make friends here. I am being ostracized for my abolitionist sympathies. My classes are interesting, mostly, but I doubt I will ever have the kind of adventures you and I had a few summers ago.

It is late. I should go to bed. See you in my dreams.

Olivia

There was plenty of white space at the bottom of the page. Rian passed the letter back and forth over her candle. Gradually, words magically appeared, all the way to the bottom but ended in mid-sentence. Rian eventually found the remainder of the sentence running vertically along the right margin. She pulled her pen and inkwell from her desk drawer and started transcribing.

SATURDAY, FEBRUARY 9

· RIAN ·

Rian was working on the crane project in her lair. As Quinton Schott had suggested, she visited pier owner Gamaliel Leonard. The man showed no interest in speaking with her until she flashed a pint of Seamus's whiskey in front of him. Leonard was initially bemused to meet with a fourteen-year-old, but the more Rian talked, the more intrigued he became with the idea of installing a crane that could lift fifteen tons.

Rian was a day or so away from presenting the entire plan to her father. Besides the knowledge that it was possible to build a crane capable of lifting thirty thousand pounds, the clincher in her presentation was a preliminary sketch of two heavy-duty horse-drawn flatbed wagons that could be hooked together like train cars and share the weight of a fully assembled locomotive.

A knock sounded on the door. *No one ever comes here.* "Come in!" she called.

A man in his mid-thirties, tall and thin, entered. Rian noted that he was plagued by a stiff neck, so when he turned his head, his torso turned as well. Added to that, he had a pinched face. A thought came unbidden: *This guy reminds me of a trout.* Rian tried to shove the unflattering thought aside but was only partially successful. "May I help you?"

"Miss Krieger, I thought I should come by and introduce myself. My name is Gerald Downing. I'm Krieger Locomotive's new foreman."

Rian's father had told her at dinner a few nights ago that he had hired a man away from Baldwin Locomotive.[23] Rian knew Matthias Baldwin had started the business a few years ahead of Krieger Locomotive and had grown his shop faster. Scuttlebutt around town was that Baldwin got clobbered during the recent depression and had not yet fully bounced back.

Rian rose to shake Downing's hand. *You have the job I wanted, but even if* Vater *had offered it to me, I couldn't have taken it because I'm afraid of steam*

---

23. Baldwin Locomotive, which in coming decades would grow to dominate the locomotive industry, built a huge factory on the corner of Broad and Hamilton Streets in 1835. By 1839, it employed 250 men.

engines. She stuffed down her residual resentment. *Plus, Seamus says I'm arrogant, impatient, and don't delegate well.* "Welcome."

"Thank you. Everyone I've met so far says it's important to get on your good side. Otherwise, I'm likely to get blown up."

Rian collapsed back into her chair, appalled by the callousness of Downing's remark. "What do you want?"

Unaware that his attempt at a joke had fallen flat, Downing continued. "I understand that my predecessor didn't allow you to work in the locomotive factory. I do not share that sentiment. As long as it's all right with your father, it's fine with me for you to work wherever you please in the shop."

"Uh, thank you? My father won't object. I've been working on the shop floor on and off since I was eleven."

"So, let's continue with this arrangement." Downing scanned a wall calendar above Rian's desk that proudly proclaimed:

Jacob Hummel's Morocco and Fancy Leather Store
No. 13 North Third St.
Buckskins, Chamois, Eastern Hogskins, Russian Leather
Suitable for Saddlers, Coachmakers, Bookbinders, Pocket-bookmakers,
Hatters, Shoemakers, Glovers, Trunk and Suspender Makers, &c.

Rian used the calendar to record the time she spent each morning on the platform above the steam engine. In the square for today's date, she had already written *44.*

Downing pulled his gaze away from the calendar. "Is it true that you're afraid of steam engines?"

Jaysus, the new guy already knows. "For the moment. I'm trying to change that."

Downing peered over Rian's shoulder at her sketch of the two heavy-duty wagons. "What are you working on?"

Rian moved to interpose herself between Downing and the sketch. "Nothing much. Just an idea I had."

Downing smiled. "Come on, impress me, Miss Krieger. Everyone I've spoken with says you have many talents—bookkeeper, pattern maker, lathe operator, wheelwright. I hear Heinrich Aldridge even gave you first crack at designing some parts for the new *Standard.* Is that what you're working on now?"

Downing's laudatory report thawed Rian's initial impression. She moved aside, allowing him to view her sketch. "It's not for a locomotive component.

It's a plan to deliver a fully assembled locomotive to our customers. You don't have to call me Miss Krieger—just Rian will do."

Downing's smile became engaging, even conspiratorial. "*Just-Rian* it is then." He peered down at the sketch. "How would it work?"

"The problem is that locomotives are a lot bigger than they were just two years ago. Now they're so heavy that the only ones we can deliver fully assembled are to the *Philadelphia & Columbia.* Our tracks roll out of this building and connect to the *P&C* at Hamilton Street. Everybody else, including the *Philadelphia & Trenton,* which ends only a couple of miles away from here, now has to take delivery of a disassembled locomotive they then have to reassemble. Both parties in the current equation lose time and money. We build the locomotive, test it, then disassemble it. If we could deliver a fully assembled locomotive to the railroad, it would reduce our production schedule, we could charge less, and we wouldn't have to send along a mechanic to supervise the reassembly."

"And how would you mount this engine onto the wagons? How would you get it off?"

"By crane."

"No crane in the city can lift that much weight."

"A man named Quinton Schott owns a factory that makes cranes. He says he can do it."

"Where would he build it?"

"Johns & Leonard Pier in Kensington. Quinton would have to build another crane here. We would have to make sure there are others built wherever we send the locos to."

"Jeesh, Rian, you're talking about a lot of weight here."

"When I was in Russia, there was a column in St. Petersburg erected in honor of the Tsar's brother. I don't know how they set it upright, but I remember it weighs over a million pounds. If the Russians can transport and set up something that big, we certainly can load fifteen tons onto a freight wagon. . . ."

"Then the locomotive would crush the wagon."

"That's what I'm working on. I did some checking . . . The Mennonites in Lancaster County make Conestoga wagons that can hold six tons of cargo. If we distributed the locomotive's weight over two of their wagons, we'd already almost be there. My wagons wouldn't be as elegant as a Conestoga, just a flatbed of oak timbers. We'd have to make beefier wheels than we've ever made, but I think I could do it."

"How many horses would you need to pull these wagons?"

"I figure twelve mules should do it. We'd have to talk to Kent's Livery across the street ahead of time so he can get the mules."

"My, my. Everything I heard about you seems to be true. I'm glad I stopped in. Just-Rian, feel free to stop into my office any time. My door will always be open to you."

As Downing left, Rian realized she hadn't asked him anything about himself. *Stupid. Well, we'll see how he does in the next couple of days. I imagine I'll know more about him soon enough.*

* * * * *

· SEAMUS ·

When Seamus strolled into McSweeney's, Braden was behind the bar, chatting with Dylan Kennedy. Braden glanced toward the door as he always did when a customer entered, muttered something to Dylan, turned, and sauntered into the kitchen.

Hmm, Seamus thought. *Normally, Braden would have started pouring me a whiskey, and it would have been sitting at my place before I got to the bar.* Seamus spotted Siobhan delivering dinners to some of the No Name boys. She shot him a smile, but she was busy and that was all she had time for. Seamus parked himself next to Dylan, who had taken over as president of the No Name Fire Brigade when Seamus went off to Russia and never ceded the title back. Dylan sipped his whiskey for a few minutes while Seamus waited for Braden to return from the kitchen. Five minutes later, Siobhan had flown in and out of the kitchen a couple of times, but still no Braden and no drink. "What's the story with McSweeney?"

"He's a touch irked at you."

"Me? How come? I'm barely here anymore. I only come in when Siobhan's working."

"That's just it. You're always at the distillery, and half our boys gravitate to your warehouse because they can sample better product at your place than they can drink here, and they're drinking for free. Braden's business is suffering."

"The boys are doing me a favor. I've pretty much figured out which one of me recipes . . . *my* recipes I'm going to produce next season because of them. I'll start selling the rest to Braden when the time comes. He'll be happy . . . eventually."

"But he ain't happy now. If you already know which recipe you'll use, why not start selling off the other batches right now?"

"They'll be better after they've aged for three years. The oldest whiskey in the warehouse is six months old . . . today, actually."

"We both know your half-year-old whiskey is better than the swill we're drinking right now. Do yourself *and* Braden a favor. Start selling him some product and put a little money in your pocket."

Seamus had no intention of deviating from his plan. "No, I wait until it's three years old. That's what Hasselbach taught me, and that's what I'm going to do."

Dylan shifted on his stool to face Seamus. "So you're telling me that what was good enough for George Washington isn't good enough for you."

George Washington? "Dylan, what are you talking about?"

"Hasselbach was in here the other day spinning tales. According to him, George Washington started making whiskey after he was president. A lot of whiskey. He never let his product sit around. He sold it right away. If he could do it, so can you."

Seamus sipped his drink and contemplated this new wrinkle. He stalled. "Hmm, I never thought my name and George Washington's would ever be mentioned in the same conversation."

Dylan pressed his point. "Let me ask you a question, Seamus. You haven't asked Siobhan to marry you yet. What's holding you up?"

"Money. Hugh said he would give me his blessing when I start making serious money."

"How serious would the money be if you started selling to Braden right now? Not your best recipe. The product you already know isn't your best."

Seamus did some quick math. "There's two hundred gallons of six-month-old whiskey—recipes I'm not using anymore—sitting there right now. There'll be two hundred more in another month, and another month after that. If I started selling those, that would be some very serious money."

"How about I go into the kitchen right now and tell Siobhan you're already sitting on a fortune? That the only thing holding up your engagement is you wanting to keep aging a product that the Father of Our Country would have sold six months ago?"

"Well, if you put it that way, she would probably kill me." At that moment, Braden came out of the kitchen. His scowl hadn't improved. Seamus gave Dylan a conspiratorial nudge with his elbow, then: "Braden, I've got a question for you. What do George Washington and I have in common?"

WEDNESDAY, FEBRUARY 13

· RIAN ·

Rian was up in Hell—what she now called her perch at the end of the platform beside the boiler. The steam engine *chooshed* rhythmically below her and drowned out much of the din and metal-on-metal clatter of the factory in production. Rian's pocket watch was open on her drafting table. *Thirty minutes down, twenty minutes to go*, she said to herself. She was sweating profusely. *But not from the boiler heat*, she acknowledged. *It's from my fear that the boiler will blow, even though I know it's unlikely.*

Okay, it's not all bad, Rian acknowledged. By now, she had logged hours in the presence of a machine that ran well. When she stuffed cotton in her ears, it filtered out a lot of noise, but it allowed her to hear sounds—almost like musical notes—normally hidden by louder notes. *Now I know what this machine sounds like when it's healthy, and I can hear notes when they aren't supposed to be there. I even feel new vibrations, and in the case of a steam engine, new is not good.* On three occasions, Rian had identified little problems and fixed them before they became big problems.

And I can actually get work done up here in Hell. She had moved all the company books up there. She had already made mechanical drawings of sixteen parts for the *Standard*, which Heinrich had approved. *Lastly, I can watch what's going on in the factory. I know who's doing what and where the bottlenecks are. That will serve me well if and when I ever run this place.*

Rian was so focused on two workers chatting at the far end of the factory that she almost missed seeing her father enter the shop through the alley door. *What's he doing here? He never comes over here unless there's a problem.* She checked her watch. *Ten o'clock sharp. Eighteen minutes left.*

Her father didn't see her up in Hell. He turned left and entered the Krieger Locomotive office. As Rian's watch marked fifteen minutes to go, Otto reappeared with Gerald Downing, the stiff-necked new shop foreman, and Heinrich Aldridge. They walked past the steam engine and stationed themselves near *Number 14*, a partially built *Eagle*-class locomotive. When completed in seven months, *Number 14* would be rechristened the *Bunker Hill*, then disassembled for shipment to the *Boston & Lowell Railroad*. Rian again checked her pocket watch. *Twelve minutes to go. Damn, I wonder what they're talking about. I'm missing something important.*

Rian stuffed the watch into her pocket seconds before her full fifty minutes in Hell had elapsed. Then, her hard-fought goal met, she raced down the wrought-iron stairs. She strode purposefully toward the trio, happy to have the lengthening ritual in Hell behind her for the day.

"What's going on?" she asked as she inserted herself between her father and Heinrich.

Heinrich leaned in toward Rian. "Trouble. Otto got a letter from Hobart Clark, the president of the *Boston & Lowell Railroad.* A man who owns a machine shop in Lowell has taken exception to our deal with the *B&L.* He thinks they should have kept their money local and he should be the one building their locomotive."

Rian frowned as she gazed at the skeleton of *Number 14.* "But the *B&L* signed a contract with us. The machine shop guy can't force them to break it."

Heinrich shrugged. "He's talked a few state legislators into proposing a law that the railroads have to buy in-state. Clark says we have to hurry delivery in order to beat the law. He also wants us to cut the price, but your father thinks that's just to give him an excuse to not buy from the machine shop."

This is a perfect opportunity to see if my crane plan will work.

She was about to speak up when Heinrich jerked his head toward Gerald Downing. "Gerald's got an interesting idea. He thinks we can deliver *Number 14* fully assembled to Boston. He thinks a pair of wagons could carry that much weight to the Johns & Leonard pier. He wants to show us some sketches that he asked you to draw up."

"No, wait, that was my plan. . . ."

Heinrich either ignored her protestation or didn't hear it above the shop's clang and clatter. "Rian, I'd like to see your drawing. Could you go get it, please?"

At sea, confused, building up a head of steam, Rian retrieved the rolled-up plans. She returned to a disaster.

Downing's head, neck, and body turned together as he addressed both Heinrich and her father. "Gamaliel Leonard and his partner are already on board to build a crane at their pier in Kensington. Of course we would have to find a pier owner in Boston who would be willing to do the same . . . Ah, Just-Rian, good." Downing held out his hand to accept Rian's plans. "I have to compliment your daughter, Herr Krieger, she is a fine draftsman . . . Herr Krieger, I know you are the chief designer of every railcar and wagon that Krieger Coach produces. If you like Rian's drawings, perhaps you could polish them up. Krieger Coach would make our wagons, of course. Rian tells me she would like to take a crack at the wheels herself. We could send a copy of the completed drawings to the B&L. It would be up to them to find a wagonmaker to build another set of wagons at their end."

Otto eyed Rian's drawings. "Rian, these are very good. The wagons do not have to be elegant, merely beefy enough that they do not collapse under the engine's weight. The wagon bed would be of oak, of course."

Rian nodded.

"And the wheels of hickory?"

Rian nodded again. "Except the hubs. They would be elm."

"Smart," said her father. "Gerald, I am impressed. Your first week on the job and you have already made a significant contribution to the way we do business. I will write to Hobart Clark. I will tell him we can offer a modest discount for *Number 14* and probably deliver it by mid-September if he can accept it fully assembled in Boston."

"Herr Krieger," said Downing, his head and body pivoting toward Otto, making him look more and more like a trout. "I appreciate your enthusiasm for my plan. I want to emphasize that Rian has given me significant assistance during this project."

Rian's father turned his attention to her. "Yes. *Liebling*, I am surprised you have not mentioned this to me." He put his hands in his pockets and rocked back and forth on his heels. "Not having to send a technician to supervise reassembly will be a great savings in the long run. Heinrich will have to go to Boston, of course, to give the new owners an orientation . . . Gerald, I think I should accompany *Number 14* to Boston. This will become a model for how we do business with a lot of railroads in the future. Perhaps I can lever more sales out of this new idea of yours."

Stymied, fuming, reeling from Downing's thievery, Rian turned on her heel and walked away. *If The Trout wants a war, that's what he'll get.* She tried to think of a place where she could calm herself. She climbed the stairs to Hell, then climbed the steeper stairs to the catwalk. High above the factory floor, she dodged first left, then right, then left around whirling pulleys and belts, heedless of the danger. At the factory's midpoint, she stopped and sat, her legs dangling in mid-air. She stuffed cotton in her ears to block out some of the notes. Then she shut her eyes and listened to the music of the machines.

THURSDAY, FEBRUARY 14

· RIAN ·

Rian felt the familiar spasm of dread as she neared the steam engine. *Not as bad as it used to be, but it's still there. Yeah . . . really, really there.* Instead of taking a right and trudging up the wrought-iron stairs, she strode straight ahead and barged into the Krieger Locomotive office without knocking.

The Trout looked up from his desk in his distinctive, stiff motion. "Just-Rian . . . You surprise me. I expected you yesterday afternoon."

Rian closed the door behind her, shutting out the clang and clatter from the shop. "You don't want me for an enemy."

"No, I certainly do not."

"Then why did you claim credit for my idea?"

The Trout held his hands out wide. "I'm the new guy. I needed to make my mark. You handed it to me on a silver platter."

"And why shouldn't I walk over to the Krieger Coach office right now and tell my father you stole my idea?"

"Why? Two reasons. First, because that's not how you deal with your problems. You solve them yourself."

Rian tried to betray no expression of surprise, no indication that The Trout's first shot hit his mark. *I wouldn't dream of running to* Vater *to help me.*

"Second," The Trout continued, "because I know what you want."

His second declaration *really* caught her attention. "What do I want?"

"You want to run Krieger Locomotive someday."

The Trout's words rocked Rian back on her heels. Sure, many of the men in the shop knew this. The late Harry Vogel certainly knew it. But the thought of The Trout—the new guy—knowing it surprised her. *This man really did his research.*

The Trout rose from his desk and started pacing. A thought crept unbidden into Rian's brain: *He has a unibody.*

"I did a lot of listening on my first day last week. I spoke with almost every man in this shop. I was merely trying to get the lay of the land, but a lot of them got around to talking about you. They all know what you want. Most of them don't like you, don't like your daddy's-daughter arrogance, don't approve of your aspirations . . . although you may be pleased to hear they begrudgingly admire your many abilities. I also heard your father has no interest in you inheriting the family business. He wants to marry you off to somebody from society so his future son-in-law will run one of the Krieger shops. So even before you told me about your plan to transport fully assembled locomotives to our customers, I concocted the proposal I'm about to reveal to you."

"And what is that?"

"An alliance. You help me, then I'll help you."

Rian seethed, but her curiosity was piqued. "How can I help you?"

"Same as you already have. Share your ideas with me."

"I'll never share another idea with you. I'll never trust you."

"Okay, let's break your problem down. Right now you're afraid of steam engines. You certainly couldn't run this shop today, even if your daddy were so inclined to let you, which we know he's not. Let's assume you'll get over your fear. How long will it take?"

"I don't know. Heinrich says a year."

"How old will you be by then?"

"Almost sixteen."

"Do you think you could run this factory at age sixteen?"

Rian stared at her shoes in the face of The Trout's verbal onslaught. "I don't know. Maybe."

"Come on, Just-Rian, be realistic. In your wildest imaginings, what is the earliest you could take over here?"

Jaysus. "Probably when I'm eighteen."

"Good. We're making progress. I know what you want. Now I'm going to tell you what I want and all will become clear to you."

"I'm listening."

"I want to go back to Baldwin Locomotive when the time comes."

The Trout's admission rendered Rian speechless.

"I didn't quit Baldwin Locomotive. I was laid off . . . How many locomotives do you think Baldwin made in 1837, the year the Panic hit?"

"I have no idea."

"Then I'll tell you. Forty."

That number astounded Rian. Krieger Locomotive's fourteenth engine—*since the day we opened!*—was sitting out on the production floor right now, and Baldwin had built three times that many in one year. "Holy mackerel."

"But Baldwin only produced twenty-six engines in '38. And it gets worse. They expect to build less than ten this year. And it's not only Baldwin. Three locomotive manufactures in the country have gone out of business since the Panic. Those left standing are at a standstill . . . except for Krieger Locomotive."

Rian sat in a chair near The Trout's desk. "Why not us?"

"Reputation, I suspect. Even when I was working at Baldwin, I knew your father and uncle valued craftsmanship. Now I see firsthand the commitment to durability. You innovate. You're willing to customize each order to suit the special needs of your customers. All laudatory attributes, especially in the middle of a depression."

"We aren't in a depression. That's behind us."

"My information says you're wrong. This depression is far from over. It gives people false hopes, then smacks them down."

"So you want to go back to Baldwin when your depression is over?"

"Yes, I do. Baldwin's factories dwarf your little family firm, and will do so even after your new factory is completed. When Baldwin finally climbs out of this nastiness, they will come roaring back and be prepared to dominate the industry. That environment suits me much better, not here. I figure we'll have to ride this unpleasantness out for three more years . . . just about the time you turn eighteen. Guess who I would be happy to recommend to replace me?"

Yana the soothsayer's words shouldered their way into Rian's foremost thoughts: *First you won't run it, then you will.* Rian hesitated, then . . . "Tell me what this alliance would be like."

"In a nutshell, if you make me look good, I will push as hard as I can for you to replace me when I leave." The Trout stuck out his hand for Rian to shake.

He's already done you dirty once, Eena. "I don't trust you."

"Understandable. But I don't trust you much, either. You've been known to have problems with authority. When Harry Vogel was foreman, you openly defied him. You embarrassed him in front of the men."

Jaysus, the workers told him a lot. "Harry didn't like having me in the shop."

"But we've already agreed you will have the run of the factory. You can move into this office when you feel comfortable doing so. I stole your idea in a moment of weakness. I'm sorry. As I said, I needed to make my mark . . . How about this? We proceed with no formal alliance. All you have to do is refrain from undermining me. As we both agreed, I don't want you as an enemy."

"And I have to wait three years to find out if you'll recommend I replace you?"

"I think you'll see the lay of the land before then, but yes, that's your payoff."

"I still don't trust you, but I'll go along with this until I have proof you aren't holding up your end."

"It seems we have a meeting of the minds . . . Have you spent your time in Hell yet?"

Rian didn't know Downing knew about Hell. "No."

"How many minutes today?"

Rian turned on her heel and headed for the door. "Fifty-two."

"Good luck."

Damnit. I have no idea if I'm making progress or if he'll betray me three years from now.

* * * * *

After Hell, Rian returned to her lair to find four local newspapers on her desk. She had read newspapers in no particular order—two in English, two in German—almost every day since she was eleven, but lately she had religiously started her morning reading with the *Philadelphia Independent*, scouring front and back, hoping to find Topper's latest letter in print. Today, she was not disappointed.

Notes from Jasper
True Stories Related by
An Enslaved Individual
Reported by Harold Foote

The Independent *has established correspondence with an individual currently in involuntary service. This person lives on a plantation in a slave state that we have chosen not to disclose. As well, this person's sex will remain a secret, although we call our correspondent Jasper and refer to him as he. Jasper swears he has personal knowledge of each incident he describes to us. Below is his latest entry.*

In my previous circumstance in another region, when slaves received a whipping, their hands were tied to a post and they were whipped on the back. That had also been the method at my new situation until my enslaver changed things. He determined that binding the hands of those being whipped resulted in undesirable injuries. When the sorry souls writhed in agony with each strike of the lash, they wrenched so violently that they broke or dislocated their own wrists. My new enslaver instructed the slavedriver to come up with another system, because those who had been punished were useless for a few days or even weeks, not because of the wounds on their backs but because of their broken wrists. The slavedriver experimented with numerous variations in the first weeks, but now has settled on a particularly cruel and humiliating method.

In an instance last spring, we had walked a mile along our road to a field to hoe and weed cotton. A young woman, who I will call Lydia, about the age of 19, carried her baby as well as her hoe that distance and parked her child in the shade at the beginning of her row. At seven o'clock the overseer blew his horn, and we all repaired to a shady area for a breakfast of water and cornbread that had been baked in ashes. Lydia instead returned to the beginning of her row to nourish her baby but was late by one minute by my reckoning getting back to her hoe.

Our workday ended after sunset when we could no longer distinguish cotton plant from weed. The strawboss assembled us all and called Lydia to come to him and remove her shift, which was her only garment. He forced her to lie prostrate on the ground, at which point he applied a dozen lashes to her buttocks, each one drawing blood. Lydia wailed with each blow but was able to walk back to the cabins, although others for the most part carried her baby for her. She worked from sunup to sunset the next day.

TUESDAY, MARCH 26

MARKET STREET,
from Front Street.

Courtesy of Library Company of Philadelphia

· CONOR ·

Conor was delivering messages along Market Street when he got distracted by a pretty girl who was shopping at the vendor kiosks between the boulevard's eastbound and westbound lanes. Not wanting to be too obvious as he gawked, he crossed the street, dodging freight wagon and a pair of horsemen coming from the east.

The kiosks thrummed with business, offering winter vegetables, chickens both alive and plucked, cheeses, household items, bolts of cloth, vegetable seeds, sweets, and hundreds of other items in no particular order. Well-to-do women were out in force with their wicker baskets, enjoying one of the first warm days of spring. *They always dress to the nines*, Conor observed, *even though they're merely shopping.*

And sometimes, some cute young thing my age comes along. The pretty girl was fingering aprons, so Conor feigned interest in a cast-iron pan at the next shed over. He stole glances at her while she shopped.

"Hi, Conor. What are you doing?"

Conor turned to find Rian approaching from the west. He decided not to mention the pretty girl. "I'm shopping for your birthday present. Happy birthday. You were out of the house early. How's it feel to be fifteen years old?"

Rian flashed him a smile that was all too rare these days. "I don't think we need another frying pan. I really don't need anything unless you're interested in killing The Trout for me."

"I stopped doing murders for birthday presents. Bad long-term plan. What'd The Trout do to you today?"

Rian gazed down the length of the kiosks. "He called me *Just-Rian* in front of the workers. When he started calling me that, I thought it was a joke between us, but I don't think it is anymore. I think he uses it to belittle me. That man really has my number. He swiped my idea and now *Vater* thinks he's the second coming of Christ. But he's a much better foreman than Harry was. He's got the shop running smoothly. The men like him. He's given me the run of the shop, which isn't saying much since I'm mostly down at the far end except the time I'm in Hell."

Conor wasn't much interested in Rian's complaints. He had heard most of this before. "Hey, did you start your day doing bookkeeping? Any problems paying bills?"

"No, not at all. We're not exactly flush, but we're okay. The depression's over . . . Why? What are you hearing?"

Conor held up his messenger bag. "Matthias Baldwin is in financial trouble. He told a lot of his creditors that if they demand payment, he'll have to fold and they'll get nothing. He's asked them to hang on and he'll pay them whenever he can."

Rian rocked back on her heels, giving Conor a small amount of pleasure that he knew something about Krieger Locomotive's gigantic competitor before she did.

"Damn, The Trout was right. Baldwin *is* in trouble. How did you hear all this?"

"I keep my ears open when I pick up messages. That's all people were talking about at the Merchants' Exchange this morning. Mostly, his suppliers are knuckling under, but Steven Griffiths—he owns the Spring Garden Tube Works—he says if Baldwin doesn't pay him, *he'll* go out of business. I'm surprised Baldwin is hurting and Krieger Locomotive seems to be doing okay. They're a lot bigger than you are."

"We *are* doing okay—better than okay. We finally received the contract for twelve locomotives from the *Utica & Schenectady*. *Vater's* taking it to the Bank of Industry loan committee today. He's ready to build a new locomotive factory across Buttonwood, but we need a loan."

Conor wondered about the propriety of a loan committee member voting on his own loan, but such decisions were far from his ability to judge. "What are you doing out and about? You should be working on more patterns."

Rian shifted her gaze to the west on Market Street. "I'm mailing a letter."

"Krieger business?"

"Nope. It's to the person I mailed the second copy of Catherine the Great's memoir to.[24] He knows that if I don't contact him every April, he's supposed to send the memoir to a newspaper."

"Jeez, that means you've been home almost a year. Nobody's tried to kill you yet. Will you send the memoir back to the Tsar?"

Rian gazed at other cast-iron household objects on display in the kiosk. "I told Kiserev ten years."

"Who is this guy you sent the memoir to?" *You've kept that secret from me for a year now, and I doubt you'll ever tell me.*

"John Quincy Adams."

"John Quincy Adams!" Conor exclaimed so loudly that he scanned around to see if anyone had overheard. No one cared. "Interesting choice. Kind of old, isn't he?"

"I don't know. I wasn't thinking about that when I concocted this plan. I was all by myself. I needed somebody I could trust who didn't live in Philadelphia. I'd met him once."

"Maybe you should rethink your plan. Unless you get blown up by another steam engine, he'll die before you do. Then what?"

"I don't know how to get the memoir back. I don't have plans to go to Boston any time soon."

"Your da is going there in September with the locomotive. Ask him to do it."

"*Vater* doesn't know as much as you do about all this."

"Maybe it's time to tell him."

---

24. In Book 3 of Rian Krieger's Journey, *The Blackmailer,* Rian read and copied the secret memoir of Catherine the Great, in which Catherine revealed that the real father of her son Paul I was an Army officer named Saltykov. Therefore, there wasn't a drop of Romanov blood in Paul, or Paul's son Nicholas I, the current Tsar. Rian blackmailed the Tsar with that information to spring Seamus, two others, and eventually her Uncle Adrian from prison. As security to make sure the Tsar didn't send operatives to kill her afterward, she made a second copy. A Russian named Kiserev sailed to America with Rian and Seamus to retrieve the first copy. At the end of their voyage, Rian informed Kiserev of the second copy.

"I've gotta go, Conor. Good luck with your messages." Rian turned and continued on her way to the post office.

Conor watched Rian as she faded into the crowd. "Happy birthday, Rian. See you tonight," he said, but he knew she didn't hear it and assumed she was already thinking of something else. *That's how she is these days.*

* * * * *

· OTTO ·

Otto sat down at the conference table, knowing the meeting would be difficult. *You scratch my back and I'll scratch yours,* George Shippen had suggested at lunch a few days ago. *You support the spur for the* Mauch Chunk & Lehigh, *I support your factory.* Otto had agreed to the collusion, but yesterday, James Mott came to him with some information that jeopardized his tentative alliance with Shippen.

"The March meeting of the loan committee of the Bank of Industry is now in session," Shippen said. "The first item on the agenda is an application from our own Otto Krieger to build a new locomotive factory across Buttonwood Street from his current shops. Mr. Schiffler will give you the specifics."

Otto leafed through his packet to assure himself he wasn't unnecessarily climbing out on a limb. He noticed James Mott and Jonas Longstreth doing the same. "Before we proceed with my application, I would like to raise a point of order. It appears that some applications are missing from my packet."

Shippen leaned forward, folded his hands, and addressed Otto. "There are only two applications on today's agenda. Krieger Locomotive and the *Mauch Chunk & Lehigh Railroad.*"

Here we go. "I was expecting two others, one from a Black hotelier for a $1,500 loan and another for $1,200 for a Black druggist—"

"Those applications were denied," said Schiffler. His words were clipped.

Otto received an encouraging nod from both Mott and Longstreth. "How could they be denied? The committee never discussed either of them."

Shippen and Schiffler simultaneously leaned back in their chairs and folded their arms. Shippen spoke. "The loan committee only deals with applications above a certain threshold. President Schiffler deals with all the smaller matters. There's no need to trouble the committee with the piddling stuff."

This is as underhanded as we suspected. "George, when we joined the committee, you told us we dealt with every loan above a thousand dollars."

"The threshold changed."

"What is the threshold now?"

"Two thousand dollars," responded Shippen.

"Who changed it?"

"Schiffler and I did."

Otto knew he was putting his loan in jeopardy, as well as all the camaraderie he had recently built up with Shippen, but still . . . "George, we made a deal last August. We okayed the loan for your brother-in-law in South Carolina. In exchange, you agreed to bring Black loan applications to the committee—"

"We granted those loans to your foreman and his apartment-owner friend. That should be enough."

"Most Black-owned businesses are small operations. They are only asking for small loans. The committee should have been told of your change."

Shippen glared at Otto but said nothing.

"If loan applications are unsound," Otto continued, "the committee will deny them. But if we deem them worthy, then these people should get a loan, no matter the color of their skin. Mr. Mott, Mr. Longstreth, and I want the threshold reduced back to a thousand dollars."

Otto could almost see Shippen machinating. *He knows James Forten will learn of this. His position as chairman of the board is in jeopardy. And he still needs my cooperation to get his loan through.*

"Edward, go get the applications," said Shippen. "We will put them on the agenda for the end of this meeting. Does that satisfy the three of you?"

Mott and Longstreth nodded, but Otto wasn't quite satisfied yet. "And the threshold will be returned to a thousand dollars?"

Otto felt the animosity radiating from Shippen. "If that is the way it has to be, yes."

We have done the right thing. If this puts my loan in jeopardy, so be it.

After five minutes of awkward silence, Edward Schiffler strode back into the room with the papers and returned to his seat. Shippen assumed an air of irritated dignity. "We are now behind schedule. Let's dispatch these items as efficiently as possible. Edward?"

Schiffler scooched his chair forward. "If you open your folders, you will find Herr Krieger's request for a loan of $40,000,[25] which the Bank of Industry would pay out in installments as construction progresses. The proposed loan is at a rate of five percent, to be fully repaid in ten years. Now, normally, as our applicants do not attend loan committee meetings, we would be working strictly from their applications. However, in this case, for efficiency and clarity's sake, I would like to yield the floor to Herr Krieger."

---

25. To gauge the magnitude of Otto's request, $40,000 in 1839 has the purchasing power of $1,357,440 in 2025.

Otto felt relieved to finally make his presentation. "Last week, Krieger Locomotive received a binding contract from the *Utica & Schenectady Railroad* for the purchase of twelve locomotives; six of our *Eagle*-class engines to be made over the course of a year starting one year from now, then six of our *Standard*-class engines the following year, starting on or about March of 1841."

"How much is the contract for?" asked Jonas Longstreth.

"For the twelve engines, the total is $66,000."

"Why did they delay so long?" Shippen knew the answer to this question, but he and Otto had worked out his role in advance. "They were supposed to make a commitment months ago."

"Their connection to the West is still incomplete. They were forced to re-route *Utica & Syracuse*, the last piece of their puzzle. Too many people were afraid cinders from the locomotives would set their buildings on fire. With the track still yet to be laid, they have delayed their merger, but the *Utica & Schenectady* decided they needed to purchase our locomotives before we cast our lot with another railroad."

"When will you break ground?" James Mott asked.

"Sadly, it will be a couple of months yet. There were no more than half a dozen outfits that could take on a project this size before the Panic, and two of them have since gone out of business. I have to wait for the contractor I settled on to finish another project. He promises me it will be under roof by December."

Longstreth leaned forward. "Mr. Chairman, I propose we grant a $40,000 loan to Krieger Locomotive at the rate of five percent to be paid back in ten years."

Shippen held up a cautionary hand. "Otto, what other contracts does Krieger Locomotive have at the moment?

Here comes the retribution. "We have three other locomotives currently in production."

"And down the road . . . any other business besides the *U&S* contract?"

"No, nothing under contract, but I feel confident others will be coming in. No matter what, those twelve locomotives will keep the new factory running at near capacity for at least two years."

Shippen smiled. "I support Mr. Longstreth's motion, except it seems a bit risky for all your eggs to be in the *U&S* basket. I think the interest should be five-and-a-half percent."

Otto did some quick math in his head. *Half a percent. That will increase my interest payment by a thousand dollars. That's what I get for bucking George.*

* * * * *

It was five o'clock, an hour before the end of the workday. Otto watched a crew of workers and four horses lift a passenger coach aloft by hauling on four sets of block-and-tackle. Jules directed the entire operation. Rian encouraged one of the horses forward by the halter.

When the coach was six feet off the factory floor, two men rolled a transport wagon beneath it. Tomorrow morning, Jules and a crew were set to deliver the passenger coach to the *Camden & Amboy Railroad* across the Delaware River.

Years ago, Otto and his brother Adrian established a tradition: Whenever a carriage, coach, or locomotive was completed, one brother or the other would "cross the alley" to admire the handiwork and share in the success. Since Adrian moved to Russia, then Saxony, Heinrich Aldridge had taken Adrian's place. He sidled up to Otto, holding a rolled sheet of vellum in the crook of his arm. "It's been a while since I crossed the alley."

"Sales are stronger than last year. I am content. We take our time. Concentrate on craftsmanship. I have been meaning to ask you a question. My daughter seems to be working most afternoons with you these days. How is she doing?"

"It's funny you asked that. I brought these drawings over to show you."

Otto held out his hand. "*Was ist das* [What is this]?"

Heinrich allowed his gaze to leave the passenger coach, which now rested on the transport wagon. "Here. Jules is busy with the men. Let's go over to his shop table and I'll show you."

Otto followed Heinrich a short distance to Jules's standing desk, and Heinrich unrolled the sheets, placing weights on each of the four corners. "This is a shop drawing of an eccentric rod for the *Standard*-class locomotive we're making for the *Utica & Schenectady*. Your daughter created this drawing. She did it in less than an hour."

"This is quite precise."

"What it is, is perfect. And once I approved the drawing, she made a wooden pattern of this same piece. The wooden pattern is also perfect. When we start building, we will embed that pattern in a sand table to cast the eccentric rod. Rian has made scores of drawings and many wooden patterns. Counting nuts, bolts, and rivets, there will be more than five thousand parts in our *Standard*. Rian will have a hand in a huge percentage of them."

"Do you think it appropriate for a young woman such as my daughter to be doing these tasks?"

"Appropriate? Yes, I think it's appropriate because she's skilled at them and she wants to do them."

"It seems to be all she wants to do."

"Otto, a week or so ago, I asked her why she's so possessed by these jobs."

"What did she say?"

"She said she has to do them because as soon as she stops, she starts thinking about other things."

"And what are these 'other things'?"

"She didn't say, and I didn't poke, but I don't think they're anything she enjoys thinking about."

* * * * *

· OLIVIA ·

When Dr. Marks designed the buildings at Barhamville, he presciently anticipated the efficient disposal of more than a hundred students' urine and excrement. Unwilling to task the few slaves he owned with carrying the contents of scores of chamber pots outside every morning, he had his contractors build a luxurious five-seat stone privy. Windows allowed ample sunlight during the day, and a whale oil sconce glowed all night. A louvered cupola provided ventilation that eliminated the stink. A hearth, banked continuously during the cold months, made the privy inviting twenty-four hours a day.

However, either oblivious or uncaring of a young woman's desire for privacy during her toilet, Dr. Marks's design allowed for no partitions between the seats. Although it took getting used to at first, Olivia accustomed herself to urinating and defecating in the presence of the other girls.

But her current circumstance added a renewed sense of unease.

Perhaps half the girls on Olivia's floor had already begun menstruating, so Olivia technically knew what would happen. But she sure as eggs is eggs didn't know what it would feel like. *Thank goodness it's Eugenie with me and not one of the other girls.*

Olivia had felt bloated since yesterday, so she suspected it might finally be her time. Part of her wanted it to happen because then Caldie Montgomery wouldn't have one more thing to lord over her. *"You really wouldn't know about that, Abo,"* Caldie had pronounced more than once. *"You're not really a woman until you start having your monthly."* When Olivia felt the first liquid warmth escape and trickle down her thighs, she grabbed Eugenie and they ran downstairs, out the back door, and to the privy. Olivia was afraid her dress, or at the very least, her petticoat, was ruined forever.

"Well?" asked Eugenie, her back to Olivia, who was sitting on the middle seat.

Olivia spread her legs and peered down into the black abyss of the pit beneath the privy. "I don't know. I can't see a thing. I think it's probably blood."

"Oh, it's blood, all right. How do you feel?"

"I feel like I just peed a gallon. I ache. Will I feel like this every month?"

"Sometimes. Sometimes not. But don't worry," Eugenie said, doing her best Caldie Montgomery imitation. "Now that you've had your monthly, you are really a woman."

Despite her embarrassment and discomfort, Olivia started to giggle.

WEDNESDAY, MAY 15

· OTTO ·

Otto and Heinrich stood in the empty field across Buttonwood Street from the three Krieger factories. Otto had arrived fifteen minutes before Heinrich and had already created stone cairns where he wanted the corners of the new locomotive factory to go.

"Otto," said Heinrich, "are you sure you want to do this? We're the only locomotive manufactury that's building right now. Baldwin cut staff again last week. I'm not sure now is the time to expand."

Otto slapped his hands back and forth to remove the dirt from his palms. "Sales in all three Krieger corporations are almost back to pre-Panic levels—strong for nine months now. If we don't build this factory, we will soon be losing business because we do not have the capacity of our competitors. Mark my words: Even though Matthias Baldwin is laying off workers, he will come roaring back. When he does, he will muscle us aside through capacity alone. We have survived this depression. Now it is time to flex our muscles. The Bank of Industry has granted us the money. If we are not growing, we are losing ground to our competitors. We must either grow bigger or die."

Heinrich shook his head and turned to Otto. "Okay, let me ask my question a different way: *Why* do you want to do this?"

Heinrich's question aroused a seed of resentment. Otto wasn't used to being challenged in this manner, at least by Heinrich. "Why? I just told you why. If we do not grow, we lose ground to our competitors."

"Otto, you only come over to our side of the alley if we have a problem. I've heard you say a hundred times: passion drives a company. Passion that comes from the top. That's you. But you're now in charge of two factories, Krieger Coach and Krieger Locomotive. You're a brilliant designer of carriages and railroad cars. Your craftsmanship and attention to detail are reflected in every landau, passenger car, and handcart that goes out the Krieger Coach door. But this factory will house Krieger Locomotive. Krieger Locomotive is your brother's baby, not yours. It's not the first thing you think about when you wake up and the last thing before you go to sleep. That space is already occupied—understandably—by your passion for Krieger Coach."

Otto felt his ire build. *This is so unfair.* "That is nonsense. I promised my brother I would take care of his business until he returns. That is what I am doing. That is why I mortgaged myself up to my eyeballs. That is why I travel all over the country making sales calls."

Heinrich responded with an incredulous "if-you-say-so" look. "I would like to point out that your brother shows no signs of returning soon."

Otto gathered his thoughts, trying to parry Heinrich's thrust another way. "I grant you: The formula for a successful enterprise requires passion and expertise, but you supply more than enough passion for locomotives, and Gerald and his men supply the expertise. I would be a fool to get in your way."

Heinrich smiled at the compliment. "If it's passion that drives our enterprises, then I suggest you include Rian in your Krieger Locomotive equation."

With the conversation taking a whole new direction, Otto felt more stabs of resentment. *But why does Rian not share my passion for Krieger Coach?* which was immediately washed away by *My daughter should not be at either factory.* For the thousandth time, he chastised himself for allowing Rian freedom of movement after the explosion. *If she keeps this up, she will end up ostracized like my mother.*

He returned his gaze to the empty lot. As he often did when procrastinating making decisions concerning his daughter, he hoped they would magically solve themselves. "My daughter will become a woman soon enough. Her passion for locomotives will wane, and she will shift her passion to finding a suitable husband . . . Where is Rian? If she were so passionate about Krieger Locomotive, she would be here."

* * * * *

· RIAN ·

Rian had allotted 206 minutes to spend in Hell today. Cotton stuffed in her ears, she was seated at her drafting table. She should have been concentrating on a mechanical drawing of a part for the *Standard*—still two years from delivery. Instead, she was trying to make lemonade out of lemons. Two hours ago, Heinrich Aldridge told her The Trout would accompany him and her father to Boston when they delivered *Number 14* to the *Boston & Lowell Railroad*.

Heinrich had to go, of course. Locomotives were such complex machines that a technician had to accompany each delivery to teach the new owners what was what. *Vater* wanted to see if he could scare up more sales for the three Krieger companies. But The Trout? The Trout was going as a reward for having such a great idea about the cranes. The reward should have been hers. She should have been the one going to Boston.

But that leaves no one in charge of Krieger Locomotive for more than a week. This will be my chance. This will be—

BAM!

Rian flinched at an explosion as loud as a gunshot. She swiveled toward the source of the blast. Fifteen feet away, the remains of a continuous belt spooled off its still-rotating pulley and cascaded to the lathe below.

Rian's brain told her she was okay. Her body, on the other hand, told her she needed to fight or flee. Unable to do either, she slid off her chair and collapsed onto the wrought-iron grillage of the platform.

The Trout came flying out of his office. He disconnected the power from the steam engine to the drive shaft by pushing the lever that shifted the belt from the drive pulley to the idler pulley. Released from its burden, the steam engine sped up its *choosh!* . . . *choosh!* . . . *choosh!* . . . and the twin flywheels continued to spin. The workers disengaged their machines before the loss of momentum made disengaging problematic. The din of the factory lessened.

"Everyone all right?" The Trout yelled from below.

Benny Holt, who had been operating the lathe, waved that he was fine but pointed up at Rian in Hell.

The Trout glanced up, saw Rian, and mounted the stairs to the platform. By the time he got to her, she had pulled herself back into her chair, but she was in no condition to put up even the remotest of brave fronts.

"Are you hurt?" The Trout asked.

Rian shook her head.

"Do you want to come down? We can talk in my office."

"I've gotta spend another ten minutes up here."

"Why don't you cut yourself a break, Just-Rian. Come down with me. You can finish your time up here later if you feel like it."

Rian followed The Trout. At the bottom of the stairs, he pulled the lever and started the drive shaft back up. One by one, the men reengaged their machines. The factory returned to its pre-bam clang and clatter. The Trout held the office door open for Rian.

She was still shaken, but her brain started to work. "What about the lathe?"

"We'll repair the belt at the end of the day. No sense shutting down the whole factory to fix one machine." The Trout settled his unibody behind his desk and indicated that Rian should sit in the chair opposite him. "Just-Rian, I'm worried about you."

"I'll be all right." *Don't trust him. Don't trust him.* "I thought it would be a straight line, that each day would be a little better than the last one."

"But it's not?"

Rian shuddered and shook her head.

"How long do you intend to work up in Hell?"

"Heinrich says that if I can do a whole day, I'll be cured."

"How long will that take?"

"Until Christmas, I suspect." Rian could hear the faint *choosh . . . choosh . . . choosh . . .* of the steam engine on the other side of the office wall. *It feels safer in here. There's a double wall of brick between me and that fooking steam engine.* "Gerald, can I move my desk in here?"

"Which one? The one up on the platform or the one in your hidey-hole at the other end of the shop?"

"The one up on the platform."

"You would be welcome to work in here. But I have to tell you, I think it's very brave of you to be doing this after what you've been through. Don't let this little setback put you back on your heels. I think you should stick to Heinrich's plan. I think you should go right back up there and finish out your minutes."

He doesn't have to be this nice. "You do?"

"Certainly. But as I told you months ago, any time you want to move in here, we can make that happen." The Trout waved toward Heinrich Aldridge's empty desk. "Heinrich would be pleased to have you as well."

"I'm going back up. Thank you for talking to me."

"Any time, Just-Rian."

Rian shut the door behind her and resolutely climbed the stairs. She was in such turmoil about the setback and Gerald Downing's unexpected kindness that she forgot about her plan to run the shop while Downing was gone. She also forgot that she and Gerald were supposed to meet her father across the street to lay out the dimensions of the new locomotive factory.

* * * * *

· SEAMUS ·

Seamus was filling another twelve bottles for delivery to McSweeney's when someone banged repeatedly on the sliding warehouse door. He walked twenty paces to the door, slid it open to find . . . James Hollingsworth, maître d' of the United States Hotel's dining room.

"Good afternoon," James said, "are you Mr. Seamus Gallagher?"

"I am," Seamus answered coldly.

"The distiller of Gallagher's Fine Whiskey?" James asked.

"Yes."

"May I come in, please? My name is—"

"I know who you are. What are you doing here?"

James's eyes widened in reaction to Seamus's coldness, but he forged ahead. "I wonder if you might be interested in a business proposition."

"You don't remember me, do you?"

The maître d' raised his eyes to the GALLAGHER'S DISTILLERY sign above the door as if it might provide a clue. He returned his gaze to Seamus. "I'm afraid you have me at a disadvantage, sir."

"Two years ago, you wouldn't let my girlfriend and me eat in your precious dining room."

James puffed himself up a bit, trying to summon all the dignity his station warranted. "Well, of course. We have rules. There's an order to things."

"You wouldn't let us in because we're Irish. 'The United States Hotel does not serve the Irish,' you said. 'In fact,' you said, 'we do not *hire* the Irish. I'm sure there are lesser establishments in the city that do, but I'm afraid that I don't know of any.' Do you remember saying those words?"

"I . . . uh . . . I have said those words before. I do not remember our encounter."

"Well, now I'm going to say to you what you said to me on that day: 'Good day to you.'" Seamus started to slide the door shut. "Consider yourself lucky that I haven't thrashed you right where you stand."

"Wait!"

Seamus stopped and glared at James. "Here's the only way I see this conversation ending: You want to buy my whiskey, but the only way I can ever enter your hotel will be through the back door. Is that true, yes or no?"

"What if I allow you to entertain your girlfriend in the dining room?"

"How many times?"

"Once. Sometime in mid-afternoon."

Seamus leaned into the handle to finish shutting the door.

"Okay! Any time you wish!"

Seamus stopped. "How many times? If you say 'whenever you want, as many times as you want,' I'll invite you in and we can continue to talk."

"You know women are only allowed to eat in our private dining rooms."

"Yes, of course. I reserved one the last time, the time you turned us away."

"There is a dress code. You must be presentable."

"We were wearing our Sunday best. Would that be suitable enough?"

James nodded. "My answer to you, sir, is: If we can reach an agreement about your whiskey, I would be pleased to have you dine at the United States Hotel, with or without your girlfriend, whenever you want, as many times as you want."

* * * * *

Seamus and James sat in Rumor Control, a circle of chairs surrounding an overturned apple crate. They had sampled three of Seamus's recipes.

Seamus gazed at the flame of the whale oil lamp on the crate. "Selling to your crowd right now is against me—*my*—better judgment. My whiskey is still too harsh."

James nodded in agreement. "Consider it a matter of comparison. The whiskey we buy now is distilled in the state's hinterlands. The farmers learned long ago that people are willing to pay quite a bit more for liquor than for corn, and liquor is much cheaper to transport. Sadly, it's loaded onto the train to Philadelphia the day after it drips out of the still. Those yokels don't have the attention to detail or the patience you exhibit."

Seamus raised his glass in acknowledgment of the compliment. "I was taught to include no corn in my recipes. Rye and barley only."

James took another sip. "I'm not sure you understand what a juggernaut you're riding. Sure, your whiskey is a little rough right now, but as you know, it will smooth out with age. I'm very impressed, as are others."

"Like who?"

"I have two younger brothers. One is an engine driver on the *Philadelphia & Columbia Railroad*. He first mentioned it to me months ago, but I didn't pay attention. My other brother works at the *Philadelphia & Trenton* station in Kensington. He asked me if I ever heard of Gallagher's Distillery, but I hadn't, and I didn't pursue it."

"They must have been served at McSweeney's Saloon on Lombard Street. That's the only place I sell at the moment."

James shook his head. "No, both of them were given bottles by a young man who asked them questions."

What young man has access to my whiskey? "What was this lad's name? What was he asking about?"

"I think he was interested in their locomotives. Honestly, I wasn't paying much attention to my brothers at the time. Then two habitués of my dining room independently asked for your whiskey within days of one another. I promised to procure a bottle but never got around to it."

"Who were the men?"

"Mr. Quinton Schott. Mr. Gamaliel Leonard. Both men who, through the trades, have made themselves into men of substance. To my discredit, I still didn't do anything."

Seamus had met neither Schott nor Leonard, nor heard of them.

"Then yesterday, Mr. Alton Vanderkemp, the owner of the United States Hotel, told me to find you and do whatever it takes to convince you to sell to us."

Seamus had never heard of Alton Vanderkemp, either. "How does he know about my whiskey?"

"It was served at the home of Mr. John Naglee, president of the *Philadelphia & Trenton Railroad*."

"And how did Naglee get his hands on it?"

"Apparently the bottle in question—only a pint, mind you—was confiscated from one of his engine drivers and somehow found its way to him. In my position, I have learned to put great credence in what I call 'the rule of three.' If I hear something from three independent sources, I assume there's some significance to it."

"Your brothers are two, Schott is three, Leonard is four, Vanderkemp is five."

"Like I said, you're riding a juggernaut."

Seamus liked James's "rule of three," but . . . "What if all five of these people lead back to one person? Does your rule of three still apply?"

"Who would that be?"

"The boy who was asking questions." *Who I bet was my cousin and primary investor, Rian Krieger. What is she up to?*

* * * * *

· OLIVIA ·

Olivia wrote the last sentence of the visible-ink part of her letter to Rian.

This will probably be my last letter for a while because my final day of classes is next week. Then I go home. Then The Squire, Mother, and I sail for Europe.

Then, for the first time, Olivia shared more of her own news in invisible ink. Previously, she transcribed only stories from Topper in vinegar.

I can't believe I'm sharing this information with you. My roommate thinks I am continuously bloated.

I bought a bottle of apple cider vinegar at the grocery store in town so I can make my invisible-ink entries, but when I write, it fills the room with that pungent, vinegary smell. No kidding, it really stinks up the whole room. Nosy Caldie Montgomery asked me what was going on, so I had to make something up. I told her I had digestive problems. I proved it by pouring a gollop of vinegar into a glass of water and drinking it. It tasted awful.

Here is Topper's latest entry.

I start this letter acknowledging a dastardly deed perpetrated by two of my brethren, one free and one a slave. They conspired to abduct the daughter of a planter who owns an extensive farm near to the one in which I am in service. This young woman was known to be the most beautiful girl in the county.

They stole her right off her horse as she and her little brother rode home from a visit to a nearby plantation. Her brother, a tad of the age of 7, escaped the ambush and alerted his father, who in turn roused numerous neighbors.

The kidnappers dragged their captive to an island in the midst of a swamp, where they tied her up and gagged her, returned to their daily responsibilities, then visited her at night. On the third evening, the kidnappers were discovered by searchers. The young woman was rescued. The kidnappers fled. One was shot twice by musket balls that broke an arm and a leg. Knowing he could not escape, the rescue party left him where he lay.

The second kidnapper eluded capture for another day but was eventually tracked down and mangled by bloodhounds. His pursuers dragged him back to where the wounded kidnapper still lay. The consensus was that a swift hanging after a trial was too lenient a penalty for both of them to suffer. After discussion of numerous tortures, the party opted to strip them naked, stuff rags in their mouths, stake them out on their backs, and let buzzards and carrion crows peck them to death.

The following Sunday, which should be our day of rest, field hands and house servants from five farms in the area were forced to walk to this site, which for many of us is miles from the plantations where we are enslaved. By this time, the bodies of both men were in significant decay. The crows had attacked the eyes first. Then they tore open the bowels and fed upon the intestines.

* * * * *

· RIAN ·

Rather than return to the shop after her time in Hell, Rian decided to check up on Seamus at the distillery. She slid aside the door, entered Gallagher's Distillery, and saw her cousin in the semi-darkness near the stacked barrels.

"Just the person I wanted to talk to," he called as she approached Rumor Control. "Cousin, have you been giving away some of our whiskey?"

Rian heard no ire in Seamus's question. "Yeah, it makes a pretty good bribe. Railroad men don't immediately warm up to a kid who asks a lot of questions about their machines. I found that when I wave a pint of our whiskey in front of them, they loosen up pretty quick."

"How much have you given away?"

Rian poured herself a sip's worth of Number 5, her cousin's current favorite. "There's a list over on that table. Probably about five gallons."

Seamus kept making notations on his slate. "All in pint bottles? That's forty bribes, forty sessions. What do you talk to them about?"

"Locomotives, whether they're Krieger locomotives or somebody else's. What they like. What breaks. Safety stuff. How we can improve the next one. We're still making changes to the design for the *Standard*. Probably will be for months." Rian took a sip of Number Five and winced. *Damn, too bad I still don't like my own product.*

Seamus, oblivious to her taste test, continued to make notations on his slate. "Did Heinrich Aldridge put you up to this?"

"No, it was my idea. I needed an excuse to get away from the factory."

Seamus glanced up from his slate. "Why is that?"

"Because of the steam engine. It's been seven months since the explosion. I thought I was getting better, but I'm not."

Seamus regarded her for a long moment. "Maybe you're in the wrong profession."

"Seamus, that's not funny. You know I want to run Krieger Locomotive someday."

"Pardon my poor attempt at levity, but I was kind of serious. Your bribes have started to build a demand for our product. The maître d' at the United States Hotel and I have just cut a deal. We're selling to the richie-riches now."

THURSDAY, JULY 25

· SEAMUS ·

"Yeah, yeah, hold your horses, I'm coming," Seamus said as the pounding persisted outside the distillery door. He slid the heavy slider aside to find Hugh Callaghan standing in the rain. Dumbfounded, he stood there for a few seconds.

Hugh made no attempt to enter. "You know, you could build a door into this sliding monstrosity so you didn't have to work so hard every time somebody pays you a visit. Jaysus, kid, I thought you were the efficiency genius in this town. I figured that one out in ten seconds."

"Yeah, but this sliding monstrosity has some advantages. It keeps out unwanted visitors."

"You going to keep me standing in the rain all day, or are you going to invite me in?"

Seamus had already considered both. Finally: "Might as well come in. I'll give you a taste of Gallagher's Fine Whiskey."

"About time," Hugh said.

Seamus led Hugh to the array of bottles and poured them both a finger. "Sip this. It's not yet as smooth as it'll be in another year."

Hugh sniffed the glass and nodded tentative approval. He sipped, then winced. "Damn, that's potent. But it's already better than the swill we drink at Clancy's half the while."

"I've been distilling sixteen barrels a month for almost a year, so there's whiskey that'll be a year old in a couple of weeks and more in the queue. You're drinking my favorite. I'm selling a case of the less-good stuff to Braden McSweeney when he needs it."

"And the United States Hotel, I hear."

Seamus nodded but didn't feel a need to elaborate.

"Your whiskey's gaining quite a reputation around town, Seamus. Some of me boyos think you should be encouraged to widen your distribution, then take a cut of your larger pie."

A cold tingle crept up Seamus's spine. Just like the No Name Fire Brigade, Hugh's Ratters occasionally engaged in extortion. *Jaysus, this is a shakedown. I should have seen it coming.* "Is that what you want to do?"

Hugh sat in a chair in Rumor Control, his back to Seamus and the array of bottles. He put his feet up on the overturned apple crate. "The truce with your No Names is still working to our advantage. 'Nope,' I said, 'I've got something better in mind.'"

Seamus remained standing near the bottles. "And what is that?"

"The new constitution, the one that denied your African friends the right to vote."

"What about it?"

"There were some other changes you might be interested in. Under the old constitution, Philadelphia's aldermen were appointed by the governor. All any governor ever did was appoint men of English stock or maybe a krautbreath. Never a single Irishman. But now, all the aldermen in Philadelphia are elected by the voters in their district."

"Who are you going to get to run for alderman?"

"Me, and I'm asking for your support. Rumors of your good work in the whiskey business are making you a very popular man amongst our people despite your affinity for the African race. I figure if the Irish unite behind me, we can outvote the Germans who live in Moya."

"Hugh, I'm not sure I even like you. Why would I want to endorse you?"

"You know, kid, I asked myself the same question." Hugh, still sitting with his back to Seamus, lifted his empty whiskey glass over his shoulder. "Then I came up with an answer I think you'll appreciate: I would promise to take it easy on your Negro friends, that's why."

Seamus turned and picked up the bottle of Number 5. "An alderman settles petty disputes, acts like a justice of the peace, controls patronage."

"Don't get ahead of yourself, kid. I wouldn't be appointing any Africans to city positions, but I would promise to be a fair dispenser of justice when it comes to Black versus white."

"What if it's Black versus Irish?"

His glass was perched over his shoulder, unrefreshed, and Hugh gave it a little waggle. "Somewhat fair."

Seamus poured him a solid three fingers this time. "And would you give Siobhan and me your blessing? You just admitted I'm making something of myself."

"I know you see my daughter at McSweeney's most days. Tell me something: When you came home from Russia, Siobhan told me that, same as ever, you still didn't know who you were. You told her you'd let her know when you figured it out. Well, Seamus, who the hell are you?"

Seamus woofed out a deep breath, then his words spilled out. "I'm just a guy trying to make my way in a hard world. I've been tossed a few lucky breaks along the way, and I feel like I've seen them and taken advantage of them. I'm a proud Irishman, but I don't think I should better myself by increasing the misery of those who want the same sort of things I do. I can be a loyal friend or an unforgiving enemy. And right now, I'm sitting atop a distilling business that will make me rich."

"Good answer, kid. I think you might be the only man in this town who could give me daughter a run for her money. Go ahead and ask her."

FRIDAY, AUGUST 9

· OTTO ·

Otto read the sign above the slider on the three-story brick building: GALLAGHER'S DISTILLERY. He was pleased when Rian invited him to the Second Whiskey Tasting Party. He had heard mention a few times at the United States Hotel about a new distillery making some fine sipping whiskey but didn't connect it with Seamus's operation until recently. Seamus had previously told him it would be at least another two years before he started selling his product.

The slider was open to the interior. The murmur of conversation punctuated by occasional laughter rippled into the evening air. Otto knocked and peered into the dimness of the cavernous building, lit solely by two whale oil lanterns.

"Uncle Otto," Seamus said as he approached, carrying one of the lanterns. "This is our Second Annual Tasting Party. How good of you to join us." Seamus grabbed Otto by the crook of his elbow and led him to a cluster of people seated around the other lantern sitting on an upside-down apple crate. "Welcome to Rumor Control, where we solve the world's problems. Let me introduce you to Ruben Hasselbach, the brains of the outfit."

Hasselbach sat away from the group. Even though the lantern light barely reached the man, Otto could tell he was unwell. Otto opted for a more upbeat greeting than his usual bow but kept his distance. "How good to see you again, sir. Rumors of your fine whiskey are already spreading around Philadelphia. I feel obligated to see for myself if they are true."

Hasselbach merely responded with a brief nod.

Seamus gestured toward Rian, who was sitting in the circle. "And of course, you know my primary investor. Turns out, it's most likely your daughter is responsible for those rumors. Apparently, she has other skills besides locomotive design."

Otto chose to ignore the locomotive design comment. "And what are they?"

"She's an advertising genius."

This was a new wrinkle for Otto. "Why? How? What has my daughter done?"

"Now, mind you, I didn't know she was doing this until recently. She's been interviewing railroad men where they work. Most of them aren't initially interested in talking with a youngster until she flashes a pint of Gallagher's Fine Whiskey. Bribe in hand, they answer her questions. But . . . and this is before my product is even aged a year yet . . . they sip our whiskey, they like it, and they're talking about it. It might not have been her intention, but your daughter is building a demand for our whiskey before it's properly aged."

Once again, Otto found himself flooded with information about Rian that did not please him. *She is meeting with men; most likely pretending to be a boy. She bribes them with whiskey. What questions could she possibly be asking them?*

Seamus continued his introductions. "These lads over here are all members of the United No Name Fire Brigade. You know Dylan, of course. That's Jimmy, Kevin Fitzpatrick, Jameson, and Silken. Braden McSweeney has taken the evening off from his saloon to sample our whiskey at the one-year mark . . . And this is my girlfriend, Siobhan."

Otto gave Siobhan a courtly bow. "I have heard about you, Miss Callaghan, but we have never met. I am happy to finally make your acquaintance." The black-haired beauty was as attractive as the rumors said she was. "I understand you are back working for Mr. McSweeney."

"I had to. The lads knew someone had to keep Braden in line."

A chorus of chuckles and *hear-hears* rippled around the circle.

Otto addressed the group. "It appears I am late to the tasting party. Have you come to any conclusions about the whiskey yet?"

All eyes turned toward Hasselbach, who cleared his throat before he spoke. "Oh, I have an opinion, but I think it's more important to hear from the man who already serves it."

Braden McSweeney wobbled a bit as he stood. "Well, of course I haven't come to any conclusion about which of the six recipes still in contention are preferable. That will take quite a bit more sampling this evening and will be a long and carefully considered process." Another chorus of *hear-hears*. "But as a saloonkeeper with a reputation to maintain, and as a connoisseur of the Water of Life, every batch I've sampled this evening is better than what I used to sell at the saloon before Seamus started supplying me with his rejects. I can only imagine what they will taste like next year, but I'm already putting in me reservation to attend next year's tasting party."

Whoops and huzzahs rose from the group amidst the clinking of glasses.

Seamus again grabbed Otto by the crook of his arm. "Come over here, Uncle. Let me get you started." He led Otto to a wide board set atop two barrels, where six bottles were arrayed. In front of each was a scrap of wooden shingle with pencil markings identifying the batch.

Otto had lost interest in the whiskey. "Seamus, why did Rian want to interview those railroad men?"

"I think she's passionate about continuing to improve your locomotives. One way to do that is to talk to the men who use them. Gotta hand it to her. I wouldn'ta thought of that."

Seamus's words harkened back to a conversation Otto had with Heinrich months ago. *Passion and expertise: the formula for a successful business. And my daughter increasingly exhibits both. When will she ever grow out of this? And what young man will ever be strong enough to take her on? And if she doesn't let up, when will the inevitable rejection happen and what form will it take?*

SATURDAY, SEPTEMBER 7

· OTTO ·

Otto grew impatient as the train inched its way down the Belmont Incline. *I know the engine driver is following safety guidelines, but I could walk the rest of the way faster than this.* For what felt like the tenth time, he consulted his pocket watch. *Six o'clock. The driver could not make up the time. Jules will have left the factory by the time I get there. I will have to tell him tomorrow.*

Otto chose not to dwell on his irritation at being late and instead focused on all that was right. *I sit in a passenger car of my own design that Krieger Coach built less than a year ago.* As the train plodded through the darkness of the covered bridge that spanned the Schuylkill, the *choosh . . . choosh . . . choosh* of the locomotive became almost deafening . . . *an* Eagle-*class Krieger locomotive.* They emerged on the east side of the river into Philadelphia twilight. Krieger cast-iron wheels screeched on Krieger rails as the train made its arcing turn onto Broad Street, a signal of the almost-end to his journey.

Yes, we have accomplished a lot. Although this depression has hurt so many, it did not kill the Krieger companies. We are very fortunate. Otto peered out the window and caught a brief glimpse of activity outside the Krieger Locomotive factory a few hundred feet to his left. *Everyone should have left by now. I wonder if Quinton is installing the crane.*

Three blocks farther on, the train came to its squeaky, smoky, jerky halt at the Vine Street station. Otto was the first one out of his passenger car. The brakeman tossed Otto's carpetbag down from the roof, and Otto caught it without breaking stride. He dodged other disembarking passengers, gaggles of people reuniting, a railroad clerk pulling mail sacks off the flatcar. Rather than head home, Otto walked north on Broad Street to investigate the activity at the factory.

Otto confirmed his suspicions from a block away: The track upon which finished locomotives were rolled out of the factory was now straddled by three giant, square, upside-down U's built of stout 12 x12 oak timbers. *Das war schnell* [That was quick], Otto thought. *They had not even started this project when I left four days ago.*

Otto had seen the plans before he left. Two massive timbers met atop the middle upside-down U and cantilevered out three feet beyond the outer U's.

Two figures, silhouetted in the waning light, sat on the cantilever that extended almost over Broad Street. One was crane builder Quinton Schott and the other was . . . Rian. *She is incessant. She makes alliances with older men who tolerate her shenanigans . . . businessmen she can mine for information.*

"We thought that might be your train," Quinton called as Otto approached. "How come you're late?"

Otto stuffed down his irritation (or was it bewilderment?) at his daughter. He liked Schott and respected his work. Otto walked within fifteen feet of the new crane, dropped his carpetbag, and gazed up at Quinton and his daughter. "Train maintenance crew fixing a rail that had come loose. Where are your men?"

"Dismissed 'em. They put in a long day. Your project's pretty much done. Gotta install the winches yet." Quinton gestured to a wooden ladder nailed onto one of the middle vertical timbers. "Come on up. If you hurry, you'll still be able to see for a mile down Broad Street from up here."

In order to get to Quinton and Rian, Otto would have to climb the twenty-five-foot ladder, walk atop the U to the cantilevered timber, and walk on the timber for twenty feet. Otto shook his head. "No thank you." He nodded at Rian, silently giving her permission to tell Schott.

"*Vater*'s afraid of heights," she said to Quinton. Then, back down to him, "Did you get the contract?"

Otto grinned up at his daughter. "Come on down and I will tell you."

Quinton rose, walked atop the horizontal timber without hesitation, turned onto the top of the U, took four more strides, swung onto the ladder, and descended. Rian sat on her perch for a few moments longer before she followed him.

Quinton shook Otto's hand. "Welcome home, Otto. I think you'll like your new crane. It's simpler than the one we're building for Gamaliel Leonard."

Otto gazed up at the new structure, admiring its simplicity. "I am happy we are doing this. I think Downing's idea will change the industry. We are the first company I know of to deliver a fully assembled locomotive to a distant customer, but we certainly will not be the last."

Quinton followed Otto's gaze, admiring the fruits of his craft, then said, "What do you mean, 'Downing's idea'?"

Otto pulled his gaze away from the crane and turned to Schott. "This was Gerald's idea. He was with us less than a week before he came up with it. It was fortunate we hired him away from Baldwin when we did."

By this time, Rian had climbed down the ladder. She picked up Otto's carpetbag. "Ready? I want to hear about your trip. Did you get the contract?"

Otto grinned. "The *Cumberland Valley Railroad* wants me to design a sleeping car. I have never heard of such a thing . . . certainly would never have thought of it, but if they like my design, we will build at least one." Otto turned to Schott and gave him a respectful salute. "Thank you for building this crane so quickly, Quinton. We expect the *Enola* back in port on the seventeenth. Will Gamaliel Leonard's crane be ready?"

"Oh, it'll be ready, but I may have to work through the night a couple of times."

"Problems?"

"My supplier of angle iron went out of business. My new guy won't deliver until he checks my credit."

Rian turned to Otto. "*Vater*, we have plenty of angle iron in the locomotive shop. Quinton could use that and then replace it."

"Talk to Gerald on Monday, Quinton. I am sure it will be fine with him."

Quinton nodded in appreciation. "I'll do that. Thank you. Otto, about Downing—"

"Quinton, it has been a long day. I am tired. It is time for us to declare our workday over. Perhaps I will see you next week when you talk to Downing. I will send a message over to him so he will be prepared with his answer."

* * * * *

· OLIVIA ·

The Tucker family's three months in Paris were characterized by an absence of conflict. The Parisian social season resoundingly eclipsed anything Philadelphia had to offer, so Mother eventually put aside her snit with Papa. With no access to concubines, Papa behaved himself—at least for a while. And away from the slave system's daily cruelties and the reminders that the Tucker wealth was built on the backs of slaves, Olivia called a hiatus to her habit of sniping at her father. The family's differences, for the summer at least, were papered over.

By day, Mother attended garden parties, met friends for coffee at streetside cafés, and strolled the many parks of Paris. In the evenings, she attended dinners, balls, the ballet, and theater. The longer Papa was away from the stresses of Long Pond, the more he relaxed. He developed a friendship with Louis Cass, America's ambassador to France, rooted in their mutual admiration for slavery, Indian removal, and brandy. Papa also traveled frequently to find markets for his Carolina Gold. Olivia suspected another motivation behind these trips—a relationship with a countess who had been flirting with Papa at one of the first balls they attended—but she refrained from saying anything.

Olivia thrived from the moment she set foot on French soil. She relished the stagecoach ride from Le Havre to Paris along the pastoral banks of the Seine. Its obligatory stop to tour the Cathedral at Rouen hinted at the grandeur to come. Each day in Paris brought a new opportunity to practice her French, shop along the Champs-Élysées, or wander aimlessly in vast museums.

She took art lessons from Monsieur Giddeaux, who spoke no English but grasped her hand and encouraged bold, confident brush strokes. He taught her much about the use of light and negative space. She stood for hours copying paintings in the Louvre, and Monsieur Giddeaux described her copies as "*Merveilleuse!*"

She toured Les Invalides and Notre-Dame, walked along the pebbled pathways of the Tuileries and through the Arc de Triomphe. She climbed to the top of Montmartre and then farther up into the basilica of Sacré-Cœur.

Best of all, the age barrier so rigidly adhered to in balls of Charleston and Philadelphia was more relaxed amongst the French, and the many American expatriates in Paris took their cues accordingly. In these gala gatherings, fifteen-year-old Olivia danced until two in the morning. She heard numerous times that she "just missed" the novelist James Fenimore Cooper, even though he had returned to the United States years ago. She waltzed in the presence of American artist Samuel F. B. Morse and the "Citizen King" Louis-Philippe.

In Paris, Olivia sensed that her body was beginning to change, and men were noticing. For the first time, she embraced, rather than resisted, wearing a corset. Her mother found a seamstress whose taste ran toward long-waisted bodices, tight sleeves, skirts that billowed under layers of petticoats, and hemlines that skimmed the floor—all of which suited Olivia's emerging silhouette.

Well-dressed swells—their fashionable cut-back swallowtail jackets and tapered pants not yet seen on the streets of Columbia and Charleston—tipped their top hats as they strolled along the pathways of the Bois de Boulogne. It was not unusual for them to give Olivia a long second gaze. They appeared to be pleased with what they saw.

Her mother, always at her side in these instances, surprised her by encouraging some degree of flirtation. "Practice in Paris, dear," Mother suggested one sunny afternoon. "But focus on the prize. Barnwell won't know what hit him." Olivia thought the off-handed statement indicated that Paris was spinning its magic on her mother as well, but she couldn't imagine flirting with Barney when she returned to America. He was far too oafish.

The end of the Tuckers' Parisian summer came all too soon. In the middle of August, they packed their trunks and embarked on their long, arduous, three-week trip home: Paris to Le Havre by stage, Le Havre to Bristol by steamship, Bristol to New York on the gigantic *Great Western* (the same steamship that brought Rian back to America on its maiden voyage the previous year), and the coastal steamer *Carolina Princess* from New York to Charleston.

Now, almost a year since she was first sent off to school, Olivia considered her brief layover at Long Pond a mere pause before she returned to Columbia for her second year at Barhamville. At Long Pond, all the papering-over of her many differences with her parents fell away. It happened because of a bolt of French silk cloth.

Mother, enamored of the legions of liveried servants who attended guests at Parisian dinner parties, bought bolt after bolt of silks in complementary colors so the Long Pond house staff could be clothed to the nines when she entertained. Olivia, thinking Cook might like to be gussied up on such occasions as well, bought enough hunter-green silk to make a dress for her.

Olivia descended the stairs from her bedroom, carrying the silk. She stepped down into the foyer as her father exited his office, shutting the door behind him. Papa had been in a mood since yesterday, when the farm supervisor presented him with a pound of East Indian rice he had bought at a store in Charleston. It cost less than Long Pond's Carolina Gold right off the plantation's dock on the Cooper River.

"What is that, Whiskey?" Papa asked. His eyes barely rose from a letter he was reading as he walked.

"It's some cloth I bought for Cook."

Papa lowered the letter. "That's silly. Cook has no need to get dressed up."

"Remember that time you entertained Governor Butler? He loved Cook's garlic crabs so much he demanded she come out and take a bow."

"Butler had guzzled too much of my brandy before dinner. He was a little drunk at the time."

Olivia hugged the silk to her chest. "But it was a sweet gesture. Cook works hard to make your dinners flawless. She cooks recipes you love. Why not give her a moment in the sun at the end of one of Mother's spectacular dinner parties. She could come out slick as a mink in her dress, take her bow, and go back to the kitchen."

"Anyone we entertain at Long Pond would frown on us giving special attention to a slave."

Olivia felt her plan, based on an innocent act of generosity, going awry. "You give special attention to Mercury when he wins races at the Jockey Club. You even put your arm around him."

"That's different."

"How?"

"It reflects well on Long Pond to have the fastest horses in the county."

"But it reflects well on Long Pond to have the best cook in the county."

"I do not want to pamper our slaves. It would not be received well by our neighbors—"

"That's what this is about? Neighbors who would disapprove of treating a slave with kindness?"

Her father freed his hands by laying his letters on a nearby table. For a moment, Olivia feared he would strike her, but she didn't shy away. Instead, her father slowly grasped the silk cloth and tried to tug it away from her. "Even if I thought this was a good idea—which I don't—Cook would be too busy in the kitchen to change in anticipation of a bow for our guests."

Olivia acknowledged her father might be right in this case. *Cook is always frazzled and cranky during dinner parties.* She clung to the silk. "Then I'll give it to Emblee."

Randolph Tucker grasped more tightly at the silk. "That won't be possible. Emblee is no longer with us."

Olivia felt the blood drain to her toes. "Why, what happened? Where is she?" Her grip on the silk loosened.

Papa pulled the silk away. "I told Mr. Boseman to take her to auction while we were in France."

"How can he do that? I thought she was being used as collateral."

Papa did a double-take at Olivia's reference to collateral. "She was." He shrugged. "It's just a name on a sheet of paper. Your uncle won't mind as long as there's six slaves available. The price of slaves is falling. You won't be here anymore for her to attend to. We figured we should get what cash we can for her before the money starts flowing back in a year from now."

Olivia felt the rage build within her. "But . . . but that's so cruel. How can you live with yourself?" She hesitated for a moment, then plunged ahead. "You know, this summer, it felt like you changed. You were softer . . . likable. It's this place, isn't it? It's Long Pond that makes you so evil. I hate this place."

Her father glared back at her; his expression unable to mask his counter-rage. "Olivia, it seems your year at school—your summer in Paris—has not yet tempered your willfulness . . . nor your misguided affection for the servants. Your actions prompt me to explore alternatives to returning to Long Pond next summer. Perhaps the Wilkinsons will put you up at Thousand Oaks. Maybe they can teach you what we have failed to do."

"And what is that?"

"Oh, there are many things." Her father held up the silk as evidence. "But what comes to mind right away is that our way of life is maintained by not confusing the help with unnecessary kindness."

* * * * *

Olivia retreated to her room and threw herself onto her bed. *I hate him. I hate him so much.*

The ramifications of her father's disclosures were huge. The loss of Emblee—sold to some unknown new owner—was a punch to the stomach. Of secondary importance, but still a bitter pill, was the realization that Olivia wouldn't be spending the summer she turned sixteen in Charleston. Papa had ripped this most important of all summers away from her. *I'll talk to Mother about this. She won't let this happen.*

For as long as she could remember, Olivia knew she would "come out" at the Charleston Debutante Ball in 1840. She knew this because her mother had rhapsodized about it endlessly. How coming out was the threshold; girlhood on one side, womanhood on the other. How her mother's own coming out was the best night of her life. Her escort. Her dress. Her dance card. Her beaus. The presentation to the cream of Charleston Society. The St. James Bow. The smell of the gardenias. The candlelight. The staircase. The music. The dancing. *"Oh, Olivia, the dancing is magical. All eyes are on the debutantes. And—and I would only say this to you, dear—I was the prettiest deb that year. All eyes were on me."*

And now all that was gone. *Mother couldn't possibly agree with Papa. "The only thing better than coming out is having your daughter come out," she told me once.* Olivia leapt off her bed, scurried downstairs, and found her mother in the tea room. "Mother, Papa says I won't be allowed to stay here next summer. That means I won't be able to come out. You have to speak up for me. Please make him change his decision. He made it on the fly . . . when he was so angry with me."

"The decision to forgo your debutante ball? Oh my goodness, dear, how could you even imagine coming out given your current sensibilities?"

"You mean my hatred of slavery?"

"I mean your distaste for our entire way of life."

Olivia turned to leave the tea room.

"But I will make you a deal, dear," her mother said before she reached the door. "You drop this nonsense . . . all of it . . . and I will talk to your father. You can still save this, but it is entirely up to you."

TUESDAY, SEPTEMBER 10

Committee Formed to Defend Slave Mutineers
Exclusive to the Philadelphia Independent
From New London, Connecticut
By Harold Foote

A committee of concerned citizens has been formed to defend 53 enslaved Africans who freed themselves by revolting aboard the Spanish ship *La Amistad*.

In early July, the Africans overwhelmed their captors as *La Amistad* approached the island of Cuba, killed the captain and most of the crew, and ordered the remaining crew members to sail them to Africa. Instead, the crew members navigated north as far as Long Island Sound. On August 26, the ship was waylaid by the crew of the USS *Washington* and escorted to New London, Connecticut.

Originally thought to be Cuban slaves born in the New World and being transported from Cuba to various plantations in the West Indies, a new and more complicated story has come to light. In fact, the Africans were kidnapped in their home continent earlier this year and transported to the West Indies, an act that was declared illegal by the United States and Great Britain more than 30 years ago, but never by Spain.

The fate of these 53 souls now hangs with the U.S. Circuit Court in Hartford, Connecticut. If convicted, they will be returned to enslavement in Cuba and tried for mutiny, which is punishable by death. However, if their act of mutiny, which they conducted to reclaim their freedom, is declared to be a human right, the ramifications of this case will reverberate nationally and internationally for decades to come.

This correspondent will return to Connecticut as events dictate to keep readers abreast of developments. Funds to support the legal defense of the Africans are being accepted by Mr. Lewis Tappan of New York City.

* * * * *

· RIAN ·

On Tuesday, Rian and a number of workers at Krieger Coach mounted the wheels on the second of the tandem freight wagons that would transport *Number 14* to the Johns & Leonard Pier. Unlike the scores of carriage wheels she had made since she was eleven, these wheels were far from elegant. They appeared almost medieval in their beefiness but would serve their purpose: supporting their one-eighth share of a fifteen-ton locomotive.

Jules moseyed over as Rian and the workers stepped back to admire their work. "Your wagons are stout enough. . . ."

Rian smiled, because her mentor was being kind. Unlike every carriage Krieger Coach had built in the past fifteen years, these two wagons were not designed as showpieces. The beds were made of six-by-six oak and had no sides. The only difference between the two wagons was that the tongue of the lead wagon was built to be hooked up to a team of twelve mules. The tongue of the following wagon would hitch to the lead wagon.

"But will your engine crush them?"

"I've done the math. Each wagon is stouter than a Conestoga wagon. Tomorrow is test day. We'll know for sure by the end of the day, but my money says they'll do their job."

"You're betting?"

"Of course. It's the only way I can shut up the doubters."

* * * * *

· OLIVIA ·

This year, with generous rainfall, the water was up and the Santee Canal was passable. The trip from Charleston to Columbia would be all by water—much more leisurely than last year's train and stagecoach ordeal. The steamboat *Granby* paused at Long Pond's landing long enough for Olivia and her mother to board, then continued on its way up the Cooper River to the Santee Canal.

Primarily a workhorse, the fifty-foot *Granby* had four passenger cabins. Had it been traveling downriver, it would have been loaded with bales of cotton—each six feet long, four feet wide, four feet tall and weighing five hundred pounds—stacked two high on its open deck. But since it was traveling upriver, the captain accepted whatever cargo was available: furniture, supplies, light machinery, a cow on a tether, and men and women traveling on the cheap who kept out of the sun under tarps they had strung willy-nilly on the deck.

Unwilling to mingle with the lesser elements, Penelope Tucker spent most of her time in her cabin. Olivia initially stayed in her cabin as well, but for a different reason: She was angry with her parents. As her feelings intensified, she sought revenge. She had a plan.

Olivia put all her anger into a letter to Rian Krieger.

Dear Rian,

I write to you from aboard the steamboat Granby. *We are on the Cooper River, heading for the Santee Canal and on to Columbia. I hope your summer has gone well. I have a lot of news from my summer in France, but that is not why I am writing this letter. Please pass this information on to you-know-who for the next publication of you-know-what.*

For years, rice from the South Carolina Lowcountry has been referred to as "Carolina Gold" as rice planters grew rich off the backs of enslaved people. However, in recent years, many foreign rice growers have started rice farms in Burma and the Dutch East Indies. Consequently, in a store in Charleston, you can now buy a pound of rice grown halfway around the world for less than the same quantity of Carolina Gold grown two miles up the Cooper River.

Rice planters, my father among them, are now in deep financial trouble. In order to make ends meet, they have taken out loans from Northern banks. Papa's is with Uncle George's Bank of Industry. They put up their slaves as collateral. However, sometimes the collateralled slaves die or get injured, and other times the planters sell them. The banks are being cheated.

Please take out any specifics that can be traced back to me, then do with this information what you will.

Love,
You-know-who

P.S. News of the slaves who rebelled aboard the Amistad *arrived here last week. Papa has been attending meetings ever since. The fear, of course, is that the slaves of South Carolina will hear about it and take inspiration. Question: Why would you oppress people when there are more of them than there are of you? Wouldn't you figure that, sooner or later, they would have their fill of your abuse and slit your throat? That's exactly what Papa fears right now.*

Olivia read and reread her letter. She dripped some candle wax onto the folded letter but used her thumb—not her *OT* stamp—to seal the letter.

At the first set of locks on the Santee Canal—a triple—she stepped off the boat and approached the lockmaster. He stood with arms crossed—idle for the moment but observing—waiting for the water gushing into the first lock to raise the *Granby* eight feet.

"Is there a post office nearby?" Olivia asked with a smile.

The lockmaster gave Olivia a quick study and pointed down the road to the south. "Moncks Corner. Three miles from here. We'll have the *Granby* through the locks long before you can get there and back." Then he spied Olivia's letter. "I can take that for you. I'm going into town tomorrow. I've got a stack of others I'm doing the same for."

Olivia surveyed the lock. Her mother was nowhere to be seen. Other passengers were admiring the lock, holding the lines as the boat rose, or stretching their legs on shore. She handed the letter to the lockmaster and fished out a few pennies from her purse. He promptly stuffed the letters and pennies into his pocket and walked away.

With her secretive mission behind her, Olivia saw no reason to spend time in her cabin except to sleep. The *Granby* steamed through the rest of the canal without incident, then headed north on the Congaree River. Expectations were that the trip would take three days, but for Olivia, they would be leisurely, spacious days spent reading on deck, not the arduous, dusty train-and-stagecoach days of a year ago.

* * * * *

· SEAMUS ·

Seamus was late for his regular meeting at McSweeney's because Siobhan's sister was late getting to him with Siobhan's Sunday dress.

When he entered the saloon, Conor was sitting at their usual table in the back, their coffees already waiting. Conor wasn't smiling. He held up only his index finger as Seamus approached.

"That's it? Only one ship?" Seamus asked as he slid into his chair. "What the hell is going on?"

Conor sipped his coffee. "They're starting to get concerned at the Merchants' Exchange. That's only five ships in the past week. We had more than forty in one day a year ago. Some people are talking about the depression coming back worse than before."

Let's get this meeting over with, Seamus said to himself. *I've got more important things to attend to today.* "Tell me about the ship."

"The brig *Daisy* entered the Delaware this morning. Forty thousand cow hides from California."

Seamus frowned. "Cowhides are tough to steal. They're heavy and cumbersome. It'll take a horse and wagon to get them off the wharf. Let's toss this one to Hugh. If he wants his boyos to work that hard for a few bucks, that's his business."

"In that case, I'm off." Conor drained his mug. "What's in the package?"

Seamus didn't want to jinx himself. "I'll tell you tomorrow." He watched Conor leave the saloon and close the door behind him. *The lack of traffic on the Delaware is concerning, but I won't worry about that today. I've got more important things to attend to.* Seamus checked his pocket watch. It was five o'clock. *Siobhan should be arriving right about now.* The door opened. *Bingo, right on time.*

Seamus's girlfriend gave him a smile and a wave but detoured into the kitchen to check in with Braden. Moments later, she reappeared and walked over to Seamus. "Braden said I'm not working tonight."

"Yeah, I asked him to give you the night off." He rose, pecked Siobhan on the cheek, and handed her the package. "Here, put this on."

Siobhan untied the string and opened the brown paper. "My Sunday dress? What's this for?"

"Put it on and you'll find out."

Seamus's plan had gone pretty well so far. Siobhan changed into her Sunday dress without asking questions. She hooked her arm tight into his on their walk north, holding him close. *She knows I'm going to propose. I know she knows. She just doesn't know where I'll ask her.*

Siobhan was all smiley and chatty until they turned left onto Chestnut Street, then she became quiet. When Seamus stopped in front of the United States Hotel, she unhooked her arm, turned, and faced him. "I am *not* going into that building. That man humiliated us the last time. I won't allow that to happen to us again."

"Trust me. It won't happen again."

"What are you thinking? What are you trying to prove?"

"Siobhan, I'm going to do what I'm going to do. You can come to your own conclusions." He offered his arm. "Come on. I think we'll enjoy this."

Seamus tried not to act like a bumpkin as they walked through the hotel lobby . . . tried not to gape at the crystal chandeliers hanging from the high ceiling or the potted palms placed next to overstuffed leather couches. Men sat,

Quintin, D. S. A. & Rea, T. C. (1840) United States Hotel, Chestnut Street, Philadelphia. United States of America Philadelphia Pennsylvania, 1840. Philadelphia: P.S. Duval Lithography. [Photograph] Retrieved from the Library of Congress

smoked cigars, and leaned into private conversations, or they stood, top hats in hand, and talked in small groups. A few men interrupted their conversations to admire Siobhan. *Eat your hearts out, you gumps.* A clerk smiled at them from behind his marble-topped registration desk. Seamus steered them to James's alcove, next to the French doors that opened to the dining room.

James looked up from his podium and smiled. "Ah, Mr. Gallagher, right on time."

"Good afternoon, James. I'd like to introduce my friend Siobhan Callaghan."

"Ah, Miss Callaghan, I've been eager to meet you. Mr. Gallagher references you frequently in our conversations. I daresay the reality exceeds his descriptions."

"I believe we met here one time before," Siobhan responded icily.

James didn't skip a beat, and the smile never left his face. "Perhaps you mistake me for one of my substitutes. I'm sure I would have remembered. Mr. Gallagher, I have the Jefferson Room reserved for you. Please follow me."

Siobhan glanced at Seamus, her eyes wide with incredulity, then followed James.

The maître d' escorted them along the periphery of the massive dining room. Silverware clinked. Plates clattered. Waiters dashed with trays held high. Men chatted and laughed and smoked cigars.

The Jefferson Room was separated from the men-only dining room by a set of French doors and a half-wall topped to the ceiling with panes of glass. James stood aside, making way for the couple to enter. The sanctum held a table for two and a breakfront. Currier and Ives prints hung on three walls. "I had the table set so you're facing one another. Some couples prefer to sit next to one another so they can see and be seen. If that would be your preference, I'll have Andrew move your place settings."

"This will be fine. Thank you, James," said Siobhan, now completely thawed.

James pulled a chair out for Siobhan, waited for her to take her seat, then scooched the chair forward for her. As Seamus sat, James placed a leather-bound menu in front of him. "Mr. Gallagher, you will see we had new menus printed for the fall. Gallagher's Fine Whiskey has been added to our extensive list of beverages . . . And now, I will take my leave. Andrew will be in shortly to take your orders. I highly recommend the squab."

Seamus reached across the table and grasped Siobhan's hands. "Siobhan. . . ."

"Yes, you amazing man," Siobhan said, "I will happily marry you."

WEDNESDAY, SEPTEMBER 11

· RIAN ·

Despite her bravado with Jules the previous day, Rian didn't sleep well. Today, the entire shop would learn if the concept of delivering an intact, fifteen-ton locomotive to a ship was viable. Today was Test Day.

Granted, the men thought all this was The Trout's idea. And granted, both Jules and her father had approved her design for the wagons. But Rian knew that if the wagons failed, everyone would blame her because she had built them (of course, with the assistance of various Krieger Coach workers). Although confident, she was relieved when The Trout demanded they test the entire delivery system by working through every step, from factory to ship.

Workers from all three Krieger factories were there to watch. Men from Krieger Rail delivered fifty sixteen-foot-long cast-iron rails—collectively far more than *Number 14*'s fifteen tons—to Quinton Schott's new three-upside-down-U's crane outside Krieger Locomotive. Under his direction, men simultaneously rotated three cranks that turned a myriad of gears and pulleys to raise three chains that lifted the entire bundle of fifty rails. The crane didn't break a sweat. Demonstrating her confidence in Quinton's design and construction, Rian led two mules that hauled the new tandem transport wagons under the bundle. Then the men reversed direction on the cranks and slowly . . . slowly lowered the bundle onto the wagons. Although the wagons creaked in protest under the weight of the load, they didn't collapse.

Rian had the satisfaction of seeing losing betters paying off winners, but feigned disinterest. She would collect her winnings later. She also noted her father standing between Jules and The Trout. They watched the proceedings with their hands in their pockets, chatting quietly. Otto was smiling, but Rian had no idea if it was because the crane worked or because the wagons worked. Either way, her father was pleased, which was good enough for her.

Quinton and Heinrich danced awkwardly around each other as they determined who was in charge of securing the rails to the wagons. Rian and Bennie Holt gathered ten more mules from Kent's Livery across Broad Street. It took an hour to hook them up to the lead transport wagon.

Jules broke away from Otto and The Trout, and approached Rian with a smile. "Will you be the driver of this expedition?"

Rian regarded the length of the twelve-mule team. "I don't know these mules. Jimmy Kent got them for us. He doesn't know which of them, if any, have been trained as lead mules. I figure I'll grab the lead mule by the halter and start walking."

Jules nodded in agreement, then held up a whistle. "I'll walk behind your wagons. If you hear this, stop."

Rian smiled back at Jules. "Think we'll need to stop?"

"If we do, it won't be because of your wagons. They're doing what they were built for."

Rian gently grabbed the lead mule by the halter and started walking. The mule, then the rest of the team, obediently followed. The wagons, creaking and groaning under their load, did the same. Eight cast-iron tires rumbled hard on cobblestones, frequently encountering a misplaced paver with a *thunk!* To Rian, each *thunk!* sounded like an opportunity for something to break.

* * * * *

· OTTO ·

The entourage departed for the Johns & Leonard Pier. Otto loved this kind of event because it was so spectacular: twelve mules, a set of tandem wagons the likes of which the city had never seen, a bundle of rails. *Yes*, Otto thought, *the city will take note, and it will be surpassed tomorrow when they see the same thing with a fully assembled locomotive.*

Gerald Downing, whose creative thinking brought this day about, led the way with two other Krieger Locomotive workers acting as outliers, keeping oncoming traffic at a distance. Following Downing, Rian led the mules in a wide arc from under the crane. The mules and the loaded wagons continued turning until they were headed east on James Street.

The wagons squeaked and creaked but held up under their load. Truth be told, there was nothing elegant about them. *But that is what their purpose calls for: a beefy sturdiness. Once again, Rian surprises me—no, she impresses me. What will I do with her? Will I ever get her out of the factories and interested in finding a husband?*

His musings were interrupted when Quinton Schott approached him. "Otto, are you walking to the pier with us?"

Otto nodded. "I would not miss this. Downing's idea puts our little shop at the forefront of the industry. It will be fun to beat Baldwin to the punch for a change."

"Yes, I want to talk to you about that," said Schott.

"Beating Baldwin to the punch?"

"No, what you refer to as 'Downing's idea.' I believe you're under a false impression. Your foreman didn't think up this plan. This whole thing was your daughter's idea."

Numerous pedestrians gawked at their procession. Some wagon drivers heading north or south on cross streets expressed irritation that twelve mules and a set of tandem wagons were delaying their missions. Otto ignored them. "No, it was Downing's idea. A few days after I hired him, I came to him with a problem and he immediately offered the solution. I remember being very impressed."

At the end of James Street, their route jigged north on Ninth, then jogged back east on Noble. Quinton followed the wagons. "When did you hire him?"

"The first week in February. Why?"

"I met Rian when I was clearing the wreckage of the Gray's Ferry bridge. She called to me from inside what remained of the bridge on the east bank and asked me how much weight my crane could lift. The flood occurred January 26. It couldn't have been more than three days later that we talked."

"No, I am sure it was Downing's idea," Otto repeated. *Downing wouldn't have lied to me.* "Rian would have told me if this had been her idea."

"You should check with Gamaliel Leonard when we get to the pier. I know Rian barged into his office soon after she talked to me. Gam didn't know she was a girl the entire time. Thought she was some ballsy boy who enticed him to meet with him with a pint of whiskey."

"Whiskey? Are you sure of this?" *At the tasting party, Seamus told me, "Most men aren't initially interested in talking with a youngster until she flashes a pint of Gallagher's Fine Whiskey in front of them."*

Quinton nodded. "Yes, I'm sure. He told me the story when we were planning his crane. I'm the one who told him Rian is a girl."

* * * * *

The Johns & Leonard Pier was located at the end of Noble Street. There, waiting for its test lift, was Gamaliel Leonard's new crane—also built by Quinton Schott. The man had designed a totally different machine than the triple-upside-down-U's crane at the locomotive factory. This one was built of wrought iron and pivoted atop a massive concrete base.

Otto watched Rian as she brought the mules to a halt next to the steamship *Enola. She has never led a large team of mules before, yet she knew what she did not know and figured out how to get the team here without an incident.* After his daughter tied the lead mule to a hitching post, Otto waved to her to join him. Her task complete, Rian nodded to Quinton as he climbed aboard the lead wagon. She scurried to Otto.

Gamaliel Leonard exited from his pier office and strode over to them. "Herr Krieger, welcome. Hello again, Rian. I see your wagons worked. And the mules cooperated?"

Rian nodded. "The pressure's off me now," she said to both her father and Leonard. "Everything I designed worked. The mules were easy. I feel like a thousand bucks."

Leonard leaned into Rian, giving her an avuncular nudge. "And how about Quinton's cranes? How do you feel about them?"

Leonard's physicalness surprised Otto. *Yet again an older man who demonstrates familiarity with her.*

Rian studied the new Johns & Leonard crane. "I guess I had great confidence in Quinton's triple-U crane back at our shop. This one? Well, I have great confidence in Quinton."

Gam Leonard chuckled. "Well said, Rian. Well said."

My daughter jokes with Leonard, a businessman three times her age, and he reacts as if she were a gifted apprentice. He knows she is a girl. He doesn't seem angry she initially deceived him.

Leonard gestured toward the crane. "And do you have money on this leg of the process? Will my new crane do its job?"

"I put a ten-dollar bet down that everything would work . . . my wagons, the mules, our new crane, and your new crane."

"Ten dollars! So perhaps your success today—and your confidence—will shut up some of your detractors at Krieger Locomotive?"

Leonard knows things about my daughter's struggles at work that she has not shared with me.

Rian hesitated; Otto assumed because he was overhearing the interplay. "Probably not, but today will give Quinton's reputation a well-deserved boost."

"Well," said Leonard, "let's see if Quinton is as good a crane man as he says he is."

* * * * *

· RIAN ·

Leonard, Rian, and her father watched Quinton finish rigging the chains that connected the crane to the bundle of rails. He climbed down from the rear wagon and signaled the crane operator. Two massive Percherons pulled on a cable, which turned a series of clattery gears, which hoisted a chain, which was connected to a horizontal steel beam, which distributed the weight out to four other chains, which lifted the bundle of rails off the wagons.

In a daring act of confidence in his system, Quinton climbed back aboard the now-empty rear transport wagon and stood with hands aloft, daring the chains to break and squash him like a bug. The chains held fast. Rian started clapping, was quickly joined by her father and Leonard, then everyone on the pier. Quinton ordered the crane operator to swing the rails over the gaping maw of the *Enola*'s hold. Everything worked.

Gerald Downing, grinning ear to ear, moseyed over to stand next to *Vater*. "Well, that's a relief. I feel like a thousand-pound weight is off my shoulders."

"Pleased?" Gam Leonard asked, although Rian had no idea if he was speaking to her, *Vater*, or The Trout.

"Amazed," her father responded. "Gamaliel, when did Rian first come to your office to talk about this crane?"

Uh-oh, Rian said to herself. She was surprised by this question and sensed that her father already knew the answer. This was the moment she had fantasized about for months. *Vater will learn the truth: The Trout lied and this was all my idea. But something's not right. Why now? Why in front of other people?*

"January 30," Leonard responded without hesitation. "Why?"

"And how do you remember the exact date?"

Gam, still unaware Otto's mood was anything but jocular, gave Rian a nudge. "Because January 30 is my birthday. Rian barged into my office with a pint of Gallagher's Whiskey. I thought she was delivering a birthday present from one of my colleagues. Turns out, she came at me with your proposal. I couldn't ignore it. I was initially surprised you put so much trust in one so young, and that was when I thought she was your son, not your daughter. But as I have gotten to know her, I now understand why."

Otto gave a jerk of his head toward Downing. "So, Gerald here did not approach you with this idea?"

Gam now sensed something was amiss that he didn't understand. "Hi, Gerald . . . Uh, no. I didn't meet Gerald until a couple of weeks after Rian stopped in. Why?"

Otto turned his attention to Downing. "Gerald, whose idea was it to build a crane heavy enough to lift a fully assembled locomotive?"

Downing stared at some middle ground halfway between them and the crane. "Uh, I'm not sure. That was six months ago."

Her father persisted. "I distinctly remember how impressed I was. You had been on the job for less than a week and you already had an idea that revolutionized the way we could deliver our engines. Yet it was not your idea, was it?"

This was Rian's fantasy come true . . . almost. Rian's *schadenfreude*[26] was tempered by the feeling something was off. She was happy to witness this confrontation but sensed she was about to get caught up in its wake.

The Trout responded to Otto. "I don't remember it that way, sir. I believe I told you your daughter and I were working on it together."

"I distinctly remember you told me it was your idea and Rian's only role was to take a first crack at designing the wagons to transport the locomotive."

Downing kept his eyes on the ground. "I'm sorry you got that impression."

"So the idea was Rian's originally?"

"I believe it was," Downing responded, then glanced up at Otto. "Yes, I believe it was."

"Gerald, when we leave for Boston tomorrow, you will not be joining us."

Nuts, thought Rian, *there goes my plan to run the shop while The Trout and Heinrich are gone.*

"Excuse me, sir?"

"You will not be accompanying Heinrich and me to Boston." Then her father turned to her. "And Rian, you allowed Gamaliel to assume you were a boy when you first met him?"

Here it comes. "Yes, I did."

"Do you understand that is the same thing as a lie?"

Rian eyed Gam Leonard, who had become wide-eyed at the turn of the conversation. "I don't think it's a lie at all. What a person assumes based on how I dress is their problem."

"The way you dress is a lie. There is no female in the country who makes the choices you do."

And there it was: What should have been a moment of victory soured to become one more rat-thought moment that gnawed away at her, reminding her that she was The Oddity. And, as was often the case, her father did the reminding.

* * * * *

· OTTO ·

Otto stood awkwardly with Gamaliel Leonard after Rian left to take charge of the mules, and Gerald Downing gathered the workers to run interference for the return trip to the factory.

---

26. *Schadenfreude* is the sense of pleasure one experiences upon hearing of the misfortune of others.

"I am curious," Otto said after a protracted silence. "My daughter deceived you, yet you treat her like so many other adult males do: more like a comrade than a child. My two brothers; my factory foreman, Jules Freeman; my nephew Seamus Gallagher, who makes the whiskey you admire. I found her and Quinton Schott sitting atop my new crane the other day. What is it you all see in her that I somehow cannot? She is a fifteen-year-old girl. She is destined to marry a young man. Her fortune . . . my fortune, such as it is . . . her dowry will position her and her husband to enter Philadelphia society. Yet she would rather bet about the success or failure of a crane than get fitted for a new dress."

Leonard put up his hands in a defensive posture. "Slow down, Otto. First of all, I do not view Rian as a comrade. She is not my equal. But I told my wife the other day that your daughter is like a sponge. She soaks up knowledge faster than anyone I've ever met. That day I met her? The day she barged into my office with a pint of whiskey? We talked about shipping traffic on the Delaware; cranes, of course; competition among the pier owners; whether the depression is really over; the Harbor Master's job. She asked questions. I could tell from her responses that she retained a flood of information. I don't expect this sort of conversation with most of the men you and I dine with at the United States Hotel. A precocious fifteen-year-old who mines me for information makes me feel . . . valuable."

"I had no idea. . . ."

"But I'll go you one better. You now acknowledge Rian was the instigator of this idea. . . ."

Otto nodded.

"The locomotive your outfit is designing now—I think you call it the *Standard*—it's going to Utica, right?"

"Yes, we hope to deliver it early in 1841."

"Well, somehow you have to get it there. And it won't fit into the hold of the *Enola*. It's too long."

"And how do you know this?"

"Rian told me. Your daughter is already thinking toward goals years ahead. Military men have a name for this. It is called strategy. Otto, your daughter is by nature a strategic thinker."

* * * * *

· RIAN ·

It was the end of a long, successful, revelatory workday. Rian and her father were walking home together, something that rarely happened these days because Rian usually stayed longer than he did. She was still smarting from her father's comment that the way she dressed was a lie.

"*Liebling*, you are the one who first approached Gam Leonard about building a crane. Why didn't you tell me the cranes were your idea?"

"I guess I always prefer to solve my own problems. I don't want to be perceived as 'daddy's little girl' in the shop." *Give him something, Eena.* "Plus, when I met with Gam, I kind of implied I was speaking for you."

"When you allowed him to think you are a boy."

There it is again: You're the Oddity. "Yes, and I knew that would irk you."

"You were right. It vexes me considerably. Do you and Gerald get along? I have not heard any rumblings like I used to with Harry."

The Trout and I made a deal: I wouldn't expose his lie and he would support me when he returned to Baldwin Locomotive. But that deal is in shambles now. "We do okay. He's a better foreman than Harry was."

"When I was under the false impression the cranes and wagons were Gerald's idea, I felt it was only fitting that he witnessed the other end of the process in Boston. As you know, I disinvited him from the trip, but it would be a shame if his ticket went unused. You should go to Boston with Heinrich and me."

Conflicted feelings welled up immediately. On one hand, Rian was pleased that her father finally learned the truth and wanted to honor her contribution to progress at Krieger Locomotive. He was apparently letting go of his ire that she allowed Gam Leonard to think she was a boy. On the other hand, she was still a little edgy around steam engines, especially one she didn't know. The *Enola* was a steamship, which, of course, was driven by a steam engine. *Two days and nights worrying that the* Enola*'s boiler will blow up on me will not be fun.*

* * * * *

· OTTO ·

Otto answered the knock at the door to find his next-door neighbor Lucretia Mott. "Good evening, dear Lucretia. How good to see you. Please come in."

Lucretia waved off his invitation. "Otto, I know thee is leaving for Boston the day after tomorrow. I have a favor to ask. Would thee be willing to hand deliver a letter to John Quincy Adams while thee is in Boston? It would require a carriage ride to Quincy, a few miles outside the city."

Having an excuse to meet with the former president excited Otto. "I would be happy to. May I ask why this letter is so important that it must be hand delivered?"

"Have thee been following the events in New London?"

"Ah, yes. Harold Foote seems to be spending more time in Connecticut than in Pennsylvania or Washington City lately. He is making quite a name for himself. His articles about the *Amistad* kidnappees are chilling. I know he is also responsible for the 'Notes from Jasper' letters causing such a stir. His sympathies for the anti-slavery movement must please you."

Lucretia's smile was short-lived. "Indeed, they do. But I have learned that President Van Buren, who we all know does not share our sentiments, is taking a personal interest in the New London case. If the mutineers are set free, he has directed the district attorney to appeal the decision. He is set to take the case all the way to the Supreme Court if necessary."

Otto sighed at the thought of a president who hailed from the North doing the bidding of the Southern slaveholders. "And the contents of this letter?"

"A plea to John Quincy to take a similar interest in the case and oppose Mr. Van Buren's efforts. And if it ever does get to the Supreme Court, to head the defense."

"I would be honored to deliver such a letter."

Lucretia nodded. "Well, now that that is settled, are thee prepared for thy trip? What will Rian do while thee is gone?"

"I am taking Rian with me. I worry about her, though. The aftereffects of the explosion still seem to haunt her."

"How so?"

"I expected her to be pleased when I told her I wanted her to accompany Heinrich Aldridge and me to Boston. She seemed ambivalent, and I suspect spending two days aboard a steamer may have something to do with it. She spends a lot of time on the scaffold next to the boiler that almost killed her. Heinrich put the idea in her head that if she spends enough time up there, she will get over her fear of steam engines."

"What does she do up there?"

"She works on projects for Heinrich. Cooks up schemes like these two new cranes we are using to get our new locomotive aboard the *Enola*. And the one after that, apparently."

"You must be proud of her."

"Proud? Perhaps. But I worry. My mother was strong like she is. Eventually, our neighbors in Stuttgart shunned her because her actions were too far outside what they were willing to accept from a woman. The shunning and the Hunger Year broke her. I don't want that to happen to Rian."

"Otto, thee is doing the best thee can. Rian is a wonderful young woman."

Otto nodded but a spasm of chagrin charged through his body. "You are very kind. The fact is I have no head for being a parent. That was Dierdre's job. Since she passed away, my method of raising my daughter has been to heed the advice of the last person I spoke to, make grand pronouncements, and then find out later that Rian has done whatever she wanted to do."

"Well, I for one applaud her pluck." Then Lucretia gave Otto a wry smile. "Although I wish thee could get her out of those horrid ragamuffin clothes she always wears."

"Rian's shop clothes irk me every day, but they should not be a problem on this trip. When she returned from Russia, we made a deal: She agreed to dress appropriately on special occasions and when we travel."

"That sounds delightful. Even normal."

"Lucretia, that is my thought as well, but my daughter persistently demonstrates she is not content with normal."

"Perhaps she could accompany thee when thee delivers my letter to John Quincy. Maybe he could inspire her in some manner."

"I cannot imagine such an important man taking time to inspire my daughter."

"Otto, I will go home and write my letter before I go to bed. I will bring it over before thee leaves for work tomorrow. Where is Rian now, by the way?"

"Oh, she and Conor went out for a walk. I'm afraid the prospect of them being apart for a week has made them both a bit wistful."

* * * * *

· RIAN ·

Rian and Conor sat atop the Sparks Shot Tower, which still had no railings, and dangled their feet to the west. Rian had told Conor about the events of the day, including the successful performance of her tandem wagons and both cranes, leading a twelve-mule team for the first time, The Trout's exposed lie, her father's contention that her shop clothes were a lie, his eleventh-hour decision to take her to Boston as a reward for coming up with the crane idea, and lastly, Rian's unease about spending two days and nights in proximity to the *Enola*'s steam engines.

They stopped talking as the sun set. The colors of Philadelphia gracefully transformed from the greens of late summer to the golds of a perfect early evening.

"Here's how I see it," said Conor, picking up the conversation from two minutes ago. "Yana—that's her name, right? The soothsayer in Russia?"

Rian nodded.

"Her prediction solves your problem. You know fire will follow you around for the rest of your life . . . fire that is out of control and fire you think is in control but isn't. She proved that. The Tsar's palace burned down. You fought that—"

"And lost," Rian interjected.

"Pennsylvania Hall burned down. You ran into the building minutes before the roof caved in to save Benjamin Lundy's papers—"

"*We* ran into that together, and the roof didn't cave in for another half-hour."

"And then the steam engine blew up. Rian, that steam engine wounded you, but it didn't kill you. If you believe some of what Yana said, then you might as well believe all of it. Have you stopped wearing dresses yet?"

"Not if *Vater* has anything to say about it . . . but as rarely as possible."

"Are you running Krieger Locomotive yet?"

"I thought I might for a week while The Trout was in Boston, but to answer your question, no."

"Well, there's your answer. If you still wear dresses—"

"Only when I have to—"

"And you're not running Krieger Locomotive, then no steam engine will kill you. You are Rian Fooking Krieger. You aren't afraid of anything. You helped Olivia Tucker's mammy escape to freedom when you were twelve—"

"We did that together—"

"You stabbed a mugger when you were thirteen. You helped free Peach and got pistol-whipped by Austin T. Slatter for your trouble. You blackmailed the Tsar of Russia. You stared down his right-hand man. Rian, you are the bravest person I know. No steam engine has killed you yet because it can't." Rian knew Conor was smiling when he added, "At least, not until the rest of Yana's prediction comes true."

"But if another one blew up on me, it would still hurt."

"Well, maybe that's a bit of a hole in me argument. But do you get me point? No steam engine is going to kill you. You are Rian Fooking Krieger. Nothing's going to kill you until you're running Krieger Locomotive."

"And I stop wearing dresses." *Hmm. Rian Fooking Krieger. I think I like that.*

THURSDAY, SEPTEMBER 12

· RIAN ·

"We had a deal, Just-Rian," Downing muttered when Rian found him in the Krieger Locomotive office. "You keep your yap shut and I tell your father he should make you foreman when I leave."

"But I didn't tell him anything. Quinton did, then Gam confirmed it."

The Trout faced his unibody toward her. "Well, that's too bad. Too bad for me and too bad for you."

"So that's it? That's the end of our deal? Gerald, you're a good foreman. You keep this place running the way it should. My father knows that, and I have no reason to fire across your bow. Let's keep the deal."

"I hear Otto's taking you to Boston instead of me. I'll think about it while you're gone."

"Are you coming to watch us load the *Number 14* onto the wagons?"

"Why should I, Just-Rian? We know the concept works. Now the whole shop knows it wasn't my idea. I've got work to do."

"Well, before I leave, I have a request. Stop calling me *Just-Rian*." *That name has become one more rat-thought that bothers me no end, especially when you call me that in front of the men. Just what I need: one more rat-thought.*

As Rian left the office, she had a new revelation. *Rian Fooking Krieger can keep all those rat-thoughts tied up in the burlap sack in the back of the wagon, right where they belong.*

* * * * *

· OTTO ·

Otto crossed the alley from Krieger Coach to celebrate the launch. This time, he invited banker and railroad executive George Shippen to join him. They stood just outside the factory slider next to the new triple-U crane.

Number 14 emerged from the factory under its own steam, its cab and boiler newly painted red with gold highlights. The finish crew had artfully hand-lettered its new name, *Bunker Hill*, on each side of the cab. The

Bunker Hill exemplified Krieger Locomotive's state-of-the-art engineering and manufacturing.

"He certainly is a beauty," said Shippen as the locomotive crawled to a halt under the crane. "I'm impressed you made a sale in Boston. Aren't there a number of locomotive manufacturers in that part of Massachusetts?"

Otto shrugged. "Some. They are machine shops trying to transition into the railroad business the way we did three years ago. We probably would not have held onto this contract if we had not kept our price down by delivering the *Bunker Hill* in one piece."

"A brilliant business move on your part. Was it your idea?"

"No," Otto said with a rueful chuckle. "It was Rian's."

"And where is she now? I'm surprised she isn't here."

"She is here." Otto nodded toward the *Bunker Hill*. "She is driving the locomotive."

"You still let her play with your machinery? Even after the explosion?"

Otto merely nodded, but a spasm of chagrin charged through his body. *That is what I do. Lay down the law with her, then neglect her, only to find out she has defied me.*

"Your daughter is the same age as my Trey. Next summer social season, they will both be old enough to attend galas and balls. That's what you want, isn't it? That's why you've been working so hard to make your enterprise a success? So that your daughter can marry well?"

"Well, yes, it is. Sometimes I lose sight of that. She is headstrong. It is often easier to let her have her way. She wants to run Krieger Locomotive someday."

"Oh, nonsense," Shippen spat out. "No woman is capable of running anything more than a laundry. Your daughter is smart, Krieger, I'll grant you that. She will make a brilliant helpmate to some young man like Trey when the time comes. But you've got to finish the job the explosion started. Knock the starch out of her."

"That explosion almost killed her," Otto responded icily.

"Oh, don't get caught up in my lack of tact. Hear my message. By allowing your daughter to persist in these fantasies, you're making it more painful for her when the inevitable realities come to the fore. She will never run your operation. She must marry. She must get out of those horrid shop clothes and start her transition into womanhood."

"Perhaps it is time we had another talk."

"I know what your little talks do. You make grand pronouncements, then she twists you around her little finger and does whatever the hell she wants. At the very least, you need to make it clear she will never run any of your factories. Once you kill that fantasy, the rest will fall into place."

"I think that is a good idea. I will talk to her on our trip to Boston."

"You're taking her with you?"

"Yes, Heinrich Aldridge and I are going."

"Why Aldridge?"

"He designs all of our locomotives. They are much more complex machines than the ones Adrian built when we got into this business. Heinrich will teach the ins and outs of the engine to the technicians at the *Boston & Lowell Railroad.*"

"You can't do that?"

"Me? No. My heart is in Krieger Coach. As far as locomotives go, I can quote horsepower, dimensions, and capabilities. I tell stories that make buying a Krieger engine sound like the wisest decision a railroad executive can make. But put me in the cab of the *Bunker Hill* over there? I could not tell you the difference between the throttle and a release valve."

"So, Mr. Salesman, sell me. Perhaps you can lure me into buying one of these fantastic machines."

Grateful to be putting their conversation about Rian behind him, Otto launched into his spiel. "Even though the *Bunker Hill* is the third *Eagle*-class engine Krieger Locomotive has produced, there are numerous small changes from its immediate predecessor and one large one: its cylinders are fifteen inches in diameter with a twenty-five-inch stroke; more aggressive dimensions than the first two. My designer, Heinrich Aldridge, extensively researched this, and I can guarantee this machine pulls a heavier load and goes faster than any machine of its weight built by our competitors."

"Not bad. Consider me enticed. And why are you taking Rian?"

Otto shook his head because he knew this would bring the conversation back to his deficiencies as a father. "I decided to include Rian as a reward for thinking up this idea in the first place."

"See?" Shippen shot back predictably. "That is exactly what you should not have done. You're dangling the possibility that if she works hard enough, has enough of her brilliant ideas, someday Daddy will see the light and let her run Krieger Locomotive. No, it's time to bring down the hammer."

"Thank you for your advice, George. My daughter is a handful. I need all the advice I can get." *And this confrontation will be ugly.*

* * * * *

· RIAN ·

Yesterday, Rian felt fifteen tons of weight melt off her shoulders when the tandem transport wagons held up during the test, but the same sense of dread returned today when the *Bunker Hill* was slowly lowered toward the wagons.

The three men turned the cranks, which did their work. The *Bunker Hill* settled onto the wagons. The wagons groaned. Everything held up.

With the engine in place, Heinrich ambled over to Rian. He and Quinton had ironed out who was in charge of tying down the *Bunker Hill*: Heinrich supervised quietly from the ground while Quinton did the actual work. The locomotive had to pivot on the wagons as they made their initial looping turn onto James Street and the right-angle turns on the streets of Philadelphia. Heinrich had anticipated this problem months ago when he pored over Rian's design while it was still on paper. His solution was relatively simple. A chain in the center of each wagon would wrap through a clevis pin in the undercarriage of the *Bunker Hill* to keep it tightly secured but able to pivot on the wagons. Additional chains wrapped over the locomotive's undercarriage to provide added security but were left loose enough to allow for pivoting.

Quinton called down to Heinrich from the rear transfer wagon after he tightened the chain on the clevis pin. "You should double-check this step when you get to Boston. Those gumps are likely to screw it up."

Rian was about to reply that she and Heinrich had already talked about that, but Heinrich nudged her, indicating she should shut up and let Quinton have his day.

The trip to the Johns & Leonard Pier proceeded much the same as the test trip, save that many pedestrians paused to gape at the sight of twelve mules pulling a thirty-thousand-pound locomotive down the street.

Quinton supervised the transfer of the *Bunker Hill* into the aft hold of the *Enola*. Rian stood on the pier, a few feet away from two of the *Enola*'s crewmen who also watched the operation. The crane did its job as expected. Rian sensed the moment when the locomotive settled into the hold: the aft of the *Enola* sank six inches into the water.

"First mate's not going to like that," Rian heard one of the sailors mutter.

Rian turned to the crewman. "How come? What's wrong?"

"First mate's in charge of the cargo," he responded. "He always wants to have his cargo balanced. Both port and starboard, fore and aft. Yer engine. It's makin' the *Enola* aft-heavy."

"Captain knows what's what," said the other sailor. "I guarantee he won't leave port with the *Enola* ridin' like this."

Heinrich emerged from the ship's hold and walked down the gangway to join Rian. "Our work here is done for the day. The *Bunker Hill*'s loaded and tied down. They're buttoning up. We leave with the tide tomorrow morning."

"Aren't they going to load more cargo in the forehold?" Rian asked.

"Apparently not," responded Heinrich.

* * * * *

· OTTO ·

That evening, as Otto reached the top of the stairs, he heard Rian and Conor talking in her bedroom. Rian was speaking. "I think your advice really made a difference. I know my brain and my body are two different things, but I think my body is listening to my brain."

Curious to hear more about this conversation, Otto stuck his head in the door to find Rian packing for the trip while Conor sat on her bed—his back to the bedstead with legs stretched out before him.

"What are you two talking about?"

Rian straightened from her task. "Conor gave me some advice last night about my fear of steam engines. I think it helped. I may even be cured."

Conor extended his arms in a "tada" gesture and gave a hint of a bow.

Otto smiled, then noticed what Rian was packing. She had folded an almost new set of shop clothes and had half-tucked it into her carpetbag. "What dresses are you bringing?"

Rian didn't look up from her folding. "I wasn't going to bring any dresses. This is a working trip."

"This is travel. One dresses up for travel. It is a special occasion. You wear dresses for special occasions. That was our deal when you returned from Russia."

Rian shoved the carpetbag away and flopped down on the bed. "Then I'm not going."

George Shippen's word rang in Otto's ears. *You've got to finish the job the explosion started. Knock the starch out of her. She must get out of those horrid shop clothes and start her transition into womanhood.* "Of course you are going. You will witness the fruition of all the planning you and Heinrich have done."

Rian folded her arms. "I don't care. I'm not going."

"This is ridiculous." Shippen again: *I know what your little talks do. You make grand pronouncements, then she twists you around her little finger and does whatever the hell she wants.* "I was planning to take you with me when I deliver a letter to President Adams."

"John Quincy Adams?" Conor asked. Otto noted that Conor nudged Rian with his toes in a gesture he couldn't interpret.

"Yes, John Quincy Adams. Lucretia asked me to hand deliver a letter to him. A plea to take an interest in this case of those mutineers in New London."

Rian stared at that damn portrait for a good ten heartbeats. He could almost see the wheels turning. She unfolded her arms. "I'll take a dress, but I won't wear it on the ship."

"You will take two dresses. A day dress and a dress for dinner, both aboard the ship and in Boston."

"But not during the day aboard the ship."

"Tomorrow when we board. And Monday when we disembark in Boston. I have reserved a suite at the American House."

Another long moment, then: "Okay. But I'm not happy about it."

FRIDAY, SEPTEMBER 13

· RIAN ·

You are Rian Krieger. You are Rian Fooking Krieger. You are fearless. You are fearless, even though you look like a court jester when you wear a dress.

Despite the dress, Rian surprised herself when she realized she was in a good mood. It was Conor's "logic" that did it. It had genuinely calmed her. Since one part of Yana's prediction proved to be true (fire had followed her numerous times), all the rest had to be true (she would one day run Krieger Locomotive, she would one day stop wearing dresses). Until that time, she couldn't die from an explosion (or, it dawned on her, any other cause).

The *Enola*'s engines built up enough steam to start idling half an hour before it left the Johns & Leonard pier. For the first time since the explosion almost a year ago, Rian wasn't constantly steeling herself in the presence of a working steam engine.

A ten-man longboat towed the *Enola* out of its berth. When the ship was safely away from the pier, the longboat released its lines and turned its bow to the ship's stern. The longboat pushed at the *Enola*, the oarsmen straining hard, until it faced downriver. Rian gave a friendly wave to the rowers, then joined her father and Heinrich at the starboard rail to watch the wharves of the Philadelphia waterfront go by. To Rian's disappointment, many of them were unoccupied.

"Are you two seeing what I'm seeing?" Heinrich asked.

Otto answered first. "The wharves are not as busy as they should be. This depression is not over for a lot of this city. We are very lucky our fate is different. Our future is bright."

Rian felt no need to add to her father's assessment. In fact, her mind was already elsewhere. To her satisfaction, she continued to feel comfortable with the rhythmic *choosh . . . choosh . . . choosh* of the *Enola*'s engines. *Maybe this will be okay.*

It was okay until four hours into their voyage down the Delaware. The *Enola* slowed as it approached the mouth of the Christina River in the state of

Delaware. The ship veered slightly toward river-left and came to a graceful stop at a floating dock loaded with scores of oak barrels.

Rian, still in her day dress, leaned on the ship's port railing as the shoremen tied the lines. The first mate stood nearby, waiting to descend the gangway as soon as it was secure.

"What's in the barrels?" she asked.

"Black powder. Two hundred barrels. About two-thirds as much as that engine of yours weighs, but the captain'll be happier with more weight up front."

"Black powder? You mean gunpowder?"

The first mate smirked at Rian's obvious discomfort. "Aye, Missy." He pointed up the Christina River. "A family named DuPont runs the largest gunpowder mill in America a couple of miles from here. We're gonna load them into the forehold to compensate for your daddy's locomotive. The coal bunkers are between the engine room and the forehold. Plenty of safety space. I wouldn't go smokin' yer pipe down there, though." The gangway secured, the first mate strode off the ship, still chuckling at his own joke.

Rian had spent such little time in a dress that she didn't know if the first mate was bandying with her because of her age, because her dress branded her as a girl, both . . . or maybe it was just his nature. No matter what his motivation, she didn't like it much.

The shoremen didn't seem concerned about the nature of the cargo. They tipped the barrels onto their sides, rolled them onto a pallet big enough to hold twelve kegs at a time, and tipped them on end again. A crane—a much smaller version of the one that loaded the *Bunker Hill* onto the *Enola* yesterday—lifted the pallet, swung it over the forehatch, and lowered it into the hold. Rian walked over to the hatch and tentatively peered into the darkness from above as four crewmembers rolled the barrels off the pallet and stacked them two high. *Yana*, Rian muttered, *you better be right about* all *your predictions. I can't get blown up because I'm not running Krieger Locomotive yet, right?*

"BOOM!" the first mate yelled in her ear as he grabbed Rian roughly from behind.

Rian jumped and her heart raced. She turned to the first mate, who was clearly amused by his prank. She pushed him in the chest with both hands. "You scared the hell out of me."

"Yer a regular wildcat, aren't ya," he responded. He smiled at her and returned his attention to the crew in the hold. "Good fer you, Missy."

Jaysus, Rian muttered to herself, *gunpowder and a crazy first mate. Rian Fooking Krieger, it's time for you to show up. Otherwise, this voyage will feel like it's a thousand years long . . . and get me out of this stupid dress.*

* * * * *

· OLIVIA ·

Despite the ease of river travel, Olivia tensed as the steamboat *Granby* approached Columbia. A myriad of challenges awaited. Her teachers at Barhamville—some known, some new—were sure to be demanding but unlikely to have a worldview as compelling as the short-tenured Miss Edwards. Stimulating subjects would need to be mastered. She would resume her clandestine visits to the rock near the capitol building. And of course, visits to the Wilkinson's Thousand Oaks included the possibility of fleeting interactions with Topper.

But most on her mind right now was Caldie Montgomery. Less than a week ago, armed with tales of her summer in Paris, she thought she would return to combat with Caldie as more of an equal. Her parents took the wind out of those sails by banning her return to Long Pond next summer, which meant she would not be coming out.

Olivia's first encounter with Caldie came as she and Eugenie unpacked their trunks in their room. The door was open.

"We're in the second form now. Most girls in our grade turn sixteen in 1840, but only members of the gentry will come out," Caldie announced as she flounced through the door. "My father will present me at the Columbia Cotillion at the Hampton-Preston House in June."

If Olivia thought Caldie was pretty before, she had turned gorgeous over the summer. And coming out was like a trump card, superseding any accomplishment, any story Olivia had in her arsenal. Thoughts of another year of combat with her tormentor curdled. She responded with her own best shot. "I spent the summer in Paris. They consider Americans quite exotic over there. I danced and danced at quite a few balls. King Louis-Phillippe was at one of them."

Caldie stiffened. "Hmm. I imagine an American girl pretending to be a woman would be considered exotic. I'm sure the king was quite amused." Caldie turned and left the room.

Deflated, Olivia removed a dress from her trunk and hung it in the armoire she shared with Eugenie. "I'm glad Caldie left. I doubt I'll come out next year, but I surely wasn't going to tell her that."

"Why aren't you coming out?"

"I don't think I'll be going home for the summer. My parents have asked the Wilkinsons to keep me here. But the ladyhood classes are in Charleston. That's where the Debutante Ball is."

Eugenie, who had been putting clothing into her dresser, turned to Olivia. "If you're not going back to Charleston, come out here, silly. Mrs. Marks gives ladyhood classes every year. Take the classes with her. That's what I'm going to do. I'm coming out and my father's only a minister, not an upper-cruster like you and Caldie. Mrs. Wilkinson will surely sponsor you. Barnwell can be your escort."

During the three days of travel from Charleston, Olivia never thought of coming out in Columbia. Every debutante had to take a lot of tutorials before she came out. Those offered in Columbia were probably similar to the ones offered in Charleston: dance classes, etiquette lessons, proper dress, dressing the dinner table, and the perfection of the St. James Bow. "How do you know all this?"

"I grew up here, remember? Columbia knows how to throw a cotillion."

Olivia immediately warmed to the idea of coming out in Columbia, at least most of it. "Barnwell Wilkinson? He's pretty gawky."

* * * * *

Olivia and Eugenie continued unpacking after dinner when a new girl from first form knocked at the door. "Is either of you Olivia Tucker? I've got a letter for her."

Olivia turned to the new girl and held out her hand. "I am." The girl handed her a letter sealed with a wax *W*, turned, and left. Olivia broke the seal, unfolded the letter, and started reading.

Friday, September 13, 1839

Olivia Dear,

We want to hear all about Paris! Please join us tomorrow morning through Sunday dinner. Barnwell will pick you up around ten. You can stay the night and we will have you back at the Collegiate Institute so you will be well rested before your first day of classes. I have written a separate note to Dr. Marks and asked for you to be excused from Chapel on Sunday.

Affectionately,
Poppy Wilkinson
Mrs. Trevor Wilkinson
Thousand Oaks

SATURDAY, SEPTEMBER 14

· RIAN ·

Unlike the *Great Western*, which was built to transport passengers across the Atlantic in luxury, the *Enola* was built to carry mostly cargo, with room for a half-dozen passengers almost as an afterthought. If you wanted to sit on the deck during the fine September weather, you had to carry a chair up from the galley. Berths were small "doubles" with bunk beds, but fortunately her father, Heinrich, and Rian were the only passengers, so no one had to share. Even so, her bed was so short she spent the night in a curled-up position.

The small passengers' dining room—next to but separate from the crew's galley—was used to store nautical charts, a surprising array of musical instruments, and pantry items. According to the first mate, the passengers ate better food than the crew, but Rian was unimpressed.

The morning after their first night at sea, Rian emerged from her bunk dressed in shop clothes, her hair tucked into her flat cap.

"Well, Missy, ain't you something," said the first mate when he walked through the dining room. "So that *was* you I saw on the docks when we were loading your daddy's engine. And this is your preferred way of spittin' in the eye of the rest of the world?"

Rian smiled at the first mate. "It is."

"Then eat yer breakfast later. I'll show you places you couldn't go in that dress you were wearing yesterday."

Rian followed the first mate around all morning. They descended into the engine room and watched the stokers shovel coal into the furnaces of the *Enola*'s twin boilers. She climbed the ladder to the catwalk above the engine. The sounds—the hissing and *chooshing*—were familiar but different from the sounds in Hell. *And thinking of Hell, I don't feel the need to steel myself. Maybe I'm cured.*

She accompanied the first mate into the forehold when he made his daily inspection, and despite his joke about smoking a pipe, he carried a whale oil lantern. "Now, mind you, if you see a barrel leaking gunpowder, back away. But we're perfectly safe. The powder's tight in its barrels."

Throughout the morning, the first mate treated her like a young boy interested in his profession, not a silly, teasable little girl. In fact, in the afternoon, he followed her into the aft hold so she could show him the *Bunker Hill*. Although most of her efforts these days went to the design of the new *Standard*-class locomotive, she certainly knew her way around the cab of *Number 14*, and she was proud to show off her knowledge. It was a good day.

The good day turned bad during dinner.

Rian reluctantly but dutifully changed into her dress and went to the dining room. While waiting for her father and Heinrich, she experimented with a violin and bow that had been lying on a shelf.

Her father entered the room and sat down at the same time a crewman placed three bowls of beef stew on the table. "*Liebling*, could you put the violin back, please. I would like to talk to you about something before Heinrich joins us."

Uh-oh. Rian did as she was told. "Good news or bad news?"

Otto tasted his stew, then reached for a pinch of salt. "I think it is time you throttled back on your involvement out in the shops . . . both Krieger Coach and Krieger Locomotive."

Rian picked up her spoon, considered taking a bite, then changed her mind. *I didn't see a fight coming. But if he wants one, he'll get one.*

"I almost lost you a year ago when the boiler blew up," her father continued. "I do not want to take a chance of that ever happening again."

Rian leaned forward. "*Vater*, it took me almost nine months, but I think I'm over my fear of steam engines. Why do you bring this up now? You know I want to someday run Krieger Locomotive—"

"No."

That's when things got complicated. Heinrich, unaware of the nature of their conversation, entered the room and sat down. "Good evening, all. I hope you had a good day. Rian, it seemed you spent a lot of time with the first mate." Heinrich took a spoonful of beef stew.

Rian ignored Heinrich and addressed her father. "No, what?"

"Running the shop is Gerald Downing's job. He may have been duplicitous about taking credit for your idea, but he runs the shop well and the men like him."

Heinrich, now aware he had entered a testy father-daughter conversation, kept quiet and continued eating.

Rian couldn't have cared less about Heinrich's presence. *Make* Vater *say it, Eena. Make him say it.* "What if Gerald were to quit?"

"Then I would find some other man to fill his position."

Make him say it. "Why not me? I proved myself with this crane idea. I know I can do it."

Heinrich was about to interject something, but Otto put up his hand to silence him and leaned across the table toward Rian. "Daughter, why must you be so tiresome? You will never run Krieger Locomotive because you are a female. Not too long from now, you will become a young woman, grow out of this foolishness, and embrace your destiny, which is to marry the brightest, most ambitious young man you can find. My share of Krieger Locomotive will become your dowry. The Panic set us back a few years, but we are climbing back. By the time you marry, I believe you and your husband can live off the profits of the Krieger factories. You will take your places near the top echelons of Philadelphia society. If your husband chooses to run either Krieger Locomotive or Krieger Coach after I am gone, that will be his decision. If he decides the two of you will travel the world, the Krieger factories should be in a position to run themselves."

Heinrich kept eating.

Stung, deflated, Rian sat back in her chair and crossed her arms. "So you want me to marry Trey Shippen. Is that it?"

"Trey would fit the bill. I want what I have always wanted: The satisfaction of seeing my daughter invited into the ballrooms, salons, and drawing rooms of Philadelphia society's elite. Remember, I came ashore in Philadelphia nineteen years ago with little more than a bag of tools. I think seeing you take your place in Philadelphia society will be a proper testament to the validity of the possibilities in this great land: Immigrant to social elite in two generations."

"*Vater*, have you ever considered that might not be what I want?"

"As I said, you are fifteen years old. I expect that any time now, you will start to envision quite a different future for yourself."

"If I'll never run Krieger Locomotive, why did you bring me on this trip?"

"I invited Gerald as a reward for his idea. Once I found out it was not his idea, I felt the reward was unwarranted. That left me with an extra ticket that the steamship company would not buy back. Rather than let the ticket go to waste, I figured you would enjoy the trip."

Heinrich put his spoon down in his bowl. "Otto, that's not entirely—"

"Stay out of this, Heinrich," Otto spat out.

Rian rose from her chair, never having taken a sip of her stew. "You know, the other night when we were walking home, you asked me why I didn't tell you the idea was mine. I didn't tell you the whole truth. I thought that if I told you, you wouldn't believe me. But I was fooling myself. My real fear—one I didn't dare think to myself then—was that if you knew the truth, it wouldn't matter to you because I'm a girl. I can't tell you how much that hurts me."

Her father threw his napkin on the table and regarded Rian with sad eyes. "This discussion did not go the way I wanted it to. I wanted to caution you to stop taking risks in the shop. As I said, I almost lost you a year ago. I do not want to go through that again."

"From now on, the risks I take will be my own." Rian heard her words come out in a jumble. Her voice was louder. "The contributions I make to the welfare of Krieger Locomotive will be my own. You say I'll never run Krieger Locomotive because I'm a female. What do you care? You love Krieger Coach." Out of the corner of her eye, she saw the first mate in the galley lean his chair back on two legs to see what the kerfuffle was all about, but she didn't care. By this time, Rian Fooking Krieger had taken over. "Krieger Locomotive has never been your passion. It's mostly Uncle Adrian's business, but he's in Saxony and you've taken responsibility for it out of duty. You almost never come over to the Locomotive side of the alley. If you really cared about it, you'd be there more often and you'd have to acknowledge what I'm doing to assure its future."

Heinrich kept eating his stew.

"Rian . . . *Liebling* . . . I—"

"Mark my words . . . someday you'll see the truth. I'm the best person for the job. And do you know what? When that time comes, I won't say thank you. I'll say, 'it's about fooking time.'"

Rian turned on her heel and climbed the three steps to get out onto the deck. *Oh, Yana, I know you said that first I wouldn't run it, then I would. But why does it have to be so hard?*

* * * * *

· OLIVIA ·

Olivia waited fifteen minutes in Dr. Marks's parlor for Mrs. Wilkinson and Barney to arrive and escort her back to Thousand Oaks. She spied Topper driving the landau up the long lane, rose to exit the main building, and descended the front steps as the landau reached the pebbled circular driveway. Topper slowed the horses. As expected, reflecting the gorgeous weather, the carriage's top was down. Surprisingly, Mrs. Wilkinson was not riding in the back. Barney bounded out almost before the carriage stopped. He gave Topper a deft signal to deal with Olivia's bags, then stepped forward to greet her.

"Olivia, I have been looking forward to seeing you again since you left for Europe." This was a Barney transformed. Last year at this time, Barney was a gawky, awkward hand-kisser. The young man standing before Olivia was smiley, more animated, more confident. *Handsome*, Olivia thought.

"How was your summer?" she asked when they were seated together in the forward-facing seat of the carriage. It wasn't a flirty question, merely a way to get him talking.

Barnwell rose from his seat next to her and shifted to the opposite seat so he could face her directly. "Interesting. The price of cotton is falling, which concerns my father. It's down to thirteen-and-a-half cents a pound in Charleston. We've opened two new fields to cultivation. My father asked me to go to Charleston with him to sit in on some of his meetings with cotton buyers. I learned a lot. How about your summer? How was Paris?"

So, Barnwell, you've finally learned the art of making conversation. "Delightful. I saw all the sights. I painted in the Louvre. I met the artist Samuel Morse. I danced until the wee hours of the morning."

"I am envious. We have two days. I want you to tell me about all of it."

Barnwell's changed demeanor demanded that Olivia envision marrying him. On the carriage ride to Thousand Oaks, she identified two problems. She wouldn't even consider marrying a slaveholder. And right at this moment, despite his new polish, she didn't yet feel any attraction to him. Whatever Barnwell was becoming—had become—it made her heart flutter nary a bit.

* * * * *

It was midnight. Topper's *hoo . . . hoo . . .* signaled his presence at the end of the corridor in the barn. Olivia rushed forward, heedless of the almost total darkness. They hugged briefly.

"How was Paris?" Topper whispered before he let her go.

Olivia gently pulled herself away. "Paris was fine. I've been worrying about you. I've been to the rock. You didn't leave any messages."

"I stopped until you got back. I've got a backlog of entries, but things have changed. South Carolina newspapers are talking about our articles. They don't say the exact words I wrote, but I know they're talking about my notes. People are angry that some enslaved person is writing bad things about slavery. They're mad that the Northern papers are reprinting the articles. They're hunting for me. Course they don't know it's me, but I know they're hunting."

"How do you know?"

"Because a man named Ashbel Molineaux was here doing the hunting. One of the house slaves heard him talking to Master Wilkinson. He's after someone named Jasper, but he allows as how that could be a made-up name."

"What got him to Thousand Oaks?"

"Some of the things I wrote were too specific. The way field hands are whipped—making them lie down and expose their backsides—there's only a few plantations that do it that way, and they're all in this neck of the woods. My murderous brethren who were staked down and pecked to death—that occurred a couple miles from here. There were a couple other things. So Molineaux has narrowed Jasper's circumstance down to three farms in the area."

"You should stop writing for good."

"No, I've got to do more. If my notes are putting their tails in a twist, then I'm doing something right. But Sister, there's one other thing. Ashbel Molineaux doesn't think Jasper can be doing this all by himself. He thinks someone else is helping him. He's hunting for you, too . . . he doesn't know who you are yet or how you're getting the information up North. I'm not the only one who's in danger. You are, same as me."

"I don't care about me. Anything they can do to me pales in comparison to what could happen to you. Give me everything you've written. I'll get it up North, even if it takes ten pretend love letters to Rian Krieger . . . Topper, Barney is like a different person. Do you have any idea why?"

"Master Barnwell? He's no different. Well, no different than any other whites the slaves can't say no to. He started taking gifts to a slave girl down in the shacks." Olivia couldn't see Topper, but she could hear the bitterness in his voice. "I call her a girl, but she's not. She's gotta be five years older than you and me. Master Wilkinson used her for a few years but got tired of her. She's teaching Trey. Everything you're seeing? That's what happens to a man when he thinks everything he sees belongs to him."

Monday, September 16

· OLIVIA ·

Olivia's first day of Natural Philosophy was a surprise in more ways than one. First of all, she expected this class to build on the debating skills she and her classmates had practiced in Moral Philosophy last year. Second, she hoped that Dr. Marks wouldn't be the teacher.

Eugenie, sitting next to Olivia, leaned over. "Caldie's sitting in the front row."

"So what?"

"She never sits in the front row of any class we've taken together. She knows something."

Moments later, a young man—twenty-something, tall, handsome, athletic, with curly brown hair that licked over his collar—strode into the room without shutting the door. "Good morning, ladies. My name is Mr. Lovewell, and I will be your Natural Philosophy teacher for the year."

Fourteen girls straightened in their seats. Fourteen pairs of hormone-fueled eyes riveted onto Mr. Lovewell.

"Natural philosophy." Mr. Lovewell continued, "is the study of the world around us. In recent years, that has come to include botany, zoology, biology, and even astronomy. My goal this year is to get you out of this classroom as often as possible to observe, measure, and compare, then use this information to experiment."

No one in the classroom moved.

Mr. Lovewell seemed not to notice. "When we are in class, it won't be unusual for you to peer through the lens of one of the three microscopes I brought with me from Richmond. You will see everyday items—table salt, hair from your brush, the skin of an onion—in a new way. I will show you one-celled animals called paramecia that live in most every pond you will ever encounter. You will see them locomoting in drops of water you place on the slides of the microscope."

Out of the corner of her eye, Olivia noticed Eugenie tucking an errant strand of hair behind her ear.

Mr. Lovewell continued. "We will also have night classes. I have brought my telescope with me. On clear nights you will observe Saturn's rings and the moons of Jupiter. It will be a great year, ladies. I look forward to getting to know you."

Nosey Caldie Montgomery raised her hand and stood. "My name is Caldwell Montgomery. I believe my father has a telescope at home that he never uses. He might be willing to loan it to the school for the year."

"Why thank you, Miss Montgomery. Perhaps you could introduce me to your father, and I could ask him."

"I would be happy to, sir. You can call me Caldie. That's what all my friends call me."

Mr. Lovewell smiled. "Then, Caldie, I hope we are already on our way to becoming friends."

Olivia and Eugenie exchanged glances and nodded in agreement. Olivia stuck her finger down her throat as if to make herself throw up. Their Natural Philosophy class was three minutes old and Caldie Montgomery was already making her play to become the teacher's pet.

* * * * *

· RIAN ·

Rian arose before dawn to avoid eating breakfast with her father. Knowing they were scheduled to arrive in Boston in the forenoon, she considered defiantly wearing her shop clothes but thought better of it. Otto showed up before her eggs-over-easy arrived. He didn't look well.

"Heinrich is sick," Otto said while standing across the table from Rian. "He thinks it might have been the beef stew. I am not feeling very well, myself. I suggest you be careful about what you eat."

Rian craned her neck to peer into the galley but saw only one man leaning over his food. "Is any of the crew sick?"

"I have no idea. I just got up. I think I will skip breakfast and go up on deck."

A small part of Rian was pleased that her father wasn't feeling well. *Serves him right*, she muttered to herself.

* * * * *

Rian emerged onto the deck in the pre-dawn twilight in time to watch a succession of lighthouses guide the *Enola* past the treacherous shoals of Cape Cod. Three hours later, she and her father hadn't said anything to one another, but she could tell he still wasn't feeling well. She checked on Heinrich in his bunk. He was sick as a dog, weak and dehydrated. The second mate, who was also the ship's doctor, assured Rian and Otto that he would get better, "But he ain't gonna see much of Boston, that's fer sure."

The *Enola* arrived outside Boston harbor at ten o'clock. It was a perfect, blue-sky September day, calm, cloudless, with temperature in the seventies. The ship idled in sight of the masts and church spires of Boston, awaiting the harbor pilot, whose job was to safely guide ships through the busy, hazardous harbor.

The pilot boat pulled alongside and the harbor pilot climbed aboard. "Quite the crowd waiting for you at the pier," he said to the first mate.

The first mate beamed. "Imagine they want to see our locomotive lifted out of the *Enola* all in one piece."

"Some do, some don't. . . ." the harbor pilot replied before the two men walked out of earshot toward the wheelhouse.

As they steamed past a succession of docks, floats, wharves, and piers, Rian assessed Boston's size and commerce as comparable to Philadelphia's—*plenty of capacity, but it's not all in use. Damn, the depression's not over here, either.*

Half an hour later, as the shoremen tied the *Enola*'s lines, Rian stood at the starboard rail, the perfect spot to survey the pier. Fifteen feet away, a shiny new crane—different than Quinton's crane at the Johns & Leonard pier in that it was steam-driven—towered above the deck. A man stoked its firebox while two others chatted nearby. A team of twelve mules patiently stood at the street-end of the pier. They were hitched to a set of tandem transport wagons—exact copies of hers.

A second crane, much smaller than the new one, was already unloading the barrels of black powder, twelve kegs at a time. Three men tipped the barrels on their sides and rolled them off the pallets, then turned them on end near a crowd that had gathered to witness the unloading of the *Bunker Hill*. Clued in by the harbor pilot's comment to the first mate, Rian surveyed the crowd. Most appeared to be happily anticipating the emergence of the *Bunker Hill*. A few looked downright sullen.

"Better give it some room, lads," one of the stevedores said to the crowd. "This is all black powder yer standin' next to, and we've got a lot more barrels to unload yet." The group backed up as advised.

Rian dashed down to the cabins and knocked on Heinrich's door.

"Come in," his weakened voice responded.

Rian entered to find Heinrich lying on his back, his knees up, one arm draped over his eyes. "Any better?"

"Maybe a little," he said without moving his arm. "Yesterday I wished I was dead. Now I'm only sorry I'm alive."

Well, he cracked a joke. At least now I know he won't die. "The *Bunker Hill* will be out in a couple of minutes. Are you well enough to supervise the tie-down once it's on the wagons?"

"I can't do it, Rian. You'll have to trust the shoremen to know what they're doing. Keep an eye on them, though. You saw what Quinton and I did in Philadelphia. It'll be the same process here."

"Can I get you anything?"

His arm still draped over his face, Heinrich shook his head. Rian turned to leave.

"Make sure they secure the *Bunker Hill* using the clevis in the center of the wagons," Heinrich said. "Otherwise, it won't pivot when they go around corners."

"How do you know they built theirs with a clevis?"

"They better have. I sent them your plans."

Rian returned to the deck, gratified that her work was being emulated and that Heinrich had confidence in it. At the same time, she was irritated that her father didn't value her work enough to envision a Krieger Locomotive future that included her.

* * * * *

When Rian returned to the deck, her father was already on the pier, chatting with some man. She walked over to the aft hatch and peered into the darkness. The chains were hooked up to the *Bunker Hill*, and the first mate was climbing the ladder out of the hold. He walked to the ship's railing, signaled to the crane operator on the pier to wait a few moments before he started lifting, joined Rian at the hatch, and peered down into the hold to ensure his men were out of the way.

"I heard you were laying bets on the worthiness of the cranes in Philadelphia," he said to Rian. "Any bets at this end?"

"No bets, but I'm hoping everything goes well."

"You going to accompany the engine to the depot?"

Rian had spent a lot of time with the first mate the previous day. This morning, it felt like he wasn't treating her any differently, even though she was wearing her day dress. "Heinrich is still sick. I guess my father and I will do it. Why?"

"Keep yer dukes up. Some fellas in that crowd don't wish ya well."

"How do you know that?"

"The harbor pilot told me. A machine shop in Worcester claims the *Boston & Lowell* should have bought local, not from out-of-staters. They hired some firemen to interrupt yer delivery."

"In Philadelphia, a lot of firemen are thugs. Is it the same in Boston?"

"That was the harbor pilot's drift. I suggest you be careful."

* * * * *

· OTTO ·

Otto hoped his ongoing queasiness was some sort of seasickness, but now, on dry land, he wasn't feeling any better. In fact, he felt worse. When Joseph Ingersoll, the pier owner, joined him to watch the proceedings, he was grateful for the distraction from his ills. *This event is as big a deal in Boston as in Philadelphia.*

Ingersoll described his new crane's task today—lifting the *Bunker Hill* out of the *Enola* and onto the transport wagons—as its "maiden voyage." He jerked his head toward the wagons. "This is their maiden voyage as well. The *Boston & Lowell Railroad* had Byron & Sons build them to take your engine to the depot."

Otto tried ignoring his increasing nausea to respond to Ingersoll's comment. Despite Otto's recent conversation with George Shippen and last night's argument with Rian, Otto's chagrin shifted to . . . *What? Amazement? Pride?* "I know." He gulped down hard, thinking he should give in to the inevitable, walk to the pier's edge, and throw up into Boston Harbor. Instead, he said, "We built a set of those wagons ourselves. We sent Byron & Sons our plans. The *B&L* hopes they will use the wagons quite a few times."

Ingersoll eyed his crane, which had by now been hooked up to the *Bunker Hill*. His operators were awaiting the signal to start lifting. "Investing in this new crane is a big risk for me, Herr Krieger. To be honest with you, if this depression doesn't end soon, I'll lose everything." He surveyed the deck of the *Enola*, where Rian was talking with the first mate. "Is that your daughter?"

Otto merely nodded as a new wave of nausea passed through him.

"How old is she? Seems like the first mate has taken a shine to her."

Otto gulped air, hoping the nausea would pass. "She is fifteen. She has an interest in steam engines. I am sure she has pried every bit of knowledge she could from him."

At that moment, Rian broke away from the first mate and descended the gangway.

"Make sure she stays out of the way when we load your locomotive onto the wagons."

"That may be rather difficult."

"And why is that?"

Otto gulped again, his nausea stripping him of any ability to stray from the truth. "She designed and built the wagons. This whole operation was her idea."

* * * * *

· RIAN ·

Rian walked down the gangway to get a closer look at the transport wagons before they accepted the burden of the *Bunker Hill*. Sure enough, the Boston wagonmaker had followed her design right down to the beefy wheels and the clevises in the middle of each of the wagons.

"Hey girlie, get away from there," a man yelled. "We're about to bring a locomotive out of this ship."

Rather than explain herself, Rian gave him a half-wave and joined her father and the man he was talking to.

"Rian," said her father, "this is Mr. Ingersoll, the owner of this pier. Mr. Ingersoll, my daughter, Rian."

Mr. Ingersoll held out his hand. "The man who just chastised you is my new strawboss, in charge of the stevedores. I'm afraid he's trying to make a good impression in front of the boss, so I apologize for his disrespect."

"The disrespect didn't surprise me," Rian said while shaking Ingersoll's hand. Then, more for her father's benefit, "I wonder if he would have spoken to me that way if I were wearing pants."

Ingersoll, ignorant of the tension between her and *Vater*, responded with a quizzical look.

Her point made, Rian turned to watch proceedings aboard the *Enola*. "In Philadelphia, the stevedores are all day workers. They show up every morning and the strawboss picks the ones he wants. Sometimes he assembles a good crew, sometimes not. Is that the same here?"

Ingersoll nodded. "Yes, it is. Don't fret. I'm familiar with most of these men. They'll get your daddy's locomotive safety onto your wagons."

The first mate, still aboard the *Enola*, signaled to the crane operator. The crane operator pulled a lever. The crane's steam engine *chooshed*. The *Bunker Hill* slowly emerged from the hold. The crane pivoted and lowered the locomotive onto the wagons. The wagons groaned, like the ones Rian built in Krieger

Coach, but they accepted the burden. A cheer went up from most, but not all, of the onlookers.

The stevedores chained the locomotive tight to the wagons, neglecting the clevis in the middle of each wagon that would allow the engine to pivot when the wagons made their turns.

"No! No!" Rian yelled as she strode toward the stevedores. "Those chains should be looser. There's a clevis in the middle of the wagons to tie it tight to—"

"Begone, girlie," the strawboss barked. "My job is to get this machine safely to the railroad yard. Your job is to shut up and get the hell out of our way."

Rian looked to her father for support. To his credit, he was about to do so when all hell broke loose.

While everyone's attention was on the *Bunker Hill*, a scruffily dressed on-looker with a red beard surreptitiously left the crowd of gawkers, turned a barrel of gunpowder on its side, rolled it near the steam-driven crane, pried the bung out of the barrel, and shook out a thick line of black powder that led directly to the transport wagons. He lifted the keg over his head and smashed it open underneath the lead wagon, then ran away. Meanwhile, a pair of day workers made their way to the crane. One sucker punched the operator while the other grabbed a coal shovel, opened the firebox, scooped up some hot coals, and tossed them onto the line of black powder, which immediately ignited. The men ran, following close behind the first conspirator.

The black powder sparked and flashed its way toward the smashed keg.

Someone in the crowd yelled, "Run away, everyone! She's gonna blow all to thunder!" When most folks started to flee, the yeller blended into the crowd and disappeared from view. Rian heard defiant whoops and hollers as the four perpetrators ran along the pier toward the city.

There was no time for anyone to do anything but react as best as they could in the seconds before the keg blew up.

The strawboss ran toward the few remaining bystanders. "Back up! Back up, everyone!" Those folks turned and ran. Some people fell over, and other people tripped over them.

Rian's father ran to the mule driver and yelled, "Get these animals moving, NOW!" The mule driver whipped at the lead mule, who protested and refused to move. The other mules, sensing danger, brayed but stayed where they were.

Joseph Ingersoll hurried to the crane operator to pull him to safety.

The sparks and flashes raced toward the wagon, yet time slowed for Rian. *Hello, Fire. I must admit I'm not surprised to see you. Have you come to test me? Me? Rian Fooking Krieger?*

Rian gauged the powder's fiery progress toward the *Bunker Hill*. *Fire will follow you.* Ignoring that she was wearing her day dress, she sprinted toward the rear transport wagon. *Fire that is out of control. Fire you think is under control but isn't.* She cut the angle to intercept the igniting powder, all the while yelling, "Rian Fooking Krieger! Rian Fooking Krieger!" She made a feet-first, diving slide between the wheels of the wagon. Her feet, then her legs, broke up the trail. Her dress rode up to her hips. The igniting gunpowder reached her a fraction of a second later, burned her dress, burned her arm, and sputtered out.

Dazed, Rian crawled out from under the wagon and scanned the wharf. The transport wagons were safe. The *Bunker Hill* was safe. People from the crowd were picking themselves up. A couple of them pointed at Rian. Her father, still gripping the lead mule's halter, was throwing up last night's dinner.

Rian brushed her hands over her day dress to return the hem to her ankles. *Pain!* The black powder had burned her right arm. *Nowhere near the nasty burns on my left arm, but I'm going to hurt for a bit.*

Stevedores filtered back. The crane operator sat near the steam engine and shook his head, trying to clear his brain after the sucker punch. Joseph Ingersoll and the strawboss stared at Rian.

Still aboard the *Enola*, the first mate leaned over the railing. "How to spit in their eye, Missy," he called down to her.

Rian gave him a quick wave and a smile, walked over to her father, grabbed him under the arm, and said, "We've got to get you and Heinrich to the American House. You're both sick as dogs."

Half an hour later, Rian had changed into her shop clothes and led her father and Heinrich down the gangway. The strawboss approached Rian when she reached the pier. "Mr. Ingersoll says I should check with you. I think I've got the locomotive tied down properly, but I'd like you to make sure I did it right."

About fooking time, Rian muttered. At her side, her father, still in food poisoning agony, nodded in silent agreement.

WEDNESDAY, SEPTEMBER 18

· OTTO ·

Otto woke from another post-food-poisoning-induced sleep. It took him a few moments to remember where he was. *Yes, the American House hotel in Boston.* He was still dressed in his nightshirt. He glanced out the window—it was light out. *Probably before noon. It has been two days since Rian hired a carriage to get us here. I assume Heinrich is still recovering. He was poisoned worse than I was.*

He shuffled out of his bedroom, hoping to find Rian in the living area. Instead, he found a letter that had been opened and left on the writing desk.

> *Mr. Krieger,*
>
> *Our contract with Krieger Locomotive states that the* B&L *will receive an orientation on the workings of the* Bunker Hill *upon delivery, which occurred two days ago. Although my Boston yard boss assures me his men can make do without an orientation, you have stated in correspondence that the* Bunker Hill *includes workings that are a leap ahead of previous generations of locomotives, whether they be yours your competitors. Therefore, please reply at your earliest convenience when you will be available to honor your commitment.*
>
> *Your humble servant,*
> *Cyrus T. Newkirk*
> *President,* Boston & Lowell Railroad

Below Newkirk's script, Rian had written, *Vater, I've gone to the* B&L *railroad yard.*

* * * * *

In his weakened state, Otto set limited goals for himself. He stuck his head in Heinrich's bedroom and found him sleeping peacefully. He wrote a note to John Quincy Adams, asking when would be an appropriate time to hand deliver a letter from Lucretia Mott. He got dressed and walked the note down to the hotel lobby. He bought a newspaper. The climb back up three flights of stairs wore him out. He read the paper, then dozed and read, dozed and read, for the rest of the day.

He found the following article during one of his reading sessions:

Young Woman Foils Plot

On Monday last, Miss Rian Krieger, a 15-year-old from Philadelphia, courageously foiled an attempt by protesters to prevent a Philadelphia-built locomotive from being delivered to the *Boston & Lowell Railroad*. She bodily threw herself in the way of a fiery line of black powder that was speeding toward a keg of gunpowder broken open under the locomotive.

Besides burns to Miss Krieger, the only other injuries during this unfortunate incident were to the fireman of a steam-operated crane who heroically attempted to defend his machine from the protesters.

"If it weren't for the quick thinking of that young woman," pier owner Joseph Ingersoll told our reporter yesterday, "people and animals would have been killed, the locomotive would have been destroyed, and my pier would have been crippled for weeks."

Although this newspaper does not condone acts of violence, this incident forces us to ask the obvious question: When the current depression is putting many local shops out of business, why is the *Boston & Lowell Railroad* buying a locomotive built in Philadelphia? Admittedly, the protest on the Ingersoll pier got out of hand, but the protestors' intention was undoubtedly to demonstrate that, had this engine been manufactured in Worcester, a struggling local machine shop would have been able to employ another fifteen honest laborers for the past year.

Nine hours later, Otto, who had been snoozing fully dressed in a wingback chair, awoke when Rian, wearing her shop clothes, entered the suite. The whale oil lamp on the table next to him cast a faint aura of light. He eyed his pocket watch. "It is ten o'clock. Where have you been?"

"Well, we started giving the orientation to the *B&L* engine drivers. They liked the *Bunker Hill* so much that we drove it to Lowell and back."

"We? Heinrich has recovered?"

"No, Heinrich was sleeping when I left. I asked Cyrus Newkirk to help me."

Otto was very confused. "The president of the *B&L*? What does he know about locomotives?"

"Nothing beyond the basics."

"Then who gave the engine drivers the orientation?"

"I did."

* * * * *

The next day, a letter arrived in the afternoon mail.

Mr. Krieger,

I hope your recovery is going well. I feel compelled to tell you that your confidence in your son is well warranted. I was initially quite skeptical that one as young as Rian could be so knowledgeable about such a complex machine. In fact, had I only heard about the orientation rather than witnessed it firsthand, I would have been irritated that you assigned a fifteen-year-old to this important task.

My engine drivers were equally impressed and are extremely pleased with the Bunker Hill. *Rest assured, when this depression eases up, you can count on us to purchase additional locomotives from Krieger Locomotive (and never the machine shop whose thugs caused the problems on the pier). Rian tells us you have an even more advanced machine in the works.*

I hope I am not being too presumptuous to comment: Perhaps someday Krieger Locomotive will be renamed Krieger & Son Locomotive.

Your humble servant,
Cyrus T. Newkirk
President, Boston & Lowell Railroad

* * * * *

· OLIVIA ·

It was the first All School Meeting of the year, held as usual in the Chapel. Dr. Marks stood at the podium. Having made his welcoming remarks, he went on to announcements. "I'm pleased to inform you that we have a number of new faculty members, all of whom I hope you get to know better as the school year unfolds. Our enrollment this year is slightly less than last year, but, in light of the return of the depression, this should be no surprise."

Dr. Marks droned on with the same platitudes he used last year, then moved on to announcements. "When we cleaned the rooms after you all left at the end of the spring semester, we found an inordinate amount of mouse droppings."

A collective "eeeew" went up from the assembled girls.

"This year, no food will be allowed in your rooms. Anyone found with food will be given extra duties . . . Also, one last announcement. I assume many of you heard of the tragic fire at the Ledbetter Rooming House in town this summer."

Olivia leaned over to Eugenie and whispered, "What tragic fire?"

"It happened while you were in Paris," Eugenie whispered back. "Three people died. The innkeeper had gone out for the night. No one knew they were in the building."

"In response," Dr. Marks continued from the podium, "we will be conducting three fire drills this semester to assure ourselves that our safety systems are in place and you girls all know your responsibilities should a real fire occur. I will be working through each of the four class presidents. Be prepared."

FRIDAY, SEPTEMBER 20

· OTTO ·

On Thursday, with the food poisoning finally behind them, Otto and Heinrich decided they felt well enough to see the sights around Boston. Just before leaving their suite in America House, Rian emerged from her bedroom wearing her shop clothes, her hair tucked into her flat cap.

"Why are you not wearing your dress?" asked Otto. "We are sightseeing. One dresses up for sightseeing."

"My day dress is ruined. My dinner dress wouldn't be appropriate. No one will pay any attention to me because they'll assume I'm a boy."

Otto's shoulders sagged in resignation. He was too tired—or perhaps, more accurately, too at sea about his thoughts and plans for his daughter—to demand that she change into something . . . anything besides her damned shop clothes. On the way out of the hotel, however, a helpful clerk at the American House front desk accepted responsibility for Rian's day dress and vowed to have it repaired and back to them the next day.

With Rian leading the way, the trio visited Boston Common, Old North Church, and Faneuil Hall.

The following day, Friday, they planned to rent a carriage and visit the battlefields at Lexington and Concord, but a note from John Quincy Adams arrived, stating he had time to meet with Otto only today and to please bring Rian. Rian seemed enthusiastic about visiting Adams despite having to wear her now-repaired day dress.

As Otto and Rian prepared to leave the suite, a letter was slipped under their door.

Dear Mr. Krieger,

As evidenced by the enclosed newspaper article, you can see that my letter dated yesterday was penned under the false impression that your daughter, Rian, was a boy. I hasten to tell you she never explicitly told me she was a boy, but she was dressed as a boy and gave every appearance in effect, deed, and knowledge that she was a boy. I must have called her "lad" or "young man" fifteen times during the day, including a trip to Lowell and back in the cab of our new locomotive, and she never corrected me.

The purpose of this letter is to correct and modify my laudatory letter of yesterday. I object to your subterfuge. I object to the fact that I was led to believe I was working with a precocious young man. I strongly recommend you examine your plans to keep your daughter on the payroll. Women are meant to be in the home, not out giving false impressions to the world.

Your humble servant,
Cyrus T. Newkirk
President, Boston & Lowell Railroad

On the buggy ride to Quincy, Otto had no idea what he would do or say to Rian because he was so at sea himself. His father was a blacksmith and cavalryman, the source of the "Warrior by name and warrior by nature" family motto. But it was his mother who kept the family together when his father went off to war and when he came back a wounded man. She was the strong one, the feisty one.

"*Liebling*, I want to tell you about my mother . . . your grandmother Gisela."

"You've told me about her. She was strong. She was a blacksmith. She raised you and Uncle Adrian and Uncle Kurt and Aunt Monika when your father was fighting in Russia."

"Yes, she was strong, but her strength was her undoing. She believed in the ideas seeping into Germany from France in those years. Revolutionary ideas about liberty and equality. I am sure I called her a blacksmith when I told you about her in the past. She shoed horses. She forged tools out of iron. She repaired things. But she could not call herself a blacksmith because she was a woman, and women were not allowed to be blacksmiths in those days. Probably are not in Stuttgart even now. Our neighbors did not like her."

"Because she was blacksmithing?"

"That was part of it—she was doing a man's work . . . a guildsman's work— but it was more than that. She was too outspoken, too free-thinking. She did not fit the mold of what a good German *hausfrau* should be."

"Did that hurt you?"

"Oh, we kids knew about it, but we loved our mother. She protected us. But then came the Hunger Year. In 1816, we had no summer to speak of in

Württemberg. It froze a couple of times in July. The crops failed. That winter, things got desperate. Everyone was starving. We ate rats and tree bark to survive. That is when our neighbors found it easy to shun us because they did not like my mother. She was too different from what they thought she should be. *Liebling*, my mother died of starvation because our neighbors turned their backs on her."

"Why are you telling me this now?"

Otto reined in the horses because two carriages blocked the road while their drivers exchanged greetings. He reached into his coat pocket and handed Rian the two letters from Cyrus Newkirk. "Because you remind me of her. And I fear that your fate will be the same as hers . . . rejected by people who are intimidated by your strength, or maybe just because you are a girl who gets things done." The carriages up front parted and Otto flipped the reins. The horses obediently returned to a trot.

Rian took a long time to read both letters in the jouncing buggy. After she read them both a second time, she held them in her lap. "I liked Mr. Newkirk."

"And he liked you—until he found out you are a young woman."

"I don't want to be a young woman."

"Here is what I see. You have already done so much in your short life. In this week alone, you brought about the delivery of a fully assembled locomotive to the *B&L*, prevented the *Bunker Hill* from being blown up, and gave an orientation to Cyrus Newkirk and his men."

"Aren't those all good things?"

"They are brave things, smart things, but you had to be lucky, or foolhardy, or deceitful to make them happen. And when the Cyrus Newkirks of the world hear about them, they reject their value because of who you are: a young woman. Rian, I want you to stop being this person."

Rian wiped her face with the palm of her hand. Otto suspected she was crying, but he kept his eyes on the carriage a hundred yards ahead of them.

"You want me to stop being me?" Rian asked.

I am totally out of my element here. "I want you to conform more to what our neighbors are willing to accept."

"Which neighbors? Quinton Schott doesn't have problems with who I am. Gam Leonard doesn't. Lucretia doesn't."

My fears . . . Tell her my fears. "But those who do will one day hurt you."

Rian was silent as they approached the bridge over the Neponset River. The buggy wheels rumbled as they bounced over the wooden planks. Once on the other side, Rian said, "No. I won't do what people I've never met think I should

256 · ROGER A. SMITH

do. I can't. If you make me, I'll run away again. This time I'll head out West. I'll make a living playing poker on a Mississippi riverboat."

Otto felt himself losing control of the argument. *As I always do.* "*Liebling,* I think I am an excellent carriage maker and a pretty good salesman. But I do not know what I am doing as a father. Your mother, rest her soul, is the one who should be handling you, not me. I just do not want you to get hurt." *Oh, Lord, what will I do with her?*

Otto expected Rian to give him the silent treatment for the rest of the ride, but she didn't.

"I never told you about a soothsayer I met in Russia. Her name is Yana. She's the aunt of the woodcutter who came to America with us. She made predictions about me that came true."

"A fortune teller. Since when do you believe in such nonsense?"

"Listen, then you tell me. Before Seamus and Uncle Adrian got arrested—when we thought we would build the Tsar's railroad and be in Russia for years—I asked her if I would live in Russia for a long time. She said no, and she said that was an easy question to answer . . . Seamus and I left Russia less than two months later."

"She had only a yes or no option. She had a fifty-percent chance of being right."

"Then she told me that fire—a lot of it—would follow me in my life."

"And then the Tsar's palace burned?"

"No, in fairness, that had already happened. But she said it would be fire that was out of control and fire I thought was in control but wasn't. Less than a month after I returned to Philadelphia, the mob burned down Pennsylvania Hall. The next night I led them away from Lucretia's house, and they burned down the Home for Colored Orphans instead. . . ."

"Those were fires you gravitated to. You could have stayed away from them. Then there would be no story."

"And then the steam engine blew me up—a fire I thought was in control but wasn't. Then four days ago you and I almost got blown up on the dock. Do you see? Yana made predictions that came true, so I know she's not a fake."

Nonsense. "Why are you telling me this now?"

"Because Yana also told me that first I wouldn't run Krieger Locomotive, then I would. She came to that prediction two different ways. So *Vater,* I know I'm going to run Uncle Adrian's shop one day, I just don't know when. And I'm telling you: Nothing you ever do will stop me."

She is bullheaded, like her grandmother. I am surprised she puts so much faith in a Russian soothsayer. "Could you at least stop being so foolhardy then? Stop throwing yourself in the way of black powder about to explode?"

"Well, that's the thing. Conor says I can't die in an explosion or any way else because all of Yana's predictions haven't come true yet. I knew I wouldn't get blown up the other day because I wasn't running Krieger Locomotive yet."

My daughter has just handed me a rare opportunity to get the best of her in an argument. "*Liebling,* you know I don't believe any bit of this nonsense, but if I did, given what you just told me, I would never let you take over Krieger Locomotive."

"Why? What are you talking about?"

"You occasionally make foolhardy, dangerous decisions, do you not?" Otto sensed Rian knew a trap was coming but didn't yet see it.

"I guess so," she said.

"Well, if you cannot die before you take over Krieger Locomotive and I want to prevent you from dying, my best gambit is to never make you foreman."

"*Verdammt noch mal* [Damnit]," Rian muttered, eliciting a smile from Otto.

* * * * *

· RIAN ·

John Quincy Adams was tending roses in front of his home when Rian and her father arrived. He laid his shears on a rickety old garden bench and strode to the front gate. "Welcome to Peacefield, Herr Krieger. Rian, how good to see you again."

Her father alighted from the buggy and greeted President Adams. Instead of greeting Adams immediately, Rian unhooked the horses and tied them to a hitching post next to a watering trough.

Adams held the gate open for Otto while he watched Rian at her task. "I lugged a couple of buckets of water out this morning. Your horses will be fine for the moment. Give them enough rope to eat the grass. The place always looks better when the horses keep it trimmed."

Rian, awkward in the hated dress, finished with the horses, walked through the gate, and shook Adams's hand. His energy and goodwill were palpable.

"Rian, the last time I saw you," said Adams, "you were five inches shorter, covered in tallow, and wearing boy's clothes. And yesterday I read about your brave exploits in one of the Boston papers. Herr Krieger, please come in, come in."

Adams preceded Rian and her father into the house, announcing, "Louisa, my guests are here! We'll be in my study!" He led them upstairs into a long, sumptuous room brightened by sunlight that radiated through pairs of windows on three walls. It reminded Rian more of an unkempt library than a study. Bookshelves lined every available inch of wall space. Although there was a door at each end of the long wall, the second door was closed and inaccessible due to books piled high in front.

A desk, flanked by two large world globes, occupied the middle of the room. Adams gestured with a sweep of his hand for his guests to sit in straight-backed chairs near an inactive fireplace. "Please, make yourselves comfortable." He carried a leather upholstered armchair from behind his desk and plopped himself down. "What is this note our dear friend Lucretia thinks is so important that it must be hand delivered?"

Rian's father reached into his inside coat pocket, retrieved their neighbor's letter, and handed it to Adams. "I believe it's about the Black kidnappees who mutinied and were recently arrested off the coast of Connecticut."

Adams broke the seal on the paper and read for a few minutes. "Hmm, there is a lot to digest here."

Rian resisted the temptation to get up and walk around, perhaps examine the globes or peruse the titles on Adams's bookcases. On Adams's desk, she spied a copy of the newspaper that contained the article about her saving the *Bunker Hill*.

Adams finished the letter. He gazed for a long moment at Rian, then turned his attention to her father. "Please tell Lucretia she is not the first person to urge me to get involved in this case. So far, I am monitoring things from a distance, and whatever influence I have must be applied delicately. I know Judge Smith has already made his ruling, but it has not yet been made public. I doubt the court will decide our Black friends are pirates. But please tell Lucretia that no matter what, I will involve myself at the proper time and place. I will not let these men be condemned to a life of slavery."

Otto started to rise out of his seat. "Well then, I guess my mission has been accomplished. We do not need to take up any more of your valuable time."

Adams smiled and put up a cautionary hand. "My roses can wait. Tarry a bit, Herr Krieger. When I entertain visitors from afar, I like to hear their news. How is business in Philadelphia?"

Otto idly picked at some horse hair that had attached itself to his suit. "The depression still lurks. It gives false hopes, then dashes them. The Krieger companies are doing well, however. We have a contract in hand for twelve locomotives and twenty-four railroad cars that will assure our prosperity for the next two years at least. We are confidently going forward and investing in a new factory across the street from our current shops."

Adams folded his arms. "Expanding during a depression. A bold move."

"Timing in business is very important, Mr. President. If we do not expand to stay ahead of our competitors, we lose ground."

"Bully for you, Herr Krieger, bully for you." Adams turned his attention to Rian. "Lucretia writes that you are still suffering from the effects of an exploding boiler." He reached for the newspaper on his desk. "This article says you broke up an ignited line of black powder with your body. I find it difficult to reconcile a fear of steam engines with a willingness to risk getting blown up a second time."

Rian hesitated. So much had changed in less than a week. *Rian Fooking Krieger showed up, and Rian Fooking Krieger isn't afraid of anything.* "I think that might be old news, Mr. President."

"How are your burns?"

Rian held up her right arm, which didn't even have a bandage. "I've had worse."

"With your fears behind you, is there anything we need to talk about?"

Yes. It's time. "I'd like to reclaim the package I sent from Russia last year."

Adams smiled, nodded, rose, and strode to a bookcase. "Good," he said over his shoulder. "I figured that was you as soon as I read Lucretia's letter. She says you ran away to Russia when you were thirteen. How long were you there?"

Rian stared back at President Adams. "Five months."

Adams retrieved the package, still wrapped in brown paper and tied with twine, and returned to his chair. With the package in his hands, he leaned forward with his elbows on his knees. "You know, I was America's first ambassador to Russia. I strolled the Neva with Tsar Alexander—Nicholas's older brother—during Napoleon's invasion. Must say, I didn't care for Nicholas much as a young man."

"I didn't care for him much as a Tsar."

"According to Mrs. Mott, your uncle and cousin ran afoul of the Tsar, and you did something to get them out of prison."

"Well, they didn't really run afoul of the Tsar. They ran afoul of the Minister of the Imperial Court."

"Ah, the dreaded Prince Volkonsky. I had doings with him as well when I served in Russia. He was one of the Tsar's closest advisors. I'm talking now about Alexander. Volkonsky was quite filled with himself at the time. And what did you, a thirteen-year-old, do to spring your relatives from prison?"

"You haven't read what's inside the package?"

"No, but I assure you, I would have before I sent it to any newspaper. Now that I know you are the source, I think we should deepen our relationship." Adams cracked a wry smile. "You can trust me. After all, I used to be the president of these United States."

Vater *is going to get an earful. He hasn't heard all this.* "That package contains proof that Tsar Nicholas isn't a Romanov by blood."

Adams leaned back in his chair. "I heard rumors to that effect when I was the ambassador. How could you have proof?"

"I copied parts of Catherine the Great's memoir. She had an affair with a military officer named Saltykov. Saltykov was the real father of Catherine's son Paul. That means his sons Alexander and Nicholas weren't either. I used the information to get Volkonsky to spring my uncle, cousin, and two other men from prison."

Adams spread his arms wide and gazed upward, as if a great revelation had dawned on him. "It was *you* who caused all that ruckus."

"Excuse me, sir?"

"My dear, please remember my employment history. I am still kept abreast of significant developments in international affairs. Ambassador Dallas sent a flurry of communications to the secretary of state. You were masquerading as a boy at the time, if I remember correctly."

"Yes, sir."

"And you angered the Tsar. He claimed Americans were meddling in Russian internal affairs. You pitted two of his ministers against one another. One was Volkonsky and the other one was . . . ?"

"General Benckendorff, head of the Third Section. He doesn't like Volkonsky either."

Adams shook his head in wonderment. "Brilliant. Ambassador Dallas had to muster all his diplomatic skills to smooth that one over."

Rian sensed her father stirring to her left. *He knew Mr. Dallas before he left for Russia.* "I never heard about that. Mr. Dallas didn't like me very much."

"And I can imagine why. Well, hopefully you won't run into him when he returns to Philadelphia."

"He's not in Russia anymore?"

"That's my understanding. He asked Secretary of State Forsyth to be brought back home. I believe he's had enough of the Russian winters. Rian, how long do you intend to hold on to this Sword of Damocles?"

"Ten years. Until 1848. I'll be twenty-four."

Adams looked ceilingward, as if calculating. "That is a long time. Too long for me. I doubt I will live to age eighty-five." He handed the memoir to

Rian. "You were smart to pen this copy of Catherine's memoir. Volkonsky is vindictive. Hopefully, his knowledge of its existence will prevent him from harming you."

"That was my thinking, sir."

"Well, please, don't get blown up again any time soon. I believe you should pass this manuscript on to someone much younger than me. If this information ever became known to the Russian nobility, they could weaken the Tsar considerably."

"I don't think that would be a bad thing. I don't like him."

"Oh, we are in agreement on that point, dear Rian." Adams nodded to Otto, referring back to his comments moments ago. "But you will find that, as in business, timing in international affairs is everything. By all means, keep your word. Return the memoir when you said you would. But if Volkonsky tries anything before then, I would say the deal is void. You could send this document to the press with a free conscience. Be sure to pick the appropriate time."

"Ahem," said her father. "Mr. President, these are heady words to a fifteen-year-old."

Adams turned to Otto. "Heady? Yes. Inappropriate? Perhaps not. Your daughter caused an international incident as a thirteen-year-old, apparently with some deftness." He again consulted Lucretia's letter. "Lucretia writes here that when Rian was eleven, she helped a woman escape from her enslavers. She stabbed a mugger in the leg when she was twelve. Last year she intentionally led a mob away from Lucretia's home when they were intent on burning it down. We have already discussed getting blown up by a steam engine. Lucretia says you saved some lives by warning men away before the boiler blew . . . Now, Lucretia editorializes here . . . She has heard Rian also excels at a card game called poker, and she is a partner in a distilling business." Adams reached behind him and grabbed the newspaper. "And just yesterday, according to this article, your daughter threw herself into the path of a line of flaming gunpowder to prevent your locomotive from being destroyed. I think your daughter's instincts are sound."

This is my opening. If I can get President Adams on my side, he can change Vater's *mind.* "Mr. President, I want to someday run Krieger Locomotive. My father doesn't think it would be appropriate."

Adams glanced alternately between father and daughter. Clearly aware he had been brought into a domestic dispute, he hesitated.

"*Liebling,*" said *Vater,* "I am not sure that we should be bothering President Adams—"

Adams held up his hand. "Like I said, when people visit me from afar, I like to hear their concerns." Then he shifted and addressed Rian. "Tell me about this."

Here we go. "I've wanted to run my Uncle Adrian's factory since I was twelve. I keep the books for all three Krieger factories, and my cousin's distillery to boot. I understand how money flows and how knowledge should be used to make future decisions. I'm the best draftsman and the second-best pattern maker in the shop. I help the designer do his research for the next locomotive we'll build. I can caulk a boiler; I can tell when something is wrong with a machine just by the sound of it. I thought up the idea of delivering a fully assembled locomotive to Boston. I designed and built wagons stout enough to carry a fifteen-ton engine to the docks. I trained a crew of men from the *Boston & Lowell* on the new engine. . . ."

Adams cocked his head. "And why didn't your father do it?"

"He and Heinrich both had food poisoning." *And* Vater *doesn't know enough about our locomotives to train anybody.*

The former president turned to Otto. "And Herr Krieger, you do not want Rian to run your brother's factory? Why doesn't your brother make that decision?"

Otto folded his hands in front of him, hesitated for a few moments, then said, "I am in charge of Krieger Locomotive while my brother is living in Saxony. There is no doubt my daughter is capable. She is also impulsive. By the time she was eleven, she had already been expelled from three schools for fighting. I brought her into the factory for lack of options. She soaked up accounting skills as fast as my bookkeeper could dish them out. But the demands of running a factory are much different than paying bills in the confines of an office. More public. More dangerous. More vulnerable to the whims and prejudices of the community. I honestly fear Rian will be harmed, and this time, it will not be by an exploding steam engine. Intolerant people turn to violence when they find the vulnerable among us who they feel are getting ahead of themselves. Rian and I have seen this when it comes to members of the Negro community. And this is certainly so for every woman in America. Not women who 'stay in their place,' but women who assume prerogatives that are not theirs by statute or by custom. I would prefer Rian redirect her energy to finding a suitable husband and let him take the lead on these tasks."

Rian was surprised at the vehemence—and the cogency—of her father's defense. She sensed the chances of her winning this argument slipping away.

"I think both sides have ably stated their case." Adams rose, walked to a cabinet, pulled a small drawer completely out of its compartment, and carried it to the desk. He sorted through scores of bundles of letters, each bound with string. "My father was away from my mother for lengthy periods from the time of the Revolution through his presidency. Neither one ever threw their letters away . . . Ah, here it is. Father was in Philadelphia on and off during much of the Revolution. He wasn't on the committee that crafted the Articles of Confederation, but he got occasional updates and wrote about them to my mother, who was living in Boston at the time. Rumors that the Second Continental Congress would soon declare independence was sweeping across the land."

Adams undid the string from one of the bundles, then unfolded a sheet of onionskin so thin that the words penned on the opposite side had bled through. "Here is what my mother wrote to my father. 'I long to hear that you have declared an independency—and by the way, in the new Code of Laws which I suppose it will be necessary for you to make, I desire you would Remember the Ladies, and be more generous and favourable to them than your ancestors. Do not put such unlimited power into the hands of the Husbands. Remember all Men would be tyrants if they could. If particular care and attention is not paid to the Ladies, we are determined to foment a Rebellion, and will not hold ourselves bound by any Laws in which we have no voice, or Representation.'"[27]

Rian stirred, feeling Adams coming down on her side of her dispute with her father. "Your mother was a woman ahead of her time."

"My mother was very capable. During my father's absences, she performed what she referred to as 'man's work,' somewhat begrudgingly but with pride. She managed the farmhands, made decisions about when and where to buy and sell livestock. She even purchased land, locally and in Vermont, although it was illegal for her to do so."

Rian tried to gauge her father's reaction, but his face was stony.

"But my mother didn't write these words to gain an equal footing with men in the world of business," Adams continued. "She knew firsthand how difficult it was to run a farm. All she was asking for was laws to be crafted so that when the man—the head of the household—was away, the wife would not be impeded from keeping the family on an even keel. She didn't seek my father's responsibilities when he was away, nor did she want them. Circumstances forced them upon her. She rose to the occasion despite the laws of the time. In retrospect, she believed her performance was unnatural, but it had to be done."[28]

27. Except for the addition of three commas, this is an exact quote of Abigail Adams's letter written to husband John Adams on March 31, 1776.

28. For a more complete view of Abigail Adams's attitude toward her domestic responsibilities, Edith Gelles, author of two biographies and editor of 430 of her letters, offers amazing insights and commentary.

"The laws at the time," Rian ventured. "Did your father encourage the committee to change the laws?"

"No, he did not. The men of that generation were concerned with getting out from under Britain's heel and birthing a new nation. They were not concerned with the rights of women. My mother's letter went unheeded."

Rian stirred, unsure of her ground. "So does your mother's letter support my aspirations or subvert them?"

Adams's eyes drilled into Rian. "I think my mother would be amazed to hear your story, impressed by what you have done in your young life, but she wouldn't support your aspirations. You, dear Rian, as capable as you are, have a role to play. The role of an extraordinary young woman, but still a woman whose exceptionality will be manifested through the successes of her husband."

Rian was crushed. Her father again tried to end the conversation. "Mr. President, we thank you for your time."

Adams again held up his hand. "I'm not finished yet. Herr Krieger, have you ever heard of the term *prodigy*?"

"No, what is that?"

"A prodigy is a person extraordinarily gifted in a particular area. Such talents are occasionally manifested as a child, but that is very rare. Mozart was such a youth—a once-in-a-generation talent. He played the pianoforte and violin by age five. Performed before royalty all over Europe by age ten. A Frenchman named Blaise Pascal, who lived in the 1600s, was equally gifted as a child but in the field of mathematics. I think you should consider this: Your daughter—your knife-wielding, bookkeeping, blackmailing, locomotive-designing, poker-playing, obstreperous Rian—may be that once-in-a-generation prodigy in the world of business." Then a smile crept over Adams's face. "Or perhaps mayhem."

"You are serious, Mr. President?" her father asked.

"Deadly serious," Adams responded. "And I think you should ask yourself whether you want to stifle that gift or let it out into the world?"

Rian's father leaned back in his chair. "I suppose that depends. Are we talking about business or mayhem?"

"That is for you and Rian to decide together."

* * * * *

· OTTO ·

Otto and Rian were lost in their own thoughts for the first fifteen minutes of the buggy ride back to Boston. Finally, he asked, "Who will you send the memoir to?"

"Maybe Hilda, your half-sister in . . . wherever it is in Pennsylvania she lives."

"Newport. I think Hilda would fit the bill. And Adams's perspective. Let us say for the moment that you are a business prodigy. How do we go about our lives—with you and your unique sense of where the Krieger businesses should go—and still get what I need, which is to make sure you do not go so far out on a limb that Philadelphia will shun you."

"That's what you're worried about? That I'll be shunned?" Her tone was dismissive, accusatory.

Otto felt the budding conversation already spinning out of control. "Well, there are other dimensions to this problem. I suppose my disapproval of you wearing your shop clothes is part of it. Your propensity to allow people to assume you are a boy. My fear you will never marry, never take your rightful place in society. But yes, at its core, I fear the people of the City of Brotherly Love will shun you at the very least and actively go out of their way to harm you, for no other reason than you are a woman attempting to do a man's job."

"I'm not a woman yet," Rian uttered without hesitation.

"But you will be soon."

Otto noted how Rian ignored his last statement. Instead, she responded to his business prodigy question. "Let's say I have an idea . . . I come to you. If you like it, you tell Gerald Downing it's your idea. As long as you and Jules know it's me, I don't care if you get the credit."

"I doubt I would take credit for one of your good ideas. I would most likely endorse it and give you credit for it. What about the dresses?"

"Same as ever. Special occasions. Travel."

"And allowing older men to think you are a young man?"

"Special occasions."

"What does that mean?"

Otto could tell Rian was smiling, even though they were both staring straight ahead. "It means I don't know. Sometimes I'll be okay with them knowing I'm a girl. Sometimes I'll let them think what their eyes tell them."

"And what if Mr. Adams's humorous comment is actually valid, that your gift may not be in business, it may be for causing mayhem?"

Rian didn't respond right away. The buggy jounced through a lengthy dried rut, forcing both Otto and his daughter to hang on to the side of the bench. Once the rut was behind them, Rian said, "How about this? If I feel the mayhem coming on, I give you as much warning as I can."

Well, at least she does not deny mayhem is what she does. "*Liebling*, you have always kept your secrets from me. Are you saying that you are willing to bring me into your circle of trust?"

"Yes, I think that's what I'm willing to do. I'll do my best."

Otto felt the ground shift under his feet. "*Liebling*, I think we have a deal."

TUESDAY, SEPTEMBER, 24

· RIAN ·

The *Enola* had completed a trip to Philadelphia and back by the time Rian, Heinrich, and her father were ready to leave Boston. Once back aboard the steamship, Rian realized how much her view of herself had changed on this trip. The incident with the black powder indicated her fear of steam engines was tamped down to a healthy caution. But it went further than that. For the first time in—*How long? Years?*—that pesky *You're The Oddity* rat-thought hadn't been regularly gnawing away in the back of her brain. It had been knocked on its heels by the welcome one-two punches of Conor's *You are Rian Fooking Krieger* speech and President Adams's prodigy/mayhem musings.

She thought Adams's talk was the kind of thing that could get her into trouble. *Thinking I'm smarter than everybody is a trap. It could be like when I played poker with the adults on the* Great Western. *I assumed I was the best player at the table, and that's when I lost almost everything I'd won on the voyage.*

So, life felt pretty good as they steamed back up the Delaware. That confidence got muted somewhat as the *Enola* steamed by so many idle Philadelphia wharves. *If this depression comes back, maybe Krieger Locomotive will* need *a prodigy.*

A letter from Olivia was waiting in the mail basket on the porch.

"Who is the letter from?" Otto asked as he inserted his key into the front door.

"Olivia. She spent the summer in France. I suspect she's back at school by now." *And she is writing love letters to me as if I were a* boy *as an excuse to pass on the information from Topper that becomes "Notes from Jasper."* Rian felt her promise to her father to bring him into the Inner Circle of Trust slip away. *Maybe* Vater *should be in the Outer Ring of the Inner Circle of Trust.*

Rian lugged her carpetbags to the second floor while holding the letter in her mouth. She sat on the bed, broke the seal, then settled in to read the letter. Olivia wrote from the steamboat *Granby*, which was on the Cooper River at the time. Her news seemed urgent and her ire, although not explicitly stated, was quite evident. The biggest item was that Olivia's father had sold slaves named as collateral on his loan agreement with the Bank of Industry. The bank was being cheated.

Since there was no reference to the *Rian-Krieger-is-a-*boy*-who-I-am-falling-in-love-with* ruse, Rian walked down the hall to her father's bedroom. "Uh, *Vater*, there's something going on you should know about."

Otto didn't bother looking up from his unpacking. "Does this have anything to do with Miss Olivia Tucker?"

"Olivia's half-brother Topper is a slave . . . a groom on a cotton plantation outside of Columbia. She sees him every once in a while. Topper has been writing things about the life of a slave. He passes them on to her, and she sends them to me. I take them to Harold Foote. He publishes them in the *Philadelphia Independent*, and they send copies to William Lloyd Garrison in Boston. Garrison reprints them. I guess they get reprinted all over the country."

Her father stopped unpacking and turned to Rian, his attention was now fully on her story. "Are these articles like 'Notes from Jasper' Harold has been writing?"

"They aren't *like* 'Notes from Jasper.' They *are* 'Notes from Jasper.'"

"And you are telling me this in light of our new agreement? I sense a wave of mayhem coming."

Rian shrugged. "Well, this little bit of mayhem kind of involves you. You sit on the Bank of Industry loan committee. This latest letter from Olivia states that the Bank of Industry is being cheated."

WEDNESDAY, SEPTEMBER 25

· RIAN ·

It was six o'clock in the morning and raining hard. Instead of walking directly to the office at Krieger Coach, Rian continued one block farther north on Broad Street. Her long, rubber-coated Mackintosh and flat cap only delayed the inevitable soaking, but she didn't care. Her mind was on the future of the Krieger companies.

The locomotive factory was taking shape across the street from the three existing Krieger factories. Previously, distracted by spending time in Hell and building the transport wagons, Rian had paid little attention to the construction. On this occasion, she wandered in and around the roofless factory shell. *Vater has taken out a huge loan—his future, my future—and bet on the success of this factory. I can see what it will be like in a few months—where every machine will be placed to best fabricate our locomotives. But the decision to build this giant, beautiful building is based on one contract. If the* Utica & Schenectady *welches on us, we are up the creek without a paddle.*

She returned to the street and turned to take in the factory's expanse. *If all goes well, Vater and I will walk to work. He will peel off to Krieger Coach, but I'll walk a little bit farther to come here. We will make the finest locomotives in the world.* Then, for the millionth time, Rian recalled Yana's prediction when Rian asked her if she would ever run Krieger Locomotive: *no, then yes.*

Rian walked to the corner, oblivious to the rain, and gazed at the factory from yet another perspective. Krieger Rail president Aaron Bassinger appeared next to her and held his umbrella above both of them. "I thought that was you. What are you doing here?"

"Half the wharves in Philadelphia and Boston are idle. This depression isn't over for a lot of people. Do you think my father is foolish for doing this?"

Aaron regarded the building. "Your father is an excellent designer of railroad coaches and a brilliant salesman."

"You didn't answer my question."

Aaron shrugged but offered no additional opinion.

"*Vater* mortgaged us up to the eyeballs after he landed that contract from the *Utica & Schenectady*. Other than the *U&S*, business has tapered off."

Aaron stood next to Rian as rain hitting the umbrella filled the silence. He turned toward the factories to the south. "Good to have you back, Rian. Make sure you get to the office before you're totally soaked."

"I'll be there for a bit. Then I've got to run some errands."

* * * * *

Rian walked in the persistent downpour to the *Philadelphia Independent* office. The steam-powered printing press *pocketa-pocketa-pocketa-ed* away, cranking out page after page of the newspaper. Harold Foote, his fingers ink stained, worked at his desk.

Foote noted Rian's approach and motioned for her to sit down. "More Notes?"

Rian shed her slicker and handed Olivia's letter to Foote. "A little different this time. It isn't from Topper. This information comes directly from Olivia."

Foote read the letter, then set it down on his desk. "Any reason not to file the story as if it were from Jasper? I can get this into print next week."

"No. I think that's a good idea. I imagine the slaveholders are trying to find Jasper." Rian rose to leave. "This will muddy the waters a bit, but don't name the Bank of Industry as one of the banks being cheated. People will figure that out on their own."

"Hey, before you go . . . Doesn't Krieger Locomotive have dealings with some of the railroads in central New York?"

"Yeah, the *Utica & Schenectady*. Why?"

"We trade courtesy copies with the *Schenectady Cabinet*. Their latest issue came in a couple of days ago. Geoffrey didn't see a need to reprint any of its articles, but he thought this might interest your father. He asked me to pass it on."

Railroad Yields to Protests
Gives in to Local Landowners' Demand to Reroute Railroad Bed

It seems no one wants noisy, ember-spewing locomotives anywhere near their livestock, barns, or hamlet centers. Sparked by protracted protests and lawsuits from landowners and business people along the proposed route of the new *Utica & Syracuse Railroad*, the railroad's Board of Directors has called a halt to further construction until a new route between the two cities can be successfully negotiated.

Rian didn't need to read any further. *This is not good.* "Can I take this?"

"We don't need it. Will you show it to your father?"

"Of course." *And it will be an unpleasant meeting.*

* * * * *

· OTTO ·

It was eleven-thirty in the morning, an hour before Otto typically walked to the United States Hotel for lunch. This morning, his first day back in the office after the Boston trip, he waded into the usual array of mail, snits, and updates, plus three notes from Nicholas Biddle, the former president of the Second National Bank, asking for a meeting. Otto sent a messenger boy to Biddle's home, suggesting an eleven o'clock meeting in the dining room of the United States Hotel. Biddle agreed to the time but not the place. He proposed instead a rendezvous upstairs in the hotel in Room 313.

Otto's umbrella sheltered him from the rain, which had remained a downpour during his two-mile walk from the factory. As he approached the hotel, he briefly contemplated the awe-inspiring eight-columned facade of the Second Bank of the United States across the street—a little bit less awesome now that the bank itself was merely a state bank and Biddle was no longer its president.

Otto entered the lobby, installed his umbrella in the rack next to the dining room, and nodded briefly to James. Otto ignored the maître d's look of surprise when he didn't enter the dining room as usual, returned to the lobby, and bounded up the stairs to the third floor. He briefly walked in the wrong direction down the hallway, turned around, found Room 313, and knocked softly on the door. Creaking floorboards indicated that someone would shortly let him in.

Biddle opened the door. "Otto, come in. Thank you for meeting me here. I assume you had much to do after such a lengthy time away from your factory."

"I must admit you have piqued my curiosity with all this cloak-and-dagger nonsense. James saw me when I entered and probably assumes I have installed a girlfriend up here."

Biddle smiled as he escorted Otto to a table and two chairs by the room's only window. The little rain-soaked light that filtered through reflected off a silver coffee pot flanked by two china cups and saucers. "Oh, I doubt that. Much of the nation's real business is conducted in these rooms, away from prying eyes. What you have observed in the dining room the past five years is merely what those same people have wanted you to see. I think your reputation is safe with James."

Biddle swept his hand toward the left-hand chair. "Please sit. You didn't respond to my notes for the longest time. I was afraid you decided to shun me like so many others."

Otto settled in and watched as his host poured coffee. "I expected to be in Boston only for a few days. The locomotive delivery turned out to be more complicated than I anticipated. Some thugs tried to blow it up, but my daughter foiled their plot. Heinrich and I were sick and unable to give the new owners an orientation."

Biddle sat back in surprise but didn't say anything.

"I found your notes on my desk this morning, my first day back at work. You will be my first dining companion. I am sorry you have been deserted."

"Well, today at least, I will not be joining you for lunch. I think it best that people not see us together for the next little bit. As far as my rejection by my former associates goes, I suppose it's to be expected. I resigned as president of the Second National Bank six months ago. I no longer have any power, any influence. Sadly, neither does the bank."

Otto fingered his coffee cup. "Yet you are still being hounded in the press."

"The Democratic press finds me a convenient demon. The jackals still dog me for alleged transgressions I never committed. It throws the people off the scent of the real culprits. I'm resolved to persevere. Perhaps even come back from the ashes like the phoenix. I have some thoughts that may interest you."

"I am listening."

"How is your business doing these days?"

"You know we are building a new locomotive factory. . . ."

Biddle nodded.

"We bottomed out two years ago. Things have steadily improved since then. Our contract with the *Utica & Schenectady Railroad* has given us confidence to proceed with the construction. The factory is shaping up nicely. When it is finished, we will be poised as a major competitor in the industry. I think we can officially put a nail in the coffin of the Panic of '37. All that unpleasantness is now behind us."

Biddle slipped a folded sheet of paper out of his coat pocket. "I'm not sure the unpleasantness *is* all behind us. I think we have some more rough weather coming."

The hairs on the back of Otto's neck stirred ever so slightly, resonating with the seed of doubt that took up residence in his mind this morning. After ten days away, he expected to return to the office to a stack of letters committing to the purchase of new locomotives, rolling stock, and rail. There were none at all. "Why do you say this?"

Biddle unfolded his paper and donned his reading glasses. "Even though I'm no longer involved with the bank, many former associates still send me information they know I'll find of interest. Today is September 25. Two weeks ago—September 11—the price of cotton on the wharves in New Orleans was twelve-and-a-half cents per pound."

Otto was momentarily distracted by a flash of lightning and thunderclap a few seconds later. The rainstorm had intensified. He returned his attention to Biddle. "As you know, I no longer do business with slaveholders. The price of cotton is of little interest to me. It does not affect me."

"Otto, two years ago, the price was nineteen-and-a-half cents. That's about a thirty-percent decline. Five days ago, at the Charleston slave auction, the top price paid for a young, healthy male field hand was four hundred dollars. That's more than a forty-percent drop."

"Good. Let the bastards rot in hell for all I care."

"I assume you're talking about the slaveholders and not the slaves. There are rumors that the Bank of England is about to raise its interest rates. As soon as they do that, the Dutch will follow. Otto, I cite a few of the many bits of information I have. The economies of the North and the South are inextricably linked to one another, Europe, South Africa, and Asia. If the South is slipping back into a depression, the North will soon follow."

Otto dismissively waved Biddle's conjecture away. "What *is* to be done? I see the American economy—the world's economy, for that matter—to be as regular as the tides on the Delaware. I bet there have been five recessions since I came to this country in 1820."

"Ah, but there is something to be done. You—we—can assure that the little bit of money circulating in this depressed economy goes to the right places."

Otto sipped his coffee, wishing Biddle would get to the point. *Wishing I were not in this discussion.* "How do we do that?"

Biddle nodded as if weighing the best way to proceed with his explanation. "As you know, William Henry Harrison is already running for president again."

"Nicholas, I pay little attention to politics."

"You should. I have it on good authority that Harrison stands firmly behind federal investment in internal improvements—railroads and canals—the first of which is your bread and butter."

"So does Mr. Clay. I see little difference between the two."

"Except that Henry Clay has no chance of getting elected."

Otto disdained political discussions, although they seemed a favorite American pastime. He watched a man on the street below wrestle with his umbrella, which had turned inside out in the wind and rain, then reluctantly turned his attention back to Biddle. "You see Martin Van Buren as vulnerable? He was Jackson's successor, and Jackson is still popular."

"The economy has been in miserable shape since Van Buren came into office, a direct result of his predecessor's policies. Like Jackson, Van Buren has also been a foe of internal improvements."

Another flash of lightning outside. "Nicholas, why are we meeting here? Now? In secrecy?"

Biddle put his elbows on the table and leaned toward Otto. "The Whig National Convention is scheduled for December in Harrisburg. Pennsylvania's Whigs held their state convention while you were gone and selected thirty delegates, but a committee was formed to name substitutes if they are needed. They quietly approached me and asked for suggestions. I would like to recommend you."

This is ridiculous. I have no interest in politics. "Why me?"

"Isn't it obvious? To get your name out there as one of the engines of the Philadelphia industrial class. If Harrison wins . . . *when* Harrison wins . . . the tap of government funds for internal improvements will open up. Otto, if you make the right connections at the Whig National Convention—also in Harrisburg—Uncle Sam's money will flow to your customers, then inexorably toward all three Krieger companies. Your success—your prosperity—will be assured."

"But why the secrecy?"

"Because it is imperative that you and I keep our distance in public. If the press learns I'm working behind the scenes to get Harrison elected, they would crucify me and use the connection to sully Harrison's campaign."

"That is all very thought-provoking. But what do you get out of this?"

"Harrison's people have assured me he is privately in favor of rechartering a national bank, but he's working hard to prevent the national bank from becoming a campaign issue. His support will only come to light after the election. Otto, if we play our cards right, we can get everything we want. A newly chartered national bank can help to stabilize the American economy and bring prosperity back to the country. If I don't return to the president's chair, at least I'll regain some of my former influence. And you, Otto, will become a very rich man."

"You know I am on the Board of Directors of the Bank of Industry. Your plan shoots directly across the bows of one of three Pet Banks in Philadelphia. A new national bank would pull funds back from the Pets."

"Of course I know about your directorship. You are a director because James Forten bought so much of Shippen's bank stock that he could name you and two others as directors. Let me ask you: What has been Shippen's reaction to your directorship?"

"Begrudging acceptance, I would say. He willingly went along with a new loan to Krieger Locomotive. He was less enthusiastic about the loans we extended to members of the Black community. They were all sterling applications, so the bank will do well. Is it not all about making money?"

"Let me phrase my question in another way. James Forten is well into his seventies. When he dies, do you know what happens to his bank stock?"

"Yes, of course. Do you?"

"Otto, I know every bit of business that goes on in this city. When Forten dies, the bank will immediately repurchase his stock at the prevailing rate. How soon after that do you think you, Mott, and Longstreth will be replaced as directors?"

Otto leaned back in his chair. "About as long as it will take me to finish this cup of coffee."

"In that case, throw your lot in with Harrison and become a very rich man."

"Nicholas, let me think about this. I have never been inclined to get involved in politics. I find it all so . . . so distasteful. Plus, although you have made a good case for supporting Harrison, I am unsure I should go to the trouble. Even if no other business comes in, my contract with the *Utica & Schenectady* assures me that my new factory will be running at capacity for the next two years. That alone should ensure we ride out any new slowdown relatively unscathed. How long can such unpleasantness last?"

"I wish I knew, Otto. I wish I knew."

＊ ＊ ＊ ＊ ＊

When Otto returned to the shop, he found a copy of the *Schenectady Cabinet* with an arrow penciled toward an article entitled "Railroads Yield to Protests" and along with the message, *Vater, we should talk about this. When was the last time we heard from Erastus Corning?*

＊ ＊ ＊ ＊ ＊

· RIAN ·

Rian spent the rest of the morning catching up on her bookkeeping in the Coach office. She ate her noontime meal at her desk, then dashed across the alley and entered the clang and clatter of the locomotive shop.

"Hi, Rian," one of the workers said as he walked by. This surprised her because he had never demonstrated any friendliness toward her in the past. "Good to have you back," said another guy who looked up from his drill press. He had previously been nothing but cold toward her.

Rian turned to head up to Hell but ran into Benny Holt before she got to the steps. "Benny, what's going on?"

Benny pointed down the aisle to the far end of the factory near her lair. "Your father just got back from his noon meal at the hotel. He's down there telling a story about you throwing yourself into a line of black powder . . . saving the *Bunker Hill*. Saving his life to boot, the way he tells it. Is it true?"

"I dunno. I guess."

"Well, Heinrich told a bunch of us another story. I asked him how his orientation with the *B&L* engine drivers went. He said he never gave it because he got sick, but you gave it instead. He said you drove the *Bunker Hill* from Boston to Lowell and back. The trainmen were happy with your lesson until they found out you were a girl. Is that one true, too?"

"That's about the size of it."

Benny put his hands in his pockets, leaned back on his heels, and smiled at her. "Well done, Rian. My hat's off to ya. Better watch your back, though."

"Why? Whataya mean?"

"The Trout was happy to be all buddy-buddy with the boss's daughter when she was afraid of steam engines, but you've come back the Big Hero of Boston. He won't like it if you start being popular with the men. He knows you want his job."

"Hi, Rian," said another man who had only muttered at her on previous occasions. "Sounds like you had a good time in Boston."

Jaysus, thought Rian. *What's happening?*

TUESDAY, OCTOBER 8

· OLIVIA ·

Olivia sat next to Eugenie in Natural Philosophy. Caldie Montgomery sat in her usual seat in the front row, the most likely to be called upon when she raised her hand.

After the last stragglers filtered in and took their seats, Mr. Lovewell rose from his chair to address the class. "Ladies, I promised I would get you out of this classroom as much as possible, but it has been so rainy lately, . . ." He shifted and pulled three weighty, oversized books from his desk and placed them on a table next to his podium. "To make up for all that inside time, I have decided you young women will do some original research on the grounds of Barhamville. The South Carolina Female Collegiate Institute has been in operation for eleven years, and it came to my attention that in all that time, we have never inventoried the many species of trees on the grounds. This is your opportunity to do original research." Lovewell paused as positive exclamations and shared smiles rippled around the classroom. "I have three books you may use as references: *Trees of South Carolina, An Atlas of Appalachian Vegetation*, and *Flora and Fauna of the South*. How delightful would it be if one of us discovered a tree not included in one of these books. I expect you to find a partner"—Olivia and Eugenie made eye contact, silently agreeing to work together—"and paste a leaf from each unique species into a page of one of these notebooks. Identify the location and description of the tree, including estimated height. The team with the most trees identified by species will win a prize."

Other girls noisily paired up, prompting Mr. Lovewell to raise his hand to quiet things. "I would like to thank Caldie's father, Representative Montgomery, for lending us two of the reference books we will be using. They wouldn't be here right now if Caldie hadn't told me about them. Please give her a round of applause."

Caldie turned in her chair to receive the gratitude of her classmates. Olivia and Eugenie once again made eye contact: *The teacher's pet gets more praise.*

What a surprise. But Olivia realized there was something else to ponder here. *Mr. Lovewell and Caldie have been having conversations outside of class. What's that all about?*

* * * * *

That evening, a girl from first form delivered a letter from Rian.

Dear Olivia,

I received your letter dated September 10. There was lots of news there, which I shared with my friends.

I would have replied sooner, but I have been in Boston, helping my father deliver a locomotive to the Boston & Lowell Railroad. *The transport wagons I designed and built held up under the weight of our locomotive. I gave the engine orientation to the* B&L *president. We drove a crew of engine drivers all the way to Lowell and back. Later on that week, we delivered a letter to John Quincy Adams for Lucretia Mott. He had some interesting things to tell me that are best told in person.*

I wonder when I will ever see you again. I miss you.

All my love,
Rian

Olivia had to admit Rian was doing a good job with her letter writing. Rian wrote her letters in the voice of a male scion of a successful industrialist. This young man fancied and missed her. His news sounded so fantastic that she wondered how much was exaggeration and how much was totally made up. *And I miss you too, dear Rian.*

* * * * *

Late that evening, the first of the fire drills occurred. Olivia was awakened by Caldie Montgomery banging on doors and yelling, "Fire drill! Everybody up! Fire drill! Everybody up!" Olivia and Eugenie groggily arose and trooped out of the dormitory with the other girls.

* * * * *

· OTTO ·

The *Philadelphia Independent* published the information in Olivia's letter on October 2. It was a doozy, headlined:

NOTES FROM JASPER
South Carolina Rice Plantations
Are Cheating Northern Banks

It described how slaves listed as collateral on loan agreements with Southern planters were being swapped out. Harold Foote had removed specifics—not naming Long Pond, for instance—but described the deception as pervasive.

Otto attended the regular monthly meeting of the Bank of Industry loan committee with the newspaper in hand but planned to raise the issue discreetly with George Shippen during their usual tête-à-tête after the meeting. However, that changed when bank president Edward Schiffler proposed that the bank call in a loan to Joseph Price, a Black druggist who had missed a payment.

"Have you contacted him?" asked Otto. He made a point of making eye contact with James Mott and Jonas Longstreth across the table. Both encouraged him with nods to continue this line of inquiry.

"Uh, no," responded Schiffler. "Our policy is to draw a hard line with these people."

"These people? Our Black clients?"

"Yes, they're unreliable."

"Excuse me," James Mott interjected. "Mr. Price is a member of the executive board of the Pennsylvania Anti-Slavery Society. I know him well. His son was recently killed in a tragic accident. He has been helping his late son's wife and children adjust to their new circumstance."

"Apparently too preoccupied to pay his bills," responded Schiffler. "Herr Krieger, this damn depression keeps flaring back to life, and we find ourselves temporarily cash-strapped. We are calling in money where we can. Mr. Price has made this an easy decision."

Otto slid his copy of the *Philadelphia Independent* toward Schiffler. "There is an article in this newspaper that says rice plantations list their slaves as collateral on loan agreements with Northern banks, then sell them and substitute them with slaves of lesser value. We have loans out to numerous plantations in the South. Have you written them to ask if this article is true?"

"Yes, we read that article as well. We have written to the rice planters to whom we have extended loans," said Schiffler, "but that article came out only a few days ago. We expect we will have responses by our next meeting."

"Are any of these rice plantations behind in their payments?"

Schiffler shuffled his papers, as if he had such information in front of him. "A few, I believe—"

"How many loans do we have to rice plantations in South Carolina, Edward? And how many of them have missed a payment?"

Schiffler glanced at George Shippen, who nodded. "I have that information in my office. Excuse me for a moment."

While Schiffler was out of the room, Shippen said, "We are aware that the Lowcountry rice farmers are going through a bit of a rough patch. Cheap rice from the Dutch East Indies has hurt their sales in Northern Europe."

"Are any of them behind in their payments?"

"Let's wait until Schiffler returns. He will have specifics."

Schiffler returned, ledger book in hand. "We have made loans to nine South Carolina rice plantations."

"And how many have missed a payment recently?"

"Uh, let me see . . . Seven are currently behind in their payments."

"How many of those are behind more than a month?"

Schiffler looked up from his ledger. "I believe all seven."

"I move that we do not call in our loan to the druggist Mr. Jonas Price, and give him as much time to get current as we have allowed the most recalcitrant of these South Carolina planters. I also move that we demand that these rice farmers get current. As well, we should ask for the status of the slaves they listed as collateral in our original agreements."

George Shippen held up a placating hand. "Think about this a bit before you demand we take action on this motion, Otto. I have some personal knowledge of our problem here. My brother-in-law is one of these mortgagees. If the Bank of Industry calls in his loans, the only way he can pay off his loans is to sell some of his slaves. You and I both know that means a life of harvesting sugarcane in Mississippi. As miserable as these people may be now, it will be worse in Mississippi, and they are likely to die a lot sooner. Is that what you want?"

"In the ideal world, slavery would have ended altogether. However, in my capacity as a member of this committee, I would like our policies to be applied equitably to everyone . . . no matter the color of their skin."

The meeting dragged on for another two hours. It was determined that no loans would be called in. Otto feared that one of the ramifications of this decision was that the price of the bank's stock would fall. *And James Forten is the bank's major stockholder. All Forten wanted was for his people to be treated fairly, and now he will pay dearly for his compassion.*

Thursday, October 10

· OTTO ·

When Otto returned to the office after his noontime meal at the United States Hotel, a letter sat on his desk from the afternoon mail.

October 2, 1839

Herr Krieger,

    Against all predictions, passenger traffic on the Utica & Schenectady Railroad *has dropped by ten percent each of the past two months. Last week, we were informed that construction of the* Utica & Syracuse Railroad *has been halted, at least temporarily, thus delaying its completion and the anticipated merger of our two railroads.*

    I regret to inform you that the board of the U&S has instructed me to reduce the purchase of the Eagle-class locomotives *from 6 to 3. We will also invoke Item XIV of our contract's terms & conditions for the* Standard-class locomotives. *As our lawyers interpret it, we are only obligated to purchase 1* Standard-*class locomotive. The remaining 5* Standard-*class locomotives are subject to our approval once we evaluate the first one of this new class, which you should be delivering to us early in 1841. Sadly, I assure you, no matter how well your engine performs, the board will invoke Article XIV.*

    We are also reducing our purchase of passenger cars from 24 to 6.

    I know this decision will affect your plans for your new factory. I hope you haven't broken ground for it yet.

    My sincere apologies for any inconvenience the board's decision may cause you.

I remain,

Erastus Corning

President, Utica & Schenectady Railroad

* * * * *

· OLIVIA ·

The first cotillion dance class had been in session for fifteen minutes, and awkwardness prevailed. Mrs. Marks stood near the piano and clapped out the beat. "ONE, two, three, ONE, two, three, ONE, two, three. . . ." Pairs of young dancers circled the room to an imagined waltz.

Mrs. Marks had recruited a number of young men from Columbia's most prominent families, but not enough future escorts had walked or ridden out to Barhamville to supply a dance partner for every future debutante. Mrs. Marks had disappeared for a few moments and returned with her husband, who now led one young dance partner around in fluid, *STEP, slide, step, STEP, slide, step* motions.

Caldie Montgomery, the perpetual queen bee, had not left the choice of partners up to Mrs. Marks or any one of the escorts. She approached Barnwell Wilkinson. "Will you practice with me, Barney? I'm afraid I'll have two left feet until I get the hang of this." This prompted Olivia to nudge Eugenie and make the now familiar Caldie's-going-to-make-me-throw-up gesture.

After Mrs. Marks had paired all the young men with a future deb, Olivia and Eugenie stood at the side of the room. "Olivia and Eugenie, you will be dancing partners for the moment," said Mrs. Marks. "One of you will have to lead. Come on now, couples. ONE, two, three, ONE, two, three. . . ."

Olivia wasn't much perturbed that she hadn't been paired with one of the boys. She saw too many toes being squashed for that. It didn't even bother her that Caldie had momentarily snaked Barney. *Now that I'm coming out in Columbia, not Charleston, Barney will be my escort come Cotillion time. The best way to twist Caldie's tail is to not let her get under my skin.*

"Lead your partner, gentlemen. STEP, slide, step, STEP, slide, step."

Olivia didn't understand what "leading your partner" meant, so she watched Dr. Marks. With his right hand, he held his dance partner lightly around the waist and extended his left hand to hold her right. His partner placed her left hand gently on his shoulder. Olivia grabbed Eugenie's left hand and theatrically draped it over her shoulder, put her right hand around Eugenie's waist, and started them off with an exaggerated first STEP. Both girls laughed.

They circled the room, their *STEP, slide, step* motions finding a rhythm that avoided squashed toes. Olivia realized she and Eugenie had been roommates for a year, and this was the first time they had touched for any length of time. She liked it.

"Partners!" called Mrs. Marks. "Don't look at your feet! Look into one another's eyes! Smile! This is supposed to be enjoyable!"

Olivia gazed at Eugenie. "I don't know about anybody else, but I'm enjoying myself." Eugenie blushed. Olivia felt something shift within her. She might as well have been struck by a lightning bolt. *I need somebody, and Eugenie is sweet and kind. But how can a person so sweet countenance the existence of slavery? I can't abandon my beliefs, but I need a friend.* She smiled at Eugenie as they continued to dance around the room.

Mrs. Marks sat down at the piano and started playing a tune that incorporated the *ONE, two, three* rhythm she had previously been clapping out. Olivia continued gazing into Eugenie's eyes. Eugenie returned her gaze with a shy smile. They circled the room, their steps more coordinated, more comfortable.

Mr. Lovewell stuck his head in the door as if to see what all the commotion was about. "Professor Lovewell!" Mrs. Marks called from the piano bench. "We need another dance partner! Please join us!"

Pairs of female eyes darted toward Lovewell as he surveyed the room. Many of Olivia's classmates secretly—or not so secretly—lusted after him, and their longing filled the room. Maybe Lovewell saw Olivia and Eugenie dancing together, and maybe he didn't. No matter—he spotted Caldie with Barney, cut in on Barney, and started leading Caldie around in polished, practiced steps. They both smiled into one another's eyes.

Olivia couldn't have cared less about Mr. Lovewell's choice, except that now Caldie had one more thing to lord over the rest of her classmates. Barnwell momentarily seemed at a loss, then spied Olivia and Eugenie as they orbited toward him. He stepped into their path. "Eugenie, do you mind if I dance with Olivia?"

Eugenie didn't let go of Olivia right away. "No," she said to Barney, "of course not," then withdrew her arm from Olivia's shoulder a long, tender second later. The moment was so fleeting Olivia could have ignored it, but . . . *what was it? Reluctance to give me up? Disappointment that Barney didn't choose her?*

I need someone, Olivia thought again to herself. *Someone special to me. Someone to whom I am special.* Barnwell started leading Olivia around the dance floor.

"ONE, two, three, ONE, two, three," Mrs. Marks called out as she banged out the tune on the piano. "Dancers, you should know the steps by now! Stop looking at your feet!"

Barney gazed at Olivia. Olivia smiled at Barney. She expected . . . *What? Electricity? Lust, like half the girls in the room were casting toward Mr. Lovewell? Well, glory be, this is interesting: I was happier with Eugenie in my arms.*

* * * * *

That evening, the second of the semester's fire drills occurred. Caldie banged on doors and yelled, "Fire drill! Everybody up!" The girls exited their rooms and filed out into the brisk night air. Class presidents counted noses and reported their numbers to Dr. Marks. Everyone was back in bed in twenty minutes.

SATURDAY, OCTOBER 12

· RIAN ·

Erastus Corning's devastating letter prompted Rian to pore over Krieger Coach's and Krieger Locomotive's accounting books. She didn't like what she found. Krieger Coach could limp along by producing the six passenger cars for the *U&S*, plus anything with wheels: farm wagons, dog carts, even wheelbarrows. The three *Eagle*-class and the one *Standard*-class locomotives would keep Krieger Locomotive busy for a while, then men would have to be let go. Her father listened to her report, shut his eyes, and nodded.

"*Vater*, I've got to get out of here and clear my head. Would you care to walk to the *P&C* station and talk to some of the workers with me?"

Her father shook his head. "Gerald Downing is coming over for a meeting. I will mention the layoffs to him. How soon must they occur?"

"Not for a while. We'll be okay through the first quarter of next year."

Rian walked south on Broad Street for a couple of blocks to the *Philadelphia & Columbia* railroad station. She hoped to watch the eastbound train from Columbia pull in, but no luck. People awaiting its arrival lounged on benches outside the ticket office. She cocked her head toward the Belmont Incline two miles away—if the train had reached the Incline, you would hear the locomotive as it crawled down the slope, even from this distance. *Even if I could hear it, it would still be fifteen minutes out.*

Not willing to wait and not interested in returning to the shop, she followed the sound of an idling steam engine in the adjacent railroad yard. She came upon craneman Quinton Schott standing atop a wrecked locomotive sitting in pieces atop a flatcar. Connected to the flatcar was a crane car. Its crane was rotating toward the wreck. Emblazoned on the side of the crane car was *Schott Cranes.*

Rian's heart sank. The wrecked locomotive was the *City of Lancaster*, an *Eagle*-class locomotive Krieger had delivered to the *Philadelphia & Columbia* four months ago. Schott was directing one of his men to position the crane over the locomotive.

"What happened?" Rian called to Schott. *This was a beautiful machine four months ago, now it's mangled pieces of junk.*

Schott eyed Rian from his perch. "Hit a cow. Jumped the tracks. Rolled over down an embankment . . . We had to take it apart to get it onto the flatcar. You want it?"

"Can't sell the ones we're making now. What would I want a wreck for?"

"I dunno. Maybe fix it up. Sell it used."

"Who would buy it?"

Schott shrugged. "A mine, maybe. Forestry outfit. Some railroad could use it as a switcher in a railroad yard."

"We built that engine for speed and long hauls. It wouldn't be happy in a railroad yard."

Schott smiled for the first time. "Do you think it would be happier gathering rust right here? That's *P&C*'s current plan. They're gonna cannibalize it for parts when the other *Eagle*-class loco you sold them breaks down."

Rian's mind started racing. "Mind if I come up and take a look at it?"

In answer, Schott waved off the crane operator.

* * * * *

Rian entered the Krieger Coach office with a passel of ideas but had to wait because her father was meeting with The Trout. Jules Freeman, sitting as his desk, sipped coffee while he buried his nose in his work. He gave the faintest shake of his head, implying he wasn't pleased with the drift of Otto and Gerald's talk. Rather than interrupt, Rian sat at her desk to return to drafting a part for the *Standard* locomotive.

"So, you are sure," Otto said to Downing. "This pains me. They have both been with Krieger Locomotive since the beginning."

"I see no alternative," Downing said.

Rian's curiosity finally got the better of her. "What's going on?"

Her father momentarily hung his head. "Gerald thinks we would be better off firing Jimmy Butter and Benny Holt immediately."

I suppose a case could be made for firing men sooner rather than later, but Jimmy and Benny? "Gerald, why would you fire Jimmy and Benny? Those two are more skilled workers than Joheim Fischer."

The Trout turned, his unibody following his head as if they were riveted together. "That isn't my sense of things. Jo is a good and loyal worker."

Loyal to you, maybe. Rian's mind raced. *The Trout was nice to me when I was a wreck, but I'm not afraid of steam engines anymore. News of my exploits in Boston have flown all over the Krieger shops. Things have changed between The Trout and me. Rian Fooking Krieger intimidates him. He chose Benny and Jimmy because they are the two Krieger Locomotive workers who like me better than him. I guess our alliance—uneasy as it was—is over.* "I have some better ideas."

"And what are those?" Downing asked.

"First of all, the locomotive we delivered to the *P&C* four months ago hit a cow and jumped the tracks. It's lying in pieces over at the *P&C* train yard. *Vater*, if you call on them right away, I bet we can sell them a new one to replace it."

Otto smiled for the first time in two days.

"Second, Jimmy and Benny know our machines well. There are three railroads with yards on the outskirts of Philadelphia: the *P&C* across the street, George Shippen's *PW&B* to the south, and the *Philadelphia & Trenton* to the north. Actually, I guess I would also include the *Camden & Amboy* across the river—"

"What is your point, Just-Rian?" The Trout interjected impatiently.

"Rather than fire anybody, we hire out teams to do repairs on our locomotives. Half the machines in this neck of the woods are at least two years old. Parts are already wearing out. Who better to repair them than the men who built them?"

The Trout tsked. "There are only fourteen Krieger Locomotives in existence, one of which has crashed. Will we send Benny to Boston when the *Bunker Hill* breaks down?"

"Probably not. But we could also repair engines built by Norris or Baldwin or Garrett & Eastwick. But that's not my big idea."

"Most railroads have their own skilled craftsmen who do repairs," countered The Trout, clearly annoyed.

"The railroad men aren't as skilled as our men are. We build the machines." Rian turned her attention—and her earnestness—to her father. "And *Vater*, here's my big idea. Last week, you got a request for bids from the *Northern Cross Railroad* in Illinois, but you didn't even bother to respond because they couldn't afford us. Well, our old *Number 12* is sitting in pieces on a siding in the *P&C* yard right now. *P&C* will sell it back to us for almost nothing. We could fix it up and sell it to *Northern Cross*. They get a four-month-old machine at a deep discount."

Otto ran his hand through his hair. "That certainly would buy us some time."

"If that idea works, I have another idea. *Vater*, when you're out on a sales call, do you ever offer to allow the railroad to trade in their old locomotives for a new one?"

288 · ROGER A. SMITH

"No, I have not. Why would I do that?"

"Because they would get a brand-new locomotive for a cheaper price. We take the old one back, recondition it, and sell it for a mark-up to a railroad that can't afford to buy new. There's a lot of those these days."

Otto became animated for the first time. "I can think of a handful of railroads right now that I could approach with a deal like that." Then Otto turned to The Trout. "Gerald, let us delay your layoffs for a bit. Give me some time to examine my daughter's proposals further."

Rian saw an opportunity to take an oblique shot at The Trout. "Uh, *Vater*, I want to make one thing clear. I wouldn't have thought of this if it hadn't been for Quinton Shott. He's the one who gave me the idea of selling used locomotives."

The Trout rose stiffly and moved to leave the office.

Otto picked up his steel-tipped pen and started writing. "One more thing, Gerald, I will be out of town for about a week, from December second to the ninth."

The Trout pivoted his unibody to face Otto. "More sales calls?"

"Not this time. I have been appointed as a delegate to the Whig National Convention in Harrisburg."

"That is quite an honor. Congratulations."

"Perhaps condolences are more in order, but nevertheless, I have agreed to go . . . and Gerald, another thing . . . I doubt this will come up, but if any big decisions arise at the locomotive factory while I am gone, I suggest you consult with Rian."

A noise came from Rian's left. Jules, who rarely let his mask down in front of whites, had spewed coffee all over his desk.

* * * * *

· OTTO ·

Rian leapt from her chair as Gerald Downing closed the office door behind him. "Are you serious?" she blurted as Jules grabbed a shop rag and mopped up spewed coffee.

"Now, now, settle down, *Liebling* . . . Jules, President Adams called Rian a business prodigy. I believe Rian just gave us three ideas that prove he is right. Rian, we should be using your sensibilities but do it in a manner that allows me to get what I need. Gerald is in charge of the shop. He gives the orders. No light will be focused on you. Therefore, I don't fear animosity from the community, the shunning my mother received, the malice. And, assuming Gerald cooperates, you get what you want: the ability to influence decisions in the factory."

Rian plopped back down in her chair and smiled at Jules, who beamed.

"Well done, Otto," said Jules. "I think it's time. It seems we've got a lot to talk about all of a sudden. Rian's new role. The convention. Perhaps we can create trade-in plans for rolling stock as well as locomotives."

At that moment, Seamus Gallagher entered the office without a knock. "Just the three I'm looking for."

"Good morning, Nephew," Otto said. "Something has put a smile on your face."

"Sure has. Siobhan and I are getting married."

All three rose for congratulatory handshakes and slaps on the back.

"It's going to be a small wedding. Family only. None of my boyos are going to be invited. Nor are any of Hugh's crew, although he doesn't know it yet."

"A wise but painful decision, I'm sure," said Otto. "Still bad blood between your No Names and the Moyamensing boys?"

"Oh, it wouldn't be a good Irish wedding if a fight didn't break out. But no. We're *not* inviting the firefighters because we *are* inviting Jules and Maddie. About the only thing that would unite our two outfits is the presence of a Black couple. Social gatherings that include Black and white aren't done, but it's a point of honor that Jules and Maddie attend. I wouldn't be the man I am today if it weren't for Jules."

Jules placed his palms together in front of him in a prayerful salute. "I believe I can speak for my wife. We will be pleased and honored to attend your wedding. I'm humbled by the gesture."

"You are an honorable man, Seamus," said Otto. "When is the date?"

"December seventh."

Otto's shoulders sagged. "Is the date set in stone?"

"Yes, it is. Why?"

"Because I will be in Harrisburg, trying to secure the nomination of William Henry Harrison as the Whig's presidential candidate in next year's election."

* * * * *

· OLIVIA ·

Olivia and Eugenie were sitting on their beds, reading books by Jane Austen. Eugenie was almost finished with *Sense and Sensibility*, which Olivia had read months ago. Olivia was a few pages into *Pride and Prejudice*.

Eugenie turned the last page, put down her book, and sighed. "They never kissed."

"Hmm?" Olivia responded, still absorbed in her book.

"Edward and Elinor. They never kissed. They get married, they move into their new house, but we never see them kiss. I'm happy for them, but I feel quite unsatisfied."

Olivia put down her book. "You expect Miss Austen to let us see such an intimate act? How would she describe it?"

"I don't know. I've never seen anyone kiss. Not even my parents. I don't know what a kiss looks like."

Olivia remembered seeing her parents occasionally give one another a chaste peck on the cheek, but that was all years in the past, ending when the bickering started. *But there were other times. . . .* "I've seen people."

"You have? What does it look like?"

Two fleeting images competed for Olivia's attention. The most recent was in Charleston a couple of years ago. Two whites—a scruffily dressed man and a woman Olivia assumed was a prostitute—both drunk in a doorway a block from the Customs House. He was smothering her with a sloppy kiss. She was running her palm up and down the front of his pants.

"Dirty," she whispered.

Then the second image pushed the first one aside. When she was little, she came upon two slaves standing in Turtle's stall. They were house servants, so they shouldn't have been in the barn. He held her head in both of his hands. She wrapped her arms around his waist and gazed up at him. He carefully lowered his face to hers and their lips met.

"Tender."

Eugenie was silent for a while as she absorbed Olivia's two responses. "Have you ever done it? Kissed a boy?"

Olivia tried to imagine herself kissing Barnwell Wilkinson. The image held none of the sordidness of the couple in the doorway and none of the sweetness of the couple in the barn. "No, of course not."

"What if I'm no good at it? What if my husband doesn't like the way I kiss?"

"Well, he'll have to teach you."

"But what if he's never done it either? How can he teach me?"

"I don't know—you'll have to make it up as you go along."

Eugenie placed her book on her bedside table. "Would you practice with me?"

"What?"

"You and me, we can make it up as we go along. We can practice."

Olivia tried to imagine kissing Eugenie. Somehow the idea felt . . . *good*. She placed her bookmark in *Pride and Prejudice*, set the book aside, and moved to sit on Eugenie's bed. Eugenie scooched her legs so she could sit next to Olivia. Olivia looked at Eugenie.

Eugenie returned Olivia's gaze. "This is just for practice, right?" she whispered.

"Of course, just for practice." *This is right . . . but wrong.*

"So we can please our husbands when we're married."

"Yes, just practice to please our husbands." *This is right because it's with a girl. It's wrong because it's with Eugenie.* Olivia shut her eyes. She leaned in toward Eugenie. Eugenie's lips were soft. The moment was as tender as anything Olivia could have imagined. And the face that came to mind was of . . . *Rian Krieger. A girl who dresses like a boy. A girl I haven't seen in two years.*

TUESDAY, OCTOBER 22

· RIAN ·

If someone had told me nine months ago that I would spend time up in Hell because it was soothing, I would have told him that he was fooking crazy. Rian checked her pocket watch as she descended the stairs. *Damn, I was up there for three hours, but that's unimportant. I got a lot of work done. I can hear the music of the machines. I'm not only cured, I'm better at my job than if that stupid explosion had never happened.*

At the bottom of the stairs, Jimmy Butter, who happened to be walking by, grabbed her by the crook of her arm and steered her toward the far end of the factory, away from the office and noise of the steam engine. When Rian asked him what was going on, he pointed toward her lair.

"Shut the door," Jimmy said when they were both inside. Rian couldn't remember Jimmy ever being in the lair before. In any case, he didn't take any time to survey the room. "I know you caused that ruckus with Harry Vogel last year to keep me off the catwalk because I was drunk."

Rian crossed her arms and leaned into her desk but said nothing.

"I haven't had a drop to drink since then. I never thanked you for that . . . You might have saved my life a second time when you moved a couple of us away from the steam engine before it exploded. So I owe you twice. My kids would be orphans if it weren't for you."

Rian still said nothing.

"You're a good guy, Rian. . . ."

Rian felt a surge of warmth toward Jimmy. *He called me a guy.*

"I like you. I owe you." Jimmy woofed out a breath as if he were about to take a big risk. "So I'm going to ask you something that will irk you."

"Ask me."

"Are you spying on the men from up in Hell?"

The conversation turned from warm to ice-cold in less than a heartbeat. "What are you talking about?"

"Gerald Downing says there's new layoffs coming because your daddy lost the contract with the *Utica & Schenectady*. He says you spy on us from your perch up there. Then you report to Otto about who's dogging it and who's not. If you ever want to run this shop, you've got to stop spying on us."

Rian was shocked on many different levels. "Jimmy, if there's layoffs coming, they're months away from now. I don't spy on the men from up there. I do my work and I listen to the machines. That's it." *And what the hell is The Trout doing spreading false rumors about me?*

"That's what I tell the men, but they don't believe me. Rian, a lot of the guys don't like having a girl on the shop floor. We're skilled craftsmen, proud of our work. There's no place for a girl here, especially one who thinks she's going to run the place someday . . . At least that's what they're saying."

Given her reception right after she and her father returned from Boston, Rian assumed she had made progress with the men. Now that illusion was dashed. "I don't spy on the men."

"Don't tell Downing I told you."

"I won't tell Gerald anything, Jimmy." *But if The Trout wants a war with me, that's what he's got.*

* * * * *

· OLIVIA ·

Mrs. Marks was supposed to introduce the dance class to the Malbrouck[29] today. Class started off on the wrong foot when Caldie reported to Mrs. Marks that her father, Representative Montgomery, had called her home on family business and she couldn't attend class this afternoon. Olivia could tell Mrs. Marks wasn't pleased to have family business override attendance at dance class, but their teacher pursed her lips and said, "Do what you have to do, Caldie. Perhaps the other girls can teach you the steps to the Malbrouck this evening."

Then the young men from Columbia filtered in, but not nearly the number needed to form four squares. Although the boys had been somewhat unreliable about attending from the start, this turnout was remarkably low, and Mrs. Marks hit the roof when she found out why. One of the boys who *did* come revealed that the missing escorts were at a cock fight across the river.

Class was further delayed as Mrs. Marks sent one of the girls to corral her husband and Mr. Lovewell to fill in, even though their participation still wouldn't balance boys and girls. The errand girl returned to report that Dr. Marks was in a meeting and Mr. Lovewell was nowhere to be found. "No matter," said Mrs. Marks, her frustration clearly growing. "We shall persevere." She

---

29. Marlbrouk is a lively quadrille (square dance) choreographed to the tune modern listeners would recognize as "The Bear Went Over the Mountain."

reorganized those in attendance into two squares, with girls filling in for the missing boys and a couple of girls left over.

By this time, the two intact squares were becoming restless and silly. Mrs. Marks sat down at the piano and started playing the tune. Before she finished the first line, a *SPROING!* resounded from inside the piano—a broken piano string that made other strings sound out of tune. The squares disintegrated into moans and laughter.

"Well," said Mrs. Marks, her irritation barely controlled. "I guess that's enough of that. Ladies—and the few gentlemen who made the trek out to Barhamville—I apologize, but apparently the stars are telling us we shouldn't be learning to dance today. Class dismissed."

The students cheered and filed out of the room, already planning what to do with their found time. With an unexpected free afternoon and beautiful weather, Olivia and Eugenie decided to proceed with their leaf project. For Olivia, being alone with Eugenie after their practice kiss—now ten days in the past and unacknowledged since—added extra allure.

An area of the grounds they had not yet explored was down near the pond at Spring Creek. They walked amidst the trees, occasionally pausing to soak in patches of sunshine. They luxuriated in each other's company, with the shared memory of their recent intimate moment an unmentioned warmth between them. Their hands bumped, their shoulders brushed. They briefly separated in a glen, Olivia to jot down a description of a tree with a big leaf they didn't have in their notebook yet, Eugenie to explore for the next tree to identify.

Eugenie reappeared at the edge of the glen. "Psst!" She made an emphatic *come here!* gesture.

Olivia closed her notebook and hurried over to Eugenie.

"Want to know what a real kiss looks like? Follow me," Eugenie whispered as she turned and moved stealthily back the way she came. One hundred yards in, she stopped and turned to Olivia. "*Regardez* down by the pond."

Olivia peeked around a huge white cedar. Mr. Lovewell was lying on his back, a blanket spread out beneath him. And lying partially atop Mr. Lovewell, kissing him deeply, was Caldie Montgomery. She was rubbing her palm on the front of his trousers, much the same way that prostitute was doing to that drunken man in Charleston two years ago.

Olivia tugged at Eugenie's sleeve. "Come on, let's go."

"What do we do?"

"I don't know. Maybe let it go. Maybe wait until Caldie calls me 'Abo' one too many times."

"So, we aren't telling anyone?"

"Not yet. Maybe not at all."

"Well, I'll tell you one thing for sure: I'm writing about it in my diary." Eugenie giggled. "This is almost as good as our practice session."

Watching Caldie and Mr. Lovewell go at it had stirred Olivia's blood. As they walked back toward the dormitory, she reached for Eugenie's hand. "Do you want to practice some more?"

"I've been afraid to ask you. Of course I do."

* * * * *

· RIAN ·

Wounded, Rian retreated, reeling from two hurts: The news of The Trout's renewed treachery and the fact that his false rumors were finding fertile ground amidst the workers in Krieger Locomotive. Hell—where she so recently had found comfort—was no longer an option because of the "spying" rumor, so she regrouped in the warm embrace of the Krieger Coach office. Jules, of course, had always been one of her advocates. More unfamiliar but extremely gratifying was her father's increasing acknowledgment of her value. It took some getting used to, but it made her happy.

Her father finished reading an article in the *Philadelphia Independent*, rose, dropped the newspaper on Jules's desk, and announced, "There is a new Jasper article in this morning's paper. I have a meeting at the hotel. *Liebling*, I will meet you at home."

Jules read the article. "James Forten says the Jasper notes are causing quite a ruckus. Abolitionist newspapers all over the country are reprinting them."

Rian feigned disinterest. "I hope they do some good."

"Rian, do you have anything to do with these articles? You mention getting letters from your friend Olivia quite often, and I know you visit with Harold Foote."

I should have known he would figure this out. "A couple of years ago, your wife taught me Rule Number 1 for the Underground Railroad. 'If somebody doesn't need to know something, you don't tell them.'"

Jules smiled. "Well, I gotta say, that rule's a lot more fun when I'm the one not doing the telling . . . Say hello to Olivia for me when you write to her next."

Rian smiled and picked up the paper. The *Independent* had led with their usual introduction, then transcribed Olivia's vinegar-written letter word-for-word.

Jasper—a frequent correspondent with the Philadelphia Independent*—is the pseudonym for a brave man or woman currently in involuntary service on a plantation in a slave state. Jasper swears he has personal knowledge of the incidents he relates to us. Below is his latest entry.*

Let us start with a basic truth. Male enslavers have their way with their captive females. These slaves have no choice in the matter. Whether their masters' advances are violent or gentle, these women are being raped. Others are being raped by their enslavers' sons or the farm supervisor or the strawboss.

This odious truth becomes the slave girl's reality about the time she turns 14. Those who become interested in her bribe her with small gifts and sweet talk. If this trickery doesn't work—if she has no desire to accept the man's advances, if she has religious principles, if she loves another—she will inevitably feel the lash or be starved into submission. The truth the young woman learns is that resistance is hopeless.

THURSDAY, NOVEMBER 7

· OLIVIA ·

Yet again, not enough boys showed up for dance class. When Mrs. Marks announced the class would be practicing the quadrille, Olivia and Eugenie could have maneuvered things so they were dance partners again, but Eugenie stood next to some gump who was a first-timer, so when the boys chose partners, he merely turned to ask her. Much to Olivia's relief, a boy named Lance walked across the room to ask her.

Now, hours later, Olivia and Eugenie lay in each other's arms in Olivia's bed. It was long past lamps-out.

"We've got to stop doing this," whispered Eugenie. "It's wrong."

Eugenie's declaration didn't surprise Olivia. Eugenie had said it before. Olivia mostly agreed with her. "When we started practicing the quadrille, I felt like I really should be dancing the figures with you."

"We can't be dancing partners," Eugenie responded. "That's not how nature works."

"Then what are we doing here? Three minutes ago, we were kissing."

Eugenie rose and shifted her legs so she could sit on the edge of the bed. "We were practicing for our future husbands."

"I think we both know we're lying to ourselves."

"Both of us?"

"Yes, both of us. We aren't practicing for our husbands anymore. We're enjoying ourselves. How can anything that feels so good be wrong?"

More silence. "How was it dancing with Lance?" Eugenie finally whispered in the darkness.

Olivia lay on her back. Her eyes were open, but she saw nothing in the pitch dark. "No sparks, if that's what you mean . . . How was it dancing with new-boy?"

"I'm so confused." There was such a long silence that Olivia thought Eugenie was about to get up and return to her own bed. Then, "Olivia, I think I'm in love with you."

There was no previous experience—no conversation she'd had, no novel she'd ever read—to give Olivia guidance on what to say at this moment. She knew Eugenie was hoping to hear "I love you, too," but she couldn't bring herself to say it. She rolled onto her side and touched Eugenie's back. "Eugenie, I care for you. I love kissing you. I suspect that what we're doing is wrong, but I don't understand how something that feels so good can be bad. If you think we should stop, then I'm okay to stop. If you want us to continue with . . . with whatever this is, whatever it's becoming, I'm okay with that as well."

In response, Eugenie lay back down on the bed with her back to Olivia, like she was a spoon nestling in with another spoon, and pulled Olivia's hand around her waist. In a few minutes Olivia could tell she was asleep.

SATURDAY, DECEMBER 7

Notes from Jasper

Jasper—a frequent correspondent with the Philadelphia Independent—*is the pseudonym for a brave man or woman currently in involuntary service on a plantation in a slave state. Jasper swears he has personal knowledge of the incidents he relates to us. Below is his latest entry.*

I was sent on an errand to a nearby farm—a cotton plantation with more than a hundred field hands in involuntary servitude—when I heard this story from the housemaid who buried the innocent little body. Knowing that I would somehow get word of this sad tale to you people in the North, I lingered long enough to assure myself this woman was telling the truth.

I previously wrote about young female slaves forced to accept the advances of their enslavers. I now write about some happenstances that readers in the North may find implausible, but I assure you, I can point to three credible instances within 50 miles of where I live right now. I refer to the effect that slavery has on the wives and daughters of the enslavers.

The wives, as you can imagine, are resentful when their licentious husbands traipse back from the slave shacks. Master and wife argue. Their daughters overhear spiteful words that reveal what liberties are taken when a man believes he owns a woman's body. The daughters question whether their fathers' or their brothers' prerogatives apply to them as well. "Can I inflict my licentious will on a handsome male slave?" she asks. YES! This happens! Imagine the fear within the meanest of the field hands when the daughter of his enslaver pushes herself upon him. Must he do this? Will he be found out? Discovery would seem almost inevitable. And what would be the consequences of such a revelation? Sold away from all he is familiar with? Whipped? Tortured? Castrated? Killed?

And the sad, misguided young woman who forced herself upon that man, what if she finds herself with child?

Slaves talk and stories spread despite our masters pretending such atrocities never happen. Dear reader, please believe me, my stories are true. Of the three instances I know of where a child of a Black father and a white mother was born, 2 were sold away and one was smothered.

* * * * *

· OLIVIA ·

Pleasure-filled evenings in Olivia's narrow bed became more frequent, then an every-night thing. The fiction that she and Eugenie might be practicing for their future husbands was no longer mentioned. Eugenie never again said anything remotely like "I love you," but Olivia knew Eugenie's feelings were deepening. Waves of conflicting emotions battered Olivia: Her affection (but not love) for Eugenie, her suspicion that what they were doing—what they were feeling—was wrong, her eager anticipation of each night's pleasure, and her fear they would be discovered. Sometimes these emotions broke over her in succession, and sometimes they hit her all at once. Her confusion felt like those foggy mornings down by the river at Long Pond when you couldn't see a thing. On such mornings, she had no idea where she was and what was one step ahead of her. But step she did . . . right into the fog.

Olivia should have known that if she didn't clear the fog herself, someone or something would clear it for her. There was so much that could go wrong. And in fact, it was already going wrong, and Olivia didn't pick up on the signs.

Like the morning Eugenie had already left the room for the privy and Caldie passed by the open door, then backtracked and peeked in to see Eugenie's bed still made from yesterday.

Like the time Caldie and one of her acolytes were talking at dinner about how dreamy Mr. Lovewell was and Oliva and Eugenie didn't nod in agreement.

Like the time her hand cradled Eugenie's ever so briefly when they were sharing a microscope in Natural Philosophy class and Caldie was there to notice.

* * * * *

"Fire drill! Everybody up!"

Before the words could work their way into Olivia's sleep, the bedroom door swung open, and Caldie Montgomery stepped in, whale oil lamp in hand. Olivia opened her eyes. Eugenie stirred next to her, then bolted upright, threw off the covers, and swung her legs to the floor.

"Well, glory be," said Caldie. "Abo and the preacher's daughter, just as I suspected." Caldie turned around in the doorway and yelled, "Hey, everyone! Come here and see what I found!"

"Caldie," said Eugenie, "Please . . . no. . . ."

Olivia tried to clear the cobwebs from her head as she climbed out of bed. *This is bad. This is really bad.* Before she could think about what she was doing, she forcibly yanked Caldie into the room and slammed the door. "Don't do this!"

Caldie, still holding the lamp, said, "Oh, Abo, what's the matter? Do you think you'll get thrown out of school for taking the preacher's daughter as your lover?"

Olivia slapped Caldie hard in the face, which wiped the smirk away. "Shut up, Caldie, or this evening will go a lot worse for you than it does for us. We saw you and Professor Lovewell down by Spring Pond when it was still warm out. If you don't walk out that door in the next minute and make something up to tell whoever's out there, we'll tell Dr. Marks and everyone else at Barhamville that you and Lovewell are lovers and you seem to know what Lovewell loves. He'll lose his job and you'll be a fallen woman. You won't even be able to come out in June. You'll be laughed right out of Richland County."

Caldie stiffened. "I'll deny it. No one will believe you."

"They'll believe me," said Eugenie. "I saw you rubbing the front of the professor's pants with your palm, and I could tell for sure it wasn't the first time you'd done it. I'll swear it to God on a stack of Bibles."

Caldie stepped back as the enormity of her potential downfall assaulted her.

Olivia piled it on, equal parts desire to shore up her defense and payback for all the little humiliations Caldie had inflicted since last year. "No man will give you the time of day, unless maybe they're sniffing around for a little of your special kind of loving."

Caldie weighed her options, then her shoulders sagged. "What will I tell the others? Half of them are probably awake."

Olivia grabbed the lamp from Caldie, walked to her desk, opened the drawer, and pulled out some crackers she had secreted out of the dining hall two nights ago. She tossed them on her desk, returned to Caldie, and handed the lamp back to her. "If anyone is out in the hall, tell them we have food in the room."

Caldie turned, opened the door, and left. "Go back to bed, everyone. It wasn't that big a deal after all."

Olivia and Eugenie turned and hugged each other tightly. "We have to quit this," Eugenie whispered in Olivia's ear. Olivia nodded, but even as the enormity of the averted disaster washed over her, she wasn't sure they could stop.

The next day, Olivia was called to Dr. Marks's office and given extra duties for the transgression of having crackers in her room.

* * * * *

· SEAMUS ·

Seamus stood with Hugh Callaghan, their backs to the growing stock of whiskey barrels lining one wall of Gallagher's Distillery.

"Gotta tell you, Seamus," said Hugh, "when I gave you and Siobhan my blessing, this isn't the kind of wedding I had in mind."

Seamus noticed Hugh used the Queen's English when speaking to him lately. It was as if Hugh had admitted him to his Inner Circle of Trust. He did his best to reciprocate. "What? Too much whiskey?"

"No, not enough guests. When you two said family only, I didn't know how rigid you would be about it. There's not a single member of the Moyamensing Hose Company here."

"Well, there are none of my No Names here either. Siobhan and I didn't want any fights to break out. That would be sure to happen once everyone got a little lubricated."

"But Jules and his wife made the guest list. . . ."

"A point of honor with me. I wouldn't be the man I am today if it weren't for him. Besides, he saved your life two years ago."

Hugh harrumphed. "And your little cousin. Look at her. Couldn't that brat have at least worn a dress?"

"Aw, Hugh, you know . . . When the cat's away, the mice will play. Siobhan and I didn't know Uncle Otto would be at the Whig Convention when we set the date. I bet Rian knew she wouldn't wear a dress as soon as she learned her father would be out of town."

"Otto should have reined her in years ago."

"Says the pot as he calls the kettle black."

Hugh took another sip of whiskey. "So now that you've made an honest woman out of my daughter, will you let her stay on at McSweeney's?"

Seamus turned to Hugh. "Since when have you or I ever been able to tell Siobhan what to do? Didn't you pay attention to the ceremony?"

"What do you mean?"

"The priest said, 'Do you agree to love and cherish your husband?' He never asked about *obeying*."

"He didn't? How'd you get him to do that?"

"Wasn't hard. It cost me a pint of Gallagher's Fine Whiskey."

"And you're okay with it?"

"Let's just say I know who I married. If she wants to work for Braden, then she works for Braden. If she wants to do something else, then that's what she'll do."

"Does she want to do something else?"

"With Siobhan, you never know until it's already happening."

TUESDAY, DECEMBER 10

· OTTO ·

After his return from the Whig Nominating Convention, Otto's first dining companion at the United States Hotel was Harold Foote. As they savored their first sips of turtle soup, George Shippen stopped by their table.

"Krieger, welcome back. It appears your sojourn into the world of politics was successful."

Otto rose, shook Shippen's hand, and sat back down. "To the degree that Mr. Harrison was nominated, I believe it was. Given your railroad involvement, I think you should be pleased as well."

"Like yours, Krieger, my business life is complex. I like to limit my railroad involvement to the regional level. My bank has a more national dimension. As one of the Bank of Industry's directors, you should also remember that. In all of your politicking, did you get wind of your man's attitude toward the resurrection of the national bank?"

Otto shook his head. "No. Nothing," he responded, trying to sound as sincere as possible. "Mr. Harrison was not at the convention, of course. None of the candidates wanted to appear so crass as to be seen actively pursuing the nomination. They all struck the posture of 'neither seek nor decline' such an honor, although everyone knows they all wanted it badly. They left the seeking to their minions. And none of Mr. Harrison's men divulged anything about Mr. Harrison's thoughts on a new national bank." *Only Biddle has talked to me about this. He was right about the return of the depression. I assume he is also right about Harrison's desire to create a new National Bank.*

"Well, we'll see. I don't trust the man, and I doubt he's electable. Mr. Clay will see to that."

Harold Foote poured some vinegar into his soup, then addressed Shippen. "Actually, I know the answer to that. I was with Mr. Clay shortly after he got the news on Sunday."

"And what was the reaction of the good senator from Kentucky?"

"My article will appear in this afternoon's *Independent*. You'll have to buy it to find out."

Shippen harrumphed and departed without a goodbye.

Otto watched Shippen leave the dining room, giving not so much as a nod to James, the maître d'. "You really do enjoy tweaking Shippen's tail."

"Otto, look at my ink-stained hands. I'm a man of the trades, one rung up from one of the mechanics in your shop. I share few values with George Shippen. He tried to have me banned from this room when I first started dining here. I'm surprised you consort with him."

"George Shippen has introduced me to people I never dreamed I would associate with. For that, I will always be grateful, and therefore I suppose I am a friend. Does he consider me a friend? I have no idea—"

"Otto," interrupted Philadelphia's Mayor John Scott as he stopped by the table, "I'm glad you joined our party on the trip back from Harrisburg. It was a pleasure getting to know you."

Otto rose and shook the mayor's hand. "It is still hard for me to believe it only takes a day to travel from Harrisburg to Philadelphia. We live in modern times."

"Well, we hope to have more opportunities to work with you."

"And I hope you consider me an ally," said Otto. "Perhaps we will see more of each other as the campaign ramps up."

Scott expanded his attention to include Harold. "Normally, I would ask you both to join my group for lunch, but city concerns demand my attention. Good day, gentlemen."

Foote watched Scott join three other diners at a distant table. "Well, well, aren't you the man of the hour. People are already telling me stories as if I hadn't been there to see them for myself. Delegate for the winning side. Mr. Harrison's railroad man at the convention. Eloquent voice of reason when tensions were getting high. You took to your role quite handily, it seems."

Otto shook his head. "Parts of it were exhilarating, others tiresome. Disillusioning. Worthwhile. Contentious. Exhausting. I didn't see you toward the end. Where did you go?"

"I wanted to be the first to record Mr. Clay's reaction when he heard the nomination went to Harrison. I left before the final gavel, before the convention went on to nominate John Tyler for vice president."

"Then your intelligence is very important. Everyone at the convention knew Clay's reaction would either assure Harrison's election or sink it. Which will it be?"

"The man was extremely disappointed, although he always knew his electability in the Northern states would be tenuous. I believe he will support the ticket."

"Which means Harrison will most likely be our next president." *And if Nicholas Biddle is right, money for internal improvements will start flowing. I made a big enough impression to assure I am consulted when those federal allocations are made, and I will become a rich man.*

Foote caught the attention of a waiter freshening patrons' coffee cups. "Tell me what you know about the vice presidential nominee."

"John Tyler? He is from Virginia. He was chosen to balance the ticket. Honestly, we were all exhausted. It took four ballots on Friday until we finally settled on Harrison after ten o'clock. We kicked the nomination of the vice president to Saturday."

"I must say, I question the choice."

Otto smiled at the waiter as he refilled their coffee cups, then returned his attention to Foote. "Scuttlebutt was that Harrison's men spent the entire night trying to line up a preferable candidate who would keep the Clay forces in the tent: Crittenden, Bell, Clayton. My intelligence is they all turned it down. I do not think you have much to worry about. The vice president's position is more ceremonial than substantive. It does not really matter who is in that position as long as Harrison gets elected."

"I hope Old Granny Harrison doesn't let us down."

* * * * *

· OLIVIA ·

Barhamville closed for the month-long break between semesters, and the Wilkinsons invited Olivia to stay with them. As usual, Mrs. Wilkinson installed Olivia in "her room," the mansion's front left bedroom.

With the sun lower in the sky and the temperature in the sixties, Olivia found that the side balcony outside her bedroom was the perfect place to enjoy the sunshine. She intended to cover herself with a blanket and get back to *Pride and Prejudice*, which she abandoned weeks ago when her involvement with Eugenie heated up. Instead, she found herself contemplating her semester. Academics had paused on a successful note, exams had gone well. Her non-academic pursuits? *Well, that would probably be more turmoil than success.* Her feud with Caldie Montgomery had become a stalemate. The thing with Eugenie, whatever it was becoming, had too many impediments. *How can something that feels so right be so shameful?*

Senator Wilkinson's two hounds sprinted down the pea-graveled lane and barked furiously to alert all of Thousand Oaks that someone was coming. Olivia craned her neck from the chaise. A rider cantered up the lane, his horse unfazed by the yapping dogs. Based on the dust on his coat and the two carpetbags strapped to the back of his saddle, he had been on the road for some time. Barnwell and his father walked out to greet the man. The traveler alighted from his horse, handed the reins to Topper, shook hands with Senator Wilkinson and Barney, and the three walked into the mansion. Topper unstrapped the carpetbags, handed them to a house servant, and led the horse toward the barn. Olivia gave Topper a wave. He acknowledged it with an almost undetectable nod of his head. Olivia returned to *Pride and Prejudice*.

* * * * *

Footsteps sounded from the front covered balcony. Olivia looked up from her book.

Barnwell appeared from around the corner, carrying a wicker chair. "I figured I would find you over here. What are you reading?"

"*Pride and Prejudice*. I'm rooting for Mr. Darcy, even though he's haughty and sarcastic. I think the author, Miss Austen, sees good in him, although she hasn't let us witness it yet."

"Darcy and Elizabeth get engaged at the end. He actually turns out to be a good guy."

Olivia let the book drop onto her blanket and leaned forward, a slight smile on her face. "You are so mean. You have deprived me of all the suspense . . . the dramatic tension." Then she slumped back into the chaise. "I'm surprised you've read it. I thought it was only popular with the ladies."

"Of course I've read it. How do you expect me to get on with any of the young women of Columbia if I don't share some common interests?"

Olivia tried to reconcile the boy who was flirting with her at this moment with the young man who slipped down to the slave shacks at night and took advantage of one of his father's castoffs. She shoved that unpleasant thought away. "Barney, you may be smart to share their interests, but allow your lady friends to discover some things for themselves." *Stop flirting, Olivia.* "Who is that man who rode up earlier? You and your father greeted him out front."

"His name is Ashbel Molineaux. He's searching for someone."

A slight spasm coursed through Olivia. *Molineaux. The investigator hunting for Jasper.* "Who's he looking for?" She picked up *Pride and Prejudice* again to feign tepid interest.

Barney shrugged. "A person who professes to be a slave is writing stories about what it's like to be a slave, and they somehow find their way North. They're appearing in Northern pennies . . . The newspapers call them Notes from Jasper. Of course, no Notes from Jasper would ever be reprinted in South Carolina, but your father sends the articles to my father. Father is all up in arms about it, so he and a couple of other legislators hired Molineaux to find the slave."

Olivia kept her nose in her book. "How's he doing so far?"

"That's the ironic thing. Molineaux thinks the slave lives near Thousand Oaks, maybe even lives right here. Everything Jasper writes about happened within twenty miles of here."

Still staring into her book but unable to read, Olivia asked, "Have you read the articles?"

"Some of them."

"Would they be of interest to me?"

"I don't think it would be appropriate. They aren't fit for feminine eyes."

Somewhat away from dangerous territory, Olivia frowned at Barnwell. "You think I'm so fragile that I'd wilt by reading these notes?"

"The women of the South need protecting. Perhaps my mission in life will be to protect you."

Barney has learned to flirt; I'll grant him that. "If that becomes your mission, then I'll warn you right now, sir: Leave room for some suspense. I, for one, want some dramatic tension in my life."

"You don't have enough of that right now?"

"Well, I do, but not with the right person."

And that pretty much summed up Olivia's life at the moment: *Plenty of tension. Not with the right person.* Added to her Caldie and Eugenie issues, now her conspiracy with Topper felt precarious. Thankfully, her flirtation with Barney seemed harmless and was destined to go nowhere.

"Well," said Barney, "maybe the right person is closer than you think."

Or maybe not as harmless as I had assumed.

WEDNESDAY, DECEMBER 18

· RIAN ·

More than a week since her father had returned from the Whig convention in Harrisburg, Rian entered the Krieger Coach office with a folded piece of paper behind her back.

She was about to speak to her father when she noticed he had taken the architect's drawing of the new locomotive factory off the wall and was rolling it up. "So you've made the decision? You won't finish the factory?"

Otto dropped the roll into a wooden crate that held many rolls of old designs, mostly railroad cars. "Only for the time being. I have told the contractor to continue working until it is under roof and the doors are on, then dismiss his men."

"How did he take the news?"

"Disappointed but not surprised." Otto lifted his gaze from the crate and regarded his daughter for the first time. "What is that behind your back?"

Rian realized that her timing wasn't the best but unfolded the paper and handed it to her father. "It's a design for a new tender."[30]

Otto barely glanced at the drawing and dropped it on his desk. "Is that what you have been doing for the past week? Designing railroad cars?"

"No, mostly Heinrich has me drawing up parts for the *Standard*. I've only designed this one car."

Otto removed his reading glasses and wiped them with a handkerchief. "I had no idea we needed a new design for a tender."

Rian pointed to the drawing. "It has a cast-iron water tank that wraps around three sides of the tender in a U-shape. The tank doubles as the tender's walls. I think there's a market for a car like this."

Her father glanced at the design anew. "Pretty big, isn't it? There's a lot of cast iron."

---

30. Steam locomotives consumed massive amounts of fuel and water. The tender car, which carried both, was always connected directly to the locomotive by a drawbar.

"Yes, it is. The *Standard* will weigh in at sixteen tons and haul as much as four hundred tons. I figured we didn't have to save weight like we used to."

"And what value does this new design bring to the marketplace? I do not see it."

Rian moved a chair close to her father's desk and sat. "Here's my thinking. We designed *Number 103* years ago to hold firewood, plus the water in barrels, of course."

"Yes, it is my design—one I am quite proud of."

"But firewood is getting scarce in the Mid-Atlantic states and much of New England. The forests are disappearing because we're burning wood to power steam engines that drive factories, ships, and locomotives, not to mention heat buildings, smelt iron, and make bricks."

Her father perused the drawing, taking in its nuances. "And we designed the *Number 104* specifically to hold coal, not firewood."

"But, *Vater*, that's the thing. Most railroads haven't converted exclusively to coal. We're in a period of transition. Coal is cheaper than firewood in some areas, or at least more readily available. In other areas, they're sticking with firewood."

Otto tapped his finger on the drawing but continued to look up at Rian. "What is your proposal?"

Rian took a deep breath. "Since our engines are so powerful these days, we don't have to worry about weight, but we do have to worry about volume."

"Agreed, go ahead."

"A short ton of anthracite coal produces approximately 19 million BTUs of energy. We figure that's enough to get a typical passenger train about thirteen miles."

"*We*? Where did you get these figures?"

"I talked to Heinrich. He didn't know the answer, so we went to the Franklin Institute."

"These are the Franklin Institute's figures?"

Rian nodded. "And a cord of seasoned firewood produces about 15 million BTUs, plus or minus—roughly the same, but here's the thing. A ton of coal is about 40 cubic feet in volume. A cord of wood is 4 by 4 by 8. That's 128 cubic feet, so you can fit 57 million BTUs of coal in the same amount of space you can fit 15 million BTUs of firewood."

"I would have to double-check your math, but go on."

"So we build a bigger tender. Rather than store the water in barrels at the rear of the tender like we do with *Numbers 103* and *104*, we wrap the outside with a U-shaped cast-iron water tank. The water tank acts as the wall of the fuel bunker. The fuel bunker is big enough that it doesn't matter if the engine is running on coal or firewood. The water tank is much bigger than either the *103* or the *104*. We can produce the same car whether the *Standard* runs on coal or wood. The railroads will like it because of its flexibility."

"How much water does this tender hold?"

Rian pointed to figures that ran down the side of the drawing. "Four hundred gallons. Enough for twenty miles, tops. I figure that will give us two water stops to each fuel stop if they're running on firewood. Of course, that ratio changes if they're running on coal."

"Who helped you with this?"

"Uh, only the folks at the Franklin Institute. Heinrich and I went over together."

"But it was your idea?"

"Yes, it was my idea. My drawing. My calculations."

"And do you have a name for this combination tender?"

"I think we should continue the series. This should be the *Number 105*."

Otto leaned back in his chair. "I'll tell you what, *Liebling*. I will check your figures and do my own analysis of the ratio between fuel capacity and water capacity. I will modify your design as I deem appropriate. Then I will kick it back to you to create a pricing structure. Assume we will build one of these tenders next year."

"Only one?"

Her father shrugged. "We will have to see. Your idea about taking used engines as trade-ins has been well received. A few orders have come in, but nothing like the contract the *U&S* welched on."

"You didn't make any contacts while you were in Harrisburg?"

"I made scores of valuable contacts during the convention. If William Henry Harrison is elected on a platform of internal improvements, the Krieger companies' fortunes will be assured. But until that time, this damned depression has come back with a vengeance and it is killing us."

"*Vater*, the presidential election is a year away. Can we last that long?"

"This depression has fooled me. It told me we are back in business, then broke my heart. William Henry Harrison may be our only way out of this fix. When he is elected, the Krieger factories will have clear sailing for at least four years." Otto returned his attention to the drawing of the tender. "Congratulations, *Liebling*. You are fifteen years old and you have already created a brilliant design for a railroad car . . . a tender, no less.

Rian beamed, soaking in the praise from her father, but he wasn't done.

"I must confess, ever since President Adams postulated that you might be a business prodigy, I have taken note of your actions. We delivered a fully assembled locomotive to the *B&L* because of you." Otto gave Rian a wry smile. "But that was three months ago—the distant past in this business. Since then, because of you, we now hire out our most skilled mechanics to four railroads to make their locomotive repairs, we take trade-ins on old locomotives and railcars, and now this design. *Liebling*, all evidence is that President Adams was right. You are a business prodigy."

Rian smiled, gratified that her father wholeheartedly acknowledged her contributions. "President Adams said I may also be gifted at causing mayhem."

Otto looked her in the eye. "Perhaps I must accept the mayhem to get the prodigy."

Rian turned to leave the office.

"Don't rush away," Otto said. He fished the factory plans back out of the bin. "There is a lot more cast iron in your design than in the *Number 104*. This car will likely be made inside the new factory when the time comes. We should talk about how that might affect the layout of the machinery."

* * * * *

· OLIVIA ·

Even though Barnwell had revealed the end of *Pride and Prejudice*, Olivia ensconced herself on her side balcony to get back to her book. Then the hounds rollicked down the lane, sounding the alarm that a stranger was coming. Olivia craned her neck, and a woman riding sidesaddle came into view. . . . *Oh glory, it's Eugenie*. Eugenie's horse was noticeably perturbed by the dogs, but she did an admirable job keeping him in check. Olivia ran down to greet her.

Topper arrived with a step stool for Eugenie to dismount from her horse, which she accomplished gracefully. She ignored Topper and the still-yapping dogs and hugged Olivia.

"Roomie, what a pleasant surprise," said Olivia. "I wasn't expecting you."

Eugenie's eyes sparkled. "I took a chance that I would catch you here. I have news."

Olivia grabbed Eugenie by both hands and smiled. "Do tell me."

"It's best spoken of in private. Is there somewhere we can talk?"

Olivia was intrigued. Even though Eugenie's father's parsonage was merely two miles away in Columbia, they had made no plans to meet over the holiday. "Let's go up to the balcony off my bedroom. We can talk there in confidence as long as we speak quietly." Olivia led Eugenie across the porch, through the front doors, into the foyer, up the stairs, down the hall, through her room, and onto the balcony. "It has only been ten days since we left school. What news has transpired in that amount of time?"

"I know what we are. There's a name for it."

Olivia could detect Eugenie's excitement but had no idea what she was referring to. "What are we?"

"We are sapphists. A sapphist is a woman who loves another woman. Olivia, my love, there's a name for what we do . . . what we are."

Olivia's eyes widened in incredulity. "How do you know this?"

Eugenie's words spilled out in a rapid jumble. "My aunt, a spinster, is visiting us from England. She moved there when I was little. She and Father had a falling out years ago, but she wrote to him and said she was coming to America for the holidays. Before she arrived, I overheard my parents arguing. My mother said she did not want a sapphist living in our house."

Olivia panicked momentarily. "You haven't told your parents about us."

"No, I could never do that. But when Auntie Ruth arrived, she seemed like a wonderful person . . . maybe a little masculine but still quite delightful. After she was here for a few days, I screwed up my courage and asked her, 'Are you a sapphist?'"

"What did she say?"

"She didn't say anything for the longest time, then asked if I knew what a sapphist is. I said no, I don't even know if it's a good thing or a bad thing. She said it's neither—it's just something that is. She loves another woman. There are others of her kind . . . of our kind. They have to meet clandestinely. They are all spinsters, every one of them. Well, no, that's not right. One of her friends is a widow, but a wealthy widow who put up with her husband, and when he died, she saw no need to have a man in her life. But Auntie Ruth is living with another woman named Marianna. She calls Marianna her companion, as if they live together because they enjoy each other's company, but Olivia, they sleep in the same bed together."

The revelations cascaded over Olivia like the waterfall at Spring Pond. "But your mother frowns upon this?"

Eugenie nodded. "Mother and Father both. But think of what this means for us. When we turn eighteen, we will be of age to make decisions for ourselves. We can run away to somewhere no one knows us. Savannah or Atlanta or Richmond. We can be companions. We can be the mistresses of our own fate. Isn't this wonderful?"

"It is wonderful," Olivia said quietly. Her thoughts coalesced in an instant. *There are other women who love women. I can be happy loving another woman, but my real self must be hidden from the world all my life.* But then a second wave of realizations tumbled into place. *Now that I know there are others, I admit to my chagrin that my love for Eugenie has its limits. There is no way I'll live in the South for the rest of my life. My future lies in Philadelphia. I abhor slavery. Eugenie takes its existence as gospel. I could never have a pro-slavery companion. Eugenie—as sweet as she is—is not the love of my life.*

"Eugenie, we could move to Philadelphia."

"Good Lord, no. I know you're comfortable among your abo friends, but I never could be."

"Eugenie, I—" Olivia stopped. Whatever it was she was going to say was best left unsaid for the moment. She hugged Eugenie. "There's a name for what we are. We're not alone. We're sapphists."

* * * * *

That evening, before Olivia climbed into bed, she stared at herself in the cheval mirror. *There is a name for what I am. I'm a sapphist. There are others of my kind.*

She was about to blow out her lamp and climb into bed but instead turned again to the mirror. *Philadelphia.*

* * * * *

· RIAN ·

That night, Rian prepared for bed with her father's words repeating over and over and over in her head.

"You are fifteen years old, and you have already created a brilliant design for a railroad car . . . a tender, no less."

She lit her whale oil lamp, blew out her candle, and walked out the back door to the privy by lamplight. She was barely conscious of the below-freezing temperature or the full moon rising to the east.

"I will kick it back to you to create a pricing structure."

She skipped back into the warmth of the house, raced through the kitchen, entered the parlor, and banked the Franklin stove with a generous scoop of coal.

"Let's talk about how that might affect the layout of the new factory."

She grabbed a cloth to pick up the soapstone slab off the top of the stove, wrapped the stone in the cloth, and climbed the stairs with her lamp in one hand and the soapstone in the other. Usually, the warmth of the soapstone at her hip was part of the pleasure of going to bed, but this evening, she didn't notice.

"Liebling, all evidence is that President Adams was right. You are a business prodigy."

She folded down her two quilts, placed the soapstone—still fully wrapped— on the bed and placed the quilts back over it. She checked the washstand to make sure Alice had filled the pitcher.

This is it. It has started. I will run Krieger Locomotive.

She removed her shirt, pants, and shoes but left her socks and long undershirt on.

In Russia, Yana said first I wouldn't run it, then I would. Maybe my "won't run it" period is coming to an end. All I have to do now is somehow get The Trout out of my way.

She grabbed her nightcap off the hook and pulled it down tight on her head, scooted through the cold to her bed, peeled back the covers, blew out the whale oil lamp, and crawled into the bed's blessed warmth.

"Perhaps I must accept the mayhem to get the prodigy."

With the soapstone near her hips and her torso still in need of warmth, Rian crossed her arms to hug herself, her open palms, still warm from the soapstone, on her chest.

Something felt different. Her nipples were a bit swollen. *No, more than a bit.*

Rian threw off the bed covers, fumbled around on her nightstand for the loco-focos, struck one on the sandpaper, re-lit the lamp, and turned the wick up to maximum. She removed her undershirt, bracing herself against the cold. She picked up the lamp and walked to her free-standing cheval mirror.

This can't be happening.

She never studied herself fully naked because such an examination would reveal the mottled burn along her left arm and the V-shaped scar on her neck. She leaned in close and examined her naked body for the first time in a long while.

No, no, this can't be happening.

Her eyes confirmed what she had felt in bed. Her breasts were swollen. Slight little bumps.

Little buds. I thought this day would never come. But it's started.

Unbelieving, she put her undershirt back on and pulled the fabric down tight. The bumps were visible if you really looked for them.

No, oh please, no.

She stared at her portrait—her most prized possession—the portrait that had captured her soul, her essence, her current and future self. The young man in the top hat stared back at her, the knowing smile that insinuated a shared secret now seemed to mock her: *You fool. You must have known this day would come.* She stared back at that boy, that boy who she assumed she would become, that boy she thought she could forever be, and she felt him slipping away from her with every heartbeat.

No, no, no! No! NO!

AUTHOR'S NOTES

I include these notes to help the reader separate fact from fiction.

In Philadelphia and Boston

- The Pennsylvania Constitution of 1838, including the white-only clause, was ratified by the male citizens of the Keystone State by a vote of 113,971 to 112,759. Free Black males, who technically had been able to vote since the previous century, were thus denied the right to vote until the passage of the Fifteenth Amendment to the U.S. Constitution in 1869.

- In the early years of the Steam Age, steam engine boilers exploded with some frequency, often with devastating consequences. To get a graphic idea of the power of such explosions, google "images of exploded steam engine boilers."

- Erastus Corning, who we meet as president of the *Utica & Schenectady Railroad*, was a prominent political and industrial figure in New York State. His vision led to the consolidation of a number of small railroads into the New York Central, which, for a time, became one of the largest corporations in America.

- In the 1830s, annual consumption of distilled spirits topped seven gallons per person. In comparison, today's figure is around 2.8 gallons. Whiskey has been distilled in Western Pennsylvania, Maryland, and Virginia since before the time of the Constitution. In the era described in *The Prodigy*, whiskey was still less popular than rum in America. Legend has it that sometime in the early 1800s, a distillery in Kentucky started aging whiskey in charred barrels.

- Just as James Forten bought stock to control the Bank of Industry's lending policy, there are historical precedents of wealthy Black men buying stock in banks in order to exercise some limited degree of power. My inspiration in this case was Stephen Smith of Columbia, Pennsylvania.

Although legally barred from becoming a director because he was Black, he could dictate which white man received the position.

- Thanks to the Postal Service Act of 1792, publishers could send their newspapers at no cost to other newspapers nationwide. It was a common practice for publishers to reprint articles from other newspapers during this era. They would often make changes in the text to suit their own biases.

- A string of semaphore towers built in 1809 extended from Cape May, New Jersey, to the Merchants' Exchange Building in Philadelphia. This optical telegraph facilitated the transmission of messages between the mouth of the Delaware and the city in a quarter-hour. In 1834, the optical telegraph was extended to New York City. Like so many technologies during this era, the optical telegraph's usefulness between the two cities was short-lived. The electronic telegraph, which appeared between New York and Philadelphia in November 1845, made the towers obsolete.

- On January 26, 1839, a flood destroyed the two bridges on the Schuylkill River—a floating bridge in operation since before the Revolution and the *Philadelphia, Wilmington & Baltimore Railroad* bridge—as described.

- Baldwin Locomotive's complex of factories was located very near the fictional Krieger factories at Broad and Buttonwood Streets. In the coming years, Baldwin would become a behemoth, dominating the industry but buffeted about during downturns in the American and world economies.

- Locomotive manufacturers started to accept used engines as trade-ins sometime in the late 1830s.

- Lucretia Mott and former president (and subsequent representative from Massachusetts) John Quincy Adams were well acquainted with one another. In this era, they were both well-known for their anti-slavery sympathies. He had previously attended a gathering at her home. They exchanged correspondence. In later years, she would visit him in his Washington City office.

- The mutiny aboard *La Amistad* occurred as described. President John Quincy Adams eventually inserted himself into the defense of *La Amistad*'s mutineers when the case reached the Supreme Court. Seventy-three years old, Adams spoke before the Supreme Court for nine hours and is credited with swaying the Court to free the mutineers and allowing them to return to Sierra Leone.

- Seamus and Conor briefly discuss the brig *Daisy* entering the Delaware with a load of cowhides from California. My inspiration for this tidbit was Richard Henry Dana's 1840 memoir, *Two Years Before the Mast*. Voyages to Mexican California were risky but potentially lucrative. Sailing from Boston around Cape Horn to the Pacific took five months. For the next sixteen months, his ship amassed forty thousand cowhides from missions and ranchos along the California coast. The return voyage took four months.

- Catherine the Great's memoir, with all its details and implications, did exist. It was kept under lock and key by successive Tsars: Catherine's (perhaps bastard) son, Paul I, and his sons, Alexander I and Nicholas I. Each new Tsar read the memoirs and understood their implications: No Tsar after Peter III had a drop of Romanov blood in their veins. For many reasons, copies of the memoir were penned but not made public, although rumors of their existence circulated among the Russian nobility and intelligentsia. In 1859, exiled Russian radical Alexander Herzen, living in London, published the memoirs in six languages and caused a firestorm. Various historians have made the case that the memoir's publication led directly to the freeing of the Russian serfs in 1861.

- In the 1830s, poker was not yet commonly played in America beyond New Orleans and the Mississippi. That changed dramatically in the 1840s.

- According to a historical roadside marker located in Chambersburg, PA, the *Cumberland Valley Railroad* pioneered the use of sleeping cars in the spring of 1839, a first on any American railroad, with a car named "Chambersburg." The berths were upholstered boards in three tiers held by leather straps. During the daytime, they were folded back against the walls. A couple of years later, a second car, the "Carlisle," was introduced into service.

In South Carolina

- By the 1830s, nation-state economies worldwide were impacting one another. Interest rates set in Great Britain affected Southern planters and Northern industrialists. New rice plantations in the Dutch East Indies flooded Europe with so much rice that they stole the market from American growers. In the United States, the Northern and Southern economies were inextricably intertwined, and the owners of Northern cotton mills, shipyards, banks, and insurance companies were willing to countenance the existence of slavery as long as it helped them make a profit.

- The Stono Rebellion, memorialized by Cook and her brethren, occurred in September 1739 as described. Twenty-five South Carolina colonists were murdered, and between thirty-five and fifty Blacks were killed in retribution.

- Colonel Jaudon unexpectedly arrived at the confrontation in the Tuckers' gazebo, prattling about a hundred gallons of whiskey found at Mount Vernon after George Washington's death. Rumors to that effect did circulate in this era, but I have found no corroboration. Well documented, however, was the fact that Washington became one of the largest whiskey distillers in America after his presidency. Mount Vernon produced eleven thousand gallons of whiskey in 1799, the year of Washington's death. Six enslaved men assisted two employees in the distilling process. The unaged whiskey was shipped to Alexandria and (I assume) consumed immediately.

- Hamburg, South Carolina, prospered for a couple of decades as the northern terminus of the *Charleston-Hamburg Railroad* but started to decline when the railroad was extended across the river to Augusta, Georgia. In 1876, Hamburg was the site of a massacre of both Blacks and whites at the hands of Southern "rifle clubs" intent on suppressing Black votes during the last election cycle of Reconstruction. Hamburg is now a ghost town.

- Dr. Elias Marks founded the South Carolina Female Collegiate Institute in 1828 to become one of the country's finest schools for young women. It survived the Civil War, but due to the shattered Southern economy, closed its doors two years later.

- Although I have altered some of the details of Topper's notes about his experiences as a slave, the germ of each entry originated from one of two first-hand accounts:

  ° *Fifty Years in Chains*, the memoir of Charles Bell, who was born into slavery in 1780. Bell finally escaped slavery by being spirited aboard a ship in Savannah by a sympathetic captain. He lived the rest of his life on a farm fifty miles from Philadelphia. Every day he lived in fear he would be captured and returned to slavery.

° *Incidents in the Life of a Slave Girl* by Harriet Jacobs (1813 or 1815 to 1897). Jacobs was born into slavery and sexually abused as a young woman. She escaped to the North. During the Civil War, she returned to Southern areas occupied by Union troops to help newly freed and self-emancipated Blacks.

• In our era, when young women reach puberty between ages eight and thirteen, it is hard to fathom that it hasn't always been this way. One early nineteenth-century report from Germany pegged the average age of menarche (the first occurrence of menstruation) at 16.6 years.

• My research indicates that the term *sapphist* did not become widely used until the 1890s, but I did not want to use the term *lesbian* because it sounded too modern. Both terms have evolved and become more nuanced over the years.

• This tidbit is pretty insignificant, but it illustrates how geeky my research can get. I conjured up the description of the five-seat privy at Barhamville using drawings and descriptions from an archeological excavation of an early nineteenth-century privy at Drayton Hall outside Charleston, South Carolina.

I am sure this book includes numerous historical inaccuracies. I apologize in advance and would appreciate hearing others' feedback on this. Feel free to contact me by visiting my website, rogerasmith.com.

• The only error I have purposely included is that St. Philip de Neri church was built in 1840, so Seamus could not have attended mass there in 1838.

• One error is a legacy from Books 1-3. Only as I was researching for *The Prodigy* did I learn that whiskey was not sold by the bottle until far later in the nineteenth century. In the 1830s and '40s, taverns and saloons bought whiskey directly from the distillers in barrels or, for smaller quantities, earthenware jugs. For consistency, I have chosen to continue the error forward.

Acknowledgments

Thank you to:

- The Brewster Writers Group for sandwiching criticism between praise and helping me tinker, improve, and appreciate nuance.

- Fellow authors at the Cape Cod Writers Center for sharing their wisdom, hard-learned lessons, and contacts.

- Sid and Margaret of Two Step Approach, developmental editors who made the macro-comments I needed to hear.

- My beta readers—Daniel Beltran, Jeff Drake, Christine Jenkins, Margie Luck, Sadie Petta, Susan Smith, Bailey Spencer, Ted Spevack, and Sally Wyner—for their time, perspective, insight, praise, and criticism.

- Mel Bornstein for perspective on the banking industry in this era.

- Jake Wanamaker, Finn Allen, Alex Meyers, Hayden Berger, Maureen Osborne, and Rikki Bates for assistance and perspective on transgender issues.

- The staff of the Shot Tower Recreation Center, who escorted me through accessible parts of the tower and showed me historic architectural drawings and photographs.

- The staff at Sunbury Press: Publisher Lawrence Knorr, who believed in me and the importance of Rian Krieger's Journey; Sarah Peachey, the last person to pore over this manuscript before it went to press; and book designer Crystal Devine.

- James Clark, who I met when he was acting as a docent in the engine room of the SS *Keewatin* (now a floating museum) in Kingston, Ontario. James gave me valuable information about steam engines and in turn introduced me to Donald R. McQueen, who he described as "the best expert I know of in Canada on the early development of locomotives." All correspondence with Don since then validates James's assessment.

- Sally Wyner and Steve Szarez for intel about John Quincy Adams. Also the staff at the Adams Historical Site.

- A treasured community of friends, fellow members of the First Parish Brewster UU Church, former students, fellow authors, and former colleagues who give encouragement, help me make connections, and send me articles and factoids of interest.

- Dr. Ted Spevack for intel on all things medical.

- My family—Susan, Matt, Alecia, Alex, and Courtney—for their constant support and encouragement. To Susan specifically for lore about all things planted.

ABOUT THE AUTHOR

Roger A. Smith started his professional career as a high school history teacher. After ten years of inspiring young people, he yielded to passions for which he had no formal training: co-owning a summer camp, farming, founding a participatory science museum, co-owning a wilderness expedition program for teenagers, teaching entrepreneurship at the college level, woodworking, and leading a rural arts organization. Now an author, he draws lore and wisdom from all those professions, and joy from the thought that he is once again making history come alive to his constituents.

Smith and his wife lived and worked on a farm in Central Pennsylvania for forty-one years. They currently reside in Massachusetts with their Great Dane and cat. They have three adult children and two grandchildren.

www.ingramcontent.com/pod-product-compliance
Lightning Source LLC
Chambersburg PA
CBHW011757010726
47497CB00013B/3249